Praise for Laura Frantz

"You'll disappear into another place and time and be both encouraged and enriched for having taken the journey."

—Jane Kirkpatrick, bestselling author
of *A Light in the Wilderness*

"Laura Frantz portrays the wild beauty of frontier life, along with its dangers and hardships, in vivid detail."

—Ann H. Gabhart, author of *The Innocent*

Praise for *Love's Fortune*

"Laura Frantz surely dances when she writes: the words sweep across the page with a gentle rhythm and a sure step. Her characters in *Love's Fortune* are sympathetic yet flawed, making them oh-so-easy to care for, ache for, cheer for. Her historical details are well chosen, and her sense of time and place rings true. Above all, it's Wren's journey that engages our hearts and makes the pages turn. Well done, lass!"

—Liz Curtis Higgs, *New York Times* bestselling author
of *Mine Is the Night*

"*Love's Fortune* is the last book in Frantz's captivating Ballantyne Legacy series. Her characters pop to life on the page, and her vivid descriptions add realistic historical depth to the story."

—*Booklist*

Praise for *Love's Awakening*

"Frantz's in-depth historical research combines with her fascinating characters to create a gripping romance that kept me turning pages late into the night. I highly recommend *Love's Awakening*. It is a rare find."

—Serena B. Miller, RITA Award–winning author
of *The Measure of Katie Calloway*

"Frantz's family saga is a rare treat for fans that will stay with readers long after they finish."

—*RT Book Reviews*

The
MISTRESS
OF TALL ACRE

Books by Laura Frantz

The Frontiersman's Daughter
Courting Morrow Little
The Colonel's Lady
The Mistress of Tall Acre

THE BALLANTYNE LEGACY

Love's Reckoning
Love's Awakening
Love's Fortune

The
MISTRESS
OF TALL ACRE

A *NOVEL*

LAURA
FRANTZ

Revell
a division of Baker Publishing Group
Grand Rapids, Michigan

© 2015 by Laura Frantz

Published by Revell
a division of Baker Publishing Group
P.O. Box 6287, Grand Rapids, MI 49516-6287
www.revellbooks.com

Printed in the United States of America

Library of Congress Cataloging-in-Publication Data
Frantz, Laura.
    The mistress of Tall Acre : a novel / Laura Frantz.
        pages ; cm
    ISBN 978-0-8007-2044-5 (softcover)
    1. Young women—Fiction. 2. Marital conflict—Fiction. 3. United States—Social life and customs—1783–1865—Fiction. I. Title.
    PS3606.R4226M57 2015
    813'.6—dc23   2015015864

Scripture quotations are from the King James Version of the Bible.

Published in association with Books & Such Literary Agency, 52 Mission Circle, Suite 122, PMB 170, Santa Rosa CA 94509-7953.

15   16   17   18   19   20   21   7   6   5   4   3   2   1

To the Isle of Mull
where this story was born
and the rivers of Living Water
I found there

These are the things which once Possess'd
Will make a life that's truly bless'd;
A good Estate on healthy Soil,
Not got by vice, nor yet by Toil;
Round a warm fire, a Pleasant Joke,
With Chimney ever free from smoke;
A Strength entire, a Sparkling Bowl,
A quiet Wife, a quiet Soul,
A Mind as well as body, whole;
Prudent simplicity, constant Friends,
A diet which no art Commends;
A Merry night without much Drinking,
A Happy Thought without much Thinking;
Each Night by Quiet Sleep made Short;
A Will to be but what thou art;
Possess'd of these, all else defy,
And neither wish nor fear to Die.

True Happiness, authorship unknown
Found in George Washington's
boyhood copybook

1

We mutually pledge to each other our Lives, our Fortunes, and our Sacred honor.

THE DECLARATION OF INDEPENDENCE

On this day, 8 August, 1778, a child was safely delivered . . .

Nay, not safely. Anything but safely.

. . . to Anne Howard Ogilvy and Seamus Michael Ogilvy of Tall Acre, Roan County, Virginia.

Dropping his quill pen, Seamus ran callused hands through hair bereft of a queue ribbon and watched a stray droplet of ink soak into the scarred desktop. Steadying his breathing, he picked up the pen and pressed on as if time was against him.

The infant's name is . . .

The heavy scratch of the nib against the family Bible's fragile page was halted by a knock on his study door. A servant to tell him he could finally see his firstborn? Or that his wife was dead? Or the both of them?

He called out with a shaky voice, but it was Dr. Spurlock who appeared, shutting the door soundly behind him. "A word with you, General Ogilvy, if I may." At Seamus's taut expression, Spurlock gave him a slight smile. "At ease, man, at ease. I'm not the undertaker."

Pulling himself to his feet, Seamus came out from behind the desk. "A word and a glass of Madeira are in order, at least." He went to a near cabinet and filled two crystal goblets as a newborn's wail rent the summer stillness, sharp and sweet as birdsong.

"'Tis about Anne," Spurlock said, a careful note to his tone.

Seamus passed him a glass. The doctor looked haggard after the lengthy ordeal, silver hair standing on end, spectacles askew, to say nothing of his waistcoat. Seamus was sure he looked equally unfit, having spent the night in his study.

"I don't need to tell you what a trial this birth has been. You've nearly worn a trail in the floor with your pacing." Spurlock regarded him with bleary, apologetic eyes. "Your wife is very weak. The baby, being so large, took a toll. Anne is a very narrow woman and continues to bleed heavily."

Blood. Wounds. Life and death. Seamus was used to such things. These were the staples of a soldier's life. Childbirth was, in a very real sense, battle. "I trust she'll recover in time."

Spurlock frowned. "Mistress Menzies, the midwife, nearly lost her at one point. If not for her presence of mind and the use of my forceps, we'd be having a very different conversation." He removed his spectacles and began cleaning them

10

with a handkerchief. "On a brighter note, your wife's sister is coming from Williamsburg to help care for her, though I do worry about you returning to duty so soon."

"Orders," Seamus said through a stitch of guilt. "General Washington wants me at reveille come morning." As it was, he'd have to ride all night to reach camp by the appointed time.

"I speak not only out of concern for your wife but for you, General. I can tell from looking at you that your own health has been compromised."

Seamus squared his shoulders. "A malaise of war, little more."

"Spoken like a true soldier." Spurlock fixed his gaze on an open window. "Very well, I'll talk plain and fast. Your wife faces a long recovery. She's always been a bit fragile, a true gentlewoman. And though it will be hard for you to hear, I'm duty bound to tell you her very life will be in danger if there's a second birth. Mistress Menzies concurs."

A second birth—and she'd barely withstood the first. The words spun round Seamus's head but made no sense. Remembering his Madeira, he took a sip, listening as the doctor explained feminine things he didn't know. Didn't want to know. Things that made him itch under his uniform collar with a heat that had nothing to do with the humid Virginia afternoon.

"Of course, husbands have certain needs, certain rights, if you will . . ." The doctor's words were becoming more labored, nearly lost as the babe's cries reached a crescendo upstairs.

"Say no more," Seamus replied. Spurlock's warning was clear as a midsummer day. All marital intimacy was at an end. "As it stands, I'll be away for the duration of the war." His outward calm belied the storm breaking inside him. "I won't—I mean, there won't be occasion to—" He stared at his boots. "I understand."

Spurlock nodded and downed the rest of his Madeira. "I knew you'd take it like the officer and gentleman you are. Now, if you're ready, your wife would like to present you with your firstborn."

Firstborn. Final born. And a robust daughter at that.

᠔

The bedchamber seemed strange since Seamus had been away so long. Stepping inside the elegant green and gilt room brought about unwanted, ill-timed memories—a crush of passionate encounters beginning on their wedding night. It was the eve of the war when he'd wed the belle of Williamsburg, three years later when their daughter was conceived on a hasty visit. He hardly remembered either. War had driven such sentimental things from his head, replacing them with the stench of smoke and powder instead.

To reorient himself, he latched onto the open corner cupboard where medicines were kept, the two wing chairs and tea table before the cold hearth. His gaze finally settled on the bed dressed with crewel embroidery.

"Seamus." Anne lay back on the bank of downy pillows, looking exhausted but triumphant. "Come meet your new daughter."

Spurs scraped the heart-pine floor before he stepped onto a lush rug and took a seat on the edge of the four-poster bed as carefully as he could. In light of the doctor's unwelcome words, the ever-delicate Anne seemed made of spun glass. If she was broken, he was to blame, at sixteen stone and over six feet.

As she settled the newborn in his arms, the catch in his

throat nearly stole all speech. One tiny hand peeked from the blanket, the plump face red and round as an orchard apple. He swallowed hard. "She's . . . beautiful."

Something wistful kindled in Anne's eyes. "You were hoping for a boy, though you never said so."

He gave a slight, dismissive shrug. "Soldiers always want sons."

"There'll be some, Lord willing. As soon as I'm well again . . ."

Her guileless words seared his heart. Spurlock hadn't told her then, but had left it up to him. Well, he wouldn't do it now. Let their dream of a large family be left intact a little longer.

Her lovely face turned entreating. "What shall we call her?"

The pride and expectancy in her eyes brought a wave of shame. He wouldn't confess he'd only entertained male names and had given little thought to a girl. Even his men had wagered on a boy, placing bold bets about the campfire till he'd ridden home to settle the matter himself.

"A name . . ." Lowering his head, he nuzzled the baby's ear, her downy neck and fuzz of dark hair. The decision came quick. He was used to thinking on his feet. As Washington's newly appointed major general, he could do little else. "Why not Lilias Catherine?"

"After my mother and yours?" Surprise shone in Anne's eyes. "Of course. 'Tis perfect."

He hesitated, looking into his daughter's face as if seeking answers. She seemed too little to merit such an onerous name. "We'll call her Lily Cate."

Nodding, Anne sank back on the pillows, her face so pale he could see the path of blue veins beneath. "I'm relieved. I didn't want you riding away without knowing."

He smiled. "Let me take her till you've slept for a few

hours. Doctor Spurlock said she won't be hungry yet, and—" He took a breath, fighting the lurch of leaving. "I don't know when I'll be back." The casual phrasing was more lie. He didn't know *if* he'd be back.

Her hazel eyes held his. "How is it on the field?"

The question wrenched him. She rarely asked. Their brief times together were too precious to be squandered on melancholy things.

"'Tis a strange war. We drill. We wait. We fight and fall back." He wouldn't tell her the biggest battle of his life was imminent, or that American forces were weak—deprived and diseased—and no match for Clinton's redcoats. Leaning forward, careful of the warm weight in his arms, he kissed her gently on the cheek. "I'll go below and introduce Miss Lily Cate to the household."

Yawning, eyes already half closed, Anne gave a last, lingering look at the baby. Down the wide, curving stair he went to a staff on tenterhooks since dawn. The birth had been—what had Spurlock said?—brutal. His people deserved a look, at least. The midwife was in the foyer preparing to leave, her daughter with her.

"Mistress Menzies, I'll settle up with you before you go." He glanced from her to her daughter, both of them looking far less disheveled than the doctor.

"There's no fee, General, not for a hero of the Revolution." Pulling on her gloves, Mistress Menzies smiled in her genteel, unruffled way, reminding him that she was no ordinary midwife.

"I have you to thank for calling in Spurlock when the situation became . . . untenable," he told her.

"You can thank my daughter for that, General. She is fleet of foot and a midwife in the making."

He took in Sophie Menzies in a glance. Dark. Plain. Clad in a fine crimson cape like her mother's.

"Then I thank you too, Miss Menzies," he said.

She smiled up at him, blue gaze fastening on the baby in his arms. "Have you named her, General Ogilvy?"

"Aye, she's to be called Lily Cate."

The pleasure in her expression seemed confirmation. "Lovely and memorable," she said with her mother's poise and a hint of her father's Scots burr. "I bid you and your wee daughter good day."

They withdrew out the front door while he went out the back, which was flung open to the river and leading to Tall Acre's dependencies. At his appearance, the steamy kitchen at the end of a shaded colonnade came to a standstill.

"Why, General Ogilvy, looks like you mustered up a fine baby." Ruby, his longtime cook, hastily left the hearth as the other servants looked on. She leaned near, and one ebony finger caressed a petal-soft cheek. "She's got your blue eyes and black hair, but I see the mistress in her pert nose and mouth."

The maids and housekeeper gathered round next on the rear veranda, cooing and sighing like the dovecote's doves. Next he went to the stables, a fatherly pride swelling his chest. By the time he returned to his study, his daughter had slept through a brief meeting with his estate manager and a first look at a prize foal. Completely smitten, he crossed to a wing chair in his study, reluctant to let her go.

"You're only a few hours old and already you've worked your way into my heart." His voice was a ragged whisper. "But there are some things you need to know. I don't want to leave you. I'm willing to die for you . . . and if I don't come back, I want you to forgive me."

The choked words staunched none of the pain. His daughter opened wide indigo eyes and stared up at him, as if she understood every syllable. He pressed his damp, unshaven cheek to hers, savoring the feathering of her warm breath on his face. Her flawlessness turned him inside out.

"Till we meet again, Lily Cate Ogilvy of Tall Acre. Never forget your loving father's words."

2

October 1783

Thank you, Lord, for an abundance of chestnuts.

The spiny treasures were strewn over the brittle October ground, thick as autumn leaves and hers for the taking. Light-headed from hunger, Sophie Menzies dropped to her knees, adding to her burgeoning basket. Her stomach growled in anticipation, gnawing from her navel to her backbone where fraying stays cinched tight. The burrs she gathered had just burst open, tickling her palm and begging for roasting.

Her only rival was a chattering, scolding squirrel.

Making a face at him, she succumbed to visions of chestnut pudding and steaming pots of tea. Not the weak, flavorless bohea tea of the Revolution but the forbidden Hyson she favored. Nary a drop had crossed her lips these eight years past. Would it ever? Tea seemed a luxury never to be had again.

When she looked up again, the sun was setting in back of Tall Acre, burnishing the brick a warm honey-gold. Sitting proudly at the end of its alley of Black Heart cherry trees, the old house looked more alive than it had in years, puffing gray smoke into clear autumn skies, its scrolled iron gates open wide.

Had General Ogilvy come home?

The snap of a twig snuffed her wondering. Scrambling to her feet, Sophie spun around. A tiny girl in a linen dress stood looking at her, fingers clutching the edges of a fine cambric apron.

Sophie smiled, trying to place her. "Good day."

"Good day," the child echoed. "Is this your woods or mine?"

Smile fading, Sophie surveyed the sagging fence that kept trespassers from Ogilvy land. "I believe the creek over there"—she pointed to a rutted ribbon of dust and rock, bone dry in late fall—"marks the boundary line between Three Chimneys and Tall Acre."

The girl looked down. Nested in her lovely apron were more nuts. She came forward and added them to Sophie's basket. Up close, Sophie felt a stirring of recognition.

Could this be the general's daughter? The one she'd helped her mother deliver years ago? The past reached out and yanked her back to anguished moans and the genteel woman who'd nearly died giving birth. Sophie studied the child's comely features, longing for a name though none was needed. The girl had her father stamped all over her. "Thank you, Miss . . . ?"

"Lilias Catherine Ogilvy." The child dropped a curtsey, her eyes huge beneath her ruffled cap. "But everyone calls me Lily Cate. I'm not yet six years old."

Sophie smiled. How could she have forgotten so bonny a name? "Well, Miss Lily Cate who is not yet six, you're very kind, but I have so many chestnuts. You're welcome to as many as you like."

"Oh, I just like to hunt them. But you—you look like you need them."

Biting her lip, Sophie hid a rueful smile. If her wants were obvious even to a child . . . "I'm glad you've come back to Tall Acre. 'Tis good to have neighbors again."

Lily Cate stayed solemn. "The general tells me to mind my manners. He'll want to know who I met in the woods today."

Joy sang through her—and then a qualm that she'd overlooked introductions. "Then tell him you met up with Sophie Menzies from Three Chimneys."

"Three Chimneys? Do you live there with your mother and father? Are you—" Worry raced through her eyes. "I'm sorry. The general says I chatter on so."

Sophie studied her, wanting to reach out and smooth a dark curl that fell free of her cap. "I like your chatter. 'Tis too quiet at Three Chimneys. My father is in Scotland, you see." She hesitated, still sore. "And my mother is in heaven."

Sorrow marred Lily Cate's pale face. "So is mine."

Sophie shifted her basket to her other arm. Mistress Ogilvy . . . dead? The last she knew, Anne Ogilvy was in Williamsburg, living with relatives.

"Do you think they're friends in heaven—my mama and yours?"

The tender question was nearly her undoing. Sophie's fingers closed around a chestnut till its spiny hull pierced her palm. "The best of friends."

"Perhaps . . ." Lily Cate seemed older than her five years. "Perhaps we can be friends too."

"Of course." As cozy as a woman of eight and twenty and a child of not yet six could be. Lily Cate was obviously lonesome. Missing her mother. Somewhat bewildered by this man she called the general. "Why don't we have a tea party? If you'll bring your doll . . ."

At this the child wilted. "My doll is in Williamsburg. The

general came to collect me in the night, and there was only room for me atop his horse. Everything got left behind." She cast a look back at Tall Acre, so much astir in her little face that Sophie's heart squeezed.

"I'm sorry," Sophie murmured. A tea party seemed suddenly silly.

"I'd best go. He doesn't like to go looking for me." Lily Cate turned without saying goodbye, her fine slippers kicking up autumn leaves as the wind sent more swirling down around them.

⁂

Sophie ran all the way home, feeling no older than Lily Cate. The back lane to Three Chimneys wasn't long but seemed endless this memorable day. The hedgerow, splashed red with Virginia creeper and bittersweet, went unnoticed, as did the showy oaks and sugar maples in all their autumn glory. Glynnis stood in their pilfered vegetable garden in back of the summer kitchen, a turnip in one gnarled hand, dismay in her expression.

Sophie burst through the open gate, nearly spilling her chestnut basket. "General Ogilvy. He's back!"

The housekeeper's gaze slanted east, as if fearful Sophie could be heard clear to Tall Acre. "The fighting's over then." Glynnis looked dazed, as if doubting the eight-year war would have an end. "Since we've had no *Gazette* . . ."

"Cornwallis's surrender to General Washington *must* be true." For once Sophie wished for a newspaper to prove it. They hadn't been able to afford the small expense, though they had heard rumors each market day when Glynnis went to Roan.

"Cornwallis and Washington, indeed!" Glynnis's mouth

twisted into a more hopeful smile. "What's all this about General Ogilvy?"

Sophie expelled a breath. "I met his wee daughter in the woods. They've recently come from Williamsburg." Delight filled her to the brim again despite the sad news about Tall Acre's mistress. "There's no other reason he'd be home. He's not been back in years."

The elderly woman studied her, looking doubtful. "You think he'll stop here?"

"I should hope so, given he's Curtis's commanding officer. Perhaps he'll bring some word—even a letter."

Glynnis's glum look reminded her the last letter they'd received was two very long years ago. Her brother, bless him, wasn't even aware their mother was dead. A melancholy silence returned the housekeeper to the kitchen, Sophie trailing after her.

"If he doesn't call soon, I'll ride to Tall Acre," Sophie told her. A bit forward, perhaps. Yet mightn't General Ogilvy allay their fears with a few well-timed words? "I've invited his daughter to a party."

"A party? Mercy!" Glynnis nearly threw up her hands. "And what will you be serving? Air? There's no tea to speak of either."

"Well, we should celebrate the war's end in some meaningful way." Sinking down atop a stool, Sophie looked to the barren larder, imagining it full again. "Flour can be ground from these chestnuts. Enough for a few biscuits, at least. We can pretend about the tea." She tried to stem Glynnis's displeasure by drawing attention to her burgeoning basket. "Lily Cate was kind enough to help me gather these today."

"Lily Cate, is it?" Glynnis's face softened. "Is she as lovely as her name?"

"Lovelier . . . perhaps a tad befuddled at being back."

Glynnis nodded. "She was just a babe when she was whisked away to Williamsburg." Her mood soured. "I suppose her high-minded mother is with her."

Sophie expelled a breath. "I'm afraid Mistress Ogilvy has passed away."

"Has she now?" Glynnis's wrinkled brow creased in consternation. "I never figured the general would come home a widower with a little daughter."

"Perhaps he'll bring us glad news."

Glynnis went to a window. "I'll be on the lookout then. Some glad news would be most welcome."

$\partial\!\!\!\!)$

By the light of a costly parlor candle Sophie worked, the slow drip of the wax reminding her of the pence she didn't have to replace it. The case clock chimed midnight in the chill, silent foyer. She needed to be abed—her fingers were stiff from the cold, and protesting—but the mere memory of Lily Cate's entreating face kept her at her task.

Earlier, a search in the attic and a prayer had turned up her old wax doll in a dusty trunk. Yellowed with age, the velvet dress worn in places, the doll had once been the height of French fashion. Snipping a length of lace from one of her mother's old gowns, Sophie began embellishing the barest places. A few brushstrokes of paint had revived the doll's dull face, her smile in place. Sophie sighed. Was she glaikit to feel such excitement over a well-loved doll, or making sure a little girl had one again?

No doubt Lily Cate's Williamsburg doll was much finer. She might reject this relic out of hand. If she was as particular as her mother, preferring the fancy over the familiar, she would. There was no guarantee the child would ever return to the woods. Or that General Ogilvy would pay them a call.

Both might turn out as badly as her volatile afternoon.

Her impulsive walk to the village of Roan and back had been her undoing. But the two-mile jaunt wasn't time enough for second thoughts. Usually she wasn't given to such rashness. Spirits high, she'd dared to think with the war won, all would be forgiven and forgotten.

'Twas market day. Easy enough to blend in with the crowd. By mid-morning the tiny hamlet was overflowing with vendors and shoppers hawking anything from fresh fish to men's queue ribbons. Small fires in blackened fire pits glowed like fireflies among the walkways, warming any who cared to tarry.

Hands clammy despite the cold, Sophie sent her gaze toward the milliner's. She'd taken care to make her rare visit to the village a success, praying and packing samples of her needlework to show the Roan seamstress. But once she stood in the tidy shop, the portly woman regarded her with smug dislike.

"You're Lord Menzies's daughter, ain't you?" The seamstress looked her over as if she was the village doxy, her refusal in her face. "I've no work for any Tories, mind you."

"I'm not a Tory," Sophie replied hastily. "My loyalties lie with the Patriots. 'Tis why I remained at Three Chimneys during the war."

"But you quartered British soldiers, the same ones who did damage to this shop."

"Those soldiers forced their way into my home too." Sophie swallowed, trying a different direction. "If you'll allow me to show you my needlework—"

"There's little need for fancy needlework in Roan."

"I could take in mending then."

"I've already hired that out."

"Is there—" Her heart was jumping about so the words came out half choked. "Anything else you need?"

"I need you to take your leave, lest someone see you here and decide my loyalties are in question." The seamstress pointed to the door, voice cresting. "Roan has long memories where your father is concerned."

Lowering her head, Sophie went out, a hasty retort withering. She didn't blame the seamstress. Her father had been insufferable and arrogant, supporting British taxes that caused many in the village undue hardship. Even her mother's fine reputation for midwifery had been tarnished because of him. And now the loathing lingered.

Face still heated from humiliation hours later, she hemmed the doll's dress in the security of Three Chimneys' parlor. The night boasted a brilliant harvest moon, coming up now through the east-facing windows. Glynnis had forgotten to close the shutters. Perhaps the room wouldn't be so cold if they would remember. But Glynnis, in her old age, was increasingly forgetful. Setting her sewing aside, Sophie closed all but the one framing the moon. Tonight its beauty and light kept her company in a house all too spare and still.

Stifling a yawn, she returned to the monotony of her sewing. She nodded off, nearly piercing her finger, then shot upright at the sound of shattering glass.

Standing, she sent the doll tumbling from her lap, her stool overturning, her eyes on the flames licking at the plank floor a few paces to her right. A leather water bucket was by the door, so she doused the fire, her woolen skirts and shoes splattered in the process. She was barely aware of Glynnis in a nightdress standing in the doorway behind her.

"What on earth?" Her housekeeper's cry was indignant as she surveyed a far parlor window, a sudden wind whooshing in uninvited.

Bending down, Sophie touched the pitch-covered paper that had been afire moments before. Beneath it was a heavy jagged rock, capable of breaking the best British crown glass. A soggy note was attached, penned by a heavy hand.

Yer Tory house will be burnt to Hades.

She started for the window, gleaming shards crunching underfoot, but Glynnis's equally sharp hiss kept her away.

"Don't be inviting more trouble, mind you." Taking her by the arm, Glynnis led her into the foyer, both of them shaking. "I'll fetch Henry to board it up."

Sophie sent her gaze to the front and back entry of Three Chimneys. "Are the doors locked?" But what did it matter when the parlor now lay open?

"Tighter than a drum. You go on up to bed, and I'll join you. 'Twill be just like when the Lobsterbacks invaded and we were quarantined in your room."

"But the war's been won," Sophie murmured. "All hostilities should cease."

"Mayhap in time." Glynnis patted her hand. "You should have stayed away from Roan today. Likely there's some who took offense at the sight of a Menzies."

"I only meant to earn coin enough for some sugar for the tea party." Sophie turned back at the foot of the staircase. "I forgot Lily Cate's doll—"

Glynnis almost scoffed. "D'ye truly think the child's father, a high and mighty American general, will let his daughter darken your door? Or darken it himself?"

"I do." She refused to let go of the hope, however small. The general had had a special fondness for Curtis, hadn't he? Her brother had been an avowed Patriot, no matter their father's rabid Tory sentiments.

Returning to the parlor with Glynnis's bulky form between her and the shattered glass, Sophie bent and picked up the doll and her scattered sewing, trying to stave off that old, insidious fear that had begun with the Revolution.

There had been other rocks, other damage. Ugly words and jeers. Why had she thought that the peace treaty General Washington had signed would restore peace to her own tattered world?

The war might be won for America, but it still raged on in Roan, Virginia.

3

Glynnis stood in the bedchamber doorway the next afternoon, looking nearly as disbelieving as when Sophie had told her the war was won. "He's come."

Sophie turned back to her dressing table, a cameo and ribbon in hand, and bit her lip to keep from saying, "I know."

She'd heard the clip of hooves and rustle of leaves through her open casement window. Spied the sleek black stallion tied to the hitching post below. Felt that peculiar tightness in her chest and the dampness of her palms the general always wrought, whether in newsprint or in person. Now here he was on her very door, the hero of Brandywine and Germantown and Monmouth and who knew what else.

Heroics be hanged.

'Twas her own reputation she was worried about. Would he shun her as they did in Roan? Turning back to the looking glass, Sophie fiddled with the cameo about her throat.

"Do I look presentable?" she asked, startling slightly when Glynnis came closer and pulled viciously at a stray thread on her skirt.

"You're in your best gown, though 'tis hardly in fashion. Your shoes look fit for the dung heap. And your hair is in need of covering. Other than that, you'll do." Turning, Glynnis plucked some pins from the dressing table and secured a lace cap atop Sophie's hastily upswept hair. "Mercy, but you're pale as dust. But since this isn't a social call, it hardly matters."

Sophie tried not to frown at the mirror, finding her reflection far from pleasing. "Where is the general? Not in Father's study, I hope."

"Ha! I've better sense than that. No need to remind him of your father's Tory sins. I put him in the front parlor as the rear parlor window is boarded up."

Mumbling thanks, Sophie started down the curving staircase, feeling like she'd swallowed a swarm of butterflies.

Like the shunned woman she was.

∞

Three Chimneys had seen better days. But then, so had he. Seamus's gaze roamed the once-grand room, now shabby and frayed as a militiaman's coat. The milk paint was peeling in places, the Wilton carpet thin, the damask drapes a tired silver-blue. Sophie Menzies's beautiful home had been used to quarter British soldiers, their angry spur marks cutting across the heart-pine floor beneath his boots. More than a few rooms had been ransacked, or so he'd heard, while Tall Acre sat untouched to the west, a locked treasure chest amidst sheltering trees.

He tunneled a hand through unruly hair, cocked hat tucked under one arm, and wished for a little warmth. The big house was cold and no fire had been laid, nor had there been in recent days. Swept clean without a speck of ash, the tiled hearth looked neat enough to crawl into and nap. He appreciated a good fire and would have lit one himself had there been some wood. In his tenure in the army, the poverty of continual cold outweighed an empty belly every time. Since his return, every chimney at Tall Acre was belching smoke as he vowed he'd never be cold again.

"General Ogilvy, welcome back."

The gentle voice spun him around. He gave a slight bow, the gallant gesture a bit stiff after so long unpracticed. Should he kiss her hand? But they were caught behind her back, denying him the privilege.

Sophie Menzies was hardly the lass he remembered.

Tall. Slim as a riding whip. Beneath a creamy cap, her hair was caught back, a few sooty strands escaping, framing a milk-glass complexion and a bone structure far too fragile. She was smiling at him, but that seemed fragile too, as if she expected he had come to wipe any fine feeling from the room with dire news.

He reached into his pocket and extracted a small tin of tea. "In honor of war's end, Miss Menzies. And a reminder of how the whole miserable mess began."

She took the offering, delight filling in the lean lines of her face. "Thank you." Bringing the gift to her chest, she held it as if it were worth its weight in gold—which it nearly was. "I've had no real tea since '76."

Nay? He wagered she'd had no guests since then either. If memory served, Roan folks reviled her father. But he was gone and gone for good, nearly tarred and feathered upon his exit. Perhaps the ill feeling against the Menzies family would follow.

"Would you like refreshments?" Gesturing to twin wing chairs, she invited him to sit. But she was looking at him as if hospitality was the last thing on her mind—and his.

"Nay," he said abruptly as if communicating to one of his men. She drew back a bit, the play of hope and dismay in her face tugging at him. "Tea then," he amended reluctantly. Virginia hospitality guaranteed a lengthy visit.

She pulled on a bell cord, making him glad she still had a servant at least. With a swish of her skirts she settled opposite him, tea tin in hand. Best come to the point posthaste.

"I have little news, I'm afraid." He spoke slowly, trying to let her down gently. "I don't know of your brother's whereabouts, though I wish I did. Captain Menzies was under my command until Richmond. Matters became confusing in the aftermath. Men were unaccounted for . . ."

She looked to her lap, struggling visibly for a response. "I've heard many soldiers died of disease and others lay aboard prison ships."

"Aye, but some are on their way home again. Your brother might be one of them. If I hear anything more, you'll be the first to know." He eyed the parlor door and changed course. "Is it just you and your housekeeper here, Miss Menzies?"

"I've a hired man, Henry."

A hired man? The one who looked to be a hundred years old? The housekeeper wasn't much younger. As Seamus thought it, the door pushed open and she appeared, carrying a tea service with shaking hands, the silver slightly tarnished. Thanking her, Sophie popped open the fragrant tin.

When the older woman left, he resumed the thread of conversation. "I remember your mother, Midwife Menzies, helped deliver my daughter."

"My mother, yes." She kept her hands busy making the tea, her words surprisingly candid. "She passed away last year. The end of April."

Had she? He'd lost touch with all sorts of things since

he'd left Tall Acre, including his neighbors. "I'm sorry. I didn't know."

"The doctor said it was her heart. But she was more broken in spirit than body, I think."

This he understood. He'd lost more men on the field to heartache and hopelessness than enemy fire and disease. Setting his jaw, he watched as Sophie readied chipped china cups. No sugar was in sight, but he liked his tea plain, even if Anne didn't. *Hadn't.* The bruising thought was cut off by the sight of Sophie's bony, slightly reddened fingers. Not a lady's hands by any stretch. What exactly had happened to Lord Menzies's genteel daughter?

"You're no stranger to mourning yourself, General. I'm very sorry about your wife." She kept her eyes down, her tone dulcet. "I also want to express my gratitude, my heartfelt thanks, for your service to the cro—colonies."

She'd nearly said *crown*, but it was an honest slip. They all needed time adjusting to the fact that they were no longer under British rule but a thoroughly American one.

"I'm relieved to have escaped the noose as a traitor, aye," he murmured, still amazed he had.

She looked up suddenly, catching him off guard. Open admiration shone in her face, so much so that he felt a discomfort bone deep.

A hero in the field. A failure at home. If she only knew . . .

He filled the taut silence. "And you, Miss Menzies? Have you no desire to return home to Scotland?"

Surprise flashed in her eyes, making him regret the quick question. "My home is here, General Ogilvy, come what may. I'm an American now, no matter my father's loyalties."

He nodded. "I'm simply trying to gauge how you're going to get along here at Three Chimneys by yourself."

"Till my brother returns?" She paused, tongue between her teeth as she concentrated on pouring the tea. "I may try to resume indigo production. We were quite successful before the war, till British raiders set fire to our fields and storehouses." She spoke quietly but confidently, as if she'd given the matter much thought. "Three Chimneys also has a fine mulberry grove. I'm considering raising silkworms."

"Silk cultivation?" He studied her, slightly disbelieving. "Do you have any idea how labor intensive that is?"

"I'm not afraid of hard work. I've heard a woman and three children can make ten pounds of raw silk for fifty dollars in five weeks' time."

"Until a blight afflicts your mulberry trees and cotton surpasses silk." At her startled look he continued wryly, "Not to mention your lack of three children."

She drew back. "You're not very encouraging, sir."

"Nay. But I am pragmatic." He tried a different tack. "I remember your mother saying you were a midwife in the making."

She shook her head, and he felt another door close. "I'm no howdy, mind you. My mother hoped I would follow in her footsteps, but I merely assisted at a few births. The truth is no one in Roan County wanted my help given my father's Tory leanings. And in the end few wanted my mother's either. But you needn't worry about Three Chimneys." She gave him a steaming cup—and a disarming smile. "We'll get along here as we have these eight years past."

"Of course," he murmured, unconvinced. He wagered she'd had a hard time getting any supplies in Roan or elsewhere given the ill feeling against them. And her telling leanness was proof.

She changed course. "On a lighter note, I've met your wee daughter."

"So she told me." He glanced down at his injured hand, wondering if she'd noticed . . . if she'd respond in revulsion like Lily Cate. "She wants to see you again, but I don't want her to be a nuisance."

"Nuisance?" Again her gaze met his, awash with protest. "She's no nuisance!" She looked oddly hurt—and had likely crossed him off her list of admirable persons. "Is she a bother to you, General Ogilvy?"

He looked to the cold hearth, afraid she'd read the answer in his eyes. His maimed hand clenched. He wouldn't say Lily Cate was afraid of him. That she sometimes refused to even speak to him. "Obviously she's a different child with you."

"She's enchanting. She even curtsied. Her manners are very fine." Her entreating tone lured him to look at her again. "I invited her to a tea party, just the two of us, only we had no tea. Till now."

He paused. Was she so starved for company that even a little girl would suffice? "You sent over a doll for her. She won't part with it. Even talks to it."

"I should hope so, sir. That's what little girls do."

Her continual if respectful use of *sir* seemed to drive a wedge between them, as did his near fatal misstep about his daughter. "Very well. She can come for a visit. Just send word when you want her."

"I shall." She got up and crossed to a desk beneath a wide Palladian window. He followed the blue swish of her skirts longer than he should have. With her spartan leanness, she reminded him of his scrawniest soldiers. Focusing on the hearth, he was glad there was no fire lulling him with its warmth. As it was, he wanted to stay longer, spill out the problems pressing in on him from Williamsburg. Sophie

Menzies seemed a sensible young woman who might help him untangle the trouble he was in.

She returned and passed him a piece of paper with Lily Cate's name written in an elegant hand. "Tea is at four o'clock on the morrow. Her doll is invited too."

"That would be Sophie."

She looked at him, momentarily perplexed. "The doll bears my name?"

"According to my daughter."

Softness filled her face, turning her touchingly girlish. More like the Sophie Menzies he remembered. "I'm honored, truly, General."

They finished their tea in silence, making him glad the cups were small. She was likely still thinking of Curtis, probably ruing the lack of news. His gut twisted at not bringing her a good report. He hadn't felt so rattled since he'd helped rout Cornwallis at Yorktown. Yet there was a strange peace in this cold, war-stripped parlor—and something else he couldn't explain.

He'd come here expecting the plump, pampered daughter of his nemesis, but this lass had engaged him on every level.

Standing, he tossed aside his query of why she had no fire and made ready to leave. "Thank you for the tea, Miss Menzies."

"Nay, General Ogilvy. Thank *you*."

Sophie stood at the parlor window and watched Seamus Ogilvy ride away till he was no more than a black streak across the brilliant autumn ground. His rich blue uniform with its buff facings and yellow buttons commanded a second look and no small dose of respect. Having a seamstress's eye, she was drawn to all the braw details. The silken sash draping his chest and the gold epaulettes spanning his shoulders with their silver stars were a heady reminder of his rank. As if she needed reminding. She'd always been partial to rebel blue.

Despite the rigors of war, he'd somehow managed to emerge more handsome, if a bit weathered. His years away had faded the remarkable eyes she remembered to a weary yet still vibrant indigo. She'd even glimpsed silver threads in his black hair.

There was no denying his noble cause had cost him dearly. When she'd spied his severed fingers, it had taken all her will not to gasp. If she had, she'd have only injured him further. She'd noticed how he'd self-consciously turned his wrist so that the wound was hidden beneath his coat sleeve, as if it pained him to look at it, or he rued her reaction.

She reached for the bell cord above her mother's favorite chair and rang for Glynnis again. Never had her gout-ridden housekeeper come round so fast, her amazement almost amusing. "Tea, ooh-la-la! Not bland bohea but fine congou!"

"The general simply wanted to soften the news about Curtis."

Glynnis's smile vanished. "What news?"

"No news really." The hurt of it was hard to mask. "General Ogilvy doesn't know where Curtis is. Not since the debacle with Benedict Arnold in Richmond."

Clucking her displeasure, Glynnis gathered up the tea tray and led the way to the kitchen. The sweet, nutty fragrance of roasting chestnuts invited them in, banishing any melancholy. "I've scored all the nuts and they're cooking over the coals." She sniffed. "Mercy, but they're done in a hurry!"

"Here, have a wee sit," Sophie told her. "The chestnuts

are better peeled when warm. I'll manage that while you enjoy your tea."

As Glynnis took a stool, Sophie poured her a cup of congou, her practiced poise dissolving with another thought of Curtis. Tepid liquid splashed into the saucer, and Glynnis sipped with relish. "Remember when the general used to pasture sheep in the chestnut grove and they'd crack open the burrs with their hooves?"

"Oh aye," Sophie replied, thinking of better days. "Perhaps he'll bring sheep back to Tall Acre now that he's home."

"I overheard you telling him you'd be fine here with just me and Henry, even if it was more a fib. I didn't expect you to say we nigh starved last winter and have no hopes of putting in a crop come spring."

"We can get by on the apples we've harvested and the root vegetables in the cellar," Sophie murmured as she emptied the pot of steaming chestnuts onto a cloth atop the kitchen table. "Though someone stole our milk cow, we still have a few chickens. Once Curtis comes home, all will be well again."

"Perhaps." Glynnis's hands shook as she lifted her cup, the rattling cough she'd gotten from a summer cold still astir in her chest. "I wasn't eavesdropping, but I did hear you say something more about a tea party."

"Tea for three on the morrow. Just me, Lily Cate, and her doll." Sophie felt a catch in her chest. "Mama always did that, remember?"

"I'll not forget." For a rare moment Glynnis turned wistful. "'Twas always in spring when she'd spread her first tea in the garden beneath the rose arbor, a signal that it was warm enough for you and Curtis to go barefoot. And then again in autumn right before the weather turned. She always seemed to know somehow when things were about to change."

The arbor was overgrown now, the roses mostly lost to disease. Perhaps with a little care, she could coax them back to life come spring. Sophie plunged ahead, away from the past. "I've set a little molasses by, enough to sweeten our biscuits. I'll even lay a fine linen tablecloth, some of Mama's Wedgwood china—"

"What little the redcoats didn't destroy, you mean."

"Surely there's something left. I even spied a few late-blooming roses for a bouquet."

Glynnis made a face. "Perhaps it won't be such a flop after all. Henry's just brought round a crock of cream."

"Oh?" The mention made Sophie frown. Henry's habit of collecting things was uncanny. Though she'd never say so, she feared he was meirleach. A fine thief.

Glynnis seemed to read her thoughts. "He traded it for some pheasant he shot, he said, though I wonder." Her voice fell to a whisper. "His eyesight is so poor and he's deaf as a post . . ."

"Well, neither of you have drawn wages since the war began, so anything you're inclined to do is welcome."

But stolen or otherwise?

Lord, forgive us.

"Well, this is our home nearly as much as yours. Three Chimneys has kept us fed and a roof o'er our heads, even if it's a leaky one." Eyeing the nearly empty porcelain teapot, Glynnis muttered, "I wonder how the general came by such fine tea?"

"Really, Glynnis. Given he's just conquered England, I'm not surprised."

"Ha!" Glynnis sputtered. "You make it sound like he won the war single-handedly!"

Sophie's skin crawled with warmth. Was her admiration so

obvious—and ridiculous? "All I'm saying is that he has connections. And now that the war's over, trading can resume."

"I must say 'tis good to have a young man about again, especially with rocks being hurled through parlor windows."

"Young?" Sophie began fanning the chestnuts with her apron. Seamus Ogilvy was nigh on thirty, at least. "I wouldn't call the general young."

"Young or no, he'll have his hands full returning Tall Acre to its former glory, and no mistress to boot, just a motherless child."

Sophie held her peace and poured the remaining tea, breathing in its intoxicating fragrance and wishing for a little loaf sugar.

A question rose in Glynnis's eyes even as a smile hovered. "You wouldn't, by any chance, have designs on the general by way of his little daughter?"

Sophie set the kettle down so hard the table rattled. "Glynnis! You make the situation sound so—conniving!" A sick feeling swirled in her belly. Is that what Seamus Ogilvy thought? She prayed not. "The truth is I'm lonely. I've always loved children. We've had no merriment at Three Chimneys for ages, even if it is a humble tea party." Other than Reverend Hopkins and his wife, they'd had no visitors at all save a beggar or two they'd fed in the kitchen. "Don't you dare think I'm glaikit enough to set my sights so high. There are plenty of wealthy widows from the war, not to mention wealthy spinsters. Even if I did have designs on him, he'd never consider the penniless daughter of a Tory."

"Tories aside, there are no wealthy widows or spinsters on hand who show an interest in his daughter. And he hardly needs a rich wife. Young and virile as he is, any warm, willing one will do—"

"Glynnis, please." Though Sophie set her jaw, the storm inside her threatened to break.

"Call me a matchmaker if you will, but I've always had your matrimonial interests at heart. And I'll forever begrudge heaven for allowing a war to steal away your best prospects. You were the belle of Williamsburg once."

"'Twas long ago. What's done is done." Sophie moved beyond herself and her stack of regrets, recalling the general's ravaged hand. "We've all made sacrifices, every one."

They fell silent, each locked in thoughts too personal to share. Canny Englishwoman that she was, did Glynnis really believe Sophie was smitten? If so, she'd attempt to dispel that notion all she could.

Thinking it left her feeling steamy as the tea.

The sun was in back of Three Chimneys, setting fire to its mulberry grove as it blazed from sight. Turning her dreams of silk production to ashes in light of Seamus Ogilvy's dismissive words. From her bedchamber window, Sophie had a heartrending view of the tumbled-down dependencies and untilled fields that had once been proud and thriving. What had the general thought of the change when he'd ridden over? That this was merely a consequence of war? Just recompense for her father's fleeing Virginia?

"Glynnis, who is that strange man by the arbor?" She put a hand to her throat, fighting the near breathless fear that outsiders always wrought.

Glynnis's chuckle set her at ease as she put away clean linens in the clothespress. "He's a guard. General's orders."

"*What?*"

Her housekeeper all but crowed in satisfaction. "The

general asked Henry about the broken parlor window. Seems like Seamus Ogilvy does not miss much. And Henry was only too happy to tell him."

"But a guard?"

"The general means to send a message to Roan and whoever else that Three Chimneys is not to be disturbed or they'll have him to tangle with. He'll lodge with Henry in the shed." At Sophie's slack-jawed silence, Glynnis burst into cackling laughter. "I mean the guard, not the general!"

Sophie stood, taking it in. The general had done that? For her? Nay, for them all. He'd obviously seen they were little more than prisoners of war at Three Chimneys and sought to do something about it. Or . . . had this guard been placed to keep an eye on her? To ferret out any suspected Tory activity? Did the general regard her as the enemy, much like Roan did?

"How long is he to stay on?" she asked indifferently, turning away from the window.

"The guard?" Glynnis lifted her shoulders in a shrug and shut the clothespress. "Best ask General Ogilvy that, Miss Sophie."

Ask? Ask she would. At the first opportunity.

4

The day of the party dawned clear, but by mid-afternoon the weather was a shambles. Rain fell so hard Sophie was forced to put a ceramic chamber pot beneath the front parlor's most incessant leak. When the wind picked up, rattling the windowpanes, she was tempted to cancel the party altogether. A little girl might catch her death going out on such a day. Torn, she summoned Henry to deliver a note, excusing Lily Cate till the weather turned in their favor.

Returning upstairs to her room she took pains dressing in case the storm cleared, resurrecting an old garment from her stale wardrobe. Sewn by Williamsburg's foremost dressmaker for her twentieth birthday, the fabric was the finest silk damask, the exquisite embroidery a palette of blues worked with silver thread. Though lovely, the gown hung on her in places, namely her bodice and waist, where the lean years had whittled her away.

She would always remember the date she was to wear it. April 19, 1775. The day the bloodshed began—the day her social season ended. She was sheltered, ignorant of the changing political landscape, so it took months for her to grasp why her father was an unpopular man in Virginia. Like Governor Dunmore and other Tories in power, he'd fled to Britain at the start of the war, though her mother stayed steadfast, refusing to leave her children and home.

Oh Mama, I miss your steady spirit.

Evelyn Baird Menzies, she'd come to realize, was a stronger soul than her nearsighted father. His political ambitions and marital neglect had taken a toll on them all but especially her mother, whom he'd abandoned and cut off despite resuming a luxurious lifestyle in Edinburgh.

Father, I'm glad you're gone.

Slipping off her scuffed everyday shoes, she sank her feet into silken slippers dyed the hue of her gown, tiny ivory rosettes at the toe. Silk stockings and garters, manifold petticoats, and a blue velvet hair ribbon completed her wardrobe.

For once she was glad of her tousled head. There was never a need for curling tongs, nor a maid. She simply swept up her hair with paste and garnet pins, leaving a few wisps spiraling down, the ribbon carelessly woven in.

Even now she recalled the barely veiled surprise in the general's eyes when he first saw her. As if he didn't believe it was she. Where was the plump, pampered girl he remembered? Sophie felt suddenly shabby despite her best dress, naught but a scarecrow in faded fabric and lace. Shutting her eyes, she cut off the thought with saber-like swiftness, glad when Glynnis called from the foyer below.

"They're here."

Truly? Despite the storm? Taking a last look in the mirror, Sophie pinched her wan cheeks, wishing for a little powder, though it would take a wheelbarrow full to coat her dark hair. Powder, some said, was decidedly British and going out of fashion.

When she reached the foyer, Glynnis was nowhere in sight. Unembarrassed by the lack of servants, Sophie opened the wide front door herself as Lily Cate got down from the Ogilvy coach and her father helped her leap over a muddy puddle.

Out of uniform today, Seamus Ogilvy was dressed like a laird, a country gentleman. The master of Tall Acre. The damp had curled the ends of his hair, adding a fine sheen to his rich broadcloth coat. His eyes sought hers as he cleared the bottom step—a thoughtful, soul-searching blue that nearly sent her spinning. Lily Cate clutched her doll, smiling shyly in expectation.

"Welcome to Three Chimneys," Sophie said as they swept inside.

Rain-speckled, Lily Cate looked up at her father, who seemed to be waiting for her to do something. Her freckled face was blank. Leaning down, he whispered in her ear and she brightened.

Drawing out her skirts with one hand, she curtsied and Sophie did the same. "I wasn't sure you'd come, but I'm very glad you did."

"If I let the weather deter me, Miss Menzies, the war would never have been won." There was wry amusement in Seamus's gaze and something akin to relief. "When would you like for me to collect her?"

Never. She smiled at Lily Cate. "Three Chimneys parties can go on for . . ." *Forever.* "Nightfall, perhaps."

"You're a gracious hostess."

She took a breath. "Before you go, sir, I wanted to ask about the guard you've posted."

His gaze was unwavering. "Is there some problem?"

"I was just wondering . . . is it truly necessary, General?"

"Necessary? Given the expense of crown glass, I'd say it was essential. The arrangement won't go on forever. Just till all hostilities cease."

Would they ever? Clasping Lily Cate's hand, she began moving toward the morning room tucked behind the stairs, a smaller, cozier spot than the front parlor where she'd first met with him. Lily Cate didn't look back or bid him goodbye, leaving Sophie to smile self-consciously in farewell, glad when he turned and retraced his way down the steps.

They stood on the threshold of the morning room, surveying the toys rescued from the attic. Sophie said, "I'm glad you've brought your doll."

"Her name's Sophie—and she's your doll, remember."

"Not anymore. She's been a bit downcast hidden away in the attic for so long. She needs a real playmate like you."

Lily Cate hugged the doll close. "I take her everywhere with me and even bring her to table. The general tells me not to, so I hide her on my lap."

Sophie smiled, sure he was well aware of the simple deception. "She might be hungry then, though I'm not sure what dolls like to eat."

"I do. Rose petals." Lily Cate reached out and plucked a spent blossom off the linen cloth.

For a moment Sophie enjoyed the pleasure filling Lily Cate's usually solemn face as she took in sparkling if chipped china and a plate of chestnut flour biscuits with molasses. A far cry from scones and clotted cream and jam. A pewter bowl of lush pink roses graced the table, the last of the season.

When they sat down, Sophie folded her hands. "Shall we give thanks for a lovely tea?"

Lily Cate blinked. "You give thanks—pray?"

"Always."

She tilted her head. "Why doesn't the general pray?"

"Perhaps he does so in secret."

"Uncle Richard and Aunt Charlotte pray." She yawned, exposing tiny kitten teeth. "Long prayers that make me sleepy."

Sophie would have smiled but for the general's prayerlessness. As it was, she stumbled on the other names. Anne's Williamsburg relations? Lily Cate's mother had had a sister, she recalled, trying to piece together what little she knew. What had Lily Cate said in the woods that day?

The general came to collect me in the night, and there was only room for me atop his horse. Everything got left behind.

With her father at war, the child had been in Williamsburg since her mother died—till he'd returned her to Tall Acre.

Lily Cate's eyes clouded. "I pray the general grows his fingers again."

"Oh?"

"I pray I can go back to Williamsburg and get my toys."

"Williamsburg is a lovely place. I used to live there too, in a townhouse at the end of England Street."

"Do you miss it?"

"Sometimes." Sophie suppressed the wistful ache. "But I'm here now, and I've met you."

Joining hands, they bowed their heads and Sophie spoke the words her mother had taught her long ago. "We thank Thee, Lord, for happy hearts, for rain and sunny weather. We thank Thee, Lord, for this our food, and that we are together. Amen."

Leaning closer, Lily Cate whispered, "You forgot to pray for the general's fingers."

Sophie closed her eyes again. "We pray too for healing for General Ogilvy's injuries, seen and unseen. And we thank

Thee that he was very brave in battle and has come home to Tall Acre at last."

Looking satisfied, Lily Cate watched as Sophie pretended to pour tea into the doll's miniature cup. "We'll serve our honored guest first."

Lily Cate peered closer. "But there's nothing coming out."

"I think she'd rather eat rose petals."

Lily Cate giggled, the sound like a chime in the quiet room. Whoever had raised Seamus Ogilvy's daughter had taught her fine manners. She sipped her tea daintily, scattered no crumbs, and declined a second biscuit. "I'll send one home to your father," Sophie told her.

"He'll be glad as we have no cook." She made a face. "Well, there's Florie, but she burns things. He's seeking another."

Sophie sipped her tea. "There's much afoot at Tall Acre then."

Lily Cate nodded. "The general has a hand in everything. He even helped with my hair." She touched her lopsided bow. "But when he brushes it, he tears out the tangles and everything."

The idea of him fussing with so simple a task made her smile. "Perhaps you should ask him to be gentler."

"I do, but he still isn't."

"Perhaps if you called him Papa and not the general he would be," Sophie ventured. What did it matter to her what she called him? But somehow it did.

Looking pensive, Lily Cate asked to be excused then slipped out of her seat, drawn to the toys. Dropping down beside her, Sophie showed her the painted Pandora dolls hidden inside the dollhouse's parlor, and the novelty of the tiny dog with its wagging tail. They began rearranging furniture and hosting a ball to which even the dog was invited, both of them unaware of Glynnis coming in to clear the table and the grumble of distant thunder.

Suddenly Lily Cate sat back on her heels. "I hope the gener—Papa—forgets to come get me."

Sophie read the worry in her honest eyes. They were the same remarkable shade of her father's and bore the same unsettling disquiet.

"If I can't go back to Williamsburg, Miss Sophie, I want to stay with you."

"Your papa would miss you if you did."

"He could come visit us sometimes . . . for tea."

Reaching out, Sophie coaxed back a wisp of midnight hair and straightened Lily Cate's awkward bow. "Even if I wanted to keep you, I couldn't."

"Do you already have a little girl?"

"Not yet, but I hope to someday." 'Twas the wrong thing to say. The light in Lily Cate's eyes was snuffed like candle flame. Sophie checked the impulse to plant a kiss on her furrowed brow. "For now 'tis just the two of us, and I'm very thankful."

Looking only slightly relieved, Lily Cate pressed a hand over her mouth and yawned. Was she in need of a nap? Glynnis napped. Henry napped. Sophie, never. Following the girl's cue, she opened her arms in invitation, feeling sleepy herself. Without a word, Lily Cate climbed onto her lap.

Warmed by the unfamiliar weight of her, Sophie shut her own eyes, as hungry for a caring touch as Lily Cate. Though she'd loved her mother with all her heart, Evelyn Baird Menzies had not been a demonstrative woman. Was the general not a demonstrative man?

"I hope she's not slept the whole afternoon."

Behind her stood Seamus Ogilvy, obviously having been

let in by Glynnis. Sophie looked to the window, the autumn darkness creeping in. Unable to turn round to greet him without waking Lily Cate, Sophie said over her shoulder, "I think all our playing wore her out."

"'Tis more than that." A soldierly stiffness tightened his tone. "She doesn't sleep much at night for crying."

"Crying?"

"Aye . . . night after night."

The complaint in his low words caught at her. "Do you not go to her? Take her in your arms?"

"I—why would I?"

"Why?" The question came soft but reproachful nonetheless. "Have your years in the field made you so hard a man you've become unmoved by your own daughter, General?"

"Mayhap." He came nearer, taking a wing chair. "The truth is she's afraid of me."

"Afraid of you? Why wouldn't she be?" She darted a glance at Lily Cate, fearing she'd awaken to their intense whispering. "She's likely never seen a man with a ravaged hand."

"She's my daughter," he shot back, as if that should resolve everything.

She took a breath. "You're a stranger to her, simply a man in uniform who's been grievously wounded. She's a wee girl, and you've been away even longer. She's lost her mother. She might have lost you—"

"But she didn't." He leaned forward, legs slightly apart, cocked hat hanging from his peg of an injured hand. "We have five years to make up for, and I can't begin to get past her fear of me."

"Taking her in your arms might help." She held his gaze, so startled by the pain in his expression she nearly backed down. "Be less the general and more a father. Hold her close at night and chase the shadows away."

A muscle convulsed in his jaw. "The only person I want in my arms at night is my wife."

The intimate detail set her face aflame. "I understand your loss—"

"Do you?"

"I've had many losses of my own, if not a husband." She looked away, finding the worn, floral weave of the carpet all too absorbing. "Though you have no wife, you do have a bewildered daughter who wants to return to Williamsburg or stay here with me. You need to do something."

"And that includes taking the advice of an unmarried woman with no children of her own." Though his tone remained measured, she nearly flinched at the steel behind it.

"I do speak from experience, General Ogilvy. My father was a military man, if you recall." She swallowed, on a precarious limb. She never spoke of past hurts, but in Lily Cate's case . . . "He had little time for a daughter and not much more for a son. I scarcely remember a kiss, a kind word. I beg you to do better—"

"Pardon me, Miss Menzies. But if I'd wanted a lecture about fatherhood, I would have asked for one." Bending down, he gathered his sleeping daughter up in his arms, his maimed hand struggling for firm hold of her. Sophie got to her feet, wanting to help but feeling helpless in the face of his temper.

The happiness of the afternoon shattered. Seamus Ogilvy was regarding her with none of the charm of before. In the span of a few minutes, with a few hasty, misplaced words, she'd become his adversary. And she, inexplicably, wanted to burst into childish tears.

He went out, striding past a wary Glynnis in the foyer, to the rain-soaked coach at the foot of the steps. Sophie stood in the open parlor doorway, wishing he'd look back. Make amends. Let her make amends. But the coach rattled away, all her hopes with it.

Glynnis studied her, mouth twisted sorrowfully. "He's a good man who bears a heavy load, coming home from a long war and trying to make a go of it again."

"I was only trying to help."

"Help? He's hardly the same man I let in a few minutes ago. What on earth happened?"

Sophie sought an explanation. How could she voice his presence, his intensity? Or her own frightful candor? "Lily Cate seems somewhat shy of him. I thought I could make him see he needs to tread lightly with her." She reached up and tore off her lace cap, sending hairpins scattering. "I suppose, my being without proper company for so long, my manners slipped and I said too much."

"Well, officers don't like to be given orders. They simply like to give them." Glynnis hooked a consoling arm through hers and led her toward the warmth and light of the kitchen. "He'll likely consider what you said in time, though he'll have to cool down first. As for you, you're as flushed as I've ever seen you. If I didn't know better, I'd say you were more moonstruck than anything."

Moonstruck? Sophie pushed a wayward strand of hair from her eye, avoiding Glynnis's probing gaze. "I'm glad you know better."

I only wish I did.

5

Seamus was willing to try it once, if only to tell his meddlesome neighbor it didn't work. After tugging off his boots, he stripped down to his linen shirt and stocking feet. The door to his bedchamber stood open despite the chill, the bed curtains parted. He'd done the same with Lily Cate's room, afraid he'd sleep through her tears. He wanted to get to her before she'd thrown up her supper as she sometimes did, crying so hard she made herself sick. Her reaction seemed extreme, and he had to continually rein himself in lest he tell her to pull herself together like he had some of his men.

She's only five . . . She's missing Williamsburg . . . I'm a strange man missing fingers . . . This house is strange too . . .

The candlelight danced across his untidy desk beneath a shuttered window, reminding him to finish the letter he'd started at dawn. He was writing a friend in Richmond to help secure a governess or nursemaid. Once Lily Cate started school, he hoped she'd find an escape in books. Till then, he'd bought her a pony and was teaching her to ride—or trying to—but she seemed as afraid of her horse as she was him so he'd nearly given up.

Finished with the letter, he lay down atop the bed, trying to chase the image of Sophie Menzies from his mind. She'd sat so serenely in her Windsor chair, her lovely skirts in a swell of silken embroidery around her, her cheek resting against Lily Cate's dark hair as she held her. As if it was something she did every day like breathing or walking or smiling. Easily. Freely. Willingly. Even joyously.

He felt none of those things with his daughter.

Sophie Menzies should have had children of her own by now. He nearly winced at the memory of slighting her unmarried state. Likely she was as touchy about spinsterhood as he was at being an inept father. She'd spoken of losses. Her brother, certainly. A fiancé, mayhap. Someone who'd died fighting? Now she was caught in a waiting game of hoping and praying Curtis would return. He hadn't the heart to tell her he'd received an unconfirmed report about Curtis and his whereabouts. He hardly believed the news himself.

Turning his head, he squinted at the mantel timepiece, making out ten o'clock through the shadows. Like clockwork he heard a little cry resembling a kitten's mewl or a lamb's bleating. His daughter had a soldier's punctuality. She never fussed when the maid first put her to bed. She only cried when she woke at ten o'clock and then all through the night after.

He was on his feet, that strange heart-pumping rush working in his chest like it always did before battle. He wished Sophie Menzies was here. Nay, 'twas Anne he wanted. Lily Cate was her child—their child—after all.

A nightlight was burning on a bedside table, the kind that made catching fire impossible with its snug globe and holder. Lily Cate was cocooned in the bedcovers, her loosened hair like spilled ink across the linen pillow.

Hiding his bad hand behind his back, he went to her, swallowing the tender words he wanted to say for fear he'd scare her, his voice too big and unfamiliar for the dark room. He sat gingerly on the edge of the mattress and stroked her brow, her loosened hair catching like silk thread against his callused palm. She quieted then began thrashing like a wounded creature, making him want to back out of the room and close the door and let her be.

Taking her in your arms might help . . . Hold her close and chase the shadows away.

She cried harder, her distress carving a deeper hole inside him, every sob more heartrending than the last. Not yet six years old, yet so weighted with misery and grief it weighted him too. He was to blame, came the familiar taunting voice.

"Lily Cate, 'tis your father."

"Papa?" Her voice warbled with the unfamiliar word. She reached out a small, searching hand.

He scooped her up, enfolding her trembling body in his hard arms, tucking her bent head beneath his bristled jaw. She tried to push away from him, but it was a sleepy, feeble protest soon spent. Holding firm, he did not let her go till all the fight had drained out of her. Till she was like she'd been as a newborn, when he'd held her briefly on that long ago summer's day before their whole world turned on end.

He'd forgotten to close the door. Forgotten to close the bed curtains. Forgotten what it was like to have a warm body beside him. Since Anne, there had been no one else. It seemed only right that it be their daughter.

He owed Sophie Menzies an apology.

⁂

The butterfly flitting about the harvested garden brought a touch of color and whimsy to the fading November landscape.

Bound in orange and amber, its arched wings were so sheer that cold sunlight filtered through. Circling Sophie's head, the creature alighted on a squat pumpkin needing to be made into pie or carved into thick rings and dried.

The basket at her feet bore the last of the turnips and carrots, a few potatoes and onions tossed in. She'd long since harvested the lavender, loving the fresh, pungent scent on her hands as she sewed it into their linens. Only the sage and thyme remained to season soups and stews, and some frost-tipped greens.

Leaning back, she rested against a cistern and looked toward Tall Acre. At five thousand acres it spread wide and proud, making Three Chimneys' mere thousand almost forgettable.

Lily Cate was never far from her thoughts. Had it truly been a fortnight since their simple party? She'd lost sleep herself, praying the general would get some rest, find peace in the embrace of his little daughter.

Forgive her.

If she'd angered him, she hadn't meant to. She'd only spoken out of her own need and longing, a sincere desire to see them settled. She wanted Lily Cate's smile to be the smile of a carefree child, unbound as a spring breeze, not pent-up and fraught with adult cares. Hers was, sadly, an old soul.

"Miss Sophie?"

Glynnis stood at the garden gate, a bemused expression on her face. The sun was slanting down so brightly Sophie couldn't see what she held in her outstretched hands. A flash of blue distracted her as the guard passed by, doffing his tricorn as he disappeared round the side of the house.

Sophie hastened down the stone path, linen skirts swirling, and took the offering in anticipation. Without another word Glynnis hurried back to the kitchen and her preserve-making, leaving Sophie alone with the package tied with twine. A gift? Or had Henry . . . ? She tore open the telltale bluish-purple paper, blinking dumbly at the plump sugar cone and charmingly crafted sugar hammer.

Lord, You know what we have need of. Sweet, indeed.

Dropping down on a near bench, she tasted a small chunk, savoring its richness on her tongue. From Tall Acre? How had the general known? Was he that in tune with their lack? The certainty nearly made her squirm. But for the moment it hardly mattered. A folded paper lay at the bottom of the bag. She slid her finger beneath the scarlet seal and drank in the bold signature, her heart stilling.

Miss Menzies,
  A fortnight of sound sleep.

  With deepest gratitude,
  Seamus Ogilvy

Eyes wide, she reread it—devoured it—till she'd memorized every letter, finally slipping it inside her shift so that it lay warm against her skin. She longed to know more. Longed to see Lily Cate at rest in his arms. Even the thought of it made her own lonesome nights more bearable.

'Twas the first note she'd ever received from a man. And though it was only a courtesy from him, she held tight to her own small piece of enchantment.

⁂

He'd sent Sophie Menzies the gift of sugar as a sort of apology. Would she think he was trying to bribe her in re-

55

turning a favor? Now at dusk the day after, he found himself on Three Chimneys' doorstep, his tethered stallion snorting behind him. There was no sign of the housekeeper. Old as she was, had she died? 'Twas Miss Menzies herself who greeted him.

"Come in, General, please." With a wave of her hand, she led him into a disheveled study down the hall. A dim memory resurfaced. He'd been here previously, arguing politics with Lord Menzies before the war. Sophie's father, he recalled, had nearly taken him by the throat.

Now, like then, he came straight to the point. "I have business in Williamsburg and Richmond and must be away a week or better." Seamus tried to hide the discomfort of asking, but Sophie Menzies was smiling at him in the sunlight of Three Chimneys' study window, making his request somewhat easier. As if his daughter wasn't a nuisance. As if their fervent exchange of before had never happened.

"So you'd like for me to keep Lily Cate here."

"I'm a bit short-staffed at Tall Acre." He wouldn't say Lily Cate had nearly begged him to ask her. "I considered taking her with me, but traveling with a child—"

"Of course, 'tis better she remain behind." She clasped her hands together as if especially pleased. "When will you bring her?"

"Day after tomorrow." He regretted the apology in his tone. "I should return as planned, barring bad weather." Could she see his relief? Though he and Lily Cate were sleeping soundly with only a few tears now and then, other problems were pressing in. He wouldn't mention his growing fear that Anne's Williamsburg relations might snatch her in his absence. Or that Lily Cate's sudden fascination with the river in back of the house made him uneasy. Here at Three

Chimneys she would be well watched even more than at Tall Acre, especially with the guard he'd posted.

He cleared his throat. "I'm also in search of a governess for her. If you happen to know of anyone suitable . . ."

She crossed her arms in contemplation, drawing attention to her ill-fitting dress. The well-rounded girl she'd been flashed to mind. But then she likely remembered a man with a whole hand. "I attended Mrs. Hallam's school for girls in Williamsburg. I can write to her and inquire. I suppose you want the usual feminine fare—deportment, music, dancing, and French conversation."

Looking down at his cocked hat, he studied its feathered cockade. "Mostly I just want my daughter to read. To grow lost in books."

"That I understand completely." Her voice held a smile. "I'll make sure I read to her while she's here. As you can see, our library is not lacking at least. I devoured nearly every book these eight years past, some of them twice. I recommend *Tristram Shandy* and *Pamela*."

Amused, he raised his gaze. "Then you've not read *The Vicar of Wakefield*." The mention brought Anne to mind, so akin to the vicar's daughter with her blinding beauty. But 'twas Sophia, the sister, who made him think of Miss Menzies herself. What had the author said?

Sophia's features were not so striking at first . . . they were soft, modest, and alluring. The one vanquished by a single blow, the other by efforts successfully repeated . . . Olivia wished for many lovers, Sophia to secure one.

Forcing the memory away, he took in the crates scattered about the masculine room. "You look . . . busy."

"I'm cleaning out the study before Curtis returns." She picked up a feather duster and ran it lightly over a thick dictionary. "This will be his now as my father isn't coming back."

"It could be yours, as mistress of Three Chimneys." Her dismayed gaze turned his way. "I only meant you seem quite capable, Miss Menzies."

"I may be good with little girls, but I know little about managing an estate, General."

"You could learn."

"Oh? You weren't very encouraging about my silk production plans, as I recall." She resumed dusting with a vengeance, making him mentally kick himself for the thoughtless remark. "At this point I simply want my brother back. Nothing more."

He took a last look at a small marble bust of George II lying on the floor beside a dusty stack of old ledgers. Everything British looked to be on its way out. She even had a small Patriot flag flying from a pewter tankard atop the massive desk. There was little doubt where her loyalties lay.

"As it stands, Three Chimneys could never be mine by law," she said quietly. "'Tis a man's domain. My brother's. My future husband's."

His gaze swiveled back to her. "Are you . . . betrothed?"

The forthright question seemed to shake her. He watched her color climb to crimson before she murmured, "Hardly that."

He took a step back, thinking it a fine time to exit. "Day after tomorrow," he said, remembering Lily Cate.

"Thank you," she replied as if he'd done her some special favor. Looking up from her dusting, she added thoughtfully, "Thank you for entrusting her to me. 'Tis far sweeter than the sugar you sent."

"Small recompense, Miss Menzies." With that, he put on his hat and turned away.

Lily Cate arrived as planned, hugging Sophie so tightly it seemed she'd never let go. Kneeling on the morning room carpet, Sophie shut her eyes, savoring the moment. Had she ever embraced her father in this way? With boundless joy and affection? Would she in time?

Lily Cate shook free of her cape and left it in a little puddle on the rug, her expectant expression dimming a bit. "Papa has gone away . . ." She leaned nearer as if it was a secret, her breath smelling of peppermint. "To get a bride."

Sophie drew back, lips parting, almost missing the fact she'd called him Papa. "A bride?"

Lily Cate nodded, her bonnet bobbing atop her head. Sophie began untying her chin ribbons, breathless with surprise. "Well, I wish him the best."

"Florie told me."

Sophie set the bonnet aside. "Florie . . . your housemaid?"

Lily Cate whispered yes, fingering the lace of Sophie's fichu. "Florie knows everything. She dusts Papa's study and reads his letters."

A cold, sick sinking spread to her breast where the general's note still rested. "So Tall Acre is to have a new mistress then." Lily Cate was looking at her, a hundred questions in her eyes. As if she needed comfort. Reassurance about this stepmother-to-be.

Sophie dredged up more words as all the implications rushed in. "Well, I'm sure she'll be good and kind . . ." And beautiful. Accomplished. Wealthy. She took a breath, her newfound happiness dwindling. Couldn't she feel even a glimmer of gladness? Tall Acre needed a mistress, the general a wife, Lily Cate a mother.

Glynnis appeared just then, a wide, satisfied smile creasing her face. "The general's sent over two hams from Tall Acre's smokehouse and a sack of Portuguese salt."

Sophie nearly sighed. Glynnis best not get used to special treatment once a new mistress was installed at Tall Acre. Great changes were afoot, the least being their brimming larder. Had Glynnis heard any news? Likely not. Her glee was too great.

Taking Lily Cate's face between her hands, Sophie spoke past a numbing ache. "I'm glad you are calling him Papa."

"I don't say it with him, only with you."

Oh? The realization was bittersweet. She'd never called her own father anything but *sir*. Perhaps Lily Cate would warm to *Papa* in time. "What shall we do first? Go for a walk, read a book? We can even make a picture as I have my old paints."

"All of it, please."

Sophie managed a smile, gladdened by the scent of tea cakes wafting from the kitchen. "I'll set everything up in the garden while you have a sweet with Glynnis."

Once Lily Cate and Glynnis padded down the hall, Sophie stepped nearer the hearth. Though the first fire of late fall glowed golden in the grate—thanks be to Henry who'd gathered some sticks—it hardly took the chill off the room. She shut her eyes, still reeling from the news. What was the general like in love? Tender? Attentive? Gallant? Or was he marrying this woman out of necessity?

She withdrew his note from her bodice and fed it to the flames, pained that a bit of paper and ink meant so much to her. 'Twas folly at her age to be even slightly enamored of a note, a man, a wee girl not hers. A bride for Tall Acre had done the trick.

Now to convince her feelings to fall in line.

6

Seamus had disliked Richard Fitzhugh from the first day he'd met him. He hated him now. Standing in the formal parlor of the Fitzhughs' grand Williamsburg townhouse, they faced each other, Anne's sister between them. Charlotte, with her corn-silk hair and hazel eyes, looked enough like Anne to be her twin, and the resemblance grated. But Charlotte was even more conniving and was likely the reason he was in this predicament to begin with.

Fitzhugh was not fond of children, and they were childless, something Charlotte found untenable but Seamus found fitting. He knew it was more Charlotte's need of Lily Cate that had him cornered here. They'd always treated his daughter oddly, kind and cruel by turns, or so he'd heard, saying things no child should hear and Seamus feared couldn't be undone. He'd never trusted them. He didn't trust them now.

His gaze wandered to the gaudily papered walls, a heavy gold and verdigris, so unlike his own serene blues and greens at Tall Acre. Everything felt oppressive, almost nauseating. Or mayhap it was only the ill feeling threading the room.

Charlotte barely glanced at him, intent on the ribbon embellishment of her sleeve. "General, I hope your trip from Tall Acre was uneventful."

Spare me the platitudes, he almost said. This was hardly a social call. "I received your summons. Now what is it that you want from me?"

Fitzhugh took control, stony-faced and powdered like the judge he was. "Let us get down to business straightaway. Regrettably, our legal counsel isn't present but will be if the matter isn't resolved to our satisfaction."

"I doubt it will be," Seamus replied, not meaning to be inflammatory, just truthful.

Charlotte was regarding him in apprehension now as if he might take out a weapon and threaten them. But he wasn't in uniform nor was he carrying so much as a simple pistol.

The judge cleared his throat. "You're well aware we want Anne's daughter returned immediately."

"I'm well aware you have no right to demand her return given I'm her father."

"General, need I remind you that you came here a month ago and took the poor child by force—"

Seamus went cold. "Only because you refused to let me see her. Explain that to your legal counsel."

"Gentlemen, please." Charlotte's face turned beseeching, though it barely masked the hardness beneath. "We're mostly concerned that Lily Cate is without a mother. You're well aware I'm the closest female relation the child has."

"You forget my sister. In Philadelphia."

"Ah, Cosima, yes. But Philadelphia is a world away. *We* were the ones who took Lily Cate in while Anne was dying and you were on the field. *We* are the most familiar. I can only imagine how terrified the child must be living with you, a virtual stranger, in a strange house with a strange staff."

"You yourselves were once strange to her." Seamus pointed out the obvious, but she simply stared at him blankly before Fitzhugh intervened.

"None of that matters." He clutched a paper in a ringed hand, shaking it as if it held some significance. "Here we have the guardianship document that Anne signed—"

"Anne?" The heated word shot across the room like musket fire. "Anne had no right." Ire gained the upper hand, making his reply tight and breathless. "Anne is dead while I, Lily Cate's father, am very much alive and making a home for her as best I can."

"Alive—and alone." Fitzhugh let the paper drop. "You cannot provide the care Anne's daughter needs, but we can. I'm confident the courts will agree. My legal counsel is preparing paperwork to that effect as we speak. 'Tis only a matter of time before the child is in our care again."

Charlotte took out a fan and flicked it open with a twist of her wrist. "You might have brought her with you, General, to visit us for an afternoon while you go about your Williamsburg business."

"I considered it, but given your disagreeable stance, I thought it wiser to keep her at home."

Disgust marred Fitzhugh's face. "*Home* is hardly the term for it. You live in a remote location devoid of civilized pursuits. Anne detested country life and thought it better Lily Cate be raised in a genteel town like Williamsburg."

Though Seamus tried to stay stalwart, the words slashed deep. He knew Anne had preferred life in town, but hearing it from the judge so bitterly was something he'd not soon forget. His heart, so torn throughout the war years by myriad things beyond his control, fractured anew. He wanted to sit down peaceably and discuss what was best for Lily Cate, arrange for her to spend time in Williamsburg or open Tall Acre to the Fitzhughs as guests. But there was no peace, no reconciliation, to be had in this parlor.

Charlotte snapped her fan shut. "Most men would be glad to relinquish the burden of a daughter's care to relatives."

"I am not 'most men.'"

"Indeed." Charlotte was almost pouting. "Our primary concern at this impasse is that you have no wife, no mother for Anne's daughter. If this was a boy, we wouldn't be so concerned. But a girl needs a woman's influence—"

"I'm about to secure a governess," Seamus interrupted, returning his hat to his head and putting an end to her weary refrain. "Every concern you have is unfounded. Now if you'll excuse me, I'm needed elsewhere."

Since Lily Cate had set foot at Three Chimneys five days before, she and Sophie had played and napped, taken tea, rearranged the dollhouse, and even sewn some new garments for the doll Sophie. A mobcap and fichu now graced her person, and a tiny folded fan made of gilt paper and lace adorned her wax hands. But most importantly, Lily Cate had begun to learn her letters.

"A . . . B . . . C . . ." They made a game and a song of it, wrote the alphabet with stylus and slate, and by week's end Lily Cate could pen her name. *Ogilvy* proved rather difficult, but even her Christian name was deemed quite an accomplishment.

Sophie hadn't forgotten the general's request for a governess. To that end, a post to Mrs. Hallam lay unfinished on her desk, sparking new questions. Was the general a progressive man? Valuing education for females? Or did he simply want Lily Cate occupied so she wouldn't be a bother? Sophie longed to give him the benefit of the doubt.

"Your papa will be so proud of you. You've made a fine start." Hugging her, Sophie glanced at the painting Lily Cate had done of her new pony, Polly, atop the morning room mantel. In one corner she'd signed her name. But Polly, sadly, inspired fear much like the girl's father.

"When will the gen—Papa—be back?" Lily Cate asked, rubbing the sleep from her eyes.

"Any time now," Sophie answered quietly, unsure what the day would bring. She braced herself for the likelihood of a new bride for Tall Acre, hating herself for her dismay. When had Seamus Ogilvy gained a foothold in her needy heart? 'Twas more than the loss of Lily Cate that rubbed her raw.

"Well, I'd like for him to stay away a little longer," Lily Cate whispered.

Sophie studied her, the soreness inside her easing not a whit. Since Seamus had left, she'd not stopped thinking of why and what it portended. Lily Cate shied from a strange father and might a strange mother too. Her small world had been turned upside down since she'd been born. Would she now have to adjust to a new mother? A new life?

As the hours passed, the waiting turned tenser. Lily Cate chewed her fingernails to little bits. Sophie's own nerves felt frayed. Even Glynnis seemed a bit on edge.

"A rider's coming down the drive, Miss Sophie." Glynnis hastened away to answer the door before Sophie could ask any questions.

Leaving Lily Cate to her letters, Sophie met a post rider in the study, news of Curtis no longer uppermost.

"From Richmond, miss."

Richmond had assumed dire proportions in her mind. She took the letter, smudged from its journey in a damp, crowded saddlebag, her thoughts whirling. Might the general have married and gone on an extended honeymoon? Left Lily Cate in her care indefinitely? The troubling uncertainty sent her to her father's desk chair, a throne-like monstrosity that was a testament to his pride. Then and there she decided to chop it into pieces and use it for firewood.

Praying for good news, she opened the post. Not the general's handwriting after all. An official letter from Richmond, it was addressed to the present occupant of Three Chimneys, the first paragraph a scolding about back taxes. She reckoned she deserved the rebuke given she'd never paid them, but she'd had no means, and with the war on no one seemed to care about collecting them either.

It was the second paragraph that stole her breath. Three Chimneys was . . . what? In the possession of the newly formed, independent American government? No longer belonging to the Menzies family, it had been confiscated as Tory property. The new occupants, yet nameless, were to move in the first of April.

Her emotions began to roil, half fury, half disbelief. She'd feared a formal notice was coming. Hope had held it at bay. Three Chimneys. Her home. The house where she'd been born. The dowry her British-born mother had brought to her ill-suited marriage. Her father had assumed ownership yet had always preferred Williamsburg and Edinburgh. But Sophie loved it, every inch, every crumbling, ivy-covered eave. She latched on to the small flag atop the desk with its stars and stripes she'd painstakingly sewn in a moment of deep desperation.

Did it not mean liberty for her too?

Letting the letter drop atop the desk, she covered her face with her hands, glad the rising wind helped mask her weeping. What of endless days and nights quartering British soldiers against her will when she feared they might burn Three Chimneys to the ground? What of her unwavering loyalty to the cause despite it all? What of Curtis's fighting with the Continental Army?

Would her brother not come? She had tried to hold on, refused to let go. Anything else seemed like giving up. Her mother was gone. She had no coin. She'd soon grow lean and tired and hungry again, only this time, save Glynnis and Henry, she'd be alone.

Could Seamus Ogilvy do something? If she swallowed what was left of her pride, she might plead for him to intervene lest she end up in the poorhouse.

Surely a hero of the Revolution had the clout she didn't.

◈

Williamsburg was as altered a place as he was a man and soldier. Since the Virginia capital had moved to Richmond, the old town had a tattered feel, still handsome but a shell of what it used to be. The high-spirited assembly days were gone, the fine livery and equipages sauntering down the shaded streets a memory. Williamsburg in its heyday was something Seamus carried around in his head like a map, reluctant to roll it up and let it go. Here he'd been young. Inexperienced. Carefree. Here he'd met Anne. Here he'd proposed. Here his fellow soldiers had feted him on news of his engagement.

And here he'd run into trouble with Anne's relatives.

He was only too glad to leave it all behind, not looking

back once he'd left the Fitzhughs' townhouse. Fury spurred him on every mile of the frost-laden distance north to Bracken Hall but blinded him to the beauty of late fall. 'Twas the first unfettered autumn he could remember. War had stolen much, including an appreciation of the seasons.

Stallion lathered, his own chest heaving, he arrived at his destination after dark, unfit for any merriment or much company, and in no mood for a wedding.

It struck him as odd to be with his fellow officers anywhere but a battlefield. Turning joyful after so much hardship and tragedy, even if they had won the war, required a new set of skills he wasn't sure he had. But this was a long-awaited occasion, after all. For a few hours at least he could play the part of the amiable, obliging best man.

Being at Bracken Hall made it somewhat easier. It had been the home of the Grayson family for over one hundred years, their vast holdings swallowing the verdant hills outside of Richmond and boasting the largest tobacco crop in Virginia. Seamus had spent an earlier visit riding round the estate, making a mental inventory of how to improve Tall Acre and turn a profit. But he wasn't sure tobacco was the cash crop it was reputed to be. He wasn't sure of anything anymore.

The next morning found him in a many-windowed parlor, better rested but still full of the bad feeling of Williamsburg. Try as he might, Seamus was unable to embrace the gaiety of Bracken Hall.

"So much fuss, a great many guests." The groom's usual calm was missing, and a faulty tenor filled the parlor instead. "Blast! I haven't felt this rattled since Brandywine." Colin Grayson appeared nervous, like he was facing a line of saber-tipped redcoats. "How do I look?"

With a wink, Seamus tried to lighten both their moods.

"At ease, Colonel, at ease. Nobody is going to be looking at you but the bride."

Colin chuckled. "I forgot you've been through this before."

"I don't remember much," Seamus admitted with a hitch of regret. Everything had been blunted that bright spring day. He'd been one and twenty, Anne only seventeen. There'd barely been time for a ceremony as he'd just enlisted.

"Ever think of doing it again?"

Reaching up, Seamus adjusted the knot of his hastily tied cravat. "Nay."

Colin studied him shrewdly. "If you're not courting now that you've returned home, how have you spent your time?"

"Trying to restore order at Tall Acre. I'm in need of a cook and a secretary—and a governess."

"A governess? There are some fine girls' schools in the east, Boston and thereabouts. Why not consider sending your daughter there?"

"Because—" Seamus struggled to make sense of the emotions swirling round his heart and head. "I'd like to be a father to Lily Cate rather than a stranger."

Colin took a seat and sent a tense breath into the silence. "Any more trouble from Anne's kin?"

"Aye, in spades." Seamus looked out a window in Williamsburg's direction. "Managing an army on campaign is one thing, disgruntled relations another."

"How so?"

"When I was discharged, Lily Cate wasn't returned to me as requested, so I went to the Fitzhughs' and took her in the night. It seems Anne's relatives had no intention of giving her back. Part of the problem is they have no children of their own—"

"So they want to keep yours."

"I understand their attachment to her, but—" He felt a bit sick navigating the emotional melee. "Lily Cate is all of Anne I have left."

"You're still in love with her."

Seamus studied him, unwilling to deny it. Everyone still remembered how Anne Howard had flirted with him behind the folds of her lace fan at a Raleigh Tavern ball as the war began. He'd won her hand over a dozen other suitors. It had been romantic. Foolish. Utterly rash. If he was still in love with her as Colin said, it was only the illusion of her, not the essence. "Her relatives have threatened to take me to court over custody of Lily Cate. In short, it's an unholy mess."

"Ah, Fitzhugh . . ." Colin eyed him sympathetically. "Your former brother-in-law is a powerful man—and a Williamsburg judge. He could well influence the courts in his favor."

Seamus rubbed his brow. "They're already making a case against me, saying I neglected Anne by rarely coming home, seldom writing letters—"

"You were fighting a war!" Colin roared, bringing his hand down on a near tabletop. "And fighting it quite well too. I dare them to take issue with your term of service. Surely *that* counts for something."

"Aye, but the war's been won and any heroics will soon fade." Forcing a slight smile, Seamus shrugged. "'Tis your wedding day. I want to forget about the trouble at home." He looked to the door, his smile broadening. "Your bride is here to help us do just that."

Colin turned round, his indignation fading. Seamus had forgotten what it was like to be in love, but Sally Lee made him want to remember. Looking up at her groom adoringly, she ran her pale fingers over the fine Mechlin lace of his stock and said in her no-nonsense way, "An eight-year engagement

70

is far too long. I'll be glad to see this done. Meanwhile, I'll be happy to play matchmaker and introduce Seamus to some of my bridesmaids."

"You'll have to act fast," Colin warned. "He's leaving for Tall Acre in the morning."

"Home?" Sally turned dismayed eyes Seamus's way. "So soon?"

"It hardly matters," Seamus returned lightly, "as you'll be on your honeymoon."

She smiled and patted his cheek. Seeing her in her yellow brocade dress, its fine lines accentuating her slender figure, Seamus was reminded of Sophie Menzies. The war years had stripped everyone and everything to bare bones. Even the new broadcloth suit he wore hung a bit loose.

Sally studied him. "I must say, Seamus Ogilvy, you're looking every bit as handsome out of uniform as in it. Now where is that charming little daughter of yours?"

"Staying with a . . . neighbor and friend."

"Well, we'll have to come down to Tall Acre soon and meet Miss Lily Cate. For now General Washington has just arrived, and the ceremony is about to begin. Shall we, gentlemen?"

7

Seamus stood before the crackling hearth's fire in back of Colin, a great many guests fanned out in the hushed parlor, all eyes on the bride and groom.

"Dearly beloved . . ." The reverend's voice skimmed over him, unleashing memories he'd thought long gone. The scent of April blooms in silver bowls. Anne's tentative smile. Their parents' pleasure. Anne's brother, Cabot, lost at Valley Forge, had been best man. Seamus couldn't recall who'd been best maid. Anne's troublesome sister, likely. Today there were too many bridesmaids standing in back of the bride as if she couldn't decide between them or didn't want to hurt their feelings.

He had the needling notion they were all too aware of him, as if Sally had reminded them behind closed doors that he was in need of a wife. They already knew about his war exploits. Colin had regaled them all at dinner the night before with tale after tale of their combined gallantry, skill, and military ardor to the point of giving Seamus indigestion.

He looked down at his mauled right hand, a knot of badly healed flesh and bone.

He should have worn his uniform. In his worn blue wool and spurs, he felt more at ease. Bereft of them, he hardly knew who he was. Raising his gaze from his boots, he caught a soft, lingering look pass between Colin and Sally. Had Anne looked at him in such an all-consuming way? As if no one else existed? Or mattered?

If she had, wouldn't he remember?

He shut his eyes as the reverend called for a kiss. He remembered his own bumbling when he'd first kissed Anne. She'd turned so shy, making him shy in return. But Colin and Sally were no mere boy and girl. They'd been loving and trysting for years, wresting from the war what it would deny them, meeting whenever and wherever they could.

The morning blurred and found him at the wedding breakfast, surrounded by too many unwed women amidst the fine napery of the dining room. Chicken, spiced ham, baked shad, and a host of other dishes lined the immense sideboard and table as if in outright defiance of war's end and Britain's penny-pinching rule. Seamus stayed quiet, self-contained even as they tried to draw him out. He could only guess the gist of their thoughts.

Wounded war hero. Grieving widower. Absentee father.

"General Ogilvy, are you staying long at Bracken Hall?" To his left, Clementine Randolph asked the question that had been broached half a dozen times already.

"Nay," he said. "I leave at first light."

"How is it returning home to Tall Acre after so long away with so much to be done?"

"Like battle," he replied with a small smile. "I'm glad to have the winter to plan for a spring offensive—planting and the like." He couldn't say the repairs needed in his absence were appalling and his former creditors in London had yet to be paid . . . and here sat the unmarried Miss Randolph whose dowry would answer for any expense he incurred.

"I've heard Tall Acre is a lovely place. I believe it's situated near the Three Chimneys estate just down from you on the Roan River?"

He raised his silver goblet. "You're familiar with Three Chimneys?"

Miss Randolph's smile was smug. In the warmth of so many candles, her wax makeup had begun to wane, though her hair with its plentiful pomade held tight. "My cousin Major John Franklin has just been awarded that confiscated property."

Seamus nearly spilled his punch.

"I believe it formerly belonged to the Tory Lord Menzies," she finished, making a disagreeable face.

He felt a sinking to his boots. "It did, aye, but is now occupied by his daughter . . . until her brother who served under my command returns home to claim it."

She dabbed at her lips with a serviette. "I'd also heard her brother has gone missing or is a casualty of war, and that the taxes on Three Chimneys haven't been paid in ages."

Emily Lee leaned in on his other side. "I believe what Miss Randolph is telling you, General, is that she'd be happy to renew your acquaintance by coming to Tall Acre once her cousin takes up residence at Three Chimneys."

They tittered conspiratorially and left him brooding. Sophie Menzies had said nothing to him of losing Three Chimneys. What else was she hiding?

Down the table General Washington was recounting news of their absent fellow officers in his quiet, self-effacing way. Several of those missing had assumed political office, others taking up residence on Tory estates seized as a reward for their wartime service. But Seamus was no longer listening.

It was now late November. The treaty ending the war had been signed in October. Congress was obviously wasting no time dealing with Tory holdings. A sad state of affairs, especially when Three Chimneys had been Sophie's mother's to begin with. Though he didn't know Sophie Menzies well, he knew her well enough to discern her loyalty to her home. And losing Three Chimneys would take her one step farther away from Lily Cate. The situation clawed at him, begged his help. All he could do was appeal to a higher power.

It was late in the day when he found General Washington alone. In full dress uniform, Washington cast him back to the battlefield and countless meetings with fellow officers. As always, the commander in chief listened thoughtfully as Seamus laid out the dilemma of Three Chimneys and asked him to intervene.

His expression was grave, his voice low. "You're aware of the talk surrounding Major Menzies . . . that he may have defected with Benedict Arnold?"

Seamus all but winced. Washington never cast suspicion that wasn't warranted. "I've heard unconfirmed reports. No solid proof."

Washington nodded intently and then outmaneuvered him. "Is the property—this Three Chimneys—a valuable one? Good timber, fertile fields, ample water supply?"

"Aye, all of it."

"And is the lady in question amiable? Young as you?"

Young? Seamus didn't feel young. The aches and complaints in his limbs bespoke age and adversity and more. But

Sophie, despite her painful leanness, still seemed youthful. "I believe she is."

"Is she comely? In your eyes at least?"

Seamus hesitated. He'd not thought of Sophie in those terms. Didn't want to think of her in those terms. But the general required honesty above all else. "She's lovely, aye."

"Does she share your patriotism?"

He nodded, well aware of where Washington was leading.

"And are you not a widower with a young daughter in need of a mother?" The ensuing pause was painful. And then a wry glimmer lit Washington's silver-blue eyes. "As one of my top officers, you've never needed me to spell things out for you, Seamus, so I'll simply ask—what are you waiting for?"

Seamus bit back an excuse, though he couldn't fault Washington's logic. He himself had married a young widow with two children before the war. Martha Custis Washington was as charming and amiable as they came.

Washington clapped him on the back. "Why not save me any wrangling with Congress over Tory holdings and settle the matter yourself?"

Colin appeared just then, sparing him an answer. "Time for cards and drinks in the parlor, gentlemen. We'll have a little more merriment before Sally and I are on our way."

Seamus joined in halfheartedly, so distracted he couldn't attend to the hand in front of him. He ended up losing at whist, his partner and opponents staring at him in stark surprise. With skills honed around countless smoky campfires, he was usually top of his game in terms of strategy and tactics.

His thoughts spun and refused to settle. Here he'd just told Colin he had no thought of remarrying, and Washington was making a case and trying to talk him into it.

Sophie Menzies Ogilvy.

It was too obvious, too easy a solution. Even if Lily Cate was wild about her, he didn't love Sophie Menzies. He'd never thought of her as anything but the unfortunate daughter of a despised Tory.

She'd never considered him either, he was willing to wager.

The motion of the rocking chair was soothing, the snap and pop of the fire nearly lulling Sophie to sleep. Lily Cate's warm weight spread across her like a quilt, her dark head upon Sophie's bony shoulder, her small body curled catlike in her lap. As the clock struck seven, the winter darkness crept in, moonless and deep, magnifying the night sounds.

She heard hoofbeats even before Glynnis announced someone. She knew it was the general. But alone . . . or with a bride? Though he'd only been gone a week, it felt far longer.

In a few minutes he stood before her, winded and windswept, his cocked hat tucked beneath one arm. She looked up at him, masking the way her heart jumped at his appearing. How could a man look and smell so fine after so long a ride? Almost like a . . . bridegroom.

"Come sit by the fire and warm yourself, General." She mulled the address. Her father had been a general. His rank meant very little, for it had been bought, unlike Seamus Ogilvy's. "Glynnis has gone to fetch you a toddy."

"I won't refuse you."

Still, his face showed surprise. She knew why. Despite their lack, Three Chimneys reeked of spirits. Her father was known for the finest pipes of Madeira and East Indian rum throughout Roan. What the British hadn't drunk, their hired man Henry had hidden away. For medicine and wounds and a wee dram or two.

Seamus shed his cloak and draped it over a chair back before sitting opposite her. The fire sputtered, sending a colorful spray of sparks past the andirons. His hat and gloves he placed near the heat, much as Curtis used to do. She missed that homey touch, the comfort and security a man's presence wrought. She opened her mouth to welcome him home. But this wasn't his home. And this wasn't their wee daughter.

He sat back, eyes never leaving Lily Cate. "How is she?"

Missing you, she wanted to say. But she couldn't, not honestly. Just this morning Lily Cate had cried because their time together was nearing an end. "She's well. We went riding this afternoon."

"Riding?" His brow lifted. "She won't get near a horse."

"She rode with me on one of Tall Acre's very gentle mares. But I'm afraid she got quite worn out."

"Wise to go today. The fair weather's spent."

Glynnis returned, bearing the toddy and a tray. Biscuits layered with the ham he'd provided were stacked beside a sliced apple on a pewter plate. He smiled his thanks, remembering her name. Flushing like a girl, Glynnis curtsied, leaving Sophie somewhat bemused. So the master of Tall Acre could even charm the help when he wanted, ensuring unending hospitality to come.

"You spoil me, the both of you." His glance widened to take Sophie in.

There was an alarming lilt to his voice she'd not heard before. And that smile . . . It eased all the rugged, weathered lines of him, giving her a nearly forgotten glimpse of the young man he'd been. Confident, even cocky. Self-assured yet unchallenged. He'd had little to do with her back then, before she went to Williamsburg. The war had mellowed and matured him like fine wine in Three Chimneys' cellar.

He seemed entirely too high-spirited tonight, having ridden untold miles in the cold to get here. She braced herself for some announcement, some startling revelation. Was he merely betrothed? Or had he left his bride at Tall Acre before coming here?

"How were your travels?" she blurted, wanting an end to her misery.

"Uneventful," he said, reaching for the toddy.

She stared at him, heart in her throat.

He returned her stare. "You're looking at me like I just lied."

"I hardly call a bride uneventful."

"A—*what*?" His amused astonishment brought the fire to her cheeks. "I don't remember saying anything about a bride."

"Little jugs have big ears." At his quizzical expression, she rushed on. "You'd do well to conceal your personal correspondence if you'd like to keep it that way."

He sat back and watched the steam curl round the tankard's rim, mulling her words. "Meaning my maid does more than dust my desk."

"I don't mean to meddle but thought you'd want to know." She forged ahead. There was simply no way to dance around it. "Lily Cate believes you went away to wed someone."

He took a long drink, leaving her hanging. "I went to Bracken Hall to see someone wed. A fellow officer. I was best man. It was, as I said, uneventful."

She rested her cheek against Lily Cate's hair as a strange euphoria rushed in. He was not wed. Not taken. Just looking annoyed that she had imagined it. She gave the rocking chair a gentle push with her foot, wondering what Lily Cate's reaction would be upon waking.

Lord, let her be glad to see him again.

"Have you ever considered a post as a governess?" He reached for a biscuit but didn't eat, as if awaiting her answer first.

'Twas her turn to be surprised. "You're not seeking my services, I hope."

Her distaste must have showed on her face, for he said quietly, "Is the prospect so abhorrent to you, then?"

"I . . ." She could just imagine that arrangement. First in line to observe the bride he would eventually bring home. Babies. A domestic scene long denied her. "I've posted a letter to Mrs. Hallam about a governess. Hopefully there'll be a hasty reply."

He ran a hand over his jaw, drawing attention to his shadow of beard. "You've been a great help to me with my daughter. I'd like to return the favor, if you'll let me speak freely."

She couldn't help but smile. "You seem to have little trouble on that score, General."

"Forgive me for that." He shot her an apologetic glance. "Sometimes my field manners follow me into the parlor." Setting his tankard aside, he leaned forward. "Since we're discussing the matter of personal correspondence, I need to know if you've received any word from government officials concerning Three Chimneys."

So he knew. Somehow it hurt, humiliated her, that he did. "Just yesterday a letter came," she answered, resuming her rocking. "The post is in the study. On my fa—Curtis's desk. You may retrieve it if you like."

He got up without waiting for more. In moments he sat back down, letter in hand. "I have a proposal."

Her girlish heart lifted. His words, the hushed way he said them, made her stomach spin, and then sharp reason reined her in. He didn't mean *that* kind of proposal. She tried to stem the thought of him on bended knee. Was that how he had proposed to Anne? He didn't seem like a romantic sort of suitor.

The look he gave her was all business, driving every romantic notion from her head. "I'm prepared to pay back taxes on Three Chimneys in exchange for your leasing land to me."

"A lease? Why?"

"Tobacco is no longer a good cash crop as it weakens the soil and is labor intensive. If Tall Acre is to turn profitable again, I need to diversify. My goal is to cultivate wheat and cotton—"

"Cotton?" she exclaimed. "'Tis nearly as hard to produce as silk."

"Only till someone finds a reliable way to harvest it," he countered, seeming unperturbed. "If you'll agree to the land lease, I can guarantee a profit. I cannot guarantee you'll retain Three Chimneys, but I'll do what I can."

She nearly sighed aloud. She'd rather he'd come striding in, take his daughter, and make no honorable proposals. With every bold word, he was wedding himself deeper into her head and heart, and she felt a new kind of desperation. She couldn't get lost in him, couldn't depend on him. Yet she felt herself warming, soaking up his attention like a neglected flower left too long in the shade.

Lily Cate stirred in her arms, slowly coming awake. She took her father in, her whisper soft and sleepy. "You've come back."

Sophie longed for her to show joy at his appearing. The guarded hope in his gaze rent her heart. Despite their shaky start, he loved his little daughter deeply. Couldn't Lily Cate sense that?

Bending her head, Sophie whispered so low in her ear he couldn't possibly hear. "Go to him."

Slowly Lily Cate eased off Sophie's lap and onto his. "Sir, where is she?"

He touched her sleep-flushed cheek with his good hand. "Who?"

"Your bride."

A slight pause. "I don't know . . . I've not found her yet."

Sophie began wrapping the remaining biscuit and apple in a linen napkin, turning away from the intimate scene. Already she felt a bit empty. Their presence was a warm, living thing, staving off bedtime and her dread of the dark. Nighttime was always hardest, when the darkness seemed ready to devour her.

"Miss Menzies."

Unwillingly her gaze found his again.

"We need to finish our conversation."

"Another time," she said vaguely.

"Tomorrow, mayhap."

She gave him a fleeting, noncommittal smile. "Tomorrow is the Sabbath."

"The day after, then."

She bit her lip. If he was this persistent on the battlefield, no wonder the war had been won. "Goodnight to you both." Bending down, she cupped Lily Cate's chin with one hand and pressed a kiss to her brow.

When she straightened he towered over her, making her feel as small as Lily Cate. He chuckled when she handed him the burgeoning napkin. Old habits made her forget Tall Acre's larder wasn't lacking.

"Till Monday," he said, purpose in his gaze.

8

"Sir, do you not go to church?"

Sir. Would she never call him *Papa* again?

Seamus looked up from his desk, over stacks of ledgers and quires of paper, to see Lily Cate in the doorway of his study dressed in her best, if one could call it that. A pink gown and quilted petticoat. Cardinal cloak. Green slippers and protective black pattens. A muff and bonnet. Nothing matched, but she'd taken pains with herself, clearly.

She took a wary step into the room. "'Tis the Sabbath, Miss Sophie said."

He bit the inside of his cheek. Whatever Miss Sophie said was law and long remembered. "I used to go to church," he told her. Before the war. Before death and disease and destruction darkened a searching heart. "To be honest, I'd forgotten what day it is."

She took another step, looking about his study, a place she'd not yet been, like it was some sort of dank dungeon. And then her eyes lit on the mantel where the painting of her pony rested, and she flashed him a shy smile. It was Anne's smile, reminiscent of a better time and place, and it warmed him like a spring day after a long winter.

"May I go with Miss Sophie?"

"Nay, but you can go with me," he said quickly.

"Thank you," she replied, clutching her little purse.

Her manners are very fine.

Miss Menzies was right. Whatever had happened with his daughter in Williamsburg, someone there had taught her to be mannerly.

"I'll need a few minutes to have the coach brought round, make myself presentable," he said.

In a quarter of an hour they were hurtling down the lane to Roan Church, leaving the problems and pressures of Tall Acre behind. He hoped they wouldn't be late.

"May we sit with Miss Sophie?"

"Nay." He felt a hitch of regret. He always seemed to be telling her no. "The Menzies family has their own pew, as do the Ogilvys."

"If she was my mama could we sit together?"

The coach lurched along with his heart. "Aye, but she is not, and I—I cannot marry her." Washington's words bore down on him, challenging him. But it was his daughter's stare, full of surprise and indignation, that pinned him.

"Well, why not?"

It was the sauciest he'd ever seen her, and he nearly smiled. Mayhap she did have a little of the Ogilvy fire, after all. "Because I don't love her. We're simply friends."

"Well, I love her." The words were soft. Heartfelt. And still a tad indignant.

He tugged on the window strap for fresh air, saying no more. Clouds were gathering in the east, stacked like cannonballs on the horizon, threatening rain. The oaks and hickories had lost most of their leaves, giving the valley, hailed as one of the most beautiful in Virginia, the look of a sodden gray quilt. Once again he was glad of a long winter. If he'd returned home in spring or summer, in the grip of the planting season, he'd be even more undone than he was.

The church came into view, and he studied it with a critical eye. Situated on a knoll overlooking the Roan Valley, the building was small and of stone, the pews hard, the reverend old. The church's interior had changed little since he'd attended years before, but the number of congregants seemed to be shrinking. He wagered Lily Cate would be fast asleep once the lengthy sermon began.

After shaking hands with a few people, he led Lily Cate to pew number two, used by Ogilvys for three generations. His father had donated land to establish the building, even recruiting a clergyman from England, and so earned a prominent place, the Menzies family just behind. Unless their pew had somehow been confiscated, Roan hostilities considered.

Seamus took a seat, Lily Cate beside him, but he saw no sign of Sophie Menzies. Soon Lily Cate began to squirm, craning her neck toward the door every time someone came in.

In a few minutes curiosity got the better of him, and he looked back as Sophie entered, her cheeks the crimson of her cape. Had she walked all the way? Facing forward, he fixed his eye on the communion table, wanting to settle the matter of leased lands and land taxes. But he'd have to endure a lengthy service first. The thought brought a stitch of guilt. Was he no better than the moneylenders in the temple?

Beside him, hands folded in her lap with only an occasional bout of fidgeting, Lily Cate did him proud till sermon's end. Then, "I'm hungry."

He nodded absently, trying to catch Sophie's attention

before she got away, but a few people cornered him, wanting to greet him and hear his opinion on the new government, and she escaped after a quick hug from Lily Cate. He stood answering questions, cape flapping in the late November wind, the tick of his pulse impatient.

"I need to . . ." Lily Cate was looking up at him, a plea in her blue eyes.

She needed to . . . what? Her small gloved hand gestured to the necessary behind the church.

He led her there, eyes on the road they'd soon travel. By the time Lily Cate emerged, rain was pelting down, rearranging his plans to ride about the estate and talk to his tenants. The road was quickly turning to mud, and a fine mist was snaking in among buildings and trees, further obscuring his view. Where was Miss Menzies?

"I'm hungry," Lily Cate told him.

I heard you the first time, he almost said, helping her into the coach. Climbing in after her, he shut the door but left the window cracked.

They took the first bend in the road too quickly, causing Lily Cate to slide across the leather seat. The coachman was young and inexperienced, almost reckless, and Seamus raised a hand to pound on the lacquered ceiling. To no avail. Out the half-shuttered window he caught a glimpse of a cardinal cape as they flew by. The figure jumped out of the way all too late, a wave of mud and water drenching her before the coach slowed to a stop.

Seamus got out, wanting to take the whip to the driver. Wanting to shake Sophie Menzies. What the devil was she doing walking so far on such a day? The sight of Lily Cate's anxious face at the window cooled his ire. "Are you hurt?" he asked Sophie.

"Just wet," Sophie answered with a smile as wide as Lily Cate's, as unbothered as if they'd splashed sunshine on her instead.

"Why aren't you riding?" he asked. Her face clouded, and he realized his mistake. No mount. No coach. He seized the moment. "The inn is just ahead. We'll have something to eat and you can dry out."

Lily Cate clapped her hands as he opened the door and helped Sophie inside, tossing out a warning to the red-faced coachman. "If you cannot manage an easier ride, I'll drive to Tall Acre myself and you'll walk the rest of the way."

After that, they inched along to the Kings Arms, recently renamed The George Inn, its sign freshly painted and bearing a Continental cocked hat. Squat and unadorned, it boasted decent food and a welcoming stone hearth. He'd not seen Lily Cate so delighted since he'd last taken her to Three Chimneys.

She studied the menu chalked on a board, saying letters she knew while holding tightly to Sophie's hand. He ordered for them and then led the way to a table near the fire through a haze of pipe smoke, away from the ale-soaked patrons in a far corner. Anne had never liked taverns. They were full of vile smells, vile food, and viler people, she'd said. But Sophie didn't seem to mind, sinking down on a bench as if weary from her walk.

He felt a moment of awkwardness as Lily Cate wedged her way between them. Taking Sophie's wet cape, he hung it by the fire before sitting down across from them at a scarred table.

"I never expected to spend so pleasant a Sabbath," she remarked with a smile.

Pleasant? He cast a glance at a rain-spattered windowpane,

evidence of the darkest day they'd had so far. Taking her amiable mood to heart, he said, "Perhaps now would be a good time to continue our conversation."

Her eyes widened as if she'd forgotten—or faulted him for discussing business on the Sabbath. "Leasing our land in exchange for payment of taxes?"

He nodded, noting her continuous use of *our* as if she believed Curtis would return any day.

She took a breath. "'Tis very generous of you, but I . . . I cannot."

Their eyes locked across the table. "Nay?"

She was looking at him in that intent way she had, conviction in her gaze. "You're a slaveholder, General, are you not?"

He nearly uttered an oath at the quiet question. But eight years in uniform had taught him to school his emotions, especially the exasperation firing inside him. "A great many Virginians are slaveholders, Miss Menzies, including General Washington."

"That doesn't make it right."

"Your father owned slaves at Three Chimneys."

"He did, yes, but my mother freed them once he left for Scotland."

Had she? He'd assumed they'd been sold or had run away. "By law she didn't have the right to free them. They were the property of your father when he married her, like Three Chimneys."

"She didn't see it that way. They were more her family as she'd been raised with them." Lowering her voice, Sophie glanced at Lily Cate, who seemed unaware of their personal drama. She was busy looking about, lost in the novelty of being in a tavern. "My father, on the other hand, was a cruel man who abused them."

"I'm not a cruel man."

"But you're still a slaveholder."

There was no denying it. Thankfully, the meal arrived, simple as it was. Lily Cate dug into her mutton pie like a little ploughman, good manners aside. Seamus had lost his appetite. He took a long sip of ale from a sweating pewter tankard and decided to retreat.

But Sophie Menzies was not finished. Eyes down, she swallowed a halfhearted bite of her own dinner and said, "I don't understand you Patriots, fighting for liberty yet denying it to the very people who need it most."

He exhaled, her point well taken. "What if I work your fields with indentures?"

"You'd have to put it in writing first."

"You'd make a good attorney, Miss Menzies. Don't you trust me?"

"At the moment I don't trust anyone." She toyed with her fork, tone soft but impassioned. "I've tried to be a good citizen, a patriotic American, only to have my home nearly destroyed by British raiders and now taken away with little warning—"

"That has nothing to do with you and everything to do with your father." His voice was as low and soothing as he could make it. He wouldn't—couldn't—tell her the rumors about Curtis. "As I said, I'm willing to pay your back taxes."

She returned her attention to her game pie, but he knew she was no more in the mood to eat than he. "And I've decided that would be a highly irregular arrangement."

"Irregular? Not if we have a working agreement in place." He felt defensive and a tad desperate all at once. The future of Tall Acre was at stake. Three Chimneys was at stake. Lily Cate's happiness was at stake. He needed Sophie's fields. He needed *her*.

"General Ogilvy, I cannot be beholden to you."

"Why in heaven's name not?" He let go of his temper and regretted it immediately.

"Because—" She raised her spirited gaze to his as they hovered on dangerous ground. "Because I feel—" Her voice fell to a whisper. "Like a *kept* woman."

A kept woman? His mistress? He almost smiled. "Then I am getting a very poor return in the bargain, Miss Menzies."

Her pinched expression told him he had gone too far. He felt a cold, flooding remorse for such a callous comment.

Lily Cate snapped to attention and scooted closer to Sophie, her eyes wide and accusing. They both stared at him as if he were to blame for everything.

"I'm sorry," he said, meaning it.

Sophie nodded but didn't look at him again.

9

Bible open to the Psalms, Sophie felt her heart somewhat assuaged. She'd written down her prayer requests on a scrap of paper, wishing there weren't so many. At the top she'd penned Lily Cate's name just below Curtis's homecoming. Beneath these she'd written *land taxes* and *Three Chimneys*. She supposed she'd better pray more earnestly for the master of Tall Acre too.

Taking up a quill, she used the last of her ink to draw a heart with an arrow through it. She wouldn't write Seamus Ogilvy's name. The childish symbol would suffice. Impulsively she scribbled the word *bride* beside the heart and arrow. She would pray for his bride. Only then, when he was wed, would this sudden, surprising infatuation for him end. It had begun with his gift of tea, then sugar, his hasty note, his handsome looks. And that infernal rebel blue uniform he wore so well.

The more she tried to distance herself from him and drive a wedge between them like she had in the tavern yesterday, the closer he came.

Pushing away from her desk, she went to the dressing table. Her bedchamber was the only room that had remained untouched during the British occupation. Throughout those two tense months she'd locked her door each night, and Glynnis had taken to sleeping on a cot at the foot of her bed, murmuring dire predictions about her threatened virtue. Thankfully both her room and her virtue remained intact.

She stared at herself in the looking glass, wishing for another face, another reflection. Though she'd changed remarkably since finishing school, her nightly ritual remained the same. One hundred brushstrokes of her hair. Peppermint tooth polish. A splash of rosewater. Though Glynnis protested, Sophie insisted on a bath every other day but went downstairs to the kitchen so no hot water would need hauling upstairs. At last she sank to her knees on the cold, hard floor. Tonight her heart was so full she nearly couldn't speak.

Was anyone saying prayers with Lily Cate?

She'd wondered during the long Sabbath service when Lily Cate and the general had sat in front of her, proving such a distraction Sophie could hardly mumble amen. Though Seamus sat stone still, she'd sensed his thoughts were far afield. On taxes and leases, perhaps. Or the recent wedding he'd attended.

She bent her head, blocking the image of hard shoulders and midnight hair and the flash of exasperation in his gaze when she'd aired her stance on slavery. The mettle in his tone when he'd countered her every word had only made him more appealing. So she'd dug in her heels and defied him.

She needed to distance herself from him, from Lily Cate, before their closeness was brought to an abrupt end. She couldn't stand another loss, another heartache. Not after her mother. Three Chimneys. A lost way of life.

Reaching out, she snuffed the candle and climbed into

the four-poster bed. The feather tick cradled her as it had done for years but tonight seemed lacking. She envied Lily Cate her nighttime comforting. No doubt if she were in Lily Cate's place, in Seamus Ogilvy's arms, she'd quit crying too.

At dusk the tranquility of Tall Acre was profound. Seamus walked through the lavender twilight on his nightly rounds, a large iron ring with myriad skeleton keys dangling from his good hand. Now, as then, he checked each dependency, the icehouse and smokehouse, the spinning house and summer kitchen and half a dozen other outbuildings. Years before, his father had prayed a blessing on each. Protection. Peace. When he was a lad, those prayers had etched themselves indelibly on his conscience. His soul.

But had it done any good?

The wide veranda wrapping round the main house was bare, swept clean of all but a few brittle autumn leaves. A few lights shone from favorite rooms—study, foyer, Lily Cate's upstairs bedchamber. He allowed her a light at bedtime, but his fear of fire kept one of the staff hovering till he came upstairs and snuffed it out himself.

He exhaled, breath pluming white in the night's chill. Everything was moon-washed, nearly perfect. A few slaves sang softly in the quarters. Their presence, their hushed, haunting melodies, disturbed him in fresh ways. They were his father's slaves. He could honestly say he'd not had a hand in their past. But he knew he had a hand in their future.

Leaning against the smokehouse door, he tilted his head back and looked skyward as one low hymn ended and another began. A soft, determined rebuke threaded throughout, convicting him anew.

I don't understand you Patriots, fighting for liberty yet denying it to the very people who need it most.

He'd wanted to tell Sophie he'd arranged for manumission of all fifty-two of Tall Acre's slaves in the will he'd made prior to his joining the army. But the cold truth was he needed slave labor to turn Tall Acre profitable again or he'd lose it altogether. His overarching desire was to leave a prosperous estate for his son like his father before him, for untold generations of Ogilvys, Lord willing.

Which entailed finding a bride.

In the back of his head, he heard his mother's voice, gentle yet distinct. *You need a woman, a wife, to help tend to all this, Seamus. While you cherish your acres and experiment with new crops, breed your horses, build your home, and enlarge your own earthly paradise, make sure you have a capable woman to stand by you.*

That woman hadn't been Anne.

Who, then, would she be?

Clementine Randolph hadn't been shy. Nor had Sarah Carter or Emma Fairfax, each having a word alone with him before he'd ridden away from Bracken Hall that wet morning after the wedding. All had substantial dowries, were heiresses in their own right, and were anxious to wed and get on with the life that had been denied them in wartime. But he found them only mildly interesting at best. And Clementine's near taunting about Three Chimneys turned his stomach. In their eyes, Sophie Menzies was an outsider and always would be.

Pushing away from the wall, he started down the shell path toward the quarters. A few heads poked out at his approach, mostly children lured by the music of his jingling keys as he walked.

"Evenin', General," an old man called out, the white of his clay pipe glowing cherry-red in the dusk.

"Evening, Thomas," he answered as he went past.

He wasn't a cruel man. These people were warm and well fed, had ample wood and water. A doctor was near at hand if they took ill. On the Sabbath they rested. He issued frequent passes to neighboring plantations for them to visit kin. Never would he break up a family. Never had he resorted to a whipping. He held his overseers to the strictest standards for meting out any punishment. What little dissension there was had always been dealt with straightaway. The ever-present fear of being sold to someone far less amiable kept most problems at bay.

But try explaining that to Sophie Menzies.

Indentures, she'd said. In writing.

He looked toward the house, Lily Cate never far from his thoughts, and took a left at the boxwood hedge framing the garden. As night deepened, a streak of white caught his eye, coming at him like a shooting star across the blackened lawn.

"Papa!" She flung herself against him, her arms tight around his knees, nearly knocking him backwards. The frantic rise and fall of her chest made him look back at the house in alarm. He bent down and picked her up, his arms snug about her trembling body. He held her at eye level, her nightcap askew, vulnerability etched in her heart-shaped face. Had she really called him Papa? Or had he only imagined it? His chest felt so full of both alarm and delight he couldn't breathe.

"Papa, there's a man—he's looking up at me. I can see him from my window!"

"What?"

"On the front lawn, behind that big oak tree."

"You're sure?"

She buried her face in his shoulder in answer, as if she couldn't bear to take another look. The sick sinking that had begun inside him the night he'd taken her by force from Williamsburg rekindled.

"I'll go see," he murmured, stroking her hair and cap till her breathing returned to normal and she lifted her head.

Calling for his housekeeper, he sent her and Lily Cate upstairs. The familiar pistol at his waist, worn as a precaution against prowling animals, saved him a trip inside to his gun case.

He sprinted around the west side of the house, eyes on every bush and tree. The front lawn yawned empty. Even with lanterns lit and a twelve-man search with his foxhounds, nothing turned up an hour later. The river, a chronic source of worry given someone could slip in by boat, gleamed empty in the moonlight, the water lapping gently along the leaf-littered shore.

But the rhythm of his heart stayed at a gallop, his thoughts as hard to corral.

This was a warning. From Williamsburg.

☙

"You've not seen Miss Lily Cate for a fortnight." Glynnis's voice filled the warm kitchen like the aroma of freshly baked gingerbread.

"Just in passing at church," Sophie said, trying to keep the lament from her tone. Their honest talk at the tavern still unsettled her. She feared she'd angered Seamus further by refusing to let him carry her to services and back in his coach since then. She preferred walking, she'd told him.

"Well, if you're wondering what's going on at Tall Acre, I heard on good authority from Florie that there's to be a holiday ball. The general's officer friends will be in attendance and a great many from Roan too."

96

"I'm not surprised," Sophie said quietly. "Tall Acre has a history of hospitality."

"He's hired a new cook, other staff." Glynnis sighed, a thorn in her pleasure. "My only concern is what you'll be wearing. You're down to a few good dresses, though you could don something of your dear mother's."

"I wouldn't count on an invitation."

Glynnis looked up from the gingerbread she was icing. "Why not?"

Lifting her shoulders, Sophie snatched a wayward crumb. "Our relationship has become somewhat strained."

"Whose? Yours and the general's?"

Sophie nodded. "Whenever we're together we have . . . words." Turning her back on Glynnis, she took the steaming kettle from the hearth and set it on the kitchen table. "And like you said, I've not seen Lily Cate for a fortnight. That speaks for itself."

Yet wasn't that what she wanted? A safe distance? Exasperation shot through her. From Seamus, truly, not Lily Cate. But she couldn't have one without the other. Could she?

"Well, ball or no ball, we still have a fine Christmas ham, thanks to Tall Acre. A far cry from last Christmas. The only thing we're lacking is your brother's presence."

"I'm still praying about that," Sophie murmured. Tucked in the pages of her Bible were the letters he'd sent, the ink faded and hard to decipher. With them was the letter from Richmond announcing that Three Chimneys was now lost. Glynnis was unaware of that.

Turning away, Glynnis began to cough, hiding her face in her apron.

"You should be abed." She schooled the sympathy in her

tone. Glynnis didn't like to be coddled. "You've still not recovered from that cold." She reached for a cup and poured tea. "Have you been drinking that water from the chestnuts we boiled? 'Tis beneficial for chest complaints, Mama always said. Perhaps I should send for the doctor—"

"You'll do no such thing. There's naught to be done for a cold except get over it. I'll mend." She started out of the kitchen, gnarled hands untying her apron as she went. "I'm off to the attic to see about a proper ball gown."

Sophie watched her go, words of refusal lodging in her throat.

❧

The invitation arrived at dusk. Standing alone in the foyer after a servant from Tall Acre delivered it, Sophie ran a finger over the heavy masculine scrawl that comprised her name. Half a dozen excuses allowing her a graceful exit leapt to mind. Glynnis was unwell. She was expecting company . . . though Curtis's homecoming hardly counted. With a swipe of a finger she broke the Ogilvy seal, devouring the contents like a piece of gingerbread.

Dear Miss Menzies,
    Our hope is that you will honor us with your presence as our house guest from Wednesday to Saturday next culminating in a holiday ball on the 20th.

                    Sincerely,
                    Seamus Ogilvy

Beneath his bold signature was Lily Cate's own, loping and unpracticed and hesitant, melting every shred of her resistance. She could say no to the general, but she couldn't disappoint Lily Cate.

Leaving the invitation open on an entry table, she took the wide stairs slowly, fighting her conflicted feelings every step. The truth was she was starved for a little life, a little company. What could it hurt? The general would be surrounded by friends and she would be on the fringe, more a companion to Lily Cate.

As expected, three gowns hung about Sophie's bedchamber awaiting her perusal. All were wrinkled, one yellowed with age, another torn. One glance decided the question. A pale lemon lustring with an overlay of French lace stole her breath. It had been Mama's favorite, though the immodest bodice was missing a fichu.

Still, she had no proper shoes. No jewels to go about her throat. Any remaining finery had been bartered for food last winter. The thought of a house filled to the brim with genteel men and women made Sophie cringe. These were the general's personal friends. She didn't want to embarrass him by appearing ill-dressed, even if she had been invited out of courtesy.

She could hear Glynnis approach, her slow tread on the stairs giving a warning. Her bent frame filled the doorway, invitation fluttering from her hand.

I told you so, her expression seemed to say.

"Not only a ball but a merry four days' stay!" Stepping into the room, she watched Sophie examine the lustring. "I thought you'd pick that one, though we'll have to alter the other two for you to wear while you're there."

"Is there time?"

"Perhaps, if we get to work at once."

"We'd best begin," Sophie said, eyeing the clock.

And pray I get the influenza instead.

10

Sophie could only remember two visits to Tall Acre, once when the general married and they paid a call to his bride, and then at Lily Cate's birth. Oddly, the memory of the lovely Anne Ogilvy was no longer fixed in her head as firmly as a framed miniature in oils. She only remembered the feel of her. The former mistress of Tall Acre seemed kind but condescending. Soft-spoken yet sharp-eyed. Sophie and her mother had not returned nor been invited back.

Sophie recalled it now as the new Ogilvy coach came round to collect her, giving her a taste of the refinements to come. Lined with green Morocco leather and boasting diamond-cut plate glass, the vehicle was Philadelphia made. Sophie was glad the coachman took his time on the rutted road so she could compose herself, but no amount of prayer or preparation could quiet her heart as the hundred-year-old house came into view. Three Chimneys was lovely in its own tired, genteel way, but Tall Acre was magnificent with its sweeping porches and three-storied brick facade.

She wasn't the first to arrive, but Lily Cate was waiting

for her, a servant by her side. Through the coach window Sophie could see her hopping on one foot and waving wildly, finally jumping down from the front veranda and dashing toward the mounting block. Her wordless hug told Sophie everything. Both of them had been counting down the days till they were together again.

"Papa said that I could show you to your room—'tis next to mine—and sit by you at supper." Taking Sophie's hand, she led her into a gleaming, beeswax-scented foyer with a wide staircase soaring upward, weaponry and paintings covering the paneled walls. Masculine voices and laughter seeped beneath a stalwart mahogany door to their right. "He's in his study with his army men."

Sophie hid a smile. Her prayers had been answered. She'd been spared an awkward entry and was in the company of the one who mattered most. "We'll not disturb them, then."

They climbed the central staircase, then headed down a long hall toward a door opened wide as if in welcome.

"I asked Papa to give you the room next to mine. 'Twas Mama's, Florie said."

Surprised, Sophie followed as a servant set her valise near an open, empty wardrobe. "Do you remember your mama, Lily Cate?" She regretted the question as sorrow crowded the girl's little face.

"I only remember Aunt Charlotte."

Charlotte. Anne's sister. They seldom spoke of Lily Cate's life in Williamsburg, though Sophie remembered the Fitzhughs. They'd been friends of her father's. Pockmarked and gaunt, Fitzhugh was every bit as cold and calculating. In the back of her mind lay hazy allegations. Of dishonesty. Darker deeds.

"Miss Sophie, look!" Lily Cate showed her a tester bed,

an elegant dressing table with a mirrored back, and the bank of south-facing windows overlooking the front lawn where myriad shade trees grew. All personal effects had been removed. She'd have thought it any other room but for the connecting door to Lily Cate's bedchamber.

There was another door on the opposite wall. She could only guess where that led. Her lingering gaze gave her away.

"That's Papa's room," Lily Cate told her.

Locked, most likely. Somehow being sandwiched between them made Sophie feel unsettled and secure all at once. She was a restless sleeper since British soldiers had occupied her home. Sometimes she had nightmares. The thought of waking either Lily Cate or her father was enough to keep her sleepless all week.

The crunch of wheels on the drive returned them to the windows. A line of coaches was delivering more guests, not officers but refined ladies, their capes and bonnets adding a bit of color to the dreary landscape. Would Tall Acre hold them all?

Lily Cate's face was alive with excitement. "I'm supposed to let you rest till supper, but I'd rather play." Pushing open the connecting door, she all but skipped into her bedchamber, a charming room made bright with floral wallpaper and a quilted yellow counterpane. "Papa gave me a dollhouse like yours from Richmond."

Her joy was so contagious Sophie felt her own spirits take wing. Dropping down beside her on the thick carpet, she lost herself in a tour of rooms, charmed when Lily Cate introduced the master of the house, a small wooden soldier in blue uniform.

"Where are *you*?" Sophie asked.

Peering into a miniature parlor, Lily Cate pointed to a dark-haired girl in a yellow silk dress. At her feet was a cat curled on a braided rug. What? No mistress? Grieving widower that Seamus was, Sophie almost expected to see a miniature version of Anne presiding.

As dusk darkened the windowpanes, the rich aroma of bread and roasting meat told them supper was near at hand. A maid delivered towels and hot water, replenishing the fire and helping Sophie dress. All thumbs, or all nerves, Sophie dropped her mother's cameo and sent the maid scrambling to retrieve it. Finally trussed in stays and a remade gown of apple-green brocade, she stared back at a stranger in the looking glass. The maid had done wonders with her hair, arranging it high at the back of her head with curls spiraling to her bare shoulders. Unpowdered, it held the patina of black silk, turning her skin to frost. Again that sense of dissatisfaction crept in. She was too pale. Too thin. More shadow.

Lily Cate had been fussed over with her own head of curls and rose taffeta dress. They stood gawking at each other in mutual admiration before Lily Cate took her hand and led her downstairs, the open dining room door looming large. Second thoughts rushed in, slowing Sophie's steps.

Whatever had possessed her to come?

She could hear the lilt of feminine voices mingling with the rumbling tenor of the men's. Her name, her family, made her feel small. Once her lineage was proudly bandied about; now she was ashamed of being a Menzies, daughter of a turncoat, in a roomful of Patriots.

Glad for the pressure of Lily Cate's small, warm hand, she stepped cautiously over the threshold. Across the sea of Wilton carpet, the general looked their way as if he'd been waiting. Sophie's gaze dropped to the place cards set about the immense table, wondering where they'd sit. For now Lily Cate was intent on leading her to her father standing with a few fellow officers.

"Miss Menzies." His eyes held hers. Warm. Kind. As if their last exchange hadn't been a heated one in a busy tavern. "Welcome to Tall Acre."

"Good evening, General Ogilvy." 'Twas all she could manage. Her smile felt pasted in place.

With a gesture to a servant to commence supper, Seamus pulled out a chair, seating her and then Lily Cate, as the other guests found their places. An older couple sat beside them. Had Seamus kept her separate out of courtesy because he knew she'd feel uncomfortable? They were at the end of the table, well away from the vivacious Clementine Randolph and the ladies intermingled with the officers. Relief swept aside her unease. Years before, Clementine had attended Mrs. Hallam's school briefly, but the other women were unknown to her.

As myriad dishes were served, Sophie took in glazed green woodwork and Turkey red carpet, drawn to the white damask tablecloth and Wedgwood dinner service. Without liveried servants, Tall Acre seemed less formal than other great houses, though plenty of spirits and silver abounded.

Lily Cate ate everything set before her, particularly the sweetmeats, making Sophie worry about a stomachache. But she'd be near at hand if Lily Cate had a bad night. She ate little herself, stomach rebelling, every dish rich if perfectly seasoned. She was used to bland fare or none at all.

As glasses were emptied and refilled and hot dishes replaced cold ones, all brought up or whisked away by a pair of ingenious dumbwaiters framing the fireplace, Sophie kept time by the tall case clock in the corner. Half past nine.

The women were full of gossip, the men discussing politics and the government's efforts to unify the new states for the first congress in the spring. Through the dazzle of candlelight, Sophie stole a look at the general at the head of the table. Heart-tuggingly handsome. The perfect host. The ladies obviously found him fascinating, one or two noticeably so. There was none of the intensity about him tonight that marked their personal exchanges. He seemed relaxed, more at ease. At meal's end the gentlemen remained behind in the dining room while the women passed into a room made rich with countless Palladian windows, the pier glass and striped taffeta elegant.

Stepping over the threshold, Sophie fell in love in a glance. Corner fireplaces were at each end, fire screens worked in vivid, intricate hues. By Anne's hand? A portrait of Tall Acre's former mistress hung above one marble mantel. Unsmiling but serene. Too young to perish.

The room shimmered with silk, jewels flashing and cologne overpowering. Sophie was glad to be unadorned and unpowdered, fading into the woodwork but for Lily Cate. Tonight she'd become a chatterbox, clutching Sophie's hand and proudly showing her around.

Someone sat down at a harpsichord, playing softly. Sophie listened, longing to touch the familiar keys. With Three Chimneys' music room a memory, she'd forgotten how lovely the sound. Charming, even romantic.

"We've come a long way from our days at Mrs. Hallam's, Miss Menzies." Clementine approached, waving her fan with all the drama Sophie remembered. "I'd quite lost track of you, but here you are at Tall Acre looking quite at home. General Ogilvy tells me your brother served with distinction under his command."

"As a captain, yes."

"I'd also heard he's not yet returned from the war . . ." Her eyes narrowed and took in Lily Cate, still by Sophie's side. "And Three Chimneys is no longer in your possession."

Had the general told her that too? "I still reside there. Nothing has changed in that respect."

"Oh, but it will change." Clementine seemed pleased to report it. "I have it on good authority that Three Chimneys is to go to a relative of mine."

Sophie's hand went to the cameo at her throat. "I'm hoping my brother will return in time and that won't be necessary." Admitting anything less was saying Curtis was dead—or worse. Behaving dishonorably was not to be broached.

"Oh?" Clementine's expression was nothing short of smug. "My relations say the land taxes haven't been paid either."

"Yes, they have!" Lily Cate's voice rang out, clear and bell-like across the grand room. The harpsichord ceased playing, and every feminine eye turned toward them. "Papa paid the land taxes. Florie told me he did!"

There was a stunned silence. Sophie looked at Lily Cate. Had he? Nothing else had been said about leasing the land. Why hadn't he told her?

"That day at the tavern when you were so upset—" Lily Cate turned wide eyes on her. "Papa hurt your feelings and you almost cried."

"Well, well . . ." With a sulky smile, Clementine folded her fan and moved away. "It seems I don't know *everything* after all."

Squeezing Lily Cate's hand, Sophie led her to a corner, sinking down in a chair so that they were eye level. "Those are private, grown-up matters." She trod as gently as she could, relieved the others resumed talking and turned their backs to them. "'Tis best to keep quiet about such things."

"Like the man outside my window?"

Sophie stared at her, embarrassment fading to confusion.

"There's a strange man on the lawn who watches me."

"A stranger?" Sophie looked toward the dining room doorway. "Does your father know?"

Nodding, Lily Cate moved into the warm circle of Sophie's arms. "He hasn't seen him yet, but I have."

Lord, please, let it be her imagination.

The genteel evening was in tatters. The ladies were looking at her again as if she and the general had more of an arrangement than simple taxes. Mention of a tawdry tavern hadn't helped. And Florie would have to be dealt with sooner or later. But all of it paled next to Lily Cate's revelation.

Yawning, Lily Cate laid her head on Sophie's shoulder. The gentlemen were coming in now, having had their after-dinner indulgences of Madeira and tobacco. Clementine began a few tentative notes on a flute.

Sophie took advantage of the moment. "Please tell your father I'm taking you upstairs. We'll read a story, say our prayers."

With a nod, Lily Cate went to him, but he was already looking at them as if sensing something amiss.

Lily Cate came back, face pale. "My stomach hurts."

Taking her hand, Sophie led her through a far door and entered a darkened hall, unsure of where she was. Thoughts full of Three Chimneys, she was suddenly homesick, wondering what she would do if it was lost to her, but more worried about the little girl who had far more troublesome matters brewing than a stomachache.

Once upstairs, Sophie summoned a maid to bring peppermint tea and replenish the waning fire. Soon Lily Cate was undressed and in a nightgown. While Sophie recounted *Le Chat Botté*, or *Puss in Boots*, promising to petition her father about a kitten, Lily Cate sipped from a dainty cup. 'Twas late, her yawning a signal to end the eventful evening.

Joining hands, they knelt on the carpet and bowed their

heads, saying in unison what had become Lily Cate's favorite prayer, taught to Sophie herself when she was young.

"Dear God most high, hear and bless Thy beasts and singing birds: And guard with tenderness small things that have no words. Amen."

Afterward, Sophie rocked Lily Cate by the crackling hearth, wondering if Anne had done the same in this very chair. Her gaze trailed to the windows. Drapes and shutters were drawn against the cold, ensuring no stranger would be looking in at them. She'd leave the connecting door open in case Lily Cate cried out or was sick in the night, or worse.

When Lily Cate was settled, Sophie returned to her bedchamber reluctantly. The music and laughter coming from below was like a jolt of coffee keeping her awake. Clementine's voice was easily distinguished, witty and frequent, rising above the rumble of the men.

Rubbing her arms against the cold despite the heat of the fire, she began a slow walk around the room, not wanting to climb into Anne's bed. The coverlet bore the popular tree-of-life pattern, conveying a subtle irony.

Was Lily Cate . . . conceived there?

Her fingers closed about the doorknob adjoining her room to the general's. Locked. The relief coursing through her made no sense. He was an officer, a man of honor. He had no designs on her, illicit or otherwise. Her being in Anne's room was pure happenstance, all because of Lily Cate. Likely he wanted a sound night's sleep and she would help ensure that. Farther down the hall were his many guests, filling up every nook and cranny of the upper floors.

The fire popped, making her jump. She slowed her pacing when she came to a desk, twin to her own. Amidst the heavier Chippendale furnishings, the delicate Queen Anne piece seemed an outcast, tucked beneath a shuttered window and heavy drapes.

Surprised, she ran her fingers over the polished wood. Did it contain a secret compartment like hers? Feeling beneath the panel triggered a latch. The wood gave way under her practiced hand. A small, leather-bound book lay in a hidden drawer. A Bible?

Nay . . . a diary.

She hesitated, hand hovering. The desk, the room, had been swept clean of Anne, all but this, and Sophie felt an inexplicable hunger to know the woman who had been Seamus's wife.

Picking up the diary carefully, she opened to the flyleaf.

To my beloved, Anne, wife of my heart.

Her own heart tripped. Beneath this tender dedication he had written in a bold, familiar hand, *Proverbs 19:14.* Sophie knew the Scripture well, though he'd not spelled it out. *House and riches are the inheritance of fathers; and a prudent wife is from the* LORD.

A spring date followed. Their wedding day? Had he bestowed the little book as a gift? If so, it held far more sentiment than she'd given Seamus Ogilvy credit for. She'd assumed the war years had bled all the softness out of him. Perhaps she was wrong.

Taking a breath, she turned a page. *October, 1778.* Anne's hand was fragile compared to her husband's, lacy and loping and uneven where his was tight and precise and steadfast. Her first penned words carried the lash of a whip.

I loathe Tall Acre.

Sophie's breathing thinned. She brought the diary nearer the fire so that light spilled onto the page. Suddenly the book assumed a weight it hadn't before.

Without Seamus here I have no purpose, no heart, no desire to do anything. The baby only makes matters worse. She grows fat and happier by the day while I seem to waste away. Tall Acre with all its woods and vales seems naught but a rustic outpost. I long to go to Williamsburg, but sister tells me 'tis unsafe. The British may attack the town and then where would we be?

Sophie shut the diary, stung by the tone of the words. Anne must have been writing about Lily Cate, who would have been a few months old by then. Crossing the carpet, she returned the book to the secret drawer, sorry and half ashamed she'd given in to temptation and opened it. The fact that Anne was no longer living made her feel only slightly less guilty. Seamus was certainly alive and well, and hopefully oblivious to the penned outpourings of Anne's heart.

Something her mother once said, long dismissed, broke loose.

"There's trouble at Tall Acre." Evelyn Menzies's features had been pinched with fatigue, as she'd just returned from attending a birth in the quarters. "I didn't go up to the house, but one hears things. With the general away, the mistress isn't faring well."

At the time Sophie had held her tongue, and her mother said no more.

Truly, Anne Ogilvy had not been a happy woman, a content wife.

11

Crying shook Sophie awake. In the cold silence of the unfamiliar room, the sound raked her every nerve. Thrusting aside the covers, she traded the warmth of the bed for the chill of the bedchamber, nearly tripping over the hem of her nightgown in her haste to quell the sound. The door separating them was open, and she groped her way to the curtained bed and took Lily Cate in her arms.

"Hush your crying, lamb. I'm right here . . . your father is near."

No sooner had she said it than the door opened and Seamus walked in from the hall. Ignoring him, Sophie continued stroking Lily Cate's hair, aware she was not truly awake. Eyes closed, she curled into Sophie's chest and seemed to settle. Sophie's own heart beat in her throat, more from Seamus standing beside her than Lily Cate's outburst.

The clock chimed two, a subtle reminder to return to bed, but neither of them moved. Finally Seamus faced the hearth, added several chunks of wood to the fire, and stirred the ashes till they came to life and pushed the shadows back. Despite the late hour he was still in formal dress, though he'd shed his fancy coat. Was the party still going on downstairs? A sudden burst of laughter told her so.

"Just a bad dream, perhaps," she told him, keenly aware she was missing her dressing gown, her hair spilling down without her customary nightcap. "I'll stay with her awhile if you want to return below."

He reached out and pulled a blanket from a chair back, draping it over her shoulders. "She's been sleeping fairly well till tonight. Mayhap all the excitement. Unfamiliar guests."

"Earlier she told me she's seen a strange man on the lawn."

He shot a glance at the shuttered windows. "Someone seems to be watching the house, aye."

"Have you any idea who or why?"

He looked at her for a long moment as if weighing how much to say. "Her Williamsburg relations are none too happy she's here. I suspect it's their doing."

"But you're her father. This is her home."

"There's much you don't know. 'Tis . . . complicated."

The general had been away fighting a war while Anne's kin took care of Lily Cate. Were they fighting to regain her? "'Tis none of my concern." She held Lily Cate closer, the intimacy of the moment making a mockery of her words.

Leaning back against the mantel, he ran a hand over his jaw, visibly aggrieved. Here, in the privacy of this room, he could unburden himself as he could never do among his many reveling guests. Who was she to deny him?

"You may tell me what you will—or not. It shall go no further."

He gave a nod that seemed to seal some sort of agreement between them. "When I was discharged from the army, I went to Williamsburg after sending a letter to Anne's relations regarding my intentions. They refused to let me see Lily Cate, so I had to force my way in and remove her."

She went still, imagining it. The heated scene. The sudden separation. Lily Cate's confusion. "As her father you had every right, though it must have frightened her as you were little more than a stranger."

"I'm not proud of what happened, but she's my flesh and blood, all I have of Anne."

Anne, indeed. Sophie looked down at his daughter, feeling like a third party. "You want what's best for her."

"Sometimes I'm not sure what that is. I simply want her to know me—as her father." The words seemed hard for a man unused to tender things. "To count on me . . . come to me . . . trust me."

His heartfelt words stirred an old, sad longing. She'd wanted that from her own father, but it had eluded her, yet here was a man who longed to be the center of a little girl's world and that hope was being thwarted.

A log rolled forward, sending a shower of sparks onto the delft tiles near his boots. "I don't want you burdened with this, Miss Menzies. You have enough concerns of your own."

"I have one less." She smoothed the coverlet around Lily Cate, torn between gratefulness and aggravation. "You've paid Three Chimneys' land taxes, your daughter tells me."

His gaze swung back to her, questioning. "The maids have been talking, I suppose." His look of surprise vanished at her nod. "Aye, the taxes have been paid, but that doesn't begin to unravel the rest."

"New occupants, you mean." He was obviously aware Three Chimneys would go to Clementine Randolph's kin. The very thought nettled. But for all she knew, Seamus fancied the outspoken Clementine. "Then you should know I've given more thought to your proposal. If you promise to use indentures or other labor, the land is yours to lease."

"You'll want that in writing."

"Your word is sufficient." She forced a small smile, trying to make amends for the tavern. "Agreed?"

"Agreed," he answered.

She'd expected to feel some satisfaction, some sweetness, but what did the land lease matter if her home was no longer hers?

Sore of heart, she eased Lily Cate back into bed, aware she might not have the privilege much longer. Shivering despite the blanket he'd draped around her shoulders, she looked toward the adjoining door. She didn't want to return to Anne's room, the troubling diary hidden in the desk. She'd not sleep a wink, unsettled as she was.

Without another word Seamus went out, looking as troubled as she felt despite their new agreement. She lay down with Lily Cate, thoughts full of Seamus, as the party below played out till dawn.

⁂

The day of the ball Seamus stood at his study window, watching snow shake down like salt from a saltcellar, blanketing every bush and tree and threatening to prolong his house party. Though he was glad of some company, he was ready to see it end and return to estate business. Clementine Randolph's outspokenness was beginning to wear thin. Some of his fellow officers drank too much and were in danger of draining his wine cellar. And he was preoccupied enough to worry that Lily Cate might disappear despite his precautions.

"Papa?"

He turned away from the frosted glass, warmed by the

sound of her lilting voice. She had finally stopped calling him *sir*. Why, he didn't know. He suspected it was Sophie's doing, and he was supremely thankful.

"How do I look for the ball?"

Like your mother.

For a moment he was too choked to speak. She pirouetted on the threshold in a new dress of silk and linen, a wide yellow sash about her waist. They'd left all her clothes in Williamsburg that bitter night, but a Roan seamstress had been at work making a new wardrobe since.

She came nearer till she stood in front of him. "Miss Sophie arranged my hair." Pleasure and pride shone in her eyes. She looked up at him as if needing his approval, hopeful and half shy all at once.

"You're . . ." Stooping, he took a closer look at her. "Beautiful."

She giggled, revealing freshly cleaned teeth. One was loose. She'd taken to wiggling it in odd moments but seemed to have forgotten about it for the time being.

He glanced at the door. "Where is Miss Menzies?"

"She's dressing." Lily Cate leaned nearer, her warm whisper tickling his ear. "She looks like a princess."

The tender moment passed. Lily Cate ran off. He wondered how Sophie felt about being here. She was still smiling, keeping to the shadows mostly, but showing no unease. And she was attracting attention. Clementine had made one high-handed remark about her presence, but he'd made sure there wasn't another. His fellow officers weren't so easily dismissed. What had McClintock said earlier?

"She's quite comely, Seamus, no matter her unsavory connections. Is she . . . unattached?"

Seamus had looked over the card table at his second in

command, someone he'd always liked—till now. "I wouldn't know," he replied, a slow awareness dawning. He'd asked Sophie here for Lily Cate, or so he'd thought. But mayhap there were higher hands in this than his.

"Do you think, perhaps, we could be seated together at supper? Last night she was at the end of the table with your daughter and the Melbournes. The old man is deaf as a post and Mrs. Melbourne is little better." McClintock furrowed a brow. "It's as if she's been quarantined and you don't want anybody near her."

Seamus ignored the gibe and made no promises, unsurprised when Richard Graeme soon cornered Sophie. Watching from across the room, Seamus wrestled down a desire to intervene, wondering if she was as bothered by the major's attention as he was.

"If you'd be a bit more obliging, I could have my estate on the James and acquire Three Chimneys too." McClintock sipped his drink and frowned as he watched Graeme share a cup of punch with Sophie across the room. "We would be neighbors."

Seamus didn't tell him Three Chimneys was in jeopardy, or that the idea of having him as a neighbor made him want more Madeira. The truth was that if Sophie did wed, her troubles might end. Only she needed a good man, a man unlike her father, who would be gentle and not harsh. Who could give her children, make a good home. Remove the danger of being destitute.

McClintock's voice was remarkably condescending. "I might overlook her Tory roots."

Seamus stiffened. The camaraderie he felt with his fellow officers only went so far. Somehow every one of them seemed unworthy. And none of them had a motherless daughter in need of a feminine hand.

For now the ball was about to begin and snow was still falling, and he was looking forward to a quieter house on the morrow.

Musicians, mostly itinerant fiddlers, were tuning their instruments at one end of the polished ballroom. They'd arrived despite the weather along with a few guests from Roan, all dressed in their Sabbath best and promising a good number for dancing.

He searched the room for Lily Cate and found Sophie instead.

She looks like a princess.

She was wearing blue, his favorite color. A simple cameo on a velvet ribbon graced her throat. She lacked both makeup and powder, but none were needed. Though the other women were alluring in a sophisticated way, she seemed set apart, a beguiling mix of simplicity and charm.

She glanced at him and then away. Lily Cate was holding her hand, and they turned their backs on the room to stand at a window and look out at the snow. It made him nervous, thinking someone might be watching from the lawn. But surely a stranger wouldn't be out in such foul weather, no matter the motive. This was his only solace.

McClintock was at his elbow again, bemoaning Graeme's persistence. "Since I was never fortunate enough to be Miss Menzies's supper partner, perhaps you could arrange for a dance."

"I plan on it," Seamus said.

McClintock grunted his displeasure. "With all due respect, I mean *me* and Miss Menzies, not *you* and Miss Menzies."

"Then ask her. But not until I've had the pleasure."

Most balls, be it country or town, opened with the minuet. Seamus preferred country dances but would bow to custom.

He simply needed a partner. No one would take the floor till he did. He made his way around the edges of the glittering room, his breathing shallow as he second-guessed what he was about to do. He didn't know if the lady in question would dance with him. Did she even like to dance? Mrs. Hallam's academy was said to turn out the finest footwork in Virginia. He was willing to wager Sophie hadn't danced a step since then. Not with a war on and circumstances what they were at Three Chimneys.

The ladies were watching him and fluttering their fans, thinking he'd choose one of them. He didn't give them a glance.

"Miss Menzies."

She turned from the window and faced him, surprise sketched across her features.

Lily Cate was between them, looking from him to Sophie like she would burst with delight. His daughter was young but clever, and she seemed close to accepting if Sophie didn't.

"May I have this dance?" For a second he hung between hope and fear. Sophie's wide eyes held his in hesitation. She wouldn't refuse him, would she? Her small curtsey was her answer.

They stepped onto the ballroom floor, Lily Cate staring after them, and not only her. He could feel Graeme's and McClintock's eyes on them too. Sophie, however, didn't look at him again. Not even when his hands captured hers. She kept her eyes averted, that serene smile locked in place.

He felt rusty as an old hinge, his battlefield injuries and the winter's damp leaving him a bit stiff. His first dance with Anne had been at a wedding. Their last dance . . . he couldn't remember. He'd always preferred foxhunting or fencing or shooting. Aside from a few frolics when the officers' wives were present during the war, there'd been little merriment in encampments. He'd asked Anne to accompany Martha Washington to headquarters at Valley Forge, but she'd refused.

The minuet ended too soon, and McClintock claimed Sophie.

"Near perfection," he murmured when their set was over. "By heaven but she's light on her feet."

Because there's nothing to her. Seamus bit his cheek to keep from saying it. Sophie was feather light. A good indication she'd be frail like Anne. Unable to have children, mayhap. A huge risk. But what did that matter to him?

By midnight she'd danced with every man in the room, even old Melbourne. Seamus danced with every woman, even Lily Cate. She didn't yet know the steps, but in her shy, eager-to-please way, she garnered admiring, amused glances for her efforts.

"Really, Seamus Ogilvy, you're hard on a woman's heart." With an exasperated swish of her fan, Clementine cornered him by the punch bowl.

He faced her warily in the small anteroom off the ballroom. Ever since she'd arrived she'd made a point of trying to discover where his affections lay, and he prepared himself for more of the same. Though they'd been friends since before the war, he hardly knew her now. The long, lean years had given her sharp edges, though he wagered she'd not known a tenth of the hardship many had. Once lighthearted and witty, she had turned waspish and bitter.

"Come now, you're hardly the grieving widower after all these years, are you? Louisa is quite put out you haven't asked her for a second dance . . . or anything else for that matter."

His gaze traveled unwillingly to the brunette across the

room. Just who was put out? Louisa . . . or Clementine? He had no need of a wife. Anne's memory was enough. Lily Cate was enough. Attempting anything other than getting Tall Acre up and running again was too much. "To be honest, I've yet to meet a woman my late wife's equal," he replied. It was neither gentlemanly nor entirely truthful, but it cleared the air and made it plain he wasn't interested.

"Well," she shot back, "I shan't tell Louisa *that*." Frowning, she scanned the ballroom. "There's another matter having to do with Sophie Menzies. It seems strange to me that you'd have a Tory beneath your roof."

He looked hard at her. "Once upon a time we were all Tories, Miss Randolph." The little flag flying atop Sophie's father's desk leapt to mind. Sewn by her own hand, every star and stripe in place, it seemed a small work of art. Of heart. The memory never failed to move him. "Miss Menzies is Tory no longer."

"Are you quite sure of that, General?" Clementine's arrogance held firm. "I've even heard her brother fled to England with Benedict Arnold."

The accusation, boldly stated as fact, turned him defensive. "Lots of rumors fly in the wake of war. That is one of them."

She turned away without another word, leaving a trail of pungent perfume in her wake. He watched her depart, sick at heart. Seamus had long counted Curtis more friend than fellow officer. But a turncoat? Washington had alluded to such. If true, the betrayal would be only one in a long line of them. Yet he sensed it would devastate Miss Menzies.

"Papa? How long will it be till the dancing stops?"

He looked to his left. Lily Cate sidled up to him, Sophie behind her. "Are you tired?"

"Aye—and nay." She wrinkled her nose in such a way her

freckles stood out. "Miss Sophie said if we go to bed now, we can wake up early tomorrow to play in the snow."

"That sounds better than dancing," he murmured, meaning it.

"Are you going to bed now too?" Lily Cate said.

"Not till our guests leave."

"Will they ever?"

He chuckled. "The weather may have other ideas."

"Goodnight, Papa." She curtsied, and he found himself wishing she'd kiss him goodnight. Once Sophie left she would be shy of him again. He resigned himself to that fact, wishing otherwise.

Looking on, Sophie reached out a hand, stroking Lily Cate's dark curls like she'd done in the night. Their bedchamber conversation came rushing in, everything he'd never say by day. All that he'd held back.

"Goodnight, General Ogilvy," Sophie whispered with a half smile.

The title seemed so formal. Hadn't they moved beyond that? A simple *Sophie* and *Seamus* sounded much better. But how to sidestep formalities . . . shift to something else?

"Goodnight, Miss Menzies," he finally said.

12

Snow decorated Three Chimneys like icing on white cake, requiring warmer fires and bed pans of smoldering coals. The water in Sophie's washstand threatened to freeze, and despite numerous blankets piled atop her bed, she never felt warm enough, unlike Tall Acre where every corner seemed cozy.

"You've no padding to warm you," Glynnis scolded when she returned that morning. "We need to fatten you up like a Christmas goose."

"You should have seen me at Tall Acre. I ate like a field hand!" Sophie ran her hands down the sides of her bodice, sure she was a bit thicker than when she'd left. "General Ogilvy has a new French cook. He laid the best table and turned out a delicious orange cake."

Glynnis coughed into her handkerchief. "I'm far keener on learning who the next mistress of Tall Acre will be. Florie came by to chat and said there were quite a few fine, unmarried ladies present. The general's even stopped traipsing to the mistress's grave."

So he traipsed, did he? She sighed at Florie's latest indiscretion. "Probably because the snow is a foot deep and he cannot."

"I don't suppose you noticed his favoring one lady over another?"

Sophie bit her lip. All she'd noticed was the attention the ladies had paid him. "General Ogilvy is difficult to read."

"No doubt the ball was a great success." Taking a chair by the kitchen hearth, Glynnis eyed a pot of porridge. "Did he dance with you?"

"He danced with everyone, even old Mrs. Melbourne who is nearly at death's door." The kind act had touched her. "And a fine dancer he is." Despite his protests to the contrary, he was surprisingly agile, even graceful. She wouldn't confide that he'd bucked custom, partnering with the least socially prominent woman in the room instead of the most for the opening minuet. "I expect we shall dance at his wedding soon."

Glynnis heaved a sigh. "I daresay his future's a bit brighter than ours at present. Florie said—"

"Glynnis!" Sophie sat down hard on a stool, edging her cold feet nearer the fire. "I fear Florie says too much."

"Well, tittle-tattle seems acceptable if it's about us." Glynnis gave a stir to the porridge with a long wooden spoon. "Apparently one of the general's guests has some claim on Three Chimneys, according to a Miss Randolph." She looked at Sophie squarely. "You'd do well to tell me these things. This has been my home ever since your mother's day."

"I didn't want to worry you. Miss Randolph has a cousin, an officer, who might be awarded Three Chimneys." Sophie still felt prickly. "Given Father's sentiments, it's considered enemy property and may pass into other hands."

"Well, I've had a letter from my widowed sister in Annapolis, the one who takes in mending." Glynnis sneezed and started to sputter. She could hardly manage a word without that chilling, bone-deep wheezing. "She has a spare room should we want it."

The sister who was so old she could hardly see her stitches? And so poor she couldn't rub two pence together? "'Tis very kind, Glynnis, but I won't be making any plans just yet." The quiet answer belied the maelstrom inside her. "For the moment we're warm, well fed, and have a roof over our heads. Curtis might still come home. All will be well."

"So say the fairy tales," Glynnis muttered, resuming her pot watching.

Three days before Christmas another note came. Sophie grew warm all over when she recognized Seamus's familiar scrawl. She, Glynnis, and Henry had been invited to Christmas dinner. Her heart raced. She'd only just left. Was she now invited back? She wouldn't, couldn't, court heartache. Though she hated to disappoint Lily Cate, she dashed off her regrets. And then she burned the invitation lest Glynnis push her out the door.

Quietly they sat down to their Christmas ham and an abundance of dishes reminiscent of better days. Creamed celery with pecans, acorn squash, lima beans, mince pie sweetened with a gill of molasses. Even her old favorite, spoonbread, crowned the table, its golden top rising and nearly touching the oven ceiling when baking. She tried not to dwell on how Henry had come by the costly pecans.

Her mind wandered to the winter frolic she and Lily Cate had enjoyed the morning after the ball, making angel imprints in their heavy coats and boots and mixing snow with Tall Acre's honey for a tasty treat. Seamus had watched them from an upstairs window for a few moments, leaving her to wonder what went on inside his handsome head. Yet deep down, she knew. He was missing his wife, perhaps wishing she was Anne instead, romping with their daughter in the snow, though Sophie doubted the discontented Anne had ever romped.

Nearby was the Ogilvy graveyard, hemmed in by a stone fence. Had Seamus not been able to grieve during the war? Was that why he wore a path to Anne's resting place?

The week after Christmas yet another note came from Tall Acre.

Miss Sophie,
  Thank you for the pretty gifts.

  With love,
  Lily Cate

Obviously Seamus had helped Lily Cate write such. In light of the elaborate dollhouse he'd given her, Sophie's gift seemed too simple, just knitting needles fit for a child's hands, along with some yarn and simple instructions. They'd been her needles, given to her by a grandmother when she was wee as Lily Cate. As for Seamus, she'd knitted him a scarf, a Highland plaid in her mother's family colors—purple the hue of wild heather, gray like a Scottish sky. Her heart was in every stitch, and then her courage had failed and she'd hidden it away instead, feeling the gift too familiar.

"Well, we've got Christmas over," Glynnis was saying from the open parlor doorway, eyebrows nearly touching her silver hairline in surprise. "And now we have a different sort of present standing in the parlor."

For a moment Sophie forgot to breathe. Curtis? Would her heart always leap in anticipation?

As if realizing the hopes she'd raised, Glynnis said hastily, "A Captain McClintock is here to see you."

For a moment Sophie didn't move, Lily Cate's letter slack in her hands. Captain McClintock, one of the general's officer friends? Of the two men who'd paid her any attention at Tall Acre, he'd been the most persistent.

"I don't suppose you neglected to tell me anything?" Glynnis studied her with guarded expectation. "Like he might fancy you and has come to tell you so?"

Setting aside the letter, Sophie said quietly, "I haven't any idea why he's come."

"Well, you'll soon be finding out."

Thankfully the parlor fire had been lit, though they were still woefully short on wood. Captain McClintock stood looking at the bare mantel where a portrait of her father in the dress of his Highland regiment had hung. She'd spent the last few weeks taking down any reminders of him, and the spot begged for another painting.

"Captain, welcome to Three Chimneys." She kept her voice cordial, though she was as surprised as her housekeeper to see him.

He twined her fingers in his, bringing them to his lips. His gloved hands were cold, prodding her to offer him a toddy.

"A real Scottish toddy? With whiskey enough to warm the blood?"

"Indeed," she said with a smile, pulling the bell cord for Glynnis. She motioned to the two chairs fronting the fire where she'd sat with Seamus. Had he sent the captain her way?

"How was your Christmas?" she ventured cautiously, hoping Glynnis would hurry.

"Quiet. Too quiet. And yours?"

"The same." She smiled self-consciously. "I mean, I like the quiet. Country life is very . . . tranquil."

He looked at her, a question in his eyes. "I thought you

might spend the holiday at Tall Acre. You seem quite attached to the general's daughter."

"Ah yes. Miss Lily Cate is fine company." She reached for a poker and prodded the lazy fire, which added little warmth to the room and had nothing to do with the color filling her face. "I stayed home as my housekeeper has been ill."

"I trust she's better."

Before she could answer, Glynnis came in with the toddy, looking hard at the captain as if still trying to unravel the riddle of his arrival. But she contained her coughing till she'd left the room, at least.

"Are you familiar with Ramsay, Miss Menzies? My estate on Occoquan Bay?"

"I've heard of it. A lovely place, I'm told."

"Aye, 'twas my father's before me." He took a long drink as if gathering courage. A strand of thinning hair fell forward over his high forehead. He wore the new style, cut below the collar, giving him the look of a shorn sheep. She'd always preferred a traditional queue like Seamus's own. A riot of black, it was always neatly tied with dark ribbon.

"Now that it's the new year, I'm taking the liberty of asking you if you'd like to accompany the Ogilvys to Ramsay when they come visit."

She masked her surprise, unsure of his meaning. As a companion to Lily Cate . . . or more?

Reaching out, he made himself clear by taking her left hand in his. No ring rested there, posy or otherwise, no doubt spurring him on. "I'd like to become better acquainted and show you my home . . . commence a courtship if you're willing."

She went cold. Under Seamus and Lily Cate's very eyes? Did the general know of the captain's intentions?

"I'm flattered, Captain. But I must tell you . . . ." She groped for finesse. This painful formality, all their fine-stepping around feelings, was excruciating. "My affections lie elsewhere."

"Elsewhere." The disappointment in his face cut her.

She withdrew her hand. "Forgive me, but I must be candid." For once she was glad of her silly infatuation. Only she'd go to her grave before revealing that it involved his commanding officer.

"I'm sorry too, Miss Menzies." He downed his remaining toddy in a single gulp. "I wouldn't want to intrude on a prior arrangement."

Glynnis ushered him out, then rushed back in as retreating hoofbeats resounded in the crisp winter air. "Heaven help me, but I listened through the keyhole and prayed I'd not cough once. Who on earth has stolen your heart?"

Sophie hesitated. Sometimes the boundaries between them blurred. Glynnis was more doting aunt than servant. Secrets were seldom kept at Three Chimneys.

"I do care for someone, but he doesn't care for me." Sophie spoke carefully as a deeper curiosity washed Glynnis's face.

"From your Williamsburg days, I'd wager." Her bosom heaved with a sigh. "Well, 'tis a crying shame to see you stuck here with no prospects and no promise there'll be any."

"Being a spinster isn't all that unsavory." Hadn't she finally convinced herself of that? "'Tis better than marrying a man I don't love."

"Well," Glynnis said amidst a bout of coughing, "you're a bonny, faithful lass. The man who does not return your affections is a fool."

Aye, Sophie almost said with a smile. *A high-ranking, handsome fool.*

13

Stoic, Seamus sat at his desk and stared at his maimed hand. He could finally look at it without recalling the nightmare of it happening, that stunning, irreversible moment when his world became a fog of pain and fury, three fingers severed in the blink of an eye. Making a fist, he could still feel them. If he shut his eyes they seemed not maimed at all. Only they ached. Phantom pain, the field surgeon called it.

Bad as it was and had been, the trial of physical pain was nothing compared to the stain of guilt he felt. A Hessian soldier had died because of his hand. A mere boy. Seamus wanted to take the moment back. No one should lose his life over a few missing fingers. Not even the enemy.

He'd stopped praying after that. He couldn't quiet the uneasy notion that God wouldn't hear his prayers, wouldn't answer. He'd felt unworthy and nearly soulless since.

His quill quivered and fell. Ink spattered the sheet of foolscap in front of him. He stared at what he'd written, illegible as it was.

Dear Miss Menzies . . .

"Sir, how do you make an *S*?" Lily Cate's voice reached out to him across the expanse of desk.

S . . . for Sophie?

She studied him, face solemn. Since Sophie's leaving as their houseguest, Lily Cate had begun a slow retreat into a shell he couldn't penetrate. Each day brought a bit more distance. She'd even stopped calling him Papa.

He took out a fresh sheet of foolscap and began to write out the whole alphabet for her with his injured right hand. Slowly. Waveringly. With a confidence he was far from feeling. It didn't help that she'd taken a step back. The sight of his injury always frightened her, and he understood.

"I can't remember all the letters Miss Sophie taught me," she confessed.

"No matter. We'll soon have a governess for you. I was just writing Miss Menzies about it."

It was New Year's Day. With any luck someone would be seeking a position. Someone who had reams of time and far more patience. Aye, patience. His daughter reminded him of a butterfly, flitting place to place, never landing for long. No doubt when she'd made her *S*, she'd fly away again.

He glanced at her, ricocheting between relief and regret. Relief when Lily Cate dropped her reserve and wanted to be around him. Regret when she'd had enough of his company and fled. Sometimes he felt relief at her going and regret that he did. A good father wouldn't feel that way. Would he?

For now she kept looking up at him and then down at the paper he was inking, open wonder in her eyes. "How is it having so many things in your head?"

He paused. "Letters and such?"

She nodded. "Is it very crowded?"

"Aye."

"Is there room for me?"

In answer, he took her fingers in his good hand and helped her shape a big S. "There's always room enough for you even when it looks like I'm too busy."

"General . . ." Mrs. Lamont stood on the study's threshold, smiling pleasantly. "Captain McClintock is here to see you."

Seamus thanked her, thinking he'd misheard. McClintock rarely came upriver. Was he back? "Send him in."

"Do you want me to disappear?" Lily Cate asked.

He stared at her, thoughtful. *Nay, I want McClintock to disappear.*

As he thought it, his junior officer walked in, tricorn in hand, skittering his plans to finish up accounts.

"Welcome back, Will," he said, trying to be hospitable despite the demands of the day. "I thought you were back home at Ramsay."

"I was." McClintock's vexed expression gave a warning. "But then I decided to make another trip upriver and call on Miss Menzies."

Lily Cate snapped to attention sooner than Seamus at the mention, but McClintock was staring at Lily Cate as if unwilling to say more. In the onslaught of the captain's unwelcome words, Seamus had all but forgotten her. "Go upstairs while our guest and I speak privately."

With a dutiful nod she was off, shutting the door behind her.

"Would you like a drink?" Seamus offered, wanting to cut to the chase instead.

"Nay, I had a toddy at Three Chimneys," he said, tossing

his hat onto a chair, "which helped me get over the sting of her refusal."

"Well, I'm glad you're over it, but what exactly are we talking about?"

"I asked Miss Menzies permission to call on her. Court her."

Court her? A strange heat settled in his belly. Seamus sat on the edge of his desk, swinging a booted leg, feeling like they were back in camp and McClintock had countermanded an order. But it was Sophie's response that left him hanging. "And?"

McClintock stepped toward a table and uncorked a brandy decanter, obviously still suffering the humiliation. Amber liquid splashed into a glass. He took a sip of the drink he'd just declined, clearly rattled. "She said her affections lie elsewhere."

Seamus stayed stoic while his mind whirled.

"She said quite plainly that she has another suitor, though she didn't name him." He shot Seamus a black look. "You might have warned me."

"Warned you? I had no idea." Seamus stared at the rug. Who on earth could it be? A neighbor? Someone in Roan? The guard he'd posted? Mayhap there was more to Sophie Menzies than he'd first thought.

"I even asked her to accompany you and your daughter on your visit to Ramsay for foxhunting in future, hoping she'd come round."

You what? Seamus wanted to spit. Sophie likely thought he'd sanctioned McClintock's pursuit, his unexpected proposal. "That wasn't wise."

"I realize it now. I should have consulted you first. But the truth is I was so sure she'd agree to everything, I forged ahead." McClintock cleared his throat. "I never thought to be turned away by a penniless spinster with a property soon to be confiscated, but there you have it."

"Was it Miss Menzies you wanted or Three Chimneys?"

McClintock had the grace to color slightly. "Both are a draw."

For all his bumbling, McClintock was honest. And lonely. His fiancée had died of fever during the war, and he had little family to call his own.

"There were a number of other women here in December," Seamus reminded him. "Any one of them would be glad of your suit."

"Yes, but none of them are Miss Menzies," he answered thoughtfully. "There's something about her . . ."

Something, aye. Seamus didn't like the reminder.

The next day Henry stood at the kitchen door on behalf of Glynnis, who was behind the house chasing down a chicken. "There's a visitor to see you, Miss Menzies."

"Another?" Sophie nearly laughed as she settled a pan of biscuits in the bake oven. Three Chimneys seemed like a toll station lately. "And who have we today?"

"General Ogilvy, miss."

Her levity vanished. "Is his wee daughter with him?"

"Nay, he's come alone. And he looks all business."

"Then I'd best not keep him waiting." Tearing her apron free, Sophie took a last look about the kitchen, wanting to dart up a back stair and mind her hair at least. A quick glance at a hanging copper pot reflected a dusting of flour on her chin. She supposed the general could wait.

A few minutes later she retraced her steps to the parlor, her favorite fichu about her shoulders, her hair repinned, her heart somersaulting along with her stomach. Why General Ogilvy so early in the morning? Half past nine wasn't exactly the break of day, but his sudden arrival had certainly shaken her awake.

The parlor door was ajar, but no fire was burning. They were trying to conserve wood, and the room felt like a cave. Seamus was standing by the cold hearth in a fulled-wool cloak and cocked hat. Perhaps their meeting would be blessedly brief.

"I'm sorry there's no fire. Would you like something warm to drink?" She wanted to eat the words as soon as she'd said them.

"Nay." He looked straight at her, aggravation in his gaze.

Shaking free of that look, she bit her lip. Protocol be hanged! She would have to invite him into the kitchen lest they be frostbitten . . . or her biscuits burn. "Please come with me."

He followed her without a word as she battled embarrassment and the dread of what was to come. The strange man Lily Cate had spoken of never left her thoughts. "Lily Cate . . . she's all right?"

"Aye."

She'd never seen him so brusque. He took a chair, watching her as she spun about the kitchen fetching India spirits, loaf sugar, and nutmeg. Her nutmeg grater eluded her, thanks to the befuddlement of his unexpected company. She couldn't remember where she'd put it. He removed his cocked hat and set it by the dog irons along with his gloves, gaze rising to the kitchen's leaking roof. Mercifully he made no comment.

When she finally served him the fragrant toddy, he looked like he might laugh. He took it with an amused, questioning half smile that reminded her he hadn't wanted one in the first place. Mortification stung her from head to toe. If she wasn't careful, he'd know 'twas *he* who made her so camshauchle!

Taking the toddy back, she managed a fiery swallow, nearly scorching her tongue as she did so. He did laugh then, throwing back his head in a rare show of mirth, banishing all awkwardness between them.

He gestured to the stool beside him, as if this was his kitchen and she was in need of direction. The comforting aroma from the bake oven filled the air, as did that of the simmering soup brimming with the last garden vegetables—and a chicken if Glynnis had her way.

He gave a kick to a smoldering log. "I'm aware Captain McClintock was by here yesterday. He came to see me afterward."

She bit her tongue. Had McClintock complained to him then? Was Seamus upset with her for refusing him? "Yes, the captain was kind enough to call and ask—" The word *courting* hung in her throat. "To ask if—"

"So he told me. I want you to know I was unaware of his intentions."

She glanced down at the toddy in her hands. Could he see her relief? She'd gone half a day and all night thinking he'd been matchmaking when—

"I understand you already have a suitor."

Her second sip went down the wrong way. Turning her head, she stifled a cough, sloshing hot liquid onto her apron as she did so. With one deft move he took the mug from her once and for all and set it on the kitchen table beyond her reach.

She put a hand to her throat. "Captain McClintock misunderstood me. I have no suitor."

"But he said—"

"I told him my affections lie elsewhere. What I didn't tell him is that they're not returned."

His gaze sharpened. "So the man you love doesn't love you back."

Fire scored her cheeks. "That's the long and the short of it, yes."

"I'm sorry, Miss Menzies. But I find that hard to believe."

"General Ogilvy, I'm telling you the truth. I—"

"I don't doubt that you're telling me the truth. What I question is your would-be suitor." His voice dropped a notch. "Is the man blind—or simply stupid?"

He is neither . . . He is you.

He leaned back in his chair. "I thought mayhap if you married this man, your troubles would resolve."

Oh aye, no doubt.

Could he not see 'twas *he* who turned her inside out? The mere thought of being courted by him skewered her with longing. She loved that he was here now asking after her, concerned and wanting to fix things for her. She loved especially that he didn't have any notion she was smitten with him.

Her words came soft. "Not everyone is meant to marry and have a family. Perhaps I'm one of them."

"I beg to differ," he said with less fire. "You're meant to be mistress of your own home, have children."

"I suppose you're going to order someone up for me." The teasing in her tone belied her heartache.

"Aye, I would if I could. But some matters are even beyond a rebel hero's reach."

More addled, she grabbed a rag, opened the beehive oven, and took out the leathery-looking biscuits. The sound of coughing drew her eye to the kitchen doorway. Glynnis appeared, eyes huge at the sight of the general's back. Dead fowl in hand, she hurried away, any questions about the burnt smell answered.

"Your housekeeper sounds in need of a doctor," he murmured.

"She won't let me send for one."

"Mayhap she'd be more willing if I was to send for one."

"What she needs is to go to her sister in Annapolis. Glynnis's duties here keep her from getting well."

"I could arrange for travel. But where would that leave you?"

"I only want what's best for Glynnis." She spoke honestly, though the prospect of life without her longtime housekeeper was lonesome indeed. "I fear she'll only worsen if she stays. She might recover in Annapolis."

"I'll take care of it if you'll prepare her."

She met his gaze, finding it all too steady in comparison to her own. "General Ogilvy, you cannot always be coming to my rescue."

His eyes warmed. "Why can't I?"

"Because . . ." Her voice trailed away as her heart lost more ground.

Because it makes me more enamored with you.

He was regarding her in that intent way he had, undermining her self-control. "I've looked over the taxes and this leasing of the land, and I remain in your debt. Once your housekeeper leaves, I'll send a servant over from Tall Acre to replace her, not that anyone can. But at least it will settle matters between us and hasten her to health."

"But—"

"Just say aye, Miss Menzies." He smiled, melting all resistance.

"Very well." 'Twas futile to protest. Her gaze trailed to the stubborn set of his shoulders beneath his fine wool cloak. "I have good news for you too. I finally received word from Mrs. Hallam just yesterday about a governess." She reached in her pocket and withdrew the post. "A young woman from Williamsburg is seeking a position. She's in reduced circumstances but is quite accomplished."

He took the letter. "You know her?"

"We shared French lessons long ago. She comes highly recommended."

He tucked the letter in his waistcoat, and it seemed a burden lifted along with it. "I'm in your debt again," he said as if indebtedness was a gladsome thing.

"I don't doubt you'll try to even the score."

"Straightaway." He gave her a wink and gestured toward the foyer. "Why is there no fire in your parlor?"

"Touché," she said in resignation. "We have little wood. Henry is too gout-ridden to manage it, and I'm little help with an ax."

He reached for his gloves and cocked hat. "What do you Scots say? *Lang may yer lum reek*?"

She laughed. "'May you never be without fuel for your fire'? Aye."

"I'll see to your wood, then, and we'll be even."

Together they walked slowly to the front door. Already she was wondering when she would see him again. "I'm missing Lily Cate," she admitted. "Is she well?"

"Aye, she's missing you. Her favorite letter is *S*. She writes it over and over."

"*S* stands for your name too, remember."

"Oh?" He shot a glance at her and came to a standstill in the foyer. "And what might that be?"

138

She warmed to his teasing. *This* was the man she was unsure of. Commanding and abrupt one minute, almost playfully sentimental the next.

He smiled down at her, something sad in it. "Nearly everyone calls me *General* or *sir.* 'Twould be a fine thing to hear you say *Seamus.*"

Seamus. The temptation was nearly too much for her. Oh, to hear him say *Sophie* in turn. Tenderly. From the heart. She held firm. "'Tis rather unconventional, is it not? To be on such familiar terms?"

He shrugged. "Times are changing. Friends and neighbors shouldn't stand on formalities, aye?" He hesitated as if waiting for her to reconsider. And then, "Good day, Miss Menzies."

She watched him go, her breath misting the cold glass sidelight as she stood there. He untied his fine chestnut stallion from the hitching post and swung himself effortlessly atop the horse's broad back, turning down the long oak-laden drive and disappearing from sight.

But not her thoughts.

And certainly not her heart.

14

Glynnis, 'tis only what's best for you. The doctor and I agree. Your sister agrees. She's overjoyed, in fact. You leave in the morning. General Ogilvy has kindly lent his coach for your journey, and all the arrangements have been made. Dr. Spurlock even knows of a physician in Annapolis who treats lung ailments."

Glynnis sighed and lay back against the bank of pillows in her cramped attic bedchamber. "It may be all right for me, but what about you?"

"I'll continue to wait for word of Curtis, see what becomes of Three Chimneys." Sophie smoothed the rumpled counterpane, not wanting to tell her how much she'd be missed lest she start crying and not stop. "When I get fearful about the future, I look back and see how faithful God has been."

Glynnis twisted her handkerchief. "Despite your father's forsaking you and your mother's dying and Curtis not coming home."

Sophie nodded, refusing to let despair do its dark work.

"Despite all that, yes. General Ogilvy has been more than generous, and then there's Lily Cate . . ." She bit her lip against the rush of emotion she felt whenever she thought of her. Lily Cate had brought life and color into her very monotonous world. Their time together was nearing an end too, but till then she'd savor every second.

"You'll write to me." Glynnis's own eyes shone. "Tell me everything."

"Oh aye!" She took one of Glynnis's gnarled hands in her own. "You've been devoted to our family for so long. 'Tis time for you to rest and enjoy your sister's company. I'll come visit."

Thankfully, Glynnis put up less of a fuss than she'd expected. Now that she was nearly eighty, her strength was spent. Sophie didn't know how she'd weather the long trip to Annapolis, but the general had thought of that too, even hiring a nurse to accompany her.

"I owe you," she whispered to him when the coach came round.

He smiled down at her, but it was edged with concern. He understood her feelings. When the groom opened the door, Lily Cate stepped out, chasing the shadows away. "Papa said I could come play."

Together they stood and waved as the coach rolled down the drive, all her years with Glynnis along with it. "Well then, shall we have tea? Warm up in the morning room where there's a fine fire?" Thanks to Seamus, they had wood enough to last through spring.

"All of it!" Lily Cate squeezed her hand, hurrying into the house. "My governess comes on the morrow. I wanted it to be you, but Papa said you're a lady."

"Governesses are often ladies too." Sophie helped remove

her cape and hat. "I hope you'll like Miss Townsend very much."

Her face held a worried cast. "I don't want to like her better than you."

Sophie touched her cheek. "You can like many people all at once. Your governess can have a special place in your heart, same as me."

"Does Papa have a special place in your heart?"

Did Lily Cate sense her feelings? "Your father is a kind, generous man. He knows how fond I am of you, and so he shares you with me."

"Don't you want a little girl of your own? You told me so." Without waiting for an answer, Lily Cate skipped into the morning room and knelt before the dollhouse. "What? A baby?"

Sophie dropped down beside her. "Henry carved it for you as a Christmas gift."

Delight filled her pale face. She took the tiny figure from its cradle almost reverently. "We must name him."

"So 'tis a he?"

Lily Cate nodded. "Boys are better. Aunt Charlotte told me I should have been one, that Papa didn't want a girl." The callous comment had obviously lodged like a splinter in Lily Cate's tender heart.

"But God made you a girl. And God makes no mistakes." Sophie gestured to the doll in Lily Cate's palm. "What shall we christen this wee one?"

"Moses. Last night Papa read the story to me about baby Moses in the bulrushes."

Surprised, Sophie tried to picture it—Seamus reading, Lily Cate listening, both washed in firelight. Her heart twisted anew. Despite the obstacles, he was trying to be a good father. He *was* a good father.

Lily Cate gathered all the dolls up. "They shall be a happy family."

A happy family, something Lily Cate longed for. Was she even aware of the trouble in Williamsburg? She'd said no more about the strange man watching her window. The mere thought raised goose bumps. Perhaps the trouble had blown over.

But some nagging, unwelcome presentiment told Sophie it had only just begun.

⁊⊘

He'd expected a governess. He just hadn't expected one so young. Or so comely. Weren't governesses supposed to be older and matronly and staid? Not fair and voluptuous and fashion conscious? For a moment Seamus felt Sophie had played a trick on him. Indulged in some secret matchmaking in hopes of winning a mother for Lily Cate. He was glad he was leaving on business and Sophie was coming to stay. By the time he returned, Lily Cate, Sophie, and the governess would have everything in hand.

"Your quarters are to your satisfaction, I trust." He nearly winced at sounding so gruff. As if he was speaking to a junior officer, not a governess. "I suppose I should say your rooms."

Miss Townsend smiled at him as if she found his slip amusing. "Oh yes, the adjoining sitting area is lovely, and I'm glad of the river view."

"And your supplies? Everything in order for schooling?"

"There is one small matter, General. Will you allow for a dancing master in future?"

"Isn't my daughter a little young for dancing?"

"She's nearly six, is she not?"

143

"Nearly. Well, in August, aye." Or was she almost seven? Out of his depth regarding dates, he cast about for something else to say as he took stock of the woman before him. "I suppose 'tis never too early to learn to be a lady."

"Well said, General." She looked about the room as if taking Tall Acre's measure. "With your consent, the dancing master will lodge here for a few days to teach the local children. He'll be making the rounds to neighboring plantations, and it would give Lily Cate an opportunity to be with others her age. He's well known to Miss Menzies."

Seamus let go of the paperweight he was fingering and met her gray eyes. "Well known?" Was she implying some intimacy? Might this be Sophie's love interest? Why did he feel on tenterhooks when Miss Townsend hesitated?

"Yes. Master Parks was Miss Menzies's dancing master at Mrs. Hallam's, and mine as well. He's quite proficient if rather old."

Seamus relaxed. He liked old. Old was good.

"I must say I'm glad to have civility resume at war's end." She sighed, wistfulness in the words. "'Tis truly a crime what the war has done, sweeping all gentility away. But for your benevolence I don't know where I'd be."

Probably in some wealthy lord's drawing room. Miss Townsend was, sadly, too highborn for a governess, and far too lovely. He lapsed into silence, wishing Sophie would come in and he could make ready to leave. He glanced at the mantel clock and felt the tick of anticipation. "Miss Menzies should join us shortly."

"Miss Menzies . . . here?" Her confusion underscored the strangeness of his and Sophie's relationship.

"Miss Menzies is a favorite of my daughter. She'll be staying at Tall Acre while I'm gone."

Her smile returned. "'Twill be like old times, then. I haven't seen her in years."

Turning toward the largest window, Seamus sent his gaze down the alley of cherry trees, relieved to see someone coming up the drive on foot. He would have sent a coach round, but the independent-minded Sophie wouldn't hear of it.

Miss Townsend joined him at the glass, a surprised catch in her voice. "Oh my, she's much changed. I hardly recognize her." Her gaze slid down his coat sleeve to his maimed hand, which he'd forgotten to hold behind his back. "But the war has brought irreparable changes to us all."

〰️

The mid-January day was cold, ice imprisoning each branch and bush. Tall Acre was beautiful in any season, but winter seemed to give it a special polish, highlighting every elegant brick and frosty pane. Sophie stepped lightly in her boots, passing beyond Tall Acre's open gates with anticipation. Later Henry would bring her valise once she found out how long she was to stay.

A maid let her in, showing her to an unfamiliar parlor where a fire crackled noisily in the grate. For a moment Sophie stood on the threshold and held her breath. Cream and azure brocade covered the lavishly carved walls rather than simple paper. Beneath a glistening glass chandelier, a tea table was agleam with crested china and silver. She took a breath, savoring the moment. The stillness. The sheer perfection of the room.

Where was Seamus? She shooed the thought of him away, then took it back. No matter what she did or didn't do, nothing toppled his standing in her head and heart. He'd even overtaken Curtis in thought.

"Sophie?"

The almost forgotten voice pulled her back to the doorway. "Amity?"

They stood looking at one another for a few appraising seconds, then embraced. The scent of violet water wrapped round Sophie, unleashing a host of lost memories. Amity Townsend was alarmingly pretty, fair-headed and lush of figure, and wearing a decidedly ungoverness-like gown of lilac silk.

"I must thank you without delay for my position here," she said as Sophie linked arms with her and they passed into the room.

"Think nothing of it. You came well recommended. 'Twas Mrs. Hallam's doing."

"I'm glad you'll be here while the general is away. He told me that I'm to come to you with any concerns or questions about his daughter."

Had he? A quiet pride suffused Sophie at his confidence. "Lily Cate is like sunshine to me. I think you'll find her every bit as delightful."

"She's at a riding lesson, the general said."

"Most mornings, yes. She's rather afraid of horses, but her new pony is bringing her round." Sophie gestured to the window overlooking the east pasture. A groom led Polly by the bridle, Lily Cate atop it. "'Tis been so long since I've seen you. I hope you'll come visit at Three Chimneys. I have few friends in Roan as I spent so many years in Williamsburg."

"I'll admit to being surprised at finding you unwed. Once you were Mrs. Hallam's star pupil—light on your feet, first honors in everything."

Sophie laughed. "Your recollections are rather rosy. All

that seems so long ago. I'm far more interested in you and what you've done since finishing school."

"What I've done? Precious little since '76. Who would have imagined? There we were, poised to enter society, outfitted in London's finest, and then the war stole away everything. Sadly, my father passed soon after my mother. I tutored and earned a little, but not enough to keep my parents' town-house. I have no family to speak of beyond Williamsburg."

"I understand." Sophie's thoughts swung to Curtis, the long wait leeching a little more hope from her heart.

"I lost my fiancée at the battle of Brandywine." Amity paused, taking a handkerchief from her pocket. "He served with the 1st Virginia Regiment."

"I'm sorry. I didn't know."

"Naturally the general's been very solicitous, being a wid-ower himself. Grief seems to bind people together."

Though sympathy tugged at her, Sophie's imagination made fearsome leaps. The grieving widower. A destitute governess. A motherless child. It had all the makings of a scintillating novel.

She looked to the tea table prepared for them, now no more appetizing than Tall Acre's bricks. "I hope you'll be very happy here," she heard herself say. "Perhaps in time, Tall Acre will feel like home to you."

"I think it shall." Amity had dried her eyes and was look-ing around as if finding everything to her satisfaction. "The general mentioned taking Lily Cate to Alexandria for some finer clothes. I'm going to insist on stays if she's not in them already."

"She was in thread stays, but they weren't a good fit. There's a fine seamstress in Roan—"

"Oh my, Roan is so rustic. Alexandria is much better. I'm

going to be fitted for riding clothes in the city as well. The general thought I might help with Lily Cate's horsemanship. Remember our canters down Palace Green in Williamsburg?"

Sophie said nothing. She'd locked those carefree days away much as she had Anne's diary, but Amity seemed to relish every dusty detail.

A sudden commotion at the door drew their notice. Lily Cate appeared, feather dancing atop her riding hat. She looked longingly at Sophie yet seemed noticeably shy of her new governess.

Sophie welcomed her in. "You're just in time to meet Miss Townsend."

Lily Cate came nearer and curtsied, eyeing the scones. "May I have one, Miss Sophie?"

"Best ask your new governess."

Gesturing to her muddy riding habit, Amity frowned. "You're welcome to join us once you've freshened up and changed clothes."

"I fell off as I dismounted." Brushing at a dirty sleeve, Lily Cate began backing toward the door, a hint of triumph in her eyes. "But I didn't cry."

Amity watched her leave, thoughtful. "She seems a charming child. I wasn't sure what to expect given she's been without a mother." She raised an inquiring brow. "I've heard rumors the general might remarry. Word is he's courting a woman who is very well placed."

Sophie hid her dismay. One of the women who'd come to Tall Acre before Christmas? They'd all been of good family, of notable fortune. She prayed it wasn't the lofty Clementine. She looked unwillingly at the open door of the Palladian room where the portrait of Anne hung, the uncontested mistress of Tall Acre. Would Anne be replaced?

Amity hurried on. "None of my concern, I suppose, but in my position 'tis sometimes wise to inquire."

"I understand." Being at the whim and mercy of employers was not an enviable position. Sophie's own future was nearly as bleak. "If the general remarries, I'm sure your position as governess would remain unchanged. Lily Cate would still be in need of schooling."

Lily Cate reappeared in time, washed and changed. "Papa wants to see you before he goes, Miss Sophie."

"You can take my place, then." She gestured to a chair. "'Tis a fine time for you to become acquainted with Miss Townsend."

Excusing herself, she crossed the foyer to Seamus's study. The door was open, his desk a shambles, but he was missing. Turning, she nearly bumped into a plump maid armed with a feather duster. Florie?

"The general's left for the stables," the girl said hurriedly, gesturing to a rear door tucked behind the staircase. "The weather's taken a bitter turn, and he wants to leave as soon as possible."

At that moment Henry entered, carrying her valise. She thanked him, struck by a sudden whim. Opening her belongings, she removed the scarf she'd knitted and passed out the back door before she could change her mind. The general was likely on his way to see his sweetheart, if Amity's confidence rang true. Her gift would be given in friendship, nothing more.

The walk to the stables wasn't far, and the cold filled her lungs, bracing her. Long, shadowed corridors of stalls held the earthy reek of hay and horses. Myriad stable hands were at work, cleaning tack and refilling water buckets. She barely noticed them, intent on Seamus's tall silhouette as he led out a saddled stallion at one end. In years past she'd watched him riding from afar, often bareback and with unforgettable dash. If someone had accompanied him, she couldn't recall. All her memories had been swallowed up by him.

She stopped a few paces away. "Lily Cate said you wanted to speak to me."

He swung round, holding the reins in a gloved hand. "Before I go, aye."

A groom scurried past, toting a bucket of oats. Other than that they were alone. Dust motes danced in a stray beam of light, accentuating the vibrant hue of his eyes and the fine creases at their corners. He was looking at her as if he'd forgotten what he wanted to say. Or perhaps it was the scarf in her hands. Or the fact she had on no cloak.

"You shouldn't be out here," he said, his breath a cold mist. "'Tis freezing."

She stepped toward him, holding out the gift. "You'll be needing this for your long ride." When he didn't take it, she came closer than she ever had and wrapped it around his neck, tying it into a loose knot. The handsome plaid matched the blue of his cloak and would keep some of him warm, at least.

"You made it . . . for me." He looked down at her, surprised.

She nodded. "For Christmas."

"Which you missed," he murmured. "A lonesome time we had at Tall Acre without the lovely Sophie Menzies present."

Smiling, she stepped back. "I haven't thanked you properly for the gift you sent round."

He gave a slight shrug. "'Twas nothing."

"I hardly call a silver tea service from Denzilow of London *nothing*."

His sudden grin was unsettling. "You're not still feeling like a kept woman, are you?"

"If I am, I'm a well-kept one while you, sir, have a very poor showing for all your silver."

Chuckling, he touched the scarf. "Not anymore."

A wind whipped past, and she crossed her arms against the cold, steeling herself against his leaving and the emptiness she felt in his wake.

He looked to his boots, contemplating the muddy straw, before his gaze locked with hers again. "I'll be lodging at Gadsby's Tavern in Alexandria. I don't expect any trouble from Williamsburg as we've seen no more of the trespasser for a month. But if something should happen, send word to me at once."

He was the general again. Commanding. Decisive. On the defensive. She nodded. "I'll take fine care of Lily Cate."

"I'll be back by week's end, Lord willing." A note of lament chilled his voice. "I haven't told Miss Townsend about the trouble. I'd rather it be kept quiet."

"I shan't say a word, though I can't say the same of everyone."

"My wee daughter, as you call her, has the gift of gab." The look he gave her was half amused, half exasperated. "Mayhap you can help with that too."

Turning his back, he swung himself into the saddle as another shiver of apprehension slid through her. Try as she might, she couldn't shake the feeling of being watched. But just *who* was being watched? Her? Lily Cate? Or was it Seamus himself? What if someone meant him harm? The worry in her eyes gave her away.

"You're looking at me like I might not come back," he said.

"Why not take an escort? A groom, at least?"

"No need." Parting his cloak, he revealed the weapons beneath. "Despite my bad hand, I'm still a fair shot."

Anxiety wore a hole in her. "I shall pray you there and home again."

"If I don't return, Lily Cate will go to my sister in Philadelphia. I've made out a will to that effect . . . though I'd rather she go to you."

She savored the words, surprised at how easily he said them. As if he'd given it considerable thought. She, on the other hand, had all but forgotten he had an older sister. "Godspeed, General."

"Aye. Till we meet again, Miss Menzies."

He didn't look back at her, but she continued to watch him till he was no more than a pinprick on the frozen, skeletal horizon before fading from sight.

15

A t midnight, Sophie was ensconced in Anne's bed-chamber, having stayed up late with Amity remi-niscing about their time at finishing school with a sort of awe and reverence. There'd been the gay assembly days where all of Williamsburg seemed one riotous festival, the hallowed Sabbath services at Bruton Parish Church, the charming, late-night dances at Raleigh Tavern where Martha Washington and other ladies gathered on the eve of the Revolution. Now it seemed naught but an extravagant dream. A make-believe world.

Had she really been so carefree back then? Consumed with dancing and dresses? The latest plays and diversions? How shallow she had been! She turned back to her reading. The Bible lay in her lap, open to a favorite Psalm.

O LORD, *thou hast searched me, and known me. Thou knowest my downsitting and mine uprising, thou understandest my thought afar off.*

Her thoughts drifted to Seamus in Alexandria, then Lily Cate who slept soundly through the adjoining doorway.

Amity was on the third floor. Sophie could hear muffled movements overhead as she readied for bed.

Setting the Bible aside, Sophie lay down and sank into the familiar feather mattress, strangely wide-eyed. Minutes ticked by as she counted the pleats in the high canopy overhead before moving to the intricate embroidery of the bed curtains. Had they been worked by Anne? She tried not to think of the hidden diary. Why this irresistible pull to read it?

One page.

She fought the notion. Lost. Getting up, she went to the desk. Curiosity withered to regret at the first line. Sophie felt Anne's misery as if it seeped from her pen.

January, 1780

Seamus has finally sent a letter. From a place called Morristown. There the men are falling right and left, infected with camp fever. Disease is more fatal than any redcoat could ever be. 'Tis the worst winter possible with snow six feet deep. A soldier's rations amount to one half pound of salt beef and a half pint of rice for a week. I imagine Seamus is nigh starving too. If he dies, I suppose he wants me to have warning. I want to tell him he has been dead to me since he first enlisted.

He asks about his daughter, begs me to write. But what can be said of a baby who is nothing but a sickly, crying little animal? Who wants to nurse night and day, so depleting me that I have given her over to Myrtilla to tend. The doctor says Lily Cate has the hysteric colic and advises laudanum, ten drops.

Riggs, the estate manager, looks askance at me. I know what he is thinking, that I have deprived him of his best spinner. But I have no heart or strength to

*tend to Lily Cate. Let the spinning house go to blazes! I
wish I had borne Seamus a son. A son would not have
caused so much trouble.*

Stunned, Sophie stopped reading. *Oh Anne, could you
not count your many blessings? You were warm, well fed,
home safe with your wee daughter, while your husband was
helping command a sickly, starving shadow of an army for
eight unending years.*

Snapping shut the diary, she looked toward the hearth.
Should she . . . burn it? Though it wasn't hers to dispose of,
she stood poised to surrender the book to the flames, eager to
watch it curl to ash, incapable of harm. If it was found, she
could only imagine Seamus's reaction. With a revulsion she
felt for snakes and sordid things, she locked it up in the desk.

Sleep was slow in coming when it came at all. She drifted
off, then wrenched awake. The clock struck three far below,
and through its ponderous chime she heard a noise. Seamus
. . . was he home? Someone was at the door below.

On her feet before the cobwebs left her head, Sophie made
it to the empty foyer below. To her right was the hall with
its door leading to the west lawn. The violent turning of the
knob sent her backing up a step. The trespasser Lily Cate had
spoken of? The broad mahogany door heaved and shuddered
but held fast, at least for the moment.

Turning, she fled down the hall. The blackened staircase
seemed endless as she felt her way upstairs. Lily Cate—was
she safe? Asleep? Trembling so hard she could barely bolt the
door, she locked Lily Cate's bedchamber. How had Seamus
kept down his fear in battle? She felt nigh smothered by it.

The intruder had not let up. Did no one else hear? She remembered the housekeeper lived in a cottage on the grounds.

The servants were in the quarters. Only she and Amity and Lily Cate occupied the house. Mrs. Lamont usually checked to make sure the house was locked. Had she forgotten any one of the doors?

Lord, help us. Protect us.

If something happened to Lily Cate . . . She pressed shaking hands together in a sort of prayer. Seamus would never forgive her. She would never forgive herself.

Crawling into bed, Sophie sought Lily Cate's reassuring warmth. The bedchamber door was bolted. Surely an intruder wouldn't break a window. The night watch—was he not making the rounds? Desperate for daylight, all thought of sleep chased from the night, she wanted Seamus back. His calm, steadying presence was the only anecdote.

At daybreak Sophie heard Mrs. Lamont come in. She returned to her bedchamber and dressed, still shaky from fright and lack of sleep. Amity met her on the stairs, intent on breakfast.

"How was your first night?" Sophie asked hesitantly.

"I slept so soundly I didn't wake till dawn." With that Amity went in to breakfast, ready to begin lessons with Lily Cate.

Sophie stepped outside the riverfront door to find Tall Acre already astir. The ring of a blacksmith's hammer and a rooster's crowing ushered in a flawless dawn. As she neared the kennel Lily Cate had shown her, Seamus's foxhounds began barking. Taking liberty, she bent and rubbed the largest dog's bristled face before turning him loose. If he could chase a fox, could he outfox an intruder?

She followed at a distance while the hound made for the

side entrance to the house, nose to the ground. Only in broad daylight and a dog's steady presence did she have the nerve to take in the side entrance. The west door stood stalwart, as if she'd only imagined the noise in the night, only had a bad dream.

"Miss Menzies, somethin' the matter?" The gardener was regarding her solemnly, shovel in hand.

"Someone—" Her voice warbled shamefully. She was glad Seamus couldn't see her so undone. "Someone tried to break in last night."

His eyes darkened as his knobby fingers traced the line of a fresh scar in the wood. "Mebbe the same man who was trespassing before Christmas?"

"I don't know. Whoever it was, I feared he'd break the door down."

"Miss Lily Cate safe and sound?" When she nodded, he said, "The general returns soon. He'll set everything to rights."

Oh, what faith they had in Seamus. She was an outsider yet sensed their ongoing regard for him. But she wasn't sure this was a battle he would win.

⁂

Seamus had always preferred Alexandria to Williamsburg. Alexandria held no haunting memories, no bitter family scenes and secrets. The little town was vibrant and thriving where Williamsburg was faded and wanting. Turning onto Oronoco Street, he made his way down the frozen, tree-lined avenue toward the home of Richard Ratcliffe, tax commissioner and land speculator.

A surly wind pushed against him, tearing at the scarf Sophie had carefully wound round his neck. He reached up a leather glove and tugged the scarf upward over his nose and jaw, his grim expression frozen into place. The nap of the fine wool was soft as a woman's skin. He fancied it carried her rose scent. At the thought he shoved his boots farther into his stirrups and shifted in the saddle. Dwelling on her was agony, but he'd nearly come undone when she'd given him the scarf.

Standing alone with her in the solitude of the stables, he'd hungered to reach out and touch her, clasp her wrists, and pull her close. But deep down he knew that was the wrong kind of wanting. He was simply craving companionship. Closeness. A distraction from outside pressures. Trying to blot out Anne's memory with Sophie was a terrible mistake.

Still, the wanting gnawed at him, made him wish halfheartedly that the man who spurned her would change his mind. If Sophie married, her future would be secure. It wouldn't matter so much if Curtis returned or not. And it would end the way Seamus had begun to think of her.

He blew out a frustrated breath. Best get his desires unmuddled before returning to Tall Acre lest he do something rash, something stupid. He couldn't risk driving Sophie from Lily Cate's life, not when his daughter needed her most.

His stallion was plodding now after so many miles, needing a warm stall as much as he needed an inn. He swung down from the saddle, tethered Vulcan to the iron rail at the front of a handsome townhouse, and stepped up to the door. A maid came straightaway, smiling at the sight of him, cheeks pinking. She was looking at him coyly from beneath her cambric cap, her dark coloring so like Sophie's that she stormed his thoughts again.

"General Ogilvy, do come in!"

"I'm here to see Mr. Ratcliffe, if he's available."

"Of course, sir. He's in the parlor. I'll fetch a groom to stable your horse."

Standing by a welcoming fire was the man he'd known for twenty years or better, hand outstretched, smile broad. "Seamus, what brings you to town in the dearth of winter?" Without waiting for an answer, he turned toward the maid. "Some grog and a meal for the general, if you will."

Seamus nodded his thanks and took the proffered chair nearest the fire. "I've come to discuss the military land grant awarded me in Kentucky. I may have need of it in future."

He was home. At last. Lily Cate flew down the stairs, nearly stumbling in her haste. But it was Sophie she ran toward, peering at him cautiously from the folds of Sophie's full skirts.

"You've come back," she said shyly, as if he'd been away so long he was more stranger. "And Miss Sophie must go?"

"In a little while," he answered, trying to allay her disappointment. "I've brought you something—all the children, actually." He'd felt a little foolish buying so many trinkets, but his staff had served him well while he was on the field, and there was no quicker way to their hearts than to reward their children. "The toys are in Mrs. Lamont's keeping. She'll go with you when you're ready to hand them out."

At this she began walking backwards, curiosity taking such hold that she flew away again, leaving them alone. Sophie turned back to him, her expression so wrenched with concern the joy of his homecoming was forgotten.

"I'm sorry to start off on so troubling a note, but something happened a few nights ago." She spoke calmly, but he sensed the beat of fear beneath. "Someone tried to get into the house through the west door. Thankfully it was bolted and held fast. I stayed the night with Lily Cate, locking us in."

"You saw no one? Heard no voices?"

"Nay." She looked about the empty foyer. "I've said nothing to Lily Cate or the governess, just Mrs. Lamont and the gardener."

He took a labored breath, all the wind knocked out of him. It was all coming back—Williamsburg, Fitzhugh's threats, the prowler he'd thought dealt with. Without another word, he left the study and took the private hall leading to his parents' bedchamber and the west door.

He unbolted it and pulled it open to birdsong and sunlight. The day looked anything but ominous, yet a thick sense of violation was crowding in. Sophie stood behind him, but he was barely aware of her. His attention was fixed on the door's scar, a deep groove that a saber might have left.

"I'll question the night watch." He shut the door, sliding the bolt into place. "Meanwhile I'll have my coachman take you home . . . just in case." He tried to focus, to be at ease. "Thank you for taking fine care of my daughter."

She hesitated a moment, then left to collect her belongings, leaving him alone and flummoxed. He went back to his study, his eyes roaming the walls with its myriad accoutrements and weaponry. He'd thought to have little use for them now. Flintlock and bayonet. Cartouche box and tomahawk. Musket. Saber. Sword. Pistols.

He was at war again.

16

Sophie returned home to Three Chimneys, unsurprised to find Glynnis's replacement on her heels. 'Twas a blessed, almost divine distraction.

"My name's Mistress Murdo, Miss Menzies. From Dumfries." Her lilt was rich and thick as Dumfries porridge. "I'm to cook and keep house to yer content."

A fellow Scot! Sophie couldn't contain her delight. "Welcome to Three Chimneys, Mistress Murdo. I'll show you to your room. If you have need of anything . . ."

Seamus seemed to have orchestrated events with the precision and efficiency of the officer he was, keeping Sophie's loneliness at bay like it was a line of warring redcoats instead. But it was an odd arrangement, the length of Mistress Murdo's stay uncertain, her wages paid by the general. She'd return to Tall Acre in time, but for now she settled in with an apron and a smile broad as her waistline.

"I'll get right to work in the kitchen. A hearty meal is in order." She surveyed her new domain with a keen eye, intent on the worn copper pots and larder. "Ye've plenty of neeps and tatties, I hope, and oats enough for oatcakes."

"All of the above."

"We'll get along well, then." Mistress Murdo chuckled. "Though Henry's an Englishman, I'll not hold it against him."

Truly, Mistress Murdo and Henry got on like a pair of turtledoves. Sophie often found him about the kitchen in the days to come as their new housekeeper and cook turned out an array of tasty dishes and sweets.

"Why, these scones are the best I've ever tasted." Sophie felt a tad disloyal to Glynnis saying so but helped herself to another just the same. "And your preserves are second to none."

Mistress Murdo beamed. "Tall Acre has a fine orchard. I've put up a good many crocks since the general employed me. The peach is a favorite of Miss Lily Cate's too."

Sophie sorely missed Lily Cate and the bustle of Tall Acre and tried not to think of Amity and Seamus beneath the same roof. Snow began to fall again, erasing the lane between their houses, ensuring there would be no visits in the near future.

A chill seemed to hover whenever she recalled the midnight trespasser. Sometimes she herself felt a vague uneasiness. The shadow of war was slow to shake off. The guard and Mistress Murdo's coming hadn't changed that. Would she always be wincing lest another rock come hurling through a window or someone in Roan spit at her as she passed?

Yet how could she ignore that their larder was blessedly full, the lovely Denzilow tea service and an abundance of Hyson at hand? She kept content by knitting in the parlor or reading in her room by the fire. She prayed for Curtis's homecoming. She wrote Glynnis letters.

She needed something more to do.

Though the weather kept him from another confrontation in Williamsburg, Seamus was glad of the snow. It prevented him from wandering to Three Chimneys bodily if not mentally. Try as he might, he couldn't stop thinking of Sophie. Lily Cate made sure of that. She stood in the doorway of his study, her new kitten in her arms, pouting in a most unbecoming way.

"Papa, I miss her." The kitten gave a little yowl. "I want to show her Sassy."

"Aren't you busy enough with lessons?"

"I think we should go see her."

"That's not possible. The horses tend to panic in deep snow and damage themselves on the harness."

"Why not take a sleigh?"

"We have none."

"Then you must get one—with bells."

He smiled ruefully at the order. "That requires ready cash and a long wait. By the time a sleigh arrives, it will be spring."

Her face clouded. "Then we must pray for the snow to melt."

"Aye, that would be far more practical and far less expensive."

She sighed as she approached his desk. "Let us pray, then."

She was so touchingly serious as she stood before him, her little face beseeching, he stifled the urge to laugh. "You have the makings of a fine preacher."

Setting the kitten down, she bowed her head and folded her hands. "Heavenly Father, we pray for the snow to melt so I can see Miss Sophie. Please help Papa not to be so busy. Or Miss Townsend to give me too many lessons. Amen."

It was the most direct prayer he'd ever heard. Still, she stood looking at him like he should do something, something other than bury himself in work. "You could pen Miss Menzies a letter . . . draw a picture."

Her face lit like a candle. "Will you help me?"

His gaze traveled to his desk where agricultural manuals lay open, his painstaking notes beside them. "I have a meeting with my estate manager in a few minutes. Mayhap after that."

"Papa, what if she's lonesome?"

His gaze swung back to her. "Mistress Murdo is there, remember. She's good company and an excellent cook."

She started to back away, clearly vexed by the lack of a sleigh, the snow, and his response.

"You're not thinking of running away to Three Chimneys, are you?" he queried.

Her fierce reserve broke. "I may!"

"Don't." He leaned back in his chair till it creaked, calling a truce. "Come back here after lessons and I'll help you pen a letter. Or you could have your governess help you instead."

"I cannot." With a decisive shake of her head, she lowered her voice to a whisper. "I do not think Miss Townsend likes Miss Sophie."

He studied her. "Why is that?"

"Because she—"

The study doorway darkened. Miss Townsend stood behind Lily Cate, who whirled round and faced her. "Are you ready to resume your schoolwork?"

Lily Cate nodded dutifully and scooped up the kitten.

"I'll be along shortly. Go ahead and start on your sums." Miss Townsend wasn't smiling. She looked . . . sour. "I need to have a word with your father."

Seamus stood, taking her tone to heart. He never felt quite

164

at ease around the governess, mayhap because he felt sorry for women in reduced circumstances and was rather rattled by her looks. It seemed strange to him she had not found a husband, war or no war, living in Williamsburg as she'd been. Not every eligible man in the colonies had enlisted. Plenty had paid their way out of service, even in patriotic Virginia.

"What can I do for you, Miss Townsend?"

"I heard that you might be traveling again soon. If so, I must tell you I'm fully capable of caring for your daughter in your absence. You needn't send for Miss Menzies again."

He clenched his injured hand, nearly at a loss for words. "That decision is not yours to make, Miss Townsend."

Flushing, she lowered her eyes as if realizing she'd overstepped her bounds. "Very well. But I do need to caution you about your daughter's unhealthy attachment. She seems inordinately fond of Miss Menzies, so much so that it's proving a distraction."

"Given she's been without a mother, that's no surprise, surely."

"I suppose not." Her chin firmed. She'd not given up the fight, whatever the cause. "If I might speak plainly . . ."

"By all means."

"I was thinking it might be better if Lily Cate had limited contact with your neighbor. 'Twould be less a disruption to lessons."

He frowned, gesturing toward a snow-spattered window. "They have no contact now."

"Yes, but once the weather clears, that will change. Your daughter is so taken with her that she cannot accept anyone else. I fear Lily Cate doesn't care for me."

"You're her governess, Miss Townsend. Miss Menzies is a family friend." He didn't mean to be unkind, just candid.

"Though you might wish otherwise, there is a difference and there probably always will be."

"I understand that, General. But your daughter's constant references and comparisons make it difficult for me to conduct lessons as I wish—"

"Then I'll speak with her."

"Thank you." The smile she gave him wasn't genuine. Or hopeful. She stood abruptly and left without another word.

He watched her go, his pulse picking up at the odd exchange. His gaze returned to his desk, his English-made compass near at hand. Reaching out, he uncovered the surveying papers gotten in Alexandria. If he left Virginia with Lily Cate and began a new life, he'd leave sulky governesses and warring relatives behind. He'd been awarded a vast tract of land along Kentucky's Licking River, remote and fraught with Indian activity. Few were bold enough to come through the gap that separated raw wilderness from the civilized world. But was he brave enough—or foolhardy enough—to subject Lily Cate to the danger?

"I apologize for being late, sir."

Seamus looked up to find his estate manager in the doorway, hat in hand, eye on the study clock. If not for him, Tall Acre would have fallen into such neglect in his absence Seamus doubted it would be worth returning to. "You're not late, Riggs. That clock isn't keeping good time." He went to the mantel, swung open the timepiece's glass door, and wound the workings with a little key. "What I'd like to do is turn back to 1775."

"Before the war began?" Riggs exhaled and chuckled in the same breath. "There's no going back, sir, much as we might wish to. 'Tis almost plowing season once again."

"Aye, so it is." Returning to his desk, Seamus surveyed a lengthy list he'd finished in the night. "Once the weather clears, I'd like the fieldwork to commence in preparation for oats and clover. We'll put lucerne in first, so you'll need Mulatto Jack and the others to start grubbing the west pasture. Those two plows on order from Philadelphia should arrive by the time that's done."

"I've nearly finished the plow harness."

"Good. After that the piazza floor needs replacing. I've ordered flagstone from England instead of using native Virginia rock."

"I can set that myself," Riggs said. "But we're in need of a millwright ere long. The spring rains carried off the tumbling dam last April, and it begs repairing."

Taking up a quill, Seamus made a note of it. "We're also in dire need of another blacksmith. A bricklayer and carpenter are on their way, both indentures. And I've posted an advertisement for another gardener."

"I'll see about grafting the plum and cherry trees till then."

"Leave that to me, along with rebuilding those fences we talked about."

"You, sir?"

"I'll not sit on my hands now that I'm home, Riggs. You need another able man, aye?"

Riggs chuckled, his pockmarked face easing. "If you mend fences like you run off redcoats, General, Tall Acre will be in fine shape in short order."

"So we hope." Seamus set aside his quill, and the throbbing in his hand ebbed. He pushed his troubling conversation with Miss Townsend to the back of his mind to fester. "How goes it in the quarters?"

Riggs looked to his hat, somewhat apologetic. "There's a sick spell starting. Ague, I'm afraid. And Shay's wife is laboring."

"Did you send for a doctor?"

"Neither Spurlock nor Craik can come in this weather. I usually fetch Betty from the kitchen to help, but she's ailing."

"Send for Miss Menzies then." Seamus spoke without thought, wondering if Sophie was any more accessible than the doctors. "She's a fine hand with babies from what I remember. I'll see to the fever."

"You, sir?"

Seamus smiled past his misgivings. "You keep saying that, Riggs."

"Well, General, seems like you have plenty else to do right here." His gaze roamed over the desk where fresh ink pots and a fat quire of paper lay amidst the clutter.

Seamus began shrugging on his greatcoat, fighting the feeling of falling further behind. He picked up Sophie's scarf for good measure and headed toward a corner cupboard. "If you bring round Miss Menzies, I'll take care of the rest."

He unlocked the giant cabinet, opened the door, and stood stone still, barely aware of Riggs leaving. In front of him, eye level, was a bottle of absinthe. What had Anne called it? The Green Fairy? A brilliant hue, it reeked of anise-flavored spirits. Beside it lay Anne's silver spoon and the cup she used for drinking. Bitter and mind-altering, the drug required ample sugar. Anne's fondness for it had become a thorn between them.

He'd shunned this cupboard since he'd come back, knowing it would trigger an avalanche of unwanted memories. He hadn't reckoned how many. Stomach clenching, he took the bottle in hand. Turning toward the hearth, he sent the absinthe colliding with the andirons in a startling storm of fire and glass. Green shards littered rug and fire pit yet seemed to lodge deep inside him instead.

Never again would he put himself in a position to be wounded. Betrayed. Deceived. Years of war had taught him many things, but none so needed as how to build a high wall around his heart.

✺

"The general *what?*" Sophie felt a qualm, realizing her sudden reply was less than gracious.

One of Tall Acre's grooms stood before her in the foyer, twirling his hat in his hands, an extra mount waiting in the ice and snow of early afternoon. "You're needed at a birth, Miss Menzies. General's orders. There's no doctor or midwife on hand."

So Seamus had sent for her. Needed her. She swallowed, imagining his stern summons. She hated that surprise gave way to painful pleasure. And then the dread of the coming ordeal rushed in.

Folding up the recent letter she'd received from Glynnis, she wrestled with the need to be two places at once. With a reluctant nod, she said, "I'll collect my satchel." *If* she could find it without Glynnis's help. Dusty and shelved for years now, the satchel had been her mother's mainstay. She'd forgotten what it contained. She barely recalled her role as assistant.

Lord, help me remember. Help mother and babe be safe.

✺

Tall Acre's infirmary was tucked behind the boxwood hedge near the servants' quarters, a medley of low-slung, brick buildings with crushed-shell walkways between. Sophie smelled the tang of wood smoke and heard a burst of masculine laughter from the stables as her boots made quick

169

work of the shallow drifts, her cloak trailing like a scarlet wave behind her.

"This way, Miss Menzies," the groom said.

Following, Sophie felt an odd connectedness with the past. Her mother had trod this same path alongside Seamus's mother years before. Confidence bloomed and then dissolved at the sound of Shay's wife crying through a thick brick wall. Had her ordeal just begun? The anguish returned her to Anne birthing Lily Cate while the general had nearly worn a hole in the floor with his pacing. All the little details came flooding back, intimate and unwanted. The heat of the August day. Her mother's studied patience with Anne's wailing. *The dreaded ordeal*, Anne had called childbirth. Sophie thought of it now with latent exasperation.

She opened the door, hands clammy. A young woman lay on a corner bed, her dark face beaded with sweat despite the chill, a cry catching in her throat at the sight of Sophie. Her first baby, likely.

A burly, homespun-clad man—Shay?—turned round, his pained expression spelling out his own anguish. "Miss Menzies, you come just in time. Kaye's nearly wore out."

"Not too much longer now, perhaps." Taking a deep breath, she hung her cloak from a peg, rolled up her sleeves, and washed her hands.

Her mother had been a stickler for cleanliness. She'd heard General Washington had insisted on sanitary measures in the field hospitals despite the upheaval all around him too. Even Seamus was as clean as he was commanding.

She glanced at the dwindling fire and then at Shay with a practiced smile. "Is there another woman who can assist? Or can you fetch more wood, bring hot water and clean linens?"

With a nod he passed outside. Sophie rummaged in her

satchel and took out a heavy apron, a knife for the cord cutting, and a flannel cover for the baby's tender belly. Opium tincture and a dropper came next. Sophie studied the bottle, her mother's voice in her ear. *Five drops to ease the pain— but slowly. We don't want them coming up again. Try a little water after.* She dispensed the drops, praying for her mother's composure.

The next hour became a blur of muffled crying and supervising, the sun sinking lower. Sophie had forgotten the pain, how much time a baby took, as she sponged Kaye with cool water and gauged her progress with the feel of gentle hands. Her throat grew dry from soothing words, her fingers nearly raw from wringing out cold cloths.

Glad for the shadows at so vulnerable a time, Sophie worked with Shay to keep Kaye calm and the baby's progress unimpeded. Despite the uncertainty and risk, there was a palpable excitement. Shay hoped for a boy but would be glad of a girl.

"Nearly there," Sophie reassured Kaye as the baby's head crowned.

With a prolonged push, Kaye bore down a final time. Sophie felt a warm rush and then a slippery filling of her outstretched hands. For a moment awe held her captive. She wiped the newborn clean with linen, bundled him up, and handed him to his exhausted mother, gladdened by their joy and her own small part in the process.

For a few bewildering seconds her thoughts veered to Seamus. Would she be summoned here to help deliver his son in time? Turn to him with a tiny bundle and lay a baby in his arms?

Nay, I cannot. I'll see Scotland first.

She lost herself in the necessity of changing bed linens and fetching a supper tray, glad the baby was blessedly quiet if wide-eyed. A few women from the quarters came in to tend Kaye as Sophie made ready to leave, their shared laughter and talk like a comforting quilt. She envied them their warm camaraderie.

Washing up at the basin, she gave a few last instructions to Shay before passing out the door into a windy night, the moon full and round as a copper shilling. Mindful of the icy walkway, Sophie rounded a garden wall and nearly collided with the general. He was wearing his blue cloak and the scarf she'd made him. She could make out its pattern in the moonlight, a pleasing palette of purple and gray, and felt as warm as if its snug folds graced her own throat.

He was clearly glad to see her. "How goes it with Kaye?"

"A braw son." Her voice was buoyant but threaded with weariness. "All is well."

"If so, I have you to thank."

"I can take little credit. God has a way of birthing babies with or without our help."

"You remember Lily Cate's birth."

"Every detail." But mostly she remembered the wanting. The wanting to be married. The wanting to be mistress of Tall Acre. The wish that her mother was attending her instead. A slow, startling awareness took hold. Had she been smitten with Seamus even then?

"That seems a lifetime ago."

She sensed the sad drift of his thoughts and changed course. "I'm surprised to find you out on so bitter a night."

"I always make the rounds to be sure nothing is amiss."

"No more trouble, I hope."

"None, nay." Taking her arm, he began steering her toward the house. "Come into my study and get warm."

She almost smiled. Yet another order, this one welcome. In moments he'd summoned a maid and set her satchel by the door. Her gaze strayed to the paneled walls and then the hearth where his rifle rested as she rearranged things in her mind. She'd draw back the heavy curtains. Work a new fire screen. Put away so many of the weapons that gave the room a melancholy feel. But this was his domain, after all. Despite its overbearing masculinity, the room held an intoxicating warmth and richness—or was it simply Seamus's presence?

He came behind her, removing her cloak. "I'll settle up with you before you go."

"You said the very same to my mother when Lily Cate was born." She tucked a wayward strand of hair beneath her cap, lost in the recollection. "Do you recall her answer?"

Looking bemused, he shed his own coat and scarf. "Aye. And you?"

"There is no fee, she said, not for a hero of the Revolution."

"At least let me lodge you."

She glanced at the clock. Nearly midnight. Could he sense she had no desire to leave? "Lodging, yes." Breaking free of his gaze, she added, "Perhaps breakfast with Lily Cate come morn."

"Done." He rested one arm along the mantel. "I thought, if you came and helped with the birth, you might consider following in your mother's footsteps."

Surprise pinched her. "You're trying to make a howdy out of me."

"Aye, but you're not going to oblige me, I can tell. What about a secretary then?" He gestured to his desk. "As you can see, I'm in dire need of help with paperwork."

Was he having trouble writing, given his maimed hand? Though cast in shadows, the chaos was apparent—and out of character. She felt a new tenderness for him. "If I could accomplish what you wish . . ."

"I've no doubt you'll do admirably."

"I want no payment, understand. None but your praise."

"That I can give you." He shifted, the firelight glancing off the buttons of his waistcoat. "Though I'm willing to give more."

More? Was he trying to help her earn her keep, knowing the loss of Three Chimneys was imminent? Her pride wouldn't allow her wages. Nay, not pride. All she wanted was his regard . . . his heart. The truth sent her gaze to her shoes.

"We need to begin rebuilding our lives. We have to start somewhere." He kicked at a log with his boot and sent it tumbling backwards in the grate. "We need to let go of what was and try again. Take advantage of every opportunity."

Did he feel she was holding on to the past, unwilling or unable to move forward? Or had *he* moved on . . . chosen a bride? Dread pooled in her belly. She'd known it was coming. But oh, the hurt . . .

"There's an empty cottage you can have here at Tall Acre. It belonged to my father's secretary."

A cottage. Cozy. Secure. Closer to Lily Cate. She wrestled with her longing and took a step nearer the smoldering fire, holding out her hands to its heat. "Your offer is generous, but I cannot leave Three Chimneys until I must." She felt that old, unwelcome sadness take hold. The longing for what was. The uncertain pull of the future. "Sometimes I—I feel caught between the present and the past. Waiting. Hoping."

"'Tis one of the things I admire about you, that hope." His voice dropped a notch, luring her to look at him. "Despite everything, you never let go. Never give up."

He was so near she felt the sturdy, reassuring warmth of

him. She drank in the bottomless blue of his eyes like cold, quenching water.

"You're a riddle, Sophie Menzies . . . a beautiful, bewildering riddle."

All the emotion of the moment rose up and clouded her vision. His callused fingers were surprisingly gentle as he caught the tear streaking her cheek. It sent her heart shattering into a thousand brittle bits.

A timid if distinct knock on the door drove them apart. Seamus's hand fell away. Sophie sank her hand into her pocket for a handkerchief as a maid entered, bearing a tray laden with a veritable midnight feast.

Saying no more, he seated Sophie by the fire, a small table between them. She was hungrier than she realized, glad when he began speaking of mundane matters like the paperwork that begged her help. She tried not to look at him, tried to think no more of the moment than she ought. It seemed nothing poignant had passed between them.

Finishing her meal, she brushed a bread crumb from her bodice. "I'll gladly see to your papers once I return home from Annapolis."

He set down his knife and fork. "Annapolis?"

"A letter has come from Glynnis. She's worsening and wants to see me. I thought I'd leave on the stage once the roads clear."

"You'd best take my coach. One hundred fifty miles is quite a journey, and my driver knows the route."

She was too tired to protest. "I'm not sure when I'll return."

He sat back, leaving his meal unfinished. "I'm sorry about your going, but I understand."

Did he? Glynnis needed her. It might be the last time they'd be together. In this realm, at least.

175

"Do you have funds for travel?"

"Funds enough." She wouldn't take money from him. His seemingly unending generosity must have an end.

"You wouldn't . . . stay on?" The quiet question was asked offhandedly, but a strange heat pulsed beneath. "In Annapolis, I mean."

"I hadn't thought of that."

He frowned. "I don't mean to give you any ideas. I was merely thinking of Lily Cate. Selfishly so." He started to say more, then got up abruptly and retreated behind the bulk of his desk.

She stood and retrieved her satchel, weariness pressing down on her like a blanket. "Thank you for supper. I'd best get to sleep."

"I'll be here if you need me." He lit a second candelabra and moved it nearer some ledgers. From the look of things, he'd be up till dawn.

"Do you spend the night in your study?" she queried.

"On occasion."

She almost chided him, but it wasn't her place. Only she was no longer sure what her place was. She simply knew she needed to be free of this room before her feelings ensnared her further. She needed distance, a diversion. She was glad of Annapolis, but it seemed as far away as the Orient.

Her wayward heart was already counting the hours till she'd be back.

17

Sophie awakened to utter darkness, roused by a baby's cry in the quarters. Kaye and Shay's? She got up and checked on Lily Cate. Sound asleep, the girl looked more angel in the glow of firelight, an echo of Seamus in her face. Returning to her room, Sophie lit a beeswax candle. Tall Acre had a great many candles, a luxury unknown to Three Chimneys. Still, she felt parsimonious. Old habits were hard to break. And not only old habits. New, insidious ones too.

Anne's diary was soon in hand, marked by a silk ribbon. She felt like a trespasser, a thief. Why did she keep reading? Did she hope to uncover some flaw in Seamus? Something that would lessen his hold on her heart?

8 August, 1779

Today our daughter is one year old. Seamus has likely forgotten. The Revolution rages on and I am supposed to celebrate a birthday? When all I can think of is his dying? Being hung as a traitor? I will be a widow with a fatherless child. A woman with an estate I despise.

Myrtilla makes it worse. She refuses to wean Lily Cate, probably on account of her own lost babe. Riggs blames me, saying I am keeping her from her work. I am torn. If Myrtilla returns to the spinning house, I must return to being a mother. And I have no strength. I am wasting away in this isolated place. My husband's fate torments me night and day.

27 September

A lovely start to autumn. Cooler weather becomes me. Lily Cate has learned to walk. She holds on to my hand and we go about the garden. She is especially fond of the baby ducks. I worry about her fascination with water. The river is so close.

She thinks everything is a delight. A butterfly landed on her shoulder, and she laughed and tried to catch it with her chubby hands before it flew away. She looks more and more like her father, which is bittersweet to me.

3 November

Much sickness in the quarters. I have brought Myrtilla into the house, which incenses Riggs, but I need the help. I cannot tend an active child. The spinning house, I told him, can go to blazes!

At night when all is calm, I beg the housekeeper for the key, go to the cupboard in Seamus's study, and make use of the Green Fairy. It soothes me as nothing else can. He would be angry with me if he knew, but what am I to do? He is gone, and there is no companionship or comfort in this forsaken place. Not even a letter from him of late—and no visit in over a year. Of

*course I do not write to him. How can I when I do not
even know where he is?*

*Still, I am teaching Lily Cate to say "Papa." That, at
least, I can do. Only she doesn't know what it means
and might never have the good fortune to use it.*

Rubbing her forehead with cold fingers, Sophie listened for
Seamus below. He'd not yet come to his room. What would
he think of her sitting here, Anne's diary open in her lap?
She took it up again. One blank page, then two. No more
entries had been made till spring.

19 March, 1780
*Along the alley the cherry trees are budding. I long
to smell the honeysuckle Seamus planted in honor of
our wedding day.*

*Lily Cate is running now. I cannot catch her. Myrtilla
is good with her, which eases my conscience and leaves
me to my leisure.*

3 May
I have met a man . . .

Sophie's breathing thinned. Though she had never been
courted, had never been kissed, and was untried as to the
ways of a man with a woman, she sensed what Anne's next
words would be.

There came a footfall on the stair. Seamus? She shut the
book, forgetting to mark her place. The silk ribbon slipped
to the floor and she bent to retrieve it, heart jumping. After
going to her satchel, she hid the diary in the bottom beneath
her belongings. She would take it to Three Chimneys, out

of harm's way. There she would dispose of it if it continued to haunt her.

She had no heart to read on, if only for Seamus's sake.

⁂

"More snow is falling, Papa."

Lily Cate stood in his bedchamber doorway, still clad in her nightgown, her hair hanging down in fat ringlets like sausages. It was dawn, frosty light edging the windowpanes. The house was still bitterly cold despite the near constant fires.

She was regarding him with a sort of thoughtful awe, as if he had control of the weather and could make the sun shine instead. He finished buttoning his breeches and went to her, not wanting to waste the moment. With his shirt untucked and his feet bare, he took a chair nearest the fire and set her on his knee. "What are you really telling me?"

"I want to see Miss Sophie." She looked up, her fingers plucking at the smooth seam of his linen shirt as she waited for his answer. "Can we go to Three Chimneys now?"

"At six o'clock in the morning?"

She nodded solemnly. "I'm afraid the snow will soon be so deep we cannot."

He looked to a window where the sky was leaden gray. The slight ache of his joints, his bad hand, told him they'd be snowbound for days. "She's likely still abed." The stray thought was so pleasant it sent the heat crawling up his neck. "A lady needs her rest."

"I suppose I should have my lessons first." Her chin quivered. "I would ask Miss Townsend to go with me, but you told me not to talk so much of Miss Sophie, remember?"

"All I said was that you need to attend to your schooling and be less glib."

180

She studied him. "What does *glib* mean?"

"*Glib* means 'gabby'—talking too much. You don't usually have a problem with this, but 'tis better to be quiet at lessons."

"I promise to be quiet if you take me to see Miss Sophie." Reaching up, she took his unshaven jaw in her little hands and kissed his chin. Overcome, he shut his eyes. She'd never kissed him before. Not once. And it didn't matter that it was merely a means to an end. At that moment he would have taken her to England to see the king. "Please, Papa."

He nearly couldn't speak. "You don't have to travel to Three Chimneys. Miss Menzies is right here."

"Here?" She looked about. "Where?"

He gestured toward the adjoining door. Scrambling off his lap, she started away, but he caught her hand. "She was up rather late, and I don't want her disturbed—"

The door in question cracked open and silenced him. Sophie's voice crept out. "Are you decent, General?"

"Aye." Seamus looked down at his state of undress, unwilling to refuse her entry. "Decent enough."

Lily Cate rushed toward the barely open door, the joy on her face immeasurable. He watched as Sophie peeked round the door frame, suspended in a moment he wanted to hold close forever.

And then the thought of Annapolis cut in.

Without a word, he finished dressing and went below to his study. Already his mind was taking him places he had no wish to go. What if Sophie found the city to her liking? Or Glynnis convinced her to stay on as nurse? What if she didn't come back?

What did it matter?

But somehow it did.

The only one happy with the arrangement would be Miss Townsend.

✦

Clad in her warmest cape and bonnet, Sophie left for Annapolis in the Ogilvy coach two days later, her purse holding what little money she'd gotten from the sale of her father's remaining belongings in Roan. A small marble bust of King George had brought nothing but sneers, though his collection of history books and fine thistle pipes had put a few pounds in her pocket. But would they ever get there?

The coachman shouted down at the first change of horses. "Worse weather on the way—I can feel it in my bones!"

Unconcerned, Sophie settled in, a foot warmer of hot coals beneath her feet, glad for the change of scenery. Studying the white landscape through the coach window, she found herself clinging to all the landmarks she knew by heart. The Roan River sluiced through the valley like a satin ribbon, partially frozen, the hills around it gentle and familiar. She didn't look back. Tried to ignore the urge to dwell on her midnight supper with Seamus. Yet his low words to her wouldn't let her go.

You're a riddle, Sophie Menzies . . . a beautiful, bewildering riddle.

After that, all had blurred. She'd left Shay's wife, Kaye, in good health and spirits, the baby nursing and thriving. Lily Cate had not cried, only asked when she'd be back, as if she'd been warned by her father to rein in her emotions. Somehow Lily Cate had knit herself to Sophie so tightly she feared the tie could never be unknotted.

As for Seamus, he'd simply stood a few feet from her, saying little. Anne's diary was hidden in the bottom of her valise beneath her smallclothes and dresses. She was relieved to have snuck it out of Tall Acre, out of Seamus's reach, but was troubled nonetheless. Guilt clawed at her and left her wanting to be rid of it for good.

Annapolis, unknown to her, would be a welcome diversion. Perhaps she'd find the elusive answers to her future there, gain the distance she desperately needed. Edinburgh, once a sort of prison, now seemed her only refuge.

She waited till the next change of horses to pull out Anne's diary. Reading in the coach made her queasy, but she was driven by a need to finish.

3 May

I have met a man, the erstwhile master of Early Hall, an Englishman. His name is Tobias Early. He has sent over a traveling wheelwright from Richmond, come to make me a riding chair. Strangely enough, Mr. Early reminds me of Seamus. Tall and strapping and quick to laugh. He says he will take me out once the chair is finished. He is quite fond of Lily Cate. Unmarried, he has no children of his own.

12 June

First time out in my new Windsor riding chair. Left at noon and didn't come home till half past five. The day was lovely. Just the two of us. Tomorrow we shall have a picnic. I want to show Tobias the little spot downriver rife with wild roses.

23 June

The heat leaves me quite wilted in the house. If not for my rides with Tobias, I do not know what I would do. Fresh air and exercise are good for what ails us. Isn't that what Seamus always said?

No word from him other than a short letter. He knows I do not care for his Patriot sentiments. Tobias agrees with me. He secretly hopes the British win the war. The colonies cannot resist so formidable a foe, says he. General Washington is but a man, not a god.

31 August

Tobias has gone. The rains of late summer have come, and my mood falls with them. Riggs has refused to fill my order for absinthe with the apothecary. He says Seamus forbids it. The violent fury I flew into did not move him. It never does.

11 October

I am undone. Myrtilla suspects. She will tell Seamus when he comes home. Her loyalty to him has no end. Only Seamus may not ever come back, I told her, so she can keep her secret—and mine. My sister tells me I must come to Williamsburg and go into seclusion. Seamus need never know. I tremble to think what he would do if I am found out. Still, I am not sorry to have had my time in the sun. If he was at home, none of this would have happened. He is entirely to blame . . .

There were more entries, each shorter and more scrawling as if written in the dark. Sophie tucked the diary away, harassed in spirit.

She arrived in Annapolis in the grip of an icy rain, heart full of Seamus and head full of Anne. Glynnis was sleeping, so her sister, Elizabeth, showed Sophie upstairs. A tiny attic bedchamber awaited, and she had a few moments alone as Elizabeth went below to make tea.

She opened her valise and took out the diary. She'd finally finished reading it, every word. Stepping toward the hearth, she weighed her actions, wanting to protect Seamus. Lily Cate.

If she destroyed it, would she feel a profound rush of relief? Or would the lick of guilt remain?

⁂

Could the day get any worse?

First, no Sophie Menzies. And then no governess either.

Sophie had been away for nigh on a month; Amity Townsend had been gone a mere twenty-four hours. No note. No excuses. Just a silent, secretive departure.

It was quickly apparent who was most missed.

The rattling clink of cutlery and the everlasting echo of the dining room nearly stole Seamus's appetite, as did Lily Cate's somber expression as night settled in. Across from him, she was fighting tears, pushing him nearer the cliff's edge of despair.

"Papa, why is the dining room so big?"

"'Tis not so big when it's full of people. Guests . . . a family."

"I can hear my voice come back to me." She raised damp eyes to the plasterwork ceiling with its fine flourishes and medallions that seemed high as the heavens.

"Mayhap we should start eating elsewhere," he said.

"Miss Sophie and I eat in the small parlor when she comes."

He nodded, and she returned her attention to her plate. As he cut his meat, he saw that she struggled to cut hers. Her knife slipped, and the mutton went sliding onto the linen tablecloth, creating a muddy puddle. Shamefaced, she let go of her knife and fork altogether and hung her head.

A pang of pity shot through him, and he got out of his chair. It seemed a long walk around the immense table to reach her, but once there he took her small hands in his and rescued the meat, returning it to her plate and showing her how to cut it. "From here on we'll eat side by side in the small parlor."

She took a bite, chewing pensively. He was thankful her appetite had returned. She'd taken the grippe recently, and he'd been up with her nights. She'd wanted Sophie, but he'd done the best he could.

"Are you sorry Miss Townsend is gone, Papa?"

He took his seat as a servant brought in dessert. "Sorry, nay." *Furious, aye.* "I don't want her to stay if she doesn't want to."

"Did I do something to send her away?"

"You had nothing to do with it." He'd put that thought to rest once and for all. "She is not meant to be a governess, I think."

More spy.

Since coming back from his morning ride about the estate, he'd learned Miss Townsend had fled without so much as a note. Pieces of the strange puzzle had begun to fall into place—his unease with her, her objections to Sophie, Lily Cate's subtle struggle with lessons—all turning his thoughts once again to Williamsburg. He may have won the war against England, but he was losing the one at home.

"Are you going to get another?"

He looked at Lily Cate through the haze of candlelight. "A governess?" At her nod, he softened. "What do you want me to do?"

Her eyes shone with such hope he realized his error immediately. "Can Miss Sophie be my governess?" At his hesitation, she hurried on. "Do you think she's going to stay away forever?"

He weighed the possibility. "I imagine her former housekeeper has worsened and needs her."

Worry marred her face. "Would you ask her, Papa?"

"To be your governess?" Her longing for Sophie to be here, beneath their roof, was acute. His own feelings about her, muddled as they were, were acute. "Why don't we think more about it first?"

"Will you pray, Papa?"

Pray? She was looking at him entreatingly, her eager face framed by tangled curls in need of combing. His heart felt swollen, too big for his chest. Her request, small as it was, was beyond him. He was at sea, borne on a tide of guilt and regret. He opened his mouth to refuse—

"Please, Papa?" Her eyes were stars, glistening amidst his darkness.

He bent his head. For several tense seconds the emotional words lodged inside him without release. Would God hear the plea of a little girl, if not her father?

"Lord, we deserve nothing from Thee, but we are in need of much. We ask Thee to provide us with—we ask that Miss Menzies be willing to act as governess or whatever would be best for her . . . for us. Thy will be done. Amen."

"Amen," his daughter echoed, her tears retreating.

He pushed his plate aside and took a breath. "There's another matter." He was reluctant to bring it up, but she needed to know. "Come morning I have to go away again. Myrtilla will be with you as usual, and I'll be back by week's end. Mayhap by then we'll have an answer to our prayer."

For once she said nothing, just gave a slight nod as she scraped her plate clean. He wouldn't tell her where he was going. Why. The coming confrontation left him cold. But it was past time to mount a counteroffensive.

He'd leave with both a day and a night watch in place. They were mere grooms, most of them, but excellent marksmen and hunters. He'd told them to shoot any trespasser on sight. By law he was within his rights. But he'd had enough of struggle after so long a war. He was sick to death of conflict.

Lily Cate looked over at him and excused herself from the table. He wanted so much for her. Wanted to make everything better for her. Suddenly he felt powerless. Ineffective.

And desperate to protect his daughter.

18

On this, the first of March, Seamus crossed the sodden Williamsburg street, mud oozing beneath his boots, intent on a meal at the Raleigh Tavern before going upstairs to his regular lodging.

The proprietor met him at the door. "Good afternoon, General. A pint and a pipe?"

"Aye," he answered. 'Twas what he always ordered but usually enjoyed in company. He knew a great many people in town. But today the Windsor chair opposite sat all too empty, unable to provide a distraction or a buffer against the ordeal to come. Taking a list from his pocket, he unfolded it, fingers stiff from the cold, and spread it out atop the scarred table. As soon as he returned to Tall Acre, he'd be busy making another. Getting the estate running full bore took every moment and speck of specie he had.

Fifty pounds spermaceti candles. One hundred pounds grass seed. Four pair riding gloves. One fire screen. Black satin queue ribbon. One dozen packs playing cards. One mahogany stool with place for chamber pot. Langley's *New Principles of Gardening*.

The tankard came, steam redolent of nutmeg and rum, returning him to Three Chimneys' kitchen. Sophie had ruined him on toddies. Somehow any others paled next to the ones she'd made. He sipped it gratefully all the same, languorous warmth stealing through him.

One glance out the window at the melting snow left him wishing for better weather. He didn't want to be here any longer than necessary. Already he was missing his paneled study and Lily Cate's chatter and the glow of candlelight at day's end.

She'd looked so troubled at his leaving—like she feared he wouldn't come back. She was still struggling with her riding lessons and had taken a nasty spill. The bump on her forehead had swollen her right eye shut, and it hurt him to look at her, though she had no breaks or other bruises.

He realized how fragile she was right then, how he'd torn her from her familiar world in Williamsburg and handed her Tall Acre instead. With its empty rooms and unhappy memories. Its high expectations and fearsome challenges.

Stooping so that he could meet her at eye level, his heavy cloak fanning out around him, he said quietly, "Keep praying, aye?"

She bit her quivering lip as his arms went round her. He held her close, feeling the tick of her pulse, her soft hair catching on his whiskers, her small hands holding on to him like she'd never let go. His heart turned over . . . held still.

That bittersweet moment had warmed him the entire thirty-two-mile ride to Williamsburg, making him want to hurry home lest he seem a stranger to her all over again.

If he lost her . . . if he had to give her up . . .

He'd rather have died in battle.

Sophie arrived home on a blustery day with a clear head and fresh resolve, her feelings for Seamus in check. Thankfully, Glynnis was improving and they'd had a lovely visit, making Sophie realize how much she'd missed the fellowship of friends. Even in the snow, Annapolis held a blessed noise and bustle that staved off melancholy. She'd even frequented a nearby tearoom with a few of her halfpennies. The Busy Bee was as good for the soul as the stomach, its whimsical name making her smile.

She'd also sent a letter to Edinburgh to her father, asking about his health and testing the waters of welcome. Mostly she wanted to see if he'd had any word of Curtis. 'Twas now a weary wait for a reply. And if there was none, what then?

"Och!" Mistress Murdo crowed in satisfaction at the sight of her. "Annapolis must have agreed with ye. Yer not so peely-wally now."

Sophie smoothed the bodice of the caraco jacket she'd sewn while in the city, glad to return to the size she was before the war. "You can tell I've had one too many Annapolis teacakes."

"Well, I found some lovely cloth in the attic. I thought ye might be in need of a new gown." Mistress Murdo hastened up the stairs to the dust and cobwebs and returned with a length of peach taffeta and velvet ribbon. "Between the two of us, we'll fashion a loosome dress for some future frolic."

Sophie held her tongue. She'd never unearthed such fine cloth and fripperies in her attic searches. Had the goods been gotten from Tall Acre on the sly? A new gown was hardly needed, especially one so fine, unless . . . Might Mistress Murdo be withholding some news? Amity's disclosure of

Seamus's courtship was never far from her mind. A month's absence might mean a wedding was in the offing. Though she ached to see Lily Cate and mend the distance between them, she wanted to honor her personal vow to keep Seamus at arm's length.

She left the third floor and paused at the oriel window, a flash of red catching her eye in the noon light. An express rider was coming up the long drive, barreling through slush and mud, the world outside a windy smirr of gray.

She hurried down to the foyer, every anxious step smothering the high feeling she'd returned home with. She paid him the last of her pence and then tore open the letter. Half a dozen bills fluttered to the foyer floor like broken-winged birds, but she scarcely noticed, riveted to the page. Curtis's writing hand was unforgettable, much like her father's. Loping and proud and grandly elegant.

8 October, 1783

Dear Sophie,

Forgive me for this latent letter. By now you likely know where my loyalties lie.

I hope we can set our differences aside. I have returned to Scotland to take my rightful place as heir, and marry.

She stared at the post, the hurt of betrayal rushing in. All this time she'd been waiting, wondering—and he was in Scotland?

Word has come that Mother has passed and you are alone at Three Chimneys. Now that Tory properties are

*being seized by the new American government, Father
and I agree it would be best for you to join us here in
Edinburgh.*

*Enclosed is money enough for your traveling ex-
penses. Rest assured you will be welcomed with open
arms.*

> *Your ever loving brother,*
> *Curtis*

Ever loving brother? Nay, traitor. A British resident again.
Did he care nothing about Three Chimneys?

Stooping, heart thudding beneath her stays, she began
gathering up the unwanted bills, surprised by the amount.
Her father was as frugal as he was Scottish. So they wanted
her to return to them? Oh aye! Likely Lord Menzies had
found some wealthy, doddering old suitor to foist on her in
order to further his own purposes there.

Stung, she stuffed both money and letter in a desk drawer,
tears blinding her. She wanted Curtis to walk in and make
things right. She wanted to find her way back to the girl she'd
been, full of promise and expectation. For half an hour she
paced the room, her love for her brother at war with her
anger and hurt. Curtis wasn't coming. He'd never meant to,
after all. While she'd been waiting, praying . . .

Spent, she curled up in a Windsor chair, her damp cheek
pressed against the threadbare brocade back. Never had she
felt so in need of her mother's company. Her quiet confidence
and unwavering faith. Her belief that God orchestrated all
things.

*And we know that all things work together for good to
them that love God.*

She'd clung to that verse for longer than she could remember. But she was no longer sure she believed it. There had simply been too much loss.

⠀⠀⠀⠀⠀⠀⠀⠀⠀⠀⠀⠀⠀⠀🌀

Seamus wasted no words once he'd set foot in the Fitzhughs' Williamsburg townhouse.

"I thought it only fair to tell you I've decided to take legal action against you."

"What the devil are you talking about?" Fitzhugh, for all his pomp and polish, looked apoplectic. "How dare you—"

"How dare *you*." Seamus held his temper by a hair. "There is such a thing as plain dealing, but time after time you resort to underhanded tactics that leave me little choice but to seek a higher authority."

Charlotte seemed aghast at such bluntness. "General, do sit down. Let us be civil." She flicked her fan toward a settee.

Seamus stayed standing, hat in hand.

Fitzhugh began anew. "You're well aware—"

"I'm well aware someone has been trespassing at Tall Acre, frightening my daughter and my staff."

"Someone?" Charlotte looked duly alarmed. "Whatever do you mean?"

"An unknown man has been seen on the grounds more than once. He's not yet been caught, but he will be." Seamus looked straight at Fitzhugh. "And I'm holding you responsible for any trouble incurred."

The judge stayed stony. "Would you like us to add libel to the case we're building against you, General?"

"Build any case you like," Seamus returned quietly. "Legally you don't have a leg to stand on."

"I beg to differ." Fitzhugh emerged from behind the desk, snuff box in hand. "We're working to return the child—"

"The child has a name."

Fitzhugh snorted. "As I was saying, we're working to return Anne's daughter to our care and see your mismanagement of her come to an end. We're aware you're often away from Tall Acre and she is unsupervised—"

"If I'm away, it's because of estate business as I've just returned from nearly a decade of war. As for my daughter, she's closely supervised at all times—"

"*Closely?*" Fitzhugh's voice climbed to new heights. "We're aware you cannot even keep a governess on hand—"

"And I'm well aware you sent Miss Townsend to Tall Acre, masquerading as such," Seamus shot back, his surface calm deserting him. "The least you could do is to not be so blasted stupid about spying!"

"You have no proof!" Fitzhugh flung at him. "'Tis hearsay, all of it!"

"Nay, not hearsay." Seamus's own voice rose and crested, overriding his former brother-in-law's. "I suspected something amiss from the first."

"Gentlemen, please!" Charlotte intruded, nearly as irate. "Need I remind you that we merely want Lily Cate to come for a visit? 'Tis been ages since we've seen her."

A visit? As if this was some social call? Would they never listen? Seamus didn't hide his disgust.

Fitzhugh regarded him through narrowed eyes. "A visit seems meager at best when Anne's daughter should be returned to our care permanently. If you're not agreeable to even a brief meeting, perhaps a court order will help change your mind. I'm prepared to force the issue if you deny our request—"

"You can threaten all you want. I'll not bring my daughter to Williamsburg. I've already told you that you can come to Tall Acre if you send word well ahead of the date." Even that was more than Seamus was willing to concede. And a supervised visit it would be. "I'll not bring her here—leave her here—court order or no."

"You're in grave error, General." Fitzhugh was nearly spitting in his ire, unused to being thwarted. "Anne's daughter is, per Anne's request, rightfully ours based on your history of absence and neglect. I needn't remind you that we have it in writing—"

"Nay, you needn't remind me." Seamus's tone flattened. "Anne did me a grave disservice, but that is all. Nothing you say or do will take my daughter from me."

"Gentlemen, please!" Charlotte looked at them, palms raised imploringly. "As I've said before, our main concern is that Lily Cate needs a woman's influence—"

"And she's to have one." Seamus returned his hat to his head and took a step back. "You're among the first to know I'm to wed." They stared at him, their shocked expressions giving him a small, sweet taste of victory.

Finally Fitzhugh said, "Marry? When?"

"As soon as I return to Tall Acre."

Confusion colored his face. "Who on earth are you to marry?"

"A lady from Roan County."

Charlotte frowned, her surprise giving way to petulance. "And who might that be?"

"Miss Sophie Menzies of Three Chimneys."

"The *turncoat's* daughter?" they said in unison.

Seamus gave a nod, pulse pounding. "Aye. I'm to have a

wife. Lily Cate is to have a mother. No argument you devise can stand up to that in court, so I advise you to quit your case."

He turned, ignoring the bitter barb Fitzhugh flung at him and Charlotte's gaping dismay. His elation lasted till he reached the foyer and realized just what he'd done.

Become betrothed to a woman who didn't have a clue.

❦

Passing into the cold Williamsburg night, the stars hanging like icicles in the frozen sky, Seamus made for the Raleigh Tavern, wishing he could return to Three Chimneys by the light of the moon and talk—nay, argue—Sophie Menzies into marrying him. For all he knew, she was still in Annapolis. As it was, there was no going home till morning. An unappetizing meal at the Raleigh would have to suffice till then, followed by a long, sleepless night.

Next morning, in a bold move his heart wasn't quite willing to make, he found himself at James Craig, Jewelers, hunting up a ring. As luck would have it the shop was empty, sparing Seamus any explanation of why he had come in so early, though Craig was looking at him in a bemused sort of way.

"And what exactly did you have in mind, General Ogilvy?"

"A wedding band . . . nothing too ornate. But no pinchbeck either." Anne had hated anything inferior or counterfeit. He guessed she'd been buried with the ornate ruby ring he'd given her. Or mayhap the ever-grasping Charlotte had kept it. The uncharitable thought nicked him, but he aimed for honesty, at least in the sanctuary of his own head and heart.

What would Sophie favor?

Muttering about the price of gems in the wake of war, Craig laid out a generous selection of jewelry atop the wooden counter. Seamus examined pointe native diamond rings and plainer bands, drawn to a gold and black enamel ring wide enough for engraving. Simple and elegant, it wouldn't overpower Sophie's slender hand.

He held it up to the light, wondering if he'd have need of it at all. Everything hinged on her response, and he hadn't even asked her. But he'd ride clear to Annapolis if he had to.

"If you'd engrave it with three names—Sophie, Seamus, Lily Cate."

Craig nodded and began putting the other rings away. "My congratulations, General. I wasn't aware you were to remarry."

"These things have a way of happening," Seamus murmured.

"Aye, indeed they do." Craig chuckled. "I'll have that engraving done straightaway."

Seamus hoped he wouldn't fish for details like wedding dates.

He wasn't sure there'd be one.

19

Twas candlelight when Sophie finished her supper and watched the last of daylight drain away. Rain streaked her bedchamber windowpane, but not so heavily as to obscure the long front drive with its lone rider hastening her way. Another post? Surely not. She'd yet to recover from the last.

Her heart gave an unmistakable, maddening skip. There was no mistaking this long, well-muscled rider who rode with a penetrating purpose.

Seamus.

Had he come about Lily Cate? Some maternal instinct always propelled her to fear illness or accident. Had there been more trouble with the trespasser at Tall Acre or Anne's Williamsburg kin?

Turning toward the looking glass, she raised cold hands to fiery cheeks, dizzy as a girl. Any hedges she put up round her heart always tumbled at first sight of him. Hastily taking the pins from her hair, she shook it loose and wove in a satin ribbon, tying back the waves with practiced hands. A splash of rosewater at her throat and wrists completed her hasty toilette as Mistress Murdo announced him.

"General Ogilvy is in the front parlor, miss."

Sophie thanked her, glad she'd asked Henry to lay a fire. Now was the time to tell him about Curtis. Would he think the worst of her? Shun her like Roan did?

Gripping the banister, she went below, shame pummeling her the nearer she came to the open parlor door. Yet not even the dread of confessing the betrayal could dampen her gladness that Seamus was waiting. Her every sense was heightened by the mere anticipation of him.

By the time she crossed the threshold and beheld his broad back, a dozen things she'd missed about him were satisfied. Unaware of her, he placed his cocked hat atop a settee and straightened to look into the mantel mirror and smooth his cravat. As if he cared how he looked for her. As if she were special . . . beloved. In that instant his gaze met hers in the cracked glass. She nearly forgot to breathe.

Never would she forget the sight of him rimmed in firelight, his dark hair so wind-tossed that loose strands lay about his shoulders like spilled ribbon, his eyes keen and kind and searching all at once. Slowly he turned round. His solemnity gave a warning.

He swallowed, the cords in his neck tensing. "Sophie . . ."

She went still. Never had he used her Christian name. Her heart, so sore over losing Three Chimneys and Curtis, so torn over missing Seamus yet needing distance, felt like it would burst.

He gestured toward a Windsor chair. "Mayhap you'd better sit down."

She stayed standing. "Whatever it is, please . . . just say it."

He took another step toward her. "I've come to ask you—"

He looked wildly uncertain yet determined all at once. "To marry me."

Her lips parted. No sound came.

"I know that's the last thing you expected." His intensity assured her he wasn't jesting. "I'm asking you to be my wife."

My wife. Not *my dance partner.* Not *my houseguest* or *my daughter's companion.* Breaking their gaze, she sat down in the nearest chair.

"Forgive me for being so abrupt." Disquiet deepened his voice. "Ever since you left for Annapolis, I've thought of little else."

Oh? If she was tied up in his thoughts, she'd like to know the gist of them.

"I admire and respect you. I doubt I'll ever meet another woman like you." His words held firm. "I'm indebted to you for being there for my daughter, and it's because of her I'm here."

She found words at last. "Something happened in Williamsburg."

"I told Anne's kin I'm to wed."

"You told them you were going to wed *me?*"

"I did."

"Are you so sure of me, then?" Her eyes widened at his audacity. "That I shall accept you?"

A glimmer of amusement broke through his unease. "Nay, I've never been less sure of anything in my life."

"You, sir, are a wee bit bold . . ." Pleasure stirred and then reason staggered in. "Rather, Lily Cate is in need of a mother, and you stand to lose her if you don't make a family again."

"Aye, to put it bluntly."

The truth sat squarely and unflinchingly between them, hardly the proposal of her dreams—but a proposal nonetheless.

"I understand . . ." Her voice fell away. She felt painfully, impossibly . . . joyful. "But you see, I—I'm reluctant to marry a man . . ."

"A man you don't love," he finished for her.

Nay, a man who doesn't love me.

He looked to his boots. "I know you care for someone else, but I thought perhaps, given time, you might find me . . . worthy of your hand."

Had he no inkling of her feelings for him? Did he somehow find himself lacking? Undeserving of her hand, of love and marriage? The emotion filling his face told her so. Clearly, the misunderstanding about her ghostly suitor was between them, awkward and misleading.

"Mayhap we'd better back up." Taking a seat beside her, he changed course. "How was your trip? Glynnis?"

She took a breath. "Glynnis is better. Annapolis is big . . . busy." She tried to smile, to steady her voice, to return to normalcy. "How are things at Tall Acre?"

"Well enough, though Miss Townsend left without warning."

"Amity?" Her mind whirled. "But she came well recommended from Mrs. Hallam."

His jaw firmed. "The same Mrs. Hallam who resides in Williamsburg and might well be friends with the Fitzhughs."

The truth dawned slowly. Was Amity part of their scheming? For the moment she couldn't take it in. All that filled her head was his shocking proposal.

She looked into the fire, the queasy knot in her middle expanding. How could she explain or let go of the girlish hope that she was waiting for someone, someday, who might look at her with longing? Someone who truly wanted to make her his in all the ways that mattered?

Not . . . *this*.

She folded her hands in a show of calm. "You should know that while I was in Annapolis, I wrote my father."

He said nothing, but she could sense his thoughts. *You wrote the man who abandoned you? Who hasn't inquired after you these eight years past?*

"At the time it seemed the right thing to do." It sounded logical. Practical. Yet writing to him had cost her. Her pride. Her last hope. "I'm considering going to Edinburgh."

"To Edinburgh," he echoed. There was no accusation or anger in his tone, just quiet contemplation. "You'd take Edinburgh over Tall Acre."

Would she? Her mind stayed muddled. Stunned.

"Then, when I returned home yesterday, I received word from—" Tears smarted in her eyes. She nearly couldn't speak. "Curtis."

His gaze clouded. She read a dozen things there, but prior knowledge and regret were uppermost.

"You knew." Her voice came soft, without blame. "But you didn't tell me."

"I suspected, but there had been no confirmation. I didn't want you hurt by false reports."

"He betrayed you, his commanding officer."

"Aye, but the war is won." He held her gaze, obviously as settled in spirit about the matter as she was unsettled. "We should be glad he's alive, all loyalties aside. One day it won't matter."

Wise words. Humble words. And at such cost. Men he'd trusted and would have laid down his life for had gone over to the enemy more times than he could count. But she never imagined Curtis would be one of them.

"I'm sorry, Sophie." He looked to the hat in his hands, the

once-colorful cockade faded. "If you think Curtis's loyalties make me think differently about you or my proposal, they don't. The future is yours—ours—to make of it what we will."

"Allow me time to pray about matters first."

"I won't force the issue. All I ask is that you forgive me for being so . . . sudden." He stood, averting his eyes, and with that instinctive gentlemanly courtesy she found so appealing, he said, "If you'd rather convey your answer by note, I'll be at Tall Acre waiting."

Coming into Tall Acre's foyer, Seamus found the house quiet, the immense case clock chiming ten. He'd wanted to see Lily Cate before she went to bed. By now she'd be asleep, unaware of the small storm he'd just created at Three Chimneys. Just as well. He didn't feel like talking but getting on his knees and asking forgiveness. From both heaven and Sophie Menzies.

What woman wanted a proposal like the one he'd just laid out? Heedless, he'd gone striding into her parlor and winged the question at her like he was pitching horseshoes and she was the target. Her shock and dismay would never leave him. And now her answer, or the lack of it, lay like an unexploded shell between them. He was sure she'd say no. And he didn't blame her.

But Edinburgh?

Myrtilla met him on the landing, having come from Lily Cate's room. "She's sleepin', sir. Everything's been fine here with you away, though she's been askin' when you be back. And she's missin' Miss Menzies somethin' fierce besides."

He thanked her and moved on to the second floor. He tore off his cloak and tossed his hat and gloves on a hall chair, then carefully opened the door of her room. Firelight caressed her face as she slept beneath the high canopy. The doll Sophie had given her was tucked beneath one arm.

Straddling the bed steps, he sat down, willing his pulse to settle. She looked so peaceful. So unlike Anne. Lily Cate had no memories of her mother, something that both saddened and gladdened him. His daughter was as darkly pretty as Sophie. He could well imagine people thinking they were mother and daughter at some point in future, if the impossible happened and Sophie would have him.

Lately Lily Cate had begun to open up, slowly escaping her shell of fear and confusion, reaching out to him in tentative trust. He could well imagine her joy if he were to tell her that Sophie was to be her mother. He'd give anything to shake Lily Cate awake with the news tonight.

He rubbed his whiskered jaw with stubborn resolve, forcing his unsettled emotions into retreat. He might soon be telling her Sophie was leaving for Scotland instead.

He touched her cheek, flushed with sleep, and brushed back a lock that curled over one eye. Her lashes were long and thick, fanning across the dainty planes of her face like black fringe. She was nearly perfect. She was in need of a mother. A happy home.

A far better father.

Sophie remained in the parlor, not bothering to go to bed, knowing sleep would never come. Facing the chair Seamus had sat in, she tried to reconstruct the scene. The shock of his unexpected proposal. The rush of disbelief. She felt backed into an impossible corner. Yet he was likely sleepless too, awaiting her answer.

Stiff from sitting, she went to the window, looking out through the rain-soaked night to the pinpricks of light that were Tall Acre. Could she really be its mistress? She knew something of its workings from the pages of Anne's diary, mainly Myrtilla's early bond with Lily Cate. She sensed Riggs's competence as estate manager, the constant upkeep and cash required to maintain so large an estate, Seamus's love of hearth and home, the endless cycle of seasons in which the enslaved and indentured played such a part.

She retrieved her Bible from her bedchamber and thumbed through its pages, searching, seeking answers, till her eyes crossed and her back ached. She prayed her way to daylight, but though dawn relieved her nighttime fears, it did little in the way of answers. Her choices seemed so simple yet were fraught with untold risk. She could go to Edinburgh and try to make a life there. Or she could wed Seamus and secure herself a home, a husband, right here in Roan.

She had no template for marriage, at least a happy one. Her parents' bond had been by arrangement. Oddly enough, her mother had cared for her father while he'd shown nothing but contempt for her feelings. The more loving she was, the more distant he became. Sophie had watched it play out like an unending tragedy. Always cold and indifferent, he had moved to Williamsburg and then Scotland, forsaking her altogether.

If she wed Seamus, she must keep her love hidden at all costs. She could not bear to be an object of contempt, making him feel cornered, trapped, suffocated, only to turn away from her in disgust. The prospect lined her spine with ice.

At the same time, how could she accept him and cast aside a chance for true love if it came? In Edinburgh, perhaps, or elsewhere?

She bent over the Bible, the words bearing both solace and challenge. *Let us not love in word, neither in tongue; but in deed and in truth.* The truth was she loved Seamus. He might be her only hope of a husband. She loved his daughter with all her heart. If taking a wife would ensure matters in Williamsburg would melt away, who was she to deny him what he most wanted?

At eight and twenty, Sophie Menzies would be the talk of Virginia marrying Seamus Ogilvy. Pondering it, she bit her lip till it nearly bled. She'd always hated such talk.

As dawn made an icy entrance, she returned to her room and tucked the Bible away. Her fingers and feet were numb, but her heart felt on fire as she began to dress to go to Tall Acre. She'd not make him wait a minute longer for her answer.

She must unburden herself—or burst.

20

Sophie walked toward Tall Acre and considered what to say. How to say it. By the time she turned down the familiar, cherry-lined alley, she was fisting her gloved hands so tightly her fingers ached. Pausing at the hitch rail near the front steps, she stood for a moment to catch her breath, her cape buffeted by a rising wind.

She lifted her gaze to Tall Acre's soaring eaves. A pair of doves nested there, cooing softly and adding a touch of whimsy to her situation. Everything, in light of Seamus's startling proposal, seemed to have altered. Or was she simply seeing the world with new eyes?

A smiling Mrs. Lamont met her at the door. "Good day, Miss Menzies. Up early this chilly morning, I see."

Before Sophie could answer, Lily Cate came bounding down the stairs, a look of pure rapture on her face. She threw her arms about Sophie, nearly catching her off balance. Still breathless, Sophie hugged her back, loving the warm, sweet feel of her after a month-long separation. She smelled of talc and soap, indicative of a recent bath.

"I thought you'd never come back," Lily Cate exclaimed, her embrace never lessening. "Are you here to play?"

Sophie ran a hand through the girl's tumbled curls and eyed the bruise on her face. Had she fallen? "I'm here to see your father first. But after that the day is ours, yes."

"Papa gave up on my hair," she whispered as Mrs. Lamont disappeared. "He says he is no good at making me pretty."

"Fetch me your ribbons, then."

"Then can we play?"

"Miss Menzies said she wanted to see me first." Behind them stood Seamus, wearing the same clothes he'd had on when he'd seen her last night. He'd obviously not slept any more than she, and the somber slant of his features told her he wasn't expecting an aye as her answer either.

Lily Cate released her reluctantly, scampering up the stairs and out of sight.

Seamus extended a hand toward the open door of his study. She went in ahead of him, feeling an air of finality settle about them when he shut the door. Silent, he came to stand before the fire, hands clasped behind him.

Awkwardness thickened the room like storm clouds gathering. She said softly, "I'm sorry I kept you up all night."

He gave a weary smile, his scruff of beard turning him roguish. "Rather, I kept *you* up all night."

True enough. She wanted to be witty, make light of it, but it was so emotional a moment she had no words.

His own expression was fraught with a striking uneasiness. "You can tell me nay without hesitation. I like to think I'm man enough to take it. But at the moment I'm guessing you're on the verge of saying yes, otherwise you would have sent a note. Though I sense you still have . . . questions."

She gave a nod, unsurprised he'd read her so easily.

"I've filed the court papers required to manumit all of Tall Acre's slaves. Those who wish to remain as freedmen can work for wages." He took hold of a poker and gave a jab to the fire's backlog. "'Tis a relief to have it done, even if you don't agree to marry me."

So all was in order and he'd kept his word. Freeing his slaves would cost him dearly in terms of labor, though it was the right thing, the godly thing, to do.

Setting the poker aside, he turned toward her. "If you'll have me, I promise to be faithful to you. I gladly give you my name, my house, all my worldly goods." Voice low, he seemed to be saying a vow. "You'll never be in want so long as I live. If you can abide a man with a bad hand, I'll do my best to make you content."

His humility, the earnestness in his expression, stirred her deeply. He was willing to be her husband, yet she was still drowning in the shock of it, uncertain if this was the Lord's will or her own—or merely that of a man determined to keep his daughter.

His mouth tilted into a smile. "And if we wed, it would probably be wise to leave Miss Menzies and General Ogilvy behind and use our Christian names instead."

Flushing, she looked down at her knotted hands. She'd nearly come undone when he'd spoken her name in the emotional maelstrom of her parlor. She hadn't recovered yet.

"Sophie . . . look at me."

Her chin came up. His eyes were a glittering blue, full of promise and hope and apology.

Was he wanting her to respond in kind? "Seamus . . ." His name tasted strange. Throat tight, she simply reached for his wounded hand, hoping that relayed her answer.

Relief washed his face—and embarrassment. As if he was

still struggling with his maimed hand, wanting to offer the whole one in its place. The vulnerability in his expression wrenched her. She longed to tell him his injury mattered not at all, that she'd take him no matter how maimed or unworthy he felt. If he loved her, she would. If this was a proper proposal, she would.

She let go of his hand. "When shall we wed?"

"As soon as you're willing."

"But the banns must be read, a fortnight to follow . . ."

"Reverend Hopkins has agreed to waive the banns in the wake of the war and Anglican upheaval."

Had he? "Tomorrow morning, then." She felt another qualm. Was a day's notice time enough to prepare the staff? Time enough to come to her senses, change her mind? Flee to Edinburgh after all? She hurried on as if to outrun the thought. "I have a small request, if you would." She felt a touch shy. "Might you wear your uniform?" The surprise in his eyes begged explanation, but she couldn't say she'd thought of him as her hero. It sounded foolish. Silly. And would certainly relay her hidden feelings.

"Aye, I will. We'll honeymoon at Warm Springs in western Virginia. You, me, and Lily Cate."

The three of them? Gratitude rushed in. To be alone as man and wife was a wilderness she wasn't prepared to walk into. Not yet. "I've never been to the hot springs."

"Neither has Lily Cate. Despite the bad roads, it should be well worth the trip."

"Everything sounds . . ." Sudden. Frightening. Irreversible. "Lovely."

He smiled, this time more easily. "I'll have your belongings brought to Tall Acre this afternoon, whatever you want moved."

"Fine, I'll be ready." That was an overstatement. Her head began to pound along with her heart. "But I—I don't want Anne's room, understand."

His eyes flashed surprise again. "My parents' bedchamber is on the ground floor if you'd rather. It's across from the small parlor and even has a second door to the back stair."

Sophie nodded her agreement. Her mother had occupied the first-floor bedchamber at Three Chimneys. Sophie tucked the memory away. How she missed her mother, especially on this most heartfelt of days.

He touched her sleeve. "Do you want to tell Lily Cate the glad news, or shall I?"

"Let's do so together."

He started for the door, drawing her eye. He'd soon become so familiar to her—his every expression, every mood. He was like marzipan to her hungry heart. Would he always be? Or would a dulling regularity smother all fine feeling in time?

"Lily Cate?" His voice rang out in the foyer, rising to the rafters.

The hum of little feet down the staircase was his answer. Lily Cate rushed into the study, hair ribbons clutched in one hand.

"We have some news for you." He turned toward Sophie. "I'll let Miss Menzies tell you about it."

Sophie sat down in a chair, drawing Lily Cate into the circle of her arms. "Starting tomorrow I'm going to come live here at Tall Acre. Your father and I are going to be married."

Her mouth formed a little O. "You won't go back to Three Chimneys?"

"No, promise." When would the truth of it sink in, the shock wear off?

"Will you be my new mama?"

"Always."

Her sigh of contentment robbed Sophie of all the composure she'd mustered. Lily Cate reached up a quick hand, brushing Sophie's tears away. "Why are you crying?"

"Because I'm happy you're happy." Taking the ribbons, Sophie began tying back her hair, all too aware of Seamus looking on.

"Will you bring all your playthings from the morning room too?"

"Everything, yes."

Seamus took a set of keys from his pocket. "Why don't you show Sophie the bedchamber across from the small parlor? See if it's to her liking."

Taking the keys, she clasped Sophie's hand. "I will, Papa. Don't you worry, I think she'll like it very much."

Seamus smiled down at her, then looked at Sophie again. His gaze held so much. She longed to read his every thought.

She was thankful he couldn't read hers.

21

What had she done?

Shocked the servants. Overturned Anglican law. Caused Mistress Murdo to stay up all night finishing what was now a wedding gown. Excited Lily Cate to the point that she'd thrown up all her breakfast. Sophie was half sick herself thinking of what was to come. Only Seamus seemed calm. But he was a soldier and officer, capable of handling life-altering events, even a sudden marital maneuver.

Servants from Tall Acre came to move her belongings—a beloved chair and dressing table, her mother's rocker, bed linens and a dimity counterpane, a trunk of clothes, her needlework and books, her writing desk and papers. Anne's diary was still buried in the bottom of her valise, almost forgotten.

Mistress Murdo, despite being puffy-eyed and unable to speak without yawning, was canty as could be. Even Henry danced an impromptu jig with her in the foyer.

The wedding day dawned bright, sunlight trickling through barren trees and warming everything in sight with a shy promise of spring. As Sophie crossed Tall Acre's threshold, this time as its new mistress and not a guest, she felt like sand in an hourglass, turned upside down and poured out, her circumstances shifting in record time.

The clock inched nearer ten, the wedding hour, and she sat in her new bedchamber, eying the peach taffeta gown finished and hanging in a far clothes cupboard, her mother's wedding veil across her lap. Slightly yellowed with age, it was still lovely, the Minonet lace a filmy cascade of vines and roses. In a small way, Evelyn Menzies seemed nearer.

Raising a hand, she stifled a yawn. During the long, sleepless night, she realized people married for all sorts of reasons, some passionate and some practical. But never had she heard of two people marrying with one of them being in love and one not. Seamus thought she was marrying him out of mutual need, both their backs to the wall. What he didn't know is that she'd marry him for no reason at all. Marrying him was as easy as falling in love with him.

Learning to live with a man who didn't love her scared her to death.

❧

Lily Cate stood hopping on one foot at the door of Seamus's bedchamber, testing his patience and his ability to tie his cravat. The creamy linen fumbled into an awkward knot beneath his nervous fingers.

"Papa, you should see her! She has on a beautiful gown but needs some flowers or herbs to hold, Florie said."

He gave himself a mental kick. He should have remembered flowers. Every bride deserved them, even in the dead of winter. But the hothouse had fallen into neglect, only the hardiest sago palms in evidence. He *had* remembered the pearls, though. They lay in a velvet pouch on his nightstand, an heirloom of his mother's.

When he turned, Lily Cate was studying him. She'd stopped her hopping, a new question dawning in her eyes. "May I call her Mama yet?"

He hesitated, unsure. "She'd like that, I think."

Her smile reappeared. "Have you seen the wedding cake?"

He chuckled. "Nay, have you?"

"Oh yes. 'Tis stacked quite high and is bursting with currants. Cook is still icing it." She started hopping again, her skirts swaying like she was dancing.

"Why don't you see if Sophie needs anything?" He eyed the pearls, torn between having Lily Cate deliver them or giving them to Sophie himself.

She disappeared and the room grew still. A quarter till ten. Reverend Hopkins had just arrived. His jovial laugh echoed through a mostly empty house. There'd been no time to invite many guests. Second weddings were usually quiet affairs, though there'd be a wedding breakfast to follow with a few last-minute guests from neighboring plantations.

Tension wound inside him, tight as a spring. Sophie had accepted him when he thought she wouldn't. Anne had kept him waiting a month. But she'd been younger and less sure of herself than the calm, competent Sophie. He'd never really lived with Anne. He'd simply married her and gone to war. Sophie would be the first to share his home. His life. Normalcy. As normal as two broken people could make it. Guilt nagged him that they were coming together on such odd terms. Sophie Menzies deserved far more. He was getting far more than he deserved.

His steps were measured as he took the hall and back stair

to the ground floor, trying to prepare himself, glad he was in uniform. He'd missed the clank of his spurs and sword, the familiar feel of worn wool. The fact she'd asked him to wear it gave him the confidence he lacked.

As he stepped over the threshold of the large parlor, Sophie turned toward him. Heat climbed from his too-tight cravat to his clean-shaven face. Every logical thought left his head save one. *Beautiful.* She was beautiful in her lovely gown, a filmy veil cascading about her shoulders, a perfect counterpoint to her dark hair. The little Bible and handkerchief she held seemed to shake, and he found himself wanting to reach out and steady her hands.

For the moment no one else was in the room. He heard Lily Cate and Reverend Hopkins down the hall. Coming behind Sophie, he pulled the pearls from his pocket and put them around her throat, much like the scarf she'd wound round his neck that bitter day in the stables.

"These were my mother's." *Not Anne's*, he almost said. Somehow he sensed pearls were Sophie's choice.

"Thank you, Seamus."

He looked down at her as her gaze fell to her ungloved hands. Would he ever get over the wonder of hearing her say his name? After months of *General Ogilvy* and *sir*? He was all thumbs when it came to the necklace's tiny clasp. It would be the same if he held her. In his arms she would seem no bigger than a sparrow. Fragile as eggshell. He felt like Goliath in comparison.

The reverend was smiling at them from the doorway as if this was an everyday occurrence, which to a man of the cloth it was. "Are you both ready?"

"Aye," Seamus said. Ready to have it over. Ready to make her mistress of Tall Acre. Ready to end the business in

Williamsburg. He reached for her hands and caught something he couldn't name in her expressive eyes. They held his for a second longer than ever before.

Lily Cate stood behind them, for once still as a statue, her small face turned up in expectation. Riggs was best man, the best maid the reverend's wife, as good as could be had on short notice. Later he'd give a ball and celebrate with his officer friends, ask Sophie who she'd like to invite. For now the ceremony was small. Hushed and hallowed.

Though he'd wondered in the night if what they were doing was God-honoring, today it felt right. Yet he didn't even know her full name. Didn't know how old she was. Wasn't privy to her dreams. Her fears and tears.

His words were firm, but he shook inside. "I, Seamus, take thee, Sophie, to be my wedded wife, to have and to hold from this day forward, for better, for worse, for richer, for poorer, in sickness and in health, to love and to cherish till death do us part, according to God's holy ordinance, and thereto I plight thee my troth . . ."

He wasn't even sure what love was. More than a feeling, aye. Would she come to love him in time? And he her? Cherishing her was easily managed. He already cherished their unusual friendship, the honest conversation between them, the boundless affection she had for his daughter.

"Wilt thou love her, comfort her, honor her, and keep her in sickness and in health, and, forsaking all others, keep thee only unto her, as long as ye both shall live?"

"I will." He studied her as she spoke her vows, wishing she'd meet his eyes again and quell some of his questions. Was she thinking of her mother and brother? Wishing they were here? Uncertainty gnawed a deeper hole inside him. He prayed she wasn't wishing herself in Edinburgh, regretting this very binding moment. Or worse, longing for the man she loved. But her voice stayed steadfast, and she even managed a small smile at the finish, warming him inside and out. Making him feel less a fool.

"You may kiss your bride."

He froze. He'd forgotten that part. Swallowing hard, he hesitated. He owed Sophie a kiss at least. Leaning in, he brushed back her filmy veil with his good hand and pressed his mouth to hers. She was warm . . . willing. Fragrant . . . inviting. Causing his chest to constrict so much he forgot to breathe.

Riggs clapped him on the back, ending the intimacy. Sophie bent down and embraced Lily Cate, laughing softly at something she said. Before leaving the parlor they signed the marriage certificate. Relief raced over him like rain as she penned her new name.

Sophie Menzies Ogilvy.

The wedding breakfast began, but Seamus was barely aware of what he ate, overcome by the novelty of taking a bride and not having to go to war soon after. His thoughts suddenly clouded at what lay ahead. A honeymoon loomed, fraught with complications. He hadn't thought that far. Hadn't let himself think that far.

Their trunks were soon lashed onto the coach, and the sun stayed out, turning the melting snow more brilliant. Lily Cate started hopping again, her face wreathed in smiles. By two o'clock the three of them left Tall Acre, the staff standing on the front stoop and waving till they'd rolled past the gates and out of sight.

They talked little. Amidst the coach's rocking, Sophie and Lily Cate slept till the day unraveled completely and The Golden Swan came into view. Seamus had taken care of lodging, sending a groom ahead to secure the best room. His bride would have clean linens, no bedbugs, and a decent night's sleep, at least. His daughter too.

As darkness descended, memories of his first wedding night crept in like an uninvited guest. Anne seemed to hover and he tried to push her away, glad for Lily Cate's chatter and Sophie's soft talk.

Still full from the wedding breakfast, they declined supper and went upstairs to their room. Spacious and warmed by a large corner hearth, the chamber bore one large bed with room enough for them all. Retreating behind a screen, Sophie shed her traveling clothes and helped Lily Cate into a nightgown while he undressed and pulled on a nightshirt. Unsettled by his own bare, battle-scarred legs, he got into bed, aware of them washing their hands and faces at the washstand just as he'd done minutes before.

The sweet silence was broken by Lily Cate as she climbed atop the feather tick, her voice limp with weariness. "Papa, Mama? Shall we pray . . . or just sleep?"

Snuffing the candle, he lay on his back. "Pray then sleep."

She reached for him in the darkness, and he felt not her small fingers but Sophie's as Lily Cate joined their hands. He was all too aware of this new wife of his. The ring he'd gotten for her in Williamsburg fit far better than he'd hoped and grazed his palm as he clasped her fingers.

For a moment he struggled with words enough to honor the day. "Father, we thank Thee for undeserved mercies and new beginnings. Bless us and protect us and make us fit to do Thy will. Amen."

"But Papa, that's not what you usually pray." Her voice held that charming lisp on account of her missing front tooth. "I'll say the rest."

Glad for the darkness, he listened, moved by the joy in her voice.

"Dear Jesus, be here with us. We are sorry for our sins. Please heal Papa's hand. Thank You for my new mama. Help her to be happy at Tall Acre and not homesick. Help me to have a new brother or sister . . ."

She was babbling now, and he fought the urge to clamp a hand over her mouth. Sophie intervened gently, finishing the prayer with a few more heartfelt words he couldn't comprehend. They breathed a combined amen and released hands. In moments Lily Cate was asleep, her even breathing like a cat's purr in the stillness.

He wanted to say goodnight to Sophie, but the words wouldn't come, so he gave in to an uneasy slumber, wondering if she'd do the same. Wondering if she wanted him to do more than sleep. For now he congratulated himself on getting the deed done. Theirs was a safe, suitable arrangement. She was in love with someone else. He had no wish to love again.

What could possibly go wrong?

Sophie lay completely still, not wanting to disturb her bedfellows with the slightest movement or noise. The fire had nearly spent itself, and there was only the sound of their combined breathing and what she feared was a mouse scuttling in a far corner.

She almost expected Seamus to snore. Wasn't that what men did? But he was stone still, perhaps as wide awake as she. Everything was too new, too strange, for her to let sleep have its way. The tester bed she'd known since girlhood seemed a lost, forgotten thing, tucked away like a child's toy. Though the inn's mattress was comfortable and the bed curtains enveloped them in velvety darkness, she was all too aware of Seamus beside her save for Lily Cate between them. His beloved masculine scent met her in the darkness, wooing her, bringing home his wedding kiss.

She was a bride. His bride. The pearl necklace he'd given her still lay warm about her neck. She'd forgotten to remove it but liked keeping it close, liked the sentiment and the brush of his fingers on her bare skin as he'd fiddled with the clasp.

The events of the day came floating through her conscience like dandelion down. She'd spoken her vows with all her heart, then grew almost light-headed signing her new name. She would always remember the way Seamus had reached out and steadied her shaking hands, and that tender, half-dazed way he'd regarded her all day as if he couldn't quite come to terms with what they'd done.

She longed to tell him she'd do it all over again, relive every heartrending moment when he'd ridden to Three Chimneys and asked her his stunning question. She sensed he was unsure of her, perhaps thinking she was awash in second thoughts. There'd been none since. Lord willing, there never would be. Not with love for them both filling her to the brim and crowding all doubt out.

Her thoughts leapt ahead, checked by dread. What did she ken about managing an estate? She knew even less about intimate matters. Finishing school hadn't taught such, though she did remember the giggling of girls and the whispering behind fans. Sunk into her studies, she mostly ignored them. Now she wished she'd paid attention. Her dear mother, bless her, had said little. A midwife's motivation was birthing babies, not begetting them.

Lily Cate turned over, flinging out an arm. Sophie curled into her, wishing Seamus was on her other side so that she could be nestled between her two favorite souls like they were a set of bookends.

In the wee small hours when the busy inn finally quieted, she surrendered to sleep.

⬥

Seamus remembered replenishing the fire in the night and standing by the window, measuring the light snow and weighing whether they should continue their journey come morning or turn back. But had no memory of how Sophie came to be beside him, close as his shadow.

He opened his eyes, jolted awake by the fact she was where Lily Cate had been. His daughter must have gotten up in the night to use the chamber pot and crawled back into bed, leaving Sophie in the middle. Sleep had never been this pleasurable. His new wife was all softness and French-milled soap and sighs, where Lily Cate was elbows and knees and half cries.

This close he could make out the sheer linen of her nightgown with its skim of white lace and pleated gathers. All the pins were gone from her hair. It spilled across the pillow like it had no end, begging for a brush or his hungry touch. Firelight danced across her face, and he traced her pale features with his eyes instead of his fingers, a fierce ache pooling in his chest. Fast asleep, she was stirring his senses without even trying.

With a twinge of conscience he rolled away from her, ignoring the voice that said he had every right, that she was his wife. But he couldn't wipe from his mind the fact that she loved someone else. Or what she'd surely been thinking when he proposed.

But you don't love me.

In the absence of love was lust. He'd not dishonor her with that. Nor could he lie with her knowing she thought of someone else. They were at an impasse as felt as any on the battlefield.

Near dawn Lily Cate cried out, and he could feel Sophie rouse slightly, sense her startling as she realized she lay beside him. Gently the mattress shifted and Lily Cate was in the middle again, the wall between them.

And what a high wall it was.

⚬

Seamus was being so careful with her. Had something happened between them in the night? She could remember little, only how puggled she was when she went to bed, and that somehow she'd awakened to find she was between him and Lily Cate. If they'd become one as Scripture said, *that* she would have remembered. But all she felt was her continued quiet elation at being his bride.

Lily Cate kept her preoccupied, sharing her bowl of porridge, bright-eyed as a chipmunk and eager for the next adventure. Another inn awaited after a day spent bumping along rutted roads that seemed to have no end. That night Lily Cate remained between them with no trips to the chamber pot, and they had to gently shake her awake at dawn.

A new world was opening up, Seamus leading. How sheltered her life had been, confined to Three Chimneys and Williamsburg. After fending for herself during the war years, she was only too glad to let him take care of the details.

"You're obviously well-traveled," she said once they set foot in Warm Springs.

"I've been to the continent. London and Edinburgh," he told her, ushering them into the village's only inn. "Your

Scotland is a remarkable place, full of contrasts. Somewhat like Cornwall, where my father was born."

"I was but Lily Cate's age when I left. I hardly recall it."

"If you had, you might have decided to return after all."

For a moment she was nearly upended by doubt. He made Scotland sound so tempting. Had she done wrong by marrying him? *Nay*, her heart was quick to answer.

No second thoughts. No regrets.

He led them to a corner table where they shared a hearty supper. At meal's end she caught him studying her so intently she flushed. "I suppose your best wedding gift is retaining Three Chimneys," he told her with a wink.

Stunned, she stared at him. "But the letter that came, saying the new occupants are arriving April first—"

"Not if we're married, Sophie."

In the muddle of the last few days, she'd forgotten just what matrimony meant. Joy washed through her. Though it would legally become his, Three Chimneys wasn't lost to her.

"I've written to Richmond telling them of our marriage. There's plenty more Tory property to dispense throughout these United States without touching Three Chimneys."

Curtis leapt to mind with the accompanying ache. What would he and her father have to say about her marrying the enemy, a hero of the Revolution? And retaining her mother's estate to boot?

"You're thinking about your brother, no doubt."

She took a sip of lukewarm tea, watching Lily Cate laughing with some children in a corner, where a puppet show was in progress. "Six years since I've seen him. I can't imagine how it was for you being away even longer, in the thick of the fighting."

"I've seen things no man should." He met her eyes in the

haze of candlelight. "But it was worth it, every minute, fighting for freedom, for the greater good, though I lost a great deal personally in the process."

She focused on his wounded hand as it lay fisted on the table between them. "Your injury . . . does it hurt?"

He looked surprised she would ask. "Sometimes it feels whole, nearly fooling me. Mostly it aches, aye." He extended it, and she forced herself to not look away. "Sabers are sharp things. I happened to be in the wrong place at the wrong time."

"How was it fighting under General Washington? Is he really the lion everyone says he is?"

"Everyone is in awe of him and should be. Even the king." He returned his attention to his mostly finished meal. "You'll understand when you meet him, Sophie."

"I'm glad war has an end." Yet she was no longer thinking of that but the way he spoke her name. Slow and thoughtful, as if he liked the way it sounded.

Or was she simply woolgathering?

Lily Cate came back to them, face alight. "Shall we try out the hot springs, Papa?"

"Aye, tonight in the moonlight if there is a moon."

"In my clothes?" Lily Cate asked in wonder. "In the snow?"

Sophie smiled. The prospect sounded almost magical. "You'll wear your bathing costume. One of the maids packed it for you."

"Do you have one?"

"Yes." She'd never seen such an outlandish garment and suspected it had been Anne's. She could only imagine what Seamus would wear.

"Are the pools hot?" Lily Cate persisted.

Seamus finished his ale. "Some are, some aren't."

So he had been here before. On his first honeymoon? Sophie felt an odd disappointment as she looked at the ring glinting on her left hand. Sometimes she felt she was following in Anne's very footsteps, living in her shadow. Was that always the way of it for second wives?

"Papa, how much longer do we have to wait for our room to be ready?"

Seamus got to his feet. "I'll ask."

Leaning closer, Sophie tweaked her nose playfully. "I've brought our sewing and some books till then."

Giggling, Lily Cate snuck her arms round Sophie's waist. "I'm glad you are my mama."

"And I'm glad you're my wee daughter." She kissed the top of Lily Cate's head where the curls were the thickest. Her hair was Seamus's own, black as coffee yet silky enough to pull her fingers through. In the heated traces of her imagination, she dared doing the same with his.

She watched as he made his way round tables and benches to the foyer. Over the past couple days she'd tried not to look at him overlong, but their continued closeness was wearing her down. Was she wrong to half hope that up close she'd see his flaws and the pedestal on which she'd put him would crumble?

He returned with word their room was almost ready. Lily Cate wedged her way between them, sleepy and animated by turns. Sophie's new beloved daughter had brought them together yet somehow, unwittingly, seemed to stand between them. Would she always?

And then there was Anne.

22

Clad in their bathing costumes, Sophie and Lily Cate went by lantern light to the springs behind an attendant, the vapor pluming out of the wooden building like steam from a bottomless kettle. Thankfully, the moon was most obliging, shining full and bright as they made their way along the boardwalk, a chill wind nipping at them and casting a few stray snowflakes about.

Seamus remained in their room, reading by the fire. Sometimes he was so quiet. Preoccupied. Fresh worries flirted with Sophie at every step. Was he bemoaning what they'd done? Wishing the whole affair in Williamsburg would melt away?

Standing on the threshold of the springs, Sophie took in everything in a glance. The sulphurous scent was subtle enough to not be unpleasant, the bathing pool mostly empty this time of night. Sophie smiled at two women leaving the waters, glad for the clasp of Lily Cate's hand.

"Will I be burned, Mama?" Lily Cate drew back, clearly befuddled by the small sea of smoking water.

"Let's test the springs slowly," Sophie told her. "I'll go first and you just put your toes in."

Lily Cate looked on as Sophie started down stone steps into the mist, water eddying around her bare ankles. Seamus had spoken of having a bath connected to the laundry at Tall Acre, piping in hot water to a large copper tub. The fanciful notion might make others laugh, but if it was anything like this, she'd encourage him all she could.

"Oh, 'tis wonderful," she reassured Lily Cate. Seamus had called it *invigorating*. Slowly she slid into the water up to her neck, the heavy tug of wet fabric making her want to shed her bathing costume.

Done with wiggling her toes, Lily Cate held out her arms. Sophie reached for her and lowered her gently into the steaming water.

"I feel like a fish." With a smile twin to Seamus's own, Lily Cate moved away from her, venturing fearlessly toward the other side.

The pool wasn't deep but wide, shaped like an enormous basin. The gravelly, cloudy bottom disguised the springs bubbling at its base. On all sides were changing rooms, a female attendant in waiting. Beyond the arching wooden canopy a white flag was raised, signaling the two hours allotted to the ladies. Taking the waters was indeed a treat.

Expelling a breath, Sophie relaxed as the springs did their healing work. Perhaps tonight she'd sleep. Sharing a bed with Seamus, even with Lily Cate between them, had left her restless and ruminating till breakfast.

"Mama . . ." Lily Cate was tugging at her, drawing her deeper into the water.

Sophie let go of her worries, intent on the present. On building a bond with her new daughter.

She'd best leave Seamus and their hasty marriage to the Lord.

⁂

Miraculously, the weather cleared. Sunlight touched the gentle hills around Warm Springs, coaxing them out of the inn. They shed their capes and hats, though Seamus left on the scarf she'd knitted him. On a rocky ledge looking west to the wilderness, they had a wintry picnic of sorts—cold chicken, cheese, pickles, and biscuits.

Lily Cate stared ominously at the distant mountains. "Papa, are there real Indians over there?" She looked up at him as if he could answer any question put to him. "Who want to take our scalps?"

His dark brows knit together. "Who's been filling your head with such talk?"

"Aunt Charlotte."

Sophie met Seamus's eyes before he replied quietly, "Indians aren't anything for you to worry about. You're safe in Virginia, remember."

Yawning, she nestled between them. Sophie covered her with a quilt from the coach, wishing she could lay down in the puddle of sunlight and nap with her. The springs seemed to have a languorous effect even hours later.

"I sent word to Williamsburg we've married," he said quietly. "The papers will post the announcement. But I've no idea what will happen next." Picking up a small stone, he rubbed it between thumb and forefinger. "Lately it seems pushing west might be the better choice. I've been awarded a tract of land in Kentucky for my service."

"Kentucky? You'd truly leave Tall Acre?"

"Against my will, aye, but it may come to that."

230

She fell silent, her head swimming with questions. "Seamus—" Would she always feel a flood of awkwardness when she said his name? "I would know how all this bad feeling came to be."

A wry smile worked its way across his face. "You have many merits, Sophie Menzies Ogilvy, but your candor and lack of kin are among your very best."

"Meaning relatives can be troublesome." Her thoughts veered from Curtis to Anne, then the diary, bringing a lash of guilt. Though she'd returned it to Anne's desk, the contents still haunted.

"'Tis time you knew how things stand." Seamus tossed the stone toward the western swell of mountains. "When Lily Cate was born, Anne nearly died. I don't know what you recall about that day, but the doctor—and your mother—said a second birth would likely take her life. So I stayed away. Anne became angry with me because I rarely took leave or came home."

"She didn't know about the doctor's warning?"

"I didn't tell her. I wanted to wait till she had healed. She knew I wanted a son and would have felt a failure." The rush of words came to a painful halt as if the past was catching up with him, forcing him to relive something better left alone. "When I returned to camp, I wrote a letter and asked my adjutant to give it to her in the event I died in battle. I explained what the doctor had said about future children. My distance."

She brushed back a strand of hair the wind had pulled free, meeting his eyes. "I don't blame her for being upset, but what you did was—" A great many words whirled in her head and settled. *Brave. Honorable. Even noble.* "You did nothing wrong, Seamus."

"I wonder. In hindsight . . ."

"If you could go back, would you not do the very same?"

He lifted his shoulders. "As it was, Anne became so angry with my perceived neglect, she decided she wanted our daughter raised by her sister and her husband if something happened to her. She'd always been a bit frail, so her worries weren't unfounded. She put her wish in writing and died of a fever not long after."

Sophie looked down at Lily Cate, wondering how much of Anne was in her features. Anne, for all her failings, seemed deserving of understanding too. She'd been lonely, fearful, isolated. Tempted. Unable to understand who or what Seamus was.

"'Twas a terrible, trying situation," she said softly, glad to let it go.

"Aye, what's done is done." There was no rancor in his speech, just raw regret. Though Anne had hurt him deeply by withholding Lily Cate, he was a man too decent to dishonor her memory by speaking disparagingly of her even in death.

A prayer rose in Sophie's heart. For healing. Mending. Peace.

They said no more, lost in their own private thoughts, as the sun dipped lower and a hawk cried out in its circling flight.

⁂

They returned to Tall Acre in a fortnight. Coming into the foyer, Sophie startled to hear the servants call her "Mistress Ogilvy" when she still felt like Miss Menzies.

Nothing had changed but her name.

Would it ever?

She went to her new bedchamber ahead of a servant shouldering her trunk, wondering if Seamus would follow. Leaving the door open, she took stock of her surroundings.

A rich Prussian blue, the milk-paint walls still looked fresh, unmarred by time and use. Delicate Queen Anne furniture predominated save the manly secretary along one wall she guessed had been Seamus's father's. The room was made more homey and familiar by her own counterpane and desk and the embroidered fire screen she'd worked with her own hand. A rag rug of Glynnis's making warmed the plank floor in front of the hearth, a wedding gift.

Spacious and full of light, the bedchamber overlooked the formal garden in back of the house and the Roan River beyond. 'Twas a grown-up room compared to her girlish one at Three Chimneys. She raised her eyes to the lovely plasterwork ceiling, remembering Seamus and Lily Cate were directly overhead. This room had belonged to his parents but had been draped in dust cloths and shut up since their deaths a decade before.

Her mother's bedchamber was remarkably similar. From there she'd dispensed instructions to what had once been a large staff, managing Three Chimneys as best she could. Sophie's father, rarely in residence, wasn't a part of those memories.

Was this beautiful room to be hers alone? The memory of their wedding kiss burned bright, but Seamus hadn't touched her since save handing her in and out of the coach. Might he find her unappealing? Her thinness? Her newness? All the ways she wasn't like Anne? His ring glinted on her finger. Binding. Irrevocable. And raising a hundred questions she couldn't answer.

"Is it to your liking, Sophie?"

She spun around to find him standing in the doorway. Her heart lifted. "I couldn't ask for a lovelier spot."

"My parents were content here. For forty years or better."

"I remember they passed away within a month of each other."

"Shortly before the war, aye." His gaze roamed the room. "My sister, Cosima, and I were born here."

"I've always wanted a sister."

He chuckled. "We'll see what you say after you've met her."

"Is she still in Virginia?"

"Philadelphia. Though once she gets word we've wed, we can expect a visit."

So far he hadn't crossed the threshold. She nearly invited him in but was seized with uncertainty.

"Tomorrow I thought we'd go riding. I need to show you around Tall Acre, have you meet the staff. I tend to rise early, but you may not."

She moved toward the windows and opened the shutters. "I do rise early. It seems a frightful waste of the day otherwise. And I'm always ready to ride, rain or shine."

He was regarding her in that unsettling way he had, as if she'd done or said something that pleased him. "Till tomorrow then."

"You're not going to . . . retire now, are you?"

"Nay. I have business in Roan."

She nearly asked why, but he stole away before she could. Maddening, that. He'd been known for his stealth during the war, slipping in and out and surprising enemy troops. She'd best get used to it here. Only she wasn't the enemy. She was his wife.

Yet she simply felt like his friend.

☙

"Where is Papa?"

The plaintive question brought Sophie's head up. "In

Roan," she answered, forking another bite of chicken pie. Though the words were softly spoken, her voice still resounded to the far corners. The immense dining room, though lovely, was cold and inhospitable for two people. If it was to be just her and Lily Cate, she'd rather resume eating in the small parlor opposite her bedchamber. "He should return soon."

Lily Cate sighed. "I miss him."

Oh? If so, great progress had been made. Since they'd been together night and day on the honeymoon trip till now, his sudden absence was certainly felt.

"Papa seems different when he's with you," Lily Cate said. "He seems . . ." She scrunched up her face in contemplation. "Merry."

"'Tis a nice thought. We should always strive to bring a little cheer."

"Does he make you merry?"

Sophie smiled over the rim of her teacup. More glaikit. Woozy. Upside down. "Yes, indeed."

"I fear he will make you so busy you shall have no more time to play."

Ah, so that was the gist of it. "I shan't be too busy for that."

Lily Cate returned to her meal, still pensive. "I suppose I'm to have a new governess."

Had she overheard them talking? They'd thought her asleep riding home in the coach. "I'll be your teacher till we find just the right one."

"Then I hope we never find one."

"Let's pray we find the *right* one. The dancing master is coming, by the way."

"Who is that?"

"A gentleman who teaches reels and country dances and such. I think you'll adore dancing."

Brightening, Lily Cate sat upright in her chair. "Like Papa danced with me at the ball?"

"Yes." Setting their supper trays aside, Sophie reached for a book on a near table. "What shall it be tonight? *Cendrillon*? Or *La Barbe Bleue*?"

"Not *Bluebeard*," Lily Cate whispered with a glance at the shuttered windows. "It reminds me of the man who was watching me. He had a beard—a black beard."

A rush of dismay nearly made Sophie drop the book. She'd almost forgotten the troublesome trespasser. "*Cendrillon* it is." Settling Lily Cate on her lap, she forced a calm she was far from feeling. "You needn't think of that man anymore. He's gone away."

No more was said as Sophie read aloud till Lily Cate grew sleepy. She hastened upstairs and tucked the girl into bed after prayers were said, making sure the windows were locked and shutters in place and the fire would last through the night.

She'd feel better when Seamus was home. 'Twas her first night alone in a strange bed, and even if he didn't join her, she'd rest better knowing he was near.

She returned to her room downstairs and took out the diary she'd bought at Warm Springs. The leather cover was the deep delft blue of a Continental coat, the pages pristine.

After dipping her quill into a bottle of fresh ink, she penned with disbelief,

18 March, 1784
  I am the mistress of Tall Acre.

23

Morning came, filtering through shutters and curtains and bringing a cold awareness. Though Sophie hadn't heard Seamus return from Roan, she did see him at breakfast.

He greeted her, rising from the dining room table. "You're just in time for our staff meeting."

Staff meeting?

She noticed he never said *servants*. *Staff* was a military term and seemed a more respectful one. They soon sat around the large desk in his study like officers convening. Though out of uniform, Seamus was fully functioning as a general in demeanor and tone. But Riggs and Mrs. Lamont seemed not to mind. Did these meetings occur regularly? Sophie hoped not.

Seamus looked to Riggs, his expression offering a glimpse of his wartime intensity. "I was reviewing your reports from last year, which bear revisiting." He took out some papers. "In one you wrote, 'It gives me real concern that we are making nothing—all our wheat destroyed, our mills idle, and but a short crop of corn. Bad weather, this, for lambs. We have lost more than I could have wished.'" He paused, unearthing a ledger. "We can do little about the weather, but we'll attempt to reverse the losses of past years beginning with collecting rents . . ."

Sophie listened as a plan was laid out for all facets of life at Tall Acre, including those not present but in Seamus's employ and Riggs's oversight—carpenters, bricklayers, brewers and bakers, millers and stable hands. Mrs. Lamont's duties followed and then Sophie's own. The clock struck ten, and Seamus studied it grimly as if time were more adversary than ally.

"Any questions or concerns?" he said at last, taking them in with a glance.

"Some of our children are sick, among them a boy of Alice's who I fear may die." Mrs. Lamont gathered her shawl closer. "Worms, I believe, is the cause of his malady."

"Have you tried the usual remedies? Southernwood and black currant and the like?" At Mrs. Lamont's nod, he said, "Take Mistress Ogilvy with you to see what more can be done, and then send for the doctor."

Listening, Sophie had to remind herself that *she* was the Mistress Ogilvy of whom he spoke.

"If it's more medicine you need, the Roan apothecary should oblige. Let me know by nightfall how the children are faring."

At that, Mrs. Lamont and Riggs excused themselves.

Seamus's eyes found hers. "I'll be out with Riggs this morning but will meet you at the stables around noon."

She gave him a half smile. "Aye, aye, General."

Looking amused, he took a seat on the edge of his desk. "Perhaps I should have *asked* if you would ride with me."

"Dare I defy your order?"

His answering smile was contrite. "Noon then." His gaze fell to the book in her hands. "What is that you're holding?"

"Your mother's housekeeping book." She clutched it to her chest like it was the answer to every question she'd encounter. "I found it in a bedchamber cupboard and have a feeling I'll be needing it."

He nodded thoughtfully, and she went out, stepping into her role as mistress without any inkling of how she would meet his exacting expectations.

And feeling fresh sympathy for Anne.

At noon Seamus met Sophie at the stables, surprising her with a new bay mare. The handsome horse nickered at her approach, tossing its silky head as if seeing if she would startle. With a groom's help she settled into the saddle, and they wasted little time making their way down a side lane to the river, where Seamus inspected the landing.

The wooden structure jutted out into the water on rotund pilings and looked secure, though it creaked beneath his weight as he walked the length of it. Could he swim? The Roan River was deep, but it wasn't a far crossing to the opposite shore. Meadowsweet and wild roses would soon smother its banks, lush and fragrant. Her gaze landed reluctantly on Early Hall.

"I'm expecting a supply of shingles to be delivered this afternoon by sloop. But we can ride till then." He came to stand beside her, looking out across the river at the empty mansion, noting her curiosity.

"'Tis a shame so grand a house has fallen into disrepair," she murmured. No smoke puffed from its many chimneys.

No sign of life enlivened its stony facade. Anne's diary came to bear, tainting the peace of the morning.

I have met a man, the erstwhile master of Early Hall, an Englishman . . .

Seamus bent to adjust her stirrup. "You remember the Earlys?"

"Curtis spent time there. The heir was a friend of his." She felt a bit duplicitous saying so little. Anne's diary had told her far more. Far too much.

"If you recall, the owner was a former Virginia burgess. He returned to England during the war and has been heard of no more."

"Is it confiscated Tory property?"

"Mayhap." With a shrug of his shoulders, he swung himself effortlessly into the saddle. Vulcan snorted, ready to be off.

Sophie stole a last look at the abandoned house. What had become of Anne's riding chair, the one she'd used her last summer at Tall Acre? Was it still in the stables? Perhaps it could be of use to her and Lily Cate.

As they set out down a back lane, Riggs approached, concerned with yet another domestic detail that needed to be dealt with immediately.

"I guess the moral of this story is never return from eight years of war and a fortnight's honeymoon and expect anything but chaos," Seamus remarked without exasperation as Riggs rode away.

Sophie said nothing to this, holding tight to their private time at Warm Springs, unromantic as it was, amidst the sudden busyness. Turning in the saddle, she waved at Lily Cate, who watched from an upstairs window, her face pressed to the glass.

"Seamus, there's something I need to tell you about the stranger Lily Cate has seen. It may be of little consequence, but last night she told me he has a beard. A black beard."

His eyes were sharp. "She's not seen him of late." It wasn't a question, rather a dare to say otherwise.

"She says not."

"Anything else?"

She shook her head, and he grew quiet, making her fear she'd tainted the peace of the morning with such talk. They rode west, skirting the weathered fence line that hemmed in crops and livestock, sunlight warming their backs. The bearded stranger faded to nothingness, swallowed up by the ever-changing landscape.

"Spring has always been my favorite season, in war and out," he told her.

"Oh aye," she agreed. Finally, winter was loosening its grip, and summer's heat with its oppressive swarm of insects had yet to set in. Awed by the hills and valleys stretching without end, she said, "I didn't realize Tall Acre was so vast."

"Five thousand acres is a bit ambitious for one man to manage even with the best of help."

She frowned. A great deal needed to be done to reverse the years of absence if Tall Acre was to turn profitable again. But with so many slaves freed . . .

"I know what you're thinking, Sophie. I can see it in your face. The work will get done with or without them. Half the freedmen are staying on, and new indentures are coming. There are tenants aplenty."

Indeed, cottage after cottage met her eye as they cantered past. Tall Acre lay like a brown quilt, pieced together in patches, tenants farming sections and paying rent to the estate. Minutes bled into one hour, then two. They finally stopped at a far-flung gate, where he dismounted and took tools from his saddlebag to mend it.

She looked east, thinking of her own tumbled fences. "Three Chimneys could always be sold."

"You would do that?"

"'Tis yours, Seamus, remember."

"'Tis ours, Sophie." The way he said it, the lingering look he gave her, sent her stomach somersaulting again.

Slipping free of the saddle, she gave an affectionate stroke down her mare's muzzle and watched Seamus at work. A neat row of nails and a repaired latch soon held the once sagging gate in place and the roaming sheep in. "You're a carpenter as much as a soldier, I see."

"Aye, and a planter too. We'll be sowing winter wheat by week's end, Lord willing." He returned the tools to his saddlebag. "The Almanack calls for an early spring."

He sounded so sure, so confident. "I, on the other hand, hardly know where to start."

With a wink, he handed her a canteen. "I have no trouble giving orders."

She took a long drink. "Let's hope I have no trouble following them."

"'Tis no trouble, surely. You simply need to oversee the staff and dependencies from dawn till dusk, quell any riots or runaways, and hand me regular reports about the state of each."

Amused, she pressed a hand to her lips to hold her mouthful of water in.

"The dairy and spinning house are your foremost concerns," he said, all levity gone.

Mention of the spinning house left her half sick. She wanted to scrub Anne's caustic references to it from her mind.

"Tend to Lily Cate like you're doing. That's most important of all."

"I wonder if I can be what she needs. The mother she needs."

"You might not have the makings of a midwife," he said without hesitation. "But you're a born mother if there ever was one."

Then let me give you a son.

She nearly shut her eyes as the thought stained her conscience. A wanton wish, perhaps. Yet Seamus's own words leapt to mind, mingling with her own longings to create a small storm.

She knew I wanted a son . . .

Ever since he'd shared the intimacy about Anne, Sophie's imagination had taken untold liberties. She wanted to give him the son he wanted, the son she wanted. She'd long dreamed of a houseful of children. Lily Cate was only the start.

He squinted at the sky. "I need to return to the landing, and you need to meet the rest of the staff. Mrs. Lamont will introduce you properly when you're ready." Bending, he locked his fingers, giving her boot firm footing so she could remount. "If you ever have trouble with anyone, come to me first."

There was a subtle warning in the words easily taken to heart. Anne had had trouble. With Riggs. Myrtilla. Perhaps others. Sophie prayed she'd win the staff over from the start.

※

So this was Myrtilla.

Sophie knew at first glance why she'd been troublesome for Anne. Myrtilla locked eyes with her the moment she set foot in the spinning house, erasing every hope Sophie had of her being a docile servant. Her expression was stony, but she was a handsome woman, younger than Sophie had imagined, with a proud, almost regal bearing. At sight of Sophie, she all but turned her back.

All Sophie knew of Myrtilla was what she'd gleaned from the diary and Evelyn Menzies's unfortunate role in her stillborn baby's birth. After she'd lost her own child, Myrtilla had been Lily Cate's wet nurse. She'd continued to care for Lily Cate because Anne could not or would not. She was devoted to Tall Acre, to Seamus. It was he who had saved her and her brother from an abusive slave trader before the war.

Sophie stood by Mrs. Lamont and took in the activity in the busy room. Half a dozen spinning wheels were in motion, their gentle whirr creating a slight draft. A hefty loom claimed one corner, operated by a thickset weaver. Hanging from racks were finished linens, a tablecloth, and assorted garments ready for dyeing.

"Spinning and weaving go on here from sunup to sundown," Mrs. Lamont told her. "The women are allowed regular breaks and a generous dinner hour. General Ogilvy doesn't like the girls to be too young when they start."

"Does the spun cloth provide for all of Tall Acre's needs?"

"Yes, nearly everything is made right here on the estate. There's little need to order from Philadelphia or elsewhere." With a keen eye, Mrs. Lamont examined a coverlet. "Spinning is something of a coveted spot, far preferable to field work."

Sophie could well understand why. The heat and horseflies alone made outdoor work grueling. With its wide windows and lofty ceilings, the spinning house provided a cooler workplace in the summer and a snug one in the winter.

"When Mistress Ogilvy—the first Mistress Ogilvy, mind you—was alive, she would visit each dependency, treat any sickness . . . Of course, you may do as you wish." Mrs. Lamont led her back outside.

Sophie was relieved when they parted. All their walking to and fro, the memory required for names and places, was daunting. She'd created a mental map of sorts, but in truth all the dependencies looked alike and there was a veritable maze of them. Her heart pulled her to the quiet orderliness of the stillroom situated by the summer kitchen. Once Seamus's mother's domain, the stillroom was low-ceilinged and suggested usefulness, an odor of withered herbs and flowers clinging to the air. It seemed to be waiting for her to claim it, though it was the infirmary, smelling of camphor and holding four tiny patients that needed her now.

As she checked each child for fever and administered the tonic on hand, she prayed for wisdom. One boy in particular was very ill, his mother at his side. The doctor had been sent for, but there'd been a delay.

Heartsore, she returned to the house to find Lily Cate waiting on the rear veranda in cape and bonnet. "Mrs. Lamont said I should take you to the nursery as she forgot."

The nursery? Yet another dependency? Hand in hand they traversed the shell path to another building newly painted white. Inside, two women tended a roomful of young children. Sophie was thankful to find it clean, even cozy, the upraised brick hearth burning brightly and encased with a protective screen lest the children come too close.

Lily Cate introduced her and then began playing, her delighted expression making Sophie realize how much she needed to be with other children. Once the weather warmed and they could be out of doors, she wanted Lily Cate to be the child she was, barefoot and carefree.

"Afternoon, Mistress Ogilvy." Shay's wife, Kaye, returned Sophie's greeting as she nursed her son near the hearth.

There were other newborns present, making Sophie's arms nearly ache.

"You fond o' squallin' babies, Mistress Ogilvy?" A plump, apron-clad woman gave her a near-toothless grin. "Sounds like a bunch o' calves bawlin' in a hailstorm to me."

Chuckling, Sophie sat down in an empty chair. "Reminds me of my mother's days as midwife."

"I remember too, God bless her." The woman gave a bounce to the fretting child in her lap. "My name's Granny Bea. This here's my grandbaby, Bristol."

The tiny boy looked up at Sophie, and his crying hushed. He reached out a plump hand and touched the chatelaine pinned to her bodice when Sophie took him on her lap. "Can you tell me the names of the others? I won't remember them all, but I'll try."

A bony finger pointed round the room. "There's Opey, Kitty, Doll, Paris, Truman, Cleve, Carter, Jenny, and Miss Lily Cate."

Lily Cate was kneeling now, wide-eyed over a spinning top. A girl her own size stood beside her, her ebony hair a mass of velvety ringlets. Myrtilla's daughter Jenny? Half-caste, she stood out noticeably among her darker playmates.

Despite the spilled milk and soiled clout odor, there was peace and a sense of purpose here. A vibrant heartbeat of a place. Sophie dandled the baby on her knee, speaking quietly with Bea and watching the children play. Her sense of wonder grew. She finally had a purpose. A plan. 'Twas overwhelming but . . . good.

God had given her so much. Those long, bleak years of hunger and isolation at Three Chimneys made her present circumstances seem like nothing short of a miracle.

Even without a husband's affection.

⁂

"Papa said we're to eat in the small parlor instead of the dining room, but he's not here," Lily Cate told her that night at supper. "And tomorrow is his birthday."

"Birthday?" Sophie felt a start. Yet another detail she didn't know. "Are you sure?"

With a solemn nod, Lily Cate nibbled on a biscuit. "Florie said so."

So Florie knew . . . while the mistress of Tall Acre didn't have a clue. "Then we must plan a little party for him. A surprise."

Lily Cate's brow furrowed. "What if he doesn't come?"

"Well, last night required he ride to Roan, and tonight . . ." Sophie overheard voices coming from the study. Tonight he was meeting with Riggs. Again. If Riggs wore a petticoat, she'd be green with envy.

"His supper will get cold," Lily Cate pointed out with a frown.

"No matter." Sophie tweaked her nose gently and she laughed. "Cook is keeping it warm in the kitchen. Perhaps 'tis providential he's not here. All the better for birthday surprises. Do you know what he likes best to eat? Should we have a celebratory sweet?"

"Best ask Florie."

Oh? She'd met the glib Florie and decided she was simply smitten with the master, a common happenstance in large households. An indentured housemaid, Florie had a mother in the dairy, a father in the fields, and a brother in the stables. Sophie was sorely tempted to move her to the spinning house.

As Lily Cate finished her pudding, Sophie roamed the room, leaving her own dessert half eaten. Like her bedchamber across the hall, the small parlor reminded Sophie of spring with its pale mint walls and floral wainscoting. Though it was seldom used, Seamus had left his mark here. A pair of field glasses and a chess set rested on a near table. Above the fireplace was a portrait of his parents, both bearing a marked resemblance to Seamus. Was it any wonder she missed him when everywhere she turned bore some reminder?

Seeking a distraction, she returned to her sewing basket. Lily Cate soon sidled up to her, asking for her sampler.

"Twelve stitches to the inch," Sophie reminded gently, her silver thimble glinting on her finger much as her wedding ring glinted on her hand.

As she plied the soft fabric of a petticoat, a noise sounded in the hall. Her heart jumped. Would Seamus join them? On their honeymoon she'd grown used to his slow smile and measured way of speaking, his studied patience with his little daughter, and even his occasional bumbling.

She heard his rumbling voice, measured and distinct, as he and Riggs emerged from the study.

Then the riverfront door closed, and all her hopes along with it.

24

The birthday cake had been made, a special supper prepared of Seamus's favorite dishes. Cream of peanut soup. Spiced ham. Sweet potatoes with coconut. String beans with mushrooms. Sophie recalled what Seamus's mother had penned in the back of her housekeeping book.

Let the wife make her husband glad to come home.

But Seamus did not come.

"He's been out foxhunting," Mrs. Lamont told her as night closed in. "But now he's down at the stables again as his favorite mare is foaling. I don't expect he'll be back anytime soon."

Her apologetic tone fueled Sophie's disappointment. She should have asked him about his plans for supper, given some warning, if only for Lily Cate's sake. Their wee daughter stood waiting in the small parlor, a fresh painting of a horse in hand, eyes swimming.

"We'll put your picture on his desk along with the cake so he can see we were thinking about him on his birthday," Sophie said.

"Well, he isn't thinking of us!" she exclaimed, a tear falling free.

Sophie swiped at her cheek with a handkerchief, feeling near tears herself. Being told of her husband's birthday and whereabouts by servants didn't set well, but what was she to do? Theirs was an odd arrangement. She'd known that before the wedding. Who was she to bemoan it after?

"Your father is a busy man, and we'd best get used to that. We have each other in the meantime."

Lily Cate brightened. "And Sassy!"

"Sassy, yes," Sophie echoed, smiling down at the kitten at their feet. "We have our very own list of things to do. Tomorrow we must go to Roan for new stays and pay a visit to Mistress Murdo at Three Chimneys."

"Then we shall be as busy as Papa is."

"We shall indeed."

Seemingly satisfied, Lily Cate wandered about the room, looking through the *vue d'optique* on a corner table and exclaiming over the lifelike pictures while Sophie sat down at the harpsichord, a smaller version of the one in the Palladian room. The ivory keys were cool beneath her fingers. One tentative touch to them brought the room to life. No music graced the stand, but a once beloved piece by Scarlatti played in her head. Her fingers felt rusty. Dusty. *Free*. She'd nearly forgotten the joy of it.

Lily Cate was soon by her side, and they began singing a simple tune. Lily Cate had a sweet soprano, leaving Sophie to wonder about Seamus. Did he like to sing? His voice was rich and sonorous even when he was speaking. They sang on till Lily Cate did more yawning than singing and needed to be abed.

With Lily Cate asleep, the night stretched before Sophie

without end. She returned to the small parlor, wishing she'd not made such a ridiculous effort to look nice for naught. She had on her wedding dress, his gift of pearls about her throat. A maid wielding curling tongs had added unnecessary ringlets parading down her back. She'd even been too liberal with her cologne, smelling like a veritable garden, thanks to Yardley of London.

Across from her, the chair that had been Seamus's father's was empty. Less than a month wed, had they already established a pattern of separation? The coldness of it stole over her, and she couldn't find her way past it. Had she not lost her heart to him, it wouldn't hurt so wide and deep. But if she complained or grew bitter, she'd simply push him farther away.

She focused on the portraits of his parents, somewhat solaced. If she couldn't have all of him, she could have some of him. His name. His daughter. His house. His history. She was part of a family again, however fractured.

Who was she to ask for more?

❦

By lantern light the foal emerged, bringing with it a relieved exhilaration. Sitting back on his haunches, Seamus watched as the mare nickered and nuzzled her newborn, welcoming it into the dusty confines of the stall where it would soon attempt to stand. The markings of each, whether colt or filly, were always unique. New life always renewed his sense of wonder, pushing back the punishing memories of war.

Once the foal was on its feet, Seamus left the head groom to oversee the rest. He emerged from the stables, gaze on the ground, nearly missing the moon's alluring rise. He was struck nigh speechless by the stars. Orion's belt had never been so bright, the North Star so chilling and sharp. Awed, he leaned into a near paddock, feeling small. Swallowed up by the vastness. Another light caught his eye, this one from a back window of Tall Acre.

Had Sophie not yet gone to bed? He'd heard music earlier, and it had drawn him much as his mother's playing used to. He'd given little thought to the pianoforte being one of Sophie's accomplishments. Anne had not been musical, and he gave silent thanks. Her memory couldn't interfere with his present pleasure.

He pulled his gaze from the house. Beneath a starlit sky, it was all too easy to forget there was anything pressing in, demanding notice. No rotting roof. No piazza in need of replacing. No mulish tenants and indentures. No new wife and needy daughter. No barely quelled rebellion in Rhode Island or riots in New Hampshire. The newly formed American government was on as shaky ground as he.

He bent his head, an uneasy longing stealing over him much like the drowsy silence stealing over Tall Acre. For a few seconds he gave in to the notion of asking Sophie to go to Richmond with him next, show her about town. She might want to select some things for the house. Though he could ill afford the time, being together might curb the restlessness mounting inside him.

He'd thought all he had to do was marry and the matter with Lily Cate would be settled. He hadn't anticipated a new set of obstacles. Separate schedules. Separate rooms. Sidestepping around each other. Whenever he said goodnight and retired upstairs, he felt in violation of the biblical commands regarding marriage. Yet hadn't he asked her to wed him on the most practical terms, as a mother to his daughter?

What in heaven's name had he been thinking?

Aye, it was owing to his botched handling of Sophie Menzies Ogilvy that accounted for his feeling lurched.

The big house was hushed. At almost midnight, the staff were abed. Though Mrs. Lamont had left a light burning on a sideboard in the foyer, it took Seamus a moment to get his bearings. To his right, the door to the small parlor stood ajar. Weary as he was, he almost overlooked it, intent on the sweep of staircase leading to his room. Usually closed, the door held an invitation. He stood on the threshold of what Sophie called the family parlor—somewhat ironic in light of their present circumstances—and looked within.

A fire still burned, as did a lone candle. The Windsor chairs fronting the hearth faced away from him, but he caught the shimmer of silk in the flickering light. A hint of cologne, an intoxicating blend of citrus and flowers, charged the air.

He ran a hand over his unkempt hair now missing a queue ribbon. He'd washed up in the laundry before coming in, though he still smelled of sweat and horseflesh. Mindful of his boots, he stepped into the parlor carefully. Was she sleeping?

A creak in the floorboards brought her upright. He hadn't meant to wake her, but neither could he leave her in her chair. But what would he have done? Carried her to her room?

His voice cut into the quiet. "I didn't mean to startle you."

Looking surprised, she stood and faced him. Her hand went to her hair, as disheveled as his own and coming free of its pins. He was cast back to their honeymoon when she'd come to bed with it unbound and falling to her hips. In her lovely gown with its snug bodice and lace sleeves, she looked different than on their wedding day. Fuller of figure. Not so fragile. Or mayhap he was seeing her with new eyes.

She smiled a sleepy smile. "You've been out foxhunting, Mrs. Lamont said."

"Aye, but caught nothing after a five-hour run." He rued the leisure time but had needed to curb his mounting restlessness.

"How is your new foal?"

"On its feet," he replied, stifling a yawn. Did she want to talk? At this hour? "And you? How goes it with the staff?" When she delayed answering, he said, "A woman's work is never done, aye?"

Her eyes held his. "I wasn't the one late for supper, Seamus."

He chuckled. A sense of fullness stole through him at her teasing. And then there was that chafing again, the certainty that she'd rather be standing here with someone else.

"At the end of my rounds I spent time in the nursery today," she was saying. "Lily Cate seemed glad to be there. I think she could benefit from Jenny coming up to the house. They seem to be about the same age."

"Jenny . . ." After he'd been so long away, some of the people, as his father had called them, were as new to him as they were to her. "That would be Riggs's daughter."

"Riggs, your estate manager?" She looked at him, a slow awareness dawning. "But . . ."

"A great many things went on in my absence that I'm not proud of." He left it at that. "So you think Lily Cate needs company."

"She shouldn't be raised in isolation like I was." Compassion warmed her eyes. "Until Williamsburg, I had few if any friends. The neighboring plantations were too far, and my father forbade any play with the servants."

He wasn't surprised. Lord Menzies had been rigidly class conscious, yet here sat his daughter aiming for the opposite. "Jenny's too young yet to work at anything but the simplest chores. I don't see how spending time at the house could hurt."

"I've also written about a Scots tutor but wanted you to look the letter over before I post it."

"A tutor, aye." He'd already forgotten, but Sophie seemed to have a head for the details he didn't, especially where Lily Cate was concerned. "Leave it on my desk then. If that sounds like an order, it isn't."

She gave him a half smile as he came nearer the fire, suddenly chilled. They stood an arm's length apart in the flickering amber light, her silhouette soft—and uncommonly dressy. "Did I miss something?" He felt a bit foolish, out of step. "You're in your lovely gown . . ."

"'Tis your birthday, Seamus."

So she'd dressed up . . . for him? Astonishment rushed in as the mantel clock struck midnight. "It *was* my birthday, aye." Such things meant little to him, but they obviously meant something to her.

Her eyes turned searching. "I don't even know how old you are."

"Older than you, I'll wager, at one and thirty."

"Only by a wee bit."

"You're not going to tell me, are you?" Suddenly he felt the need to know.

"Why should I?" She was regarding him in that warmly candid way she had. "Ladies don't usually reveal their age."

"But . . ." He held her blue gaze. "You're my bride."

Her expression changed. Softened. She liked that he'd called her his. He could sense it, feel it, in the very air between them. What's more, he liked saying it. Yet the words held an untested intimacy that made him want to retreat. "As your husband I would know your age, Sophie."

She sat back down, skirts rustling faintly. "Eight and twenty."

He took the chair opposite. "I would have a good deal more." At her inquiring look he continued, "We've only touched the surface."

"You sound as if we're playing parlor games, Seamus."

"Why not?"

"Well . . ." She glanced at the clock. "'Tis late. You need your rest. Sleep is obviously more appealing than sitting here questioning me."

"According to whom?" When she hesitated, he said with more conviction than he felt, "Ask me anything."

Surprise lit her eyes. "Anything? A question for a question?" At his nod, she folded her hands in her lap, thoughtful. "Why do I see a scar there below your jawline?"

His hand rose to meet it. "You'd best ask my sister, Cosima. Suffice it to say she threw a rock at me when we were small. When you meet her, you'll understand."

She let out a chuckle. "Your turn."

He studied her, memory catching fire. "Your brother never called you *Sophie*. When he talked about you he used a nickname, but I cannot recall it." For a moment he regretted mentioning it, but she gave him a pensive smile.

"When we were wee, Curtis could never pronounce *Sophie*, so he took to calling me *Posie* instead. 'Tis something I miss." Breaking their gaze, her eyes roamed the shadows. "Why have you never made any changes here at Tall Acre?"

"The staff told you that, I suppose." Suddenly he was all too aware of the portraits above the mantel, and his parents'

256

contentment with Tall Acre and each other. "This has always seemed more my father's home than mine. I still don't feel it belongs to me." He might as well admit the rest. "Anne never liked it here, so no alterations were ever made."

"'Tis a beautiful place, even more so than Three Chimneys." A new intensity shone in her eyes. "I don't understand why anyone would spurn it."

His gaze traveled to the fire. "Do you remember Anne?"

She paused. "I only remember coming here soon after you wed and then when Lily Cate was born. Perhaps Anne and I might have been friends had I come more often."

"I wonder." Doubt clouded his voice. "The two of you . . ." He left it unsaid, sorry the moment had turned melancholy. Sometimes Anne's unhappy spirit seemed to linger. He prayed Sophie's presence would drive the bitter memories out.

Her silky voice pulled him back from the brink. "Why is your horse called Vulcan?"

The soreness inside him ebbed. "Vulcan is the god of fire. My stallion was so named because he was less skittish than any other mount under fire, even cannon fire." His gaze rested on her throat. "Where did you get that cameo you're wearing?"

Her hand went to the beloved jewelry. "'Twas my grandmother's and is made of Scottish agates. I've always liked the color pink."

Did she? He made a mental note of it.

She was looking at him again, at his mangled hand half hidden in his coat sleeve, a bad habit he'd gotten into on account of Lily Cate. Her face showed a telling empathy. "How did you come by your injury?"

Their questions were becoming more personal, the hour late, but neither he nor she showed any inclination to stop.

"I was in the wrong place at the wrong time behind enemy lines. Some Hessians ambushed me—" The wound was aching again, driving home that very dangerous moment. "They tried to—um, dispatch me, but one simply ruined my hand." He couldn't tell her all the rest. His blinding fury. The boy soldier who'd died. The moment his prayers stopped.

She looked to her lap as if giving him privacy—or mayhap his injury repulsed her too. He said, "Does it bother you, being wed to a maimed man?"

The protest in her eyes quelled all doubt. "Nay, Seamus. 'Tis the man beneath that matters most. Do you question that?"

With a shrug of his shoulders, he fixed his gaze on the fire. Another far riskier query pulled at his conscience. Unasked, it was burning a hole inside him. "Why did you agree to marry me, Sophie?" He held still, giving her room to answer or not as all the obvious reasons resounded in his head.

Because I was about to lose Three Chimneys. Because Curtis isn't coming back. Because I am estranged from my father and had nowhere else to go . . .

"Because I love Lily Cate and I want you both to be happy." She spoke without reservation. "I want to be a part of that, have a family."

He warmed to the truth of it. There was no doubt she loved his daughter. But he'd had no inkling his happiness mattered to her. Emboldened, he met her eyes, fighting a sudden breathlessness. "What I really want to know is if you're still in love with the man you told me about."

She looked away, but not before he saw alarm flood her eyes. "'Tis my turn, Seamus, not yours, remember."

"Sophie, I—"

"What does it matter, truly?"

The tables were turned. He fisted his good hand.

Because the thought of another man, another man's memory, is driving me mad.

She stood in a swish of skirts and excused herself, moving toward the hall and her bedchamber. The door between them closed with a forbidding click.

A sick regret gripped him. He'd gone too far. Tried to scale too high a wall and burned a bridge instead. He knew better than to try to gain some ground between them. He'd violated his own personal vow to keep his distance, and this was his punishment.

Theirs was a marriage in name only. Nothing more. 'Twas folly to wish otherwise.

25

"So who do you think will arrive first?" Sophie broached the question the next morning over breakfast. "Your aunt Cosima or the dancing master?"

"Aunt Cosima!" Lily Cate said with relish, finishing her porridge.

"You may be right. We just received word she's on her way."

Lily Cate licked a smidgen of jam off her thumb. "Is a new governess coming too?"

"Your father has decided on a Scottish tutor like he had as a boy. But I'll teach you till he comes."

"Did Papa show you the schoolhouse?"

Sophie searched her memory and came up short. "Why don't you take me there after breakfast?"

In minutes they stood on the threshold of the sole dependency Sophie hadn't seen. Nearly obscured by the garden's boxwood hedge, the schoolhouse went largely unnoticed. Inside, the knotty pine floors and streaked windows bespoke age and disuse. Little more than a playroom with a few desks and a small hearth, it boasted several south-facing windows. Sophie was charmed outright.

"Perhaps we'll have school right here once I see if the chimney's in working order. Do you think Jenny would like to learn to read and write like you?"

"Oh aye!" Lily Cate mimicked. "I can teach Jenny her letters like you taught me!"

Sophie laughed, Lily Cate's joy contagious. Together they took stock of the peeling walls, chipped wainscoting, and scuffed floor. "I'll see about having it painted, inside and out. For now we'll hold lessons in the small parlor till everything is ready."

She was fairly confident of Seamus's support of her endeavor. Since Anne hadn't taken the initiative to do much at Tall Acre, she suspected he welcomed change, however small. Or might he be in a less than gracious mood given their midnight stalemate?

As she thought it, a roll of thunder resounded, making Lily Cate cover her ears. Lately one spring storm ran into the next. Taking her hand, Sophie led her down a shell walk into the heart of the garden beneath a fickle play of sun and clouds, the scent of rain clinging to the air.

"My favorites, the daylilies and old roses, will return soon," Sophie told her, pointing out various plantings.

Crocuses and early violets peeked from newly weeded beds while blooming cherry and pear trees branched over low brick walls, creating a lacy canopy overhead. But Lily Cate was intent on something else entirely.

"Are you looking for something?" Sophie asked her.

She expelled a little breath. "I no longer see that bearded man on the lawn. Not since Papa chased him away. Now I see a light."

"A light?"

"Sometimes I wake up in the night and see a light shining at that house across the river." Sophie followed Lily Cate's pointing finger. Like an enticing toy just beyond a child's reach, Early Hall was fixed squarely in their vision on its crest of sloping, overgrown lawn. "The light is bright like a star, but it's always gone by morning."

Sophie felt a chill. "Do you see it often?"

Lily Cate looked up at her, so much of Seamus in her face. "Sometimes it's shining. Sometimes not."

Sophie squeezed her hand. "Next time you see the light, I want you to wake me or your father so we can see it too."

Though she tried to bury the entire matter as she made her rounds that morning, Lily Cate's revelation threaded through Sophie's thoughts, needling as a thorn.

Some vagabond might be trespassing, seeking shelter beneath Early Hall's sagging roof. Even a runaway slave might take temporary refuge. So many roamed about the countryside, displaced by the war. The trespasser at Tall Acre might be nothing more than that.

But she would need to tell Seamus just in case.

※

Seamus noticed his field hands before he noticed her. They stood at attention as Sophie rode into view, coming at a half gallop across the pasture. There was no denying she was a fine figure on a horse. She sat on her mount confidently, the new sidesaddle he'd ordered from Biddle in Philadelphia beneath her. There was a sense of purpose, an aliveness in her stride that made him proud. And then apprehension rode in.

She rarely came looking for him. He feared it involved Lily Cate. While he went about estate business, Sophie usually stayed close to the house, managing things as best she could. Sometimes a day or more would pass and he wouldn't see her. If he rose early and came in late, he missed her altogether. But he couldn't dodge the guilt he felt doing so. Or his quiet delight at first sight of her today.

She'd timed her visit well. Now almost noon, the hands would be after their dinner, leaving the two of them alone. At the sound of the bell clanging across the pasture, they dispersed, bent on Tall Acre.

He was suddenly conscious that he looked like a field hand, stripped of his coat, shirtsleeves rolled up. He'd been demonstrating how he wanted the sunken ditches built, those quaintly named ha-has that hemmed in the livestock without impairing the view. Raising a sleeve, he swiped at his brow and spied his queue ribbon near his boot. He snatched it up and soon had his hair hastily tied, at least.

Perhaps now was the time to move past the unsettling question he'd put to her recently and apologize. In the privacy of the small parlor, he'd simply wanted to know if the man she loved still had a hold on her heart. But given her reaction, he'd been wrong to ask.

She flashed him a disarming smile, no hint of tension about her, and slid to the ground in one graceful motion beneath the growl of thunder and a sprinkle of rain.

"You've not come to tell me my sister is here, have you?"

"Indeed," she replied, seeming a bit remote beneath her riding hat and veil. "Cosima has just stormed Tall Acre."

He rubbed his jaw and cast a look at the house. "I don't doubt it."

"Lily Cate and I served tea and showed her to her room. She'll join us later for supper, provided it isn't mutton and includes cherry bounce."

He chuckled. Coming nearer, he wanted to brush aside the veil of her riding hat to better see her face. "Is that all you've come to tell me? No more bearded trespassers or strange lights?"

Her smile dimmed. She reached into her pocket and withdrew a letter. "Just this. From Williamsburg."

He took it grudgingly. "'Tis the second post from the Fitzhughs. They've obtained a court order that Lily Cate is to visit them."

"Oh?" Concern creased her face. "When? How long?"

"Soon. For a week."

"Perhaps if you go along with it this once, the strain will ease."

He didn't share her optimism, but he wouldn't naysay it either. "Mayhap."

"There's no way to stop her going?"

"Not unless I want to defy the Virginia court."

"Perhaps her visit will be a bridge. Mend matters with Anne's kin."

"Then why do I feel such dread at her going?" He tucked the post away, giving vent to his unease. "'Twas the same before certain battles, that sure sense we were about to lose something huge and unalterable. We always did. I never felt that way before a fight we won. Call it uncanny, but I never erred. Not once."

"Then we'll continue to pray our way through." Her calm was enviable. "Entrust her to the One who loves her most."

"I'm hardly doing that," he admitted. "Not properly."

She spread her hands entreatingly. "Since when do prayers have to be proper? The Lord hears our prayers, Seamus, fitly spoken or not." She studied him a long, dissecting moment.

"What else is troubling you? Something beyond Lily Cate, I think."

"I simply want to move forward, cut ties with the past, including Anne's relatives. I want my daughter to be my daughter, not farmed out to kin I question. I want you to be my wife, with no thought of the woman who came before you."

Or no thought of the man who came before me.

She looked suddenly troubled. He felt a nagging remorse for such plain speaking. He wanted to make the whole unsavory matter go away, but there was no fixing this. "We'll tell Lily Cate about Williamsburg once Cosima leaves. I don't want anything spoiling her visit."

"Does your sister know about the trouble in Williamsburg?"

"Nay." Knowing Cosima, she'd ride right up to Fitzhugh's chambers and argue him into changing the court order. "'Tis probably better left unsaid. My sister is a bit of a firebrand."

"I'd already gathered that." She fingered her veil as it blew in the wind, finally lifting it so he could better see her. "She is delightfully different. Lily Cate adores her. She's brought her parrot along, by the way."

He rolled his eyes. Cosima's eccentricities had long aggravated and amused him. No telling what was in store this visit. They'd not have a moment's peace—a moment alone—for some time. Emboldened by the thought, he began, "About the other night . . ."

She looked up at him, her clear gaze sending an undeniable melting through his belly.

"'Twas a rude question I asked you. I know better, and I apologize."

"I owe you an answer."

"You owe me nothing, Sophie."

A hawk swooped low, its raucous cry making her startle. He swallowed, nervous as a schoolboy, his next words broken by a sharp hallooing from the east. Turning, he saw his sister coming their way atop his prized thoroughbred, the horse barely broken, and astride to boot.

The visit had begun.

⁂

"Look, Papa! I can play the drums that Aunt Cosima brought me!" Lily Cate was beaming at him from across the small parlor, devilry in her expression. She began a rat-a-tat that rivaled the Continental Army's finest drummer boy. For a moment Seamus was cast back to long marches and transmitting orders by fife and drum on war-torn battlefields.

Glancing at his sister, who sat beside him, he asked mockingly, "What instrument *didn't* you bring my daughter?"

"I only brought the very noisy ones," Cosima replied with an impish smile that rivaled Lily Cate's.

His gaze returned to the tin trumpet and a child's fiddle strewn atop the rug, waiting to be played. Sophie was sitting near Lily Cate, admiring a whistle on a long silver chain. Seamus hoped she wouldn't blow it. "I'd rather you have hauled down a harp from Philadelphia. Fiddles and trumpets are male instruments, remember."

"Posh! Times are changing, Seamus. You, an officer of the Revolution, should know that better than anyone. Besides, you mustn't mind my spoiling her. I haven't seen her for years, not with the Fitzhughs denying me a wartime visit. She's my only niece, after all. Though I do hope you're going to rectify that in time."

"In time," he replied noncommittally, eyes on Sophie.

"You've done well with your new bride, Seamus. I never

cared for Anne, God rest her. But Sophie . . ." She smiled as a maid brought round a tea tray. "Sophie has heart."

His throat tightened. He'd never thought to hear Cosima praise her so soon. He'd always admired this new wife of his, but now, when she was near at hand, when he could study her in small, unguarded moments, his admiration—and his frustration—grew. Sophie had a curious effect on him, sitting there like a tray of treacle he couldn't have.

"Simply put, I adore her."

"Mayhap by the end of the visit, you'll find something not to your liking," he said, their familiar banter of old taking hold.

"Hush," she shot back, busying herself with sugar and cream. "Truly, Seamus. She's lovely. She's also candid and engaging and remarkably well read. She's even—"

"She's in love with someone else."

"Oh?" Her greenish gaze swiveled back to him. "Then why did you wed her? Or perhaps the better question is, why did she wed you?"

"The man she cared for didn't care for her." The words came hard, but there was no skirting the truth. "She was about to lose her home and had few options."

The drums quieted as Lily Cate switched to the fiddle, but the hammering in Seamus's chest stayed steadfast. Perhaps Sophie would have been better off in Edinburgh. If he'd not intervened, she would be on her way there now, not tied up in matters of his own making.

Cosima pulled him back to the present. "She's absolutely devoted to Lily Cate."

"That's why I married her," he admitted.

"So this isn't a love match."

He hesitated. "One day, mayhap."

Cosima sipped her tea, her prolonged pause preparing him for her next volley. "Is that why you're keeping separate chambers?"

Heat snuck up his neck. His voice was low and flat beneath the squeak of the fiddle. "I cannot wed and bed a woman without knowing she has some feeling for me besides reluctance—or duty."

"Well, removing Anne's portrait from the Palladian room might help. She is no longer the mistress of Tall Acre, mind you. Sophie Menzies Ogilvy is." There was chiding in her tone, but she was treading carefully. She knew not to push him. "Start there, Seamus."

"Your point is well taken," he said as if discussing battlefield strategy with his fellow officers. "But in my defense, that room is rarely used, and I've forgotten all about the painting."

"Perhaps Anne's Williamsburg relations would like to have it, or Lily Cate when she's older. At least put it in the attic till then."

The drums were thundering again, and Sophie gave a tentative try to the whistle. Cosima laughed as Sophie winced and switched to the trumpet instead. For a moment she seemed as winsome and childlike as Lily Cate, tugging at Seamus in fresh ways.

"How is Philip?" he asked, changing course.

"Never better. We celebrated our tenth anniversary recently, you know. He regrets business kept him in Philadelphia but hopes to join you for some foxhunting in the fall."

"He's welcome at Tall Acre anytime, as are you." He pulled himself to his feet, the weight of the pistol hidden in his waistcoat an unwelcome reminder of the bearded stranger and strange light. He'd searched Early Hall himself after Lily Cate's revelation and stirred up nothing but dust and unwanted memories. His daughter had an active imagination. The moon could easily reflect off glass and mimic a light. "Time for my nightly rounds. I leave for Richmond on business at daybreak."

"Sleep well, little brother," Cosima said, laughing again as Lily Cate began blowing the whistle *and* beating the drums.

Seamus swam upward through a swell of fog and pain. His left leg was almost useless and would bear his weight for only a moment at a time. His right hand needed to be amputated, the surgeon said. The dark blue of his uniform was torn and streaked with blood and grime. He wore no shirt, for it had long since gone for bandages. His boots were unspeakable.

Through the haze and heat of his battlefield dreams, all the fighting and falling back, *she* stayed uppermost, rising above deafening musket fire and the never-ending stench of smoke and powder.

He jerked awake, clammy despite the chill. For a few disorienting seconds the room spun and then settled into cold, unfamiliar reality. Grant's Tavern. Early morning. Late March. The war won. But his chest felt empty, as if carved out by a cannonball.

He was missing . . . Sophie.

He shut his eyes, still at war within. If he didn't love her, why did he miss her? Why this nagging need to make things right between them, move toward more of her, more of them? Why did his blood rise at the mere thought there might be something between them?

All his tattered memories of Anne rose up and made him want to retreat. Yet some small, stubborn hope challenged him to wade through the hurts of the past lest he repeat them, taking hold of what was before him. Sophie. Second chances. Not distance and coldness and regret.

He dared a tentative, heartfelt prayer. For forgiveness. Direction. Wisdom.

What now, Lord?

Turning over, pulse drumming in his chest, he hardly expected an answer.

You need to court her.

He went completely still. The thought was not his own. He hadn't the courage to court her. But aye, he needed to court her. Woo her. Make her his. But how? A strange task to woo a woman after the wedding, but there'd been no time before.

He lay on his back, staring the idea in the face like he was preparing for battle, as if determined to drive any other man from the farthest reaches of her mind. With the Lord's help, he would court her. Only with the Lord's help was he capable of courting a woman as a woman ought to be courted . . . loving Sophie as she ought to be loved.

He wanted to be an attentive, tender husband. Wanted to savor more moments like the one that had passed between them by the hearth's fire when he'd playfully called her his bride. Something had happened in that too fleeting instant that left him changed.

Had she felt it too?

<hr />

The dancing master finally arrived, a score of Roan County children in his wake. Cosima was in her element supervising, a task Sophie gladly relinquished. With her energy and enthusiasm, Cosima turned the ballroom into a fete, leaving Sophie to her stillroom and her rounds. Seamus was still in Richmond. She wasn't sure when he'd be back.

Going into his study, she returned a quill and pen knife to his desk, breathing in the fragrance of pipe smoke and leather. The lengthy list he'd made atop the cluttered mahogany top couldn't be ignored. She studied the page, noting his writing varied in intensity and clarity, finally fading to a weary scrawl.

Graft 40 cherries and plums. Sow flax in west pasture. Ready Three Chimneys' fields for planting. Finish rail fence along Roan Creek and put chariot horses there. Prepare lambing pens. Hire millwright. Rid coach house of Anne's riding chair . . .

The last sentence shook her. His wording was strong. If he knew the significance of that riding chair . . . She prayed he never would. Overwhelmed by all that needed to be done, she felt a bit shamefaced. Why had she not realized he was having such trouble writing? His maimed hand would only accommodate so much. He needed a secretary to help manage everything. Or a willing wife. She'd forgotten her promise to help him when she returned from Annapolis . . .

Her gaze landed on an ill-concealed paper. To Seamus, Riggs had written in a tight, exacting hand, "As for Molly Kennedy, a more lazy, deceitful, and impudent hussy is not to be found in the United States than she."

The new indenture. There was always drama among the staff. Seamus had threatened to send Molly back to Ireland till Sophie had intervened, moving her from the dairy to the spinning house, where another wheel had been added and the women were making striped fabric instead of drab homespun. But Sophie didn't know if the arrangement would last.

Meanwhile Mrs. Lamont was laid low with gout and Sophie had assumed her duties, supervising Florie and the other two housemaids and kitchen staff. But at the moment, none of this was on her mind. She touched Seamus's pipe with its familiar thistle Pollock, the tobacco scent pungent and pleasant. Being in his study, among his own beloved things, assuaged her need of him somewhat.

A sudden movement sent her gaze to the door. Cosima stood looking at her, a fan in hand. Composed of peacock feathers, it fluttered artfully amidst the dark decor.

Sophie smiled. "How goes it, the dancing?"

"The children have nearly mastered the country dances, but you and Seamus are needed to step the minuet and show them how it's done."

"I'll be glad to." Opening a ledger, Sophie quickly added to their order for Biddle in Philadelphia. *Loaf sugar. Best Hyson tea. One small satin Capuchin hat.* "But you'll be hard-pressed to find Seamus as he's still in . . ."

She looked up, voice fading. Cosima was no longer in the doorway. Seamus was. Dressed for dinner and looking like he'd never left the house.

"My sister's powers of persuasion know no bounds. Would you do me the honor of a dance, Sophie?"

She smiled her delight as he extended his good hand. Something about him seemed markedly different. He, who'd helped rout Burgoyne at Saratoga and laid siege to Cornwallis at Yorktown, looked touchingly unsure of her.

"Of course I'll dance with you, Seamus."

They crossed the foyer and entered the ballroom where the children were finishing a country dance. Lily Cate hurried across the floor to greet them, giggling all the way.

"Papa, are you going to dance the minuet with Mama?"

"Aye. And then I'm going to dance with you." He looked to the fiddler and dancing master as they took their places, the children watching from the edge of the floor. The music began, and Seamus gave a bow to Sophie's curtsey. One dance turned into two, three . . . six. Night set in and more candles were lit.

Sophie had heard that George Washington, despite his great height and heft, was a graceful dancer. Seamus was the same. He never missed a step, though she nearly lost her footing trying to keep her mind on the maneuvering. Flushed and slightly winded, they danced a final, joyous reel, which led them down the length of the lovely room.

Sophie looked up without thought to the marble hearth where a fire glowed. Something seemed amiss. Out of place.

The portrait of Anne had come down.

26

Keys jingling as she walked, Sophie opened the door of the spinning house the next morning, the sound of angry voices fading as she stepped into the room. Myrtilla and Molly, the Irish indenture, faced off, bickering yet again. Dismayed, Sophie mentally raced through her options. Perhaps Molly should be sent into the fields. Or returned to Ireland, if Seamus had his way.

"Molly, you're needed in the dairy." Exasperation rising, Sophie forced a calm she wasn't feeling. "Myrtilla, I'd like to speak with you next door."

Molly sauntered past, head high, while Myrtilla followed Sophie outside. A sudden burst of girlish laughter lightened the mood of the moment. Jenny and Lily Cate were playing French hoops on the side lawn, brandishing their wands as gracefully as they could as they tried to catch the flying circles. Sophie waved as she went by, wishing she could join them.

In the privacy of the schoolhouse, its walls still smelling of fresh milk paint, Sophie faced Myrtilla. "What are you and Molly quarreling about today?"

Myrtilla stood, dark arms akimbo. "You only have to look at Molly to quarrel with her."

"If it keeps happening, I'll have to pass the matter to the general, and I'd rather not."

Sophie saw the alarm in her eyes, sensed her bone-deep loyalty to Tall Acre. While she might bear Sophie a grudge regarding her mother, Myrtilla revered Seamus.

"Don't go troublin' the general none, Mistress Ogilvy."

"The general put you in charge of the spinning house, and I don't want that to change. But you and Molly must work in peace. What can be done to bring that about?"

Myrtilla bit her lip. "Let Molly spin half a day and do kitchen work the rest. She don't take to nothin' long, though she spins fine once she's settled."

"The next time Molly has an outburst, come straight to me and I'll move her. Do your best not to provoke her in the meantime."

Myrtilla nodded, eyes roaming the room. "When you goin' to start your schoolin'?"

When, indeed. Would she ever find the time? "As soon as our guest leaves and Lily Cate returns from Williamsburg."

"Williamsburg?" Wariness flooded Myrtilla's gaze, making Sophie regret the slip.

"Lily Cate doesn't know she's to go yet. The general wants it kept quiet."

"Why Williamsburg?"

"Lily Cate's kin want to see her."

Opposition curled Myrtilla's lip. "Mistress Anne's, I suppose."

Sophie wouldn't say they'd had little choice in the matter. At the same time, what could a visit hurt? "She'll return to Tall Acre in a week." Sophie forged ahead, a new plan forming. If Seamus was willing . . . "Would you consider letting Jenny go to Williamsburg with Lily Cate?"

Her hopeful question was nearly snuffed by Myrtilla's dark look. Keeping in mind Myrtilla was now a free woman, Sophie waited, sure of a refusal.

Myrtilla ran dark fingers over an old slate. "Maybe. Maybe not."

Sophie nearly sighed. Whatever grievance Myrtilla had about the past seemed to have spilled over to the present. Not even Jenny's friendship with Lily Cate had turned her temper.

Stepping onto the sunny stoop just beyond the open door, Myrtilla gave her a last dark look. "If the general wants Jenny to go, she'll go."

Sophie felt a small, surprising victory. "I'll speak with him about it then."

$$\partial\!\!\!\supset$$

Mid-afternoon, Sophie hurried to the house, the slant of the sun telling her she was late for tea. Cosima, for all her free-spiritedness, operated with a soldier's punctuality. Tea was at four o'clock and not a minute later.

She and Lily Cate were gathered round a table in the small parlor, nibbling and chatting. The fragrance of Hyson was strong and pleasant, Sophie's empty chair pulled out invitingly.

"We'd all but given up," Cosima told her, pouring her a steaming cup. "Between you and Seamus working night and day, Tall Acre will return to its former glory in no time."

Across the table Lily Cate smiled, her doll seated between them. "I saw you talking with Papa in the garden this morning."

Sophie reached for the sugar. "We were trying to decide what to plant. The gardener had questions . . ."

"Just remember, all work and no play make the master

and mistress dull indeed." Cosima gestured to the pianoforte. "Though Seamus tells me you're a fine musician, I haven't heard a note in the time I've been here so will have to take his word for it."

Sophie digested that without reply. Cosima rarely made a frivolous comment; there was always a pithy message beneath. Before Sophie could divert her, Lily Cate took up the charge.

"Aunt Cosima says I'm in need of a baby brother and sister—or a parrot."

Cosima winked. "And I'm so hoping it won't be a parrot." As the bird preened in its corner cage, Cosima shot Sophie an apologetic glance. "All I meant is that I hope you and Seamus make up for mine and Philip's lack."

Sophie didn't miss the sudden wistfulness in Cosima's eyes. Playing along, she looked at Lily Cate. "So what would you like most? A baby brother or a sister?"

"Both!"

"Best talk to your father about that," Cosima whispered conspiratorially.

Did Cosima know of their separate rooms? Separate lives? Sophie sampled the gingerbread made rich with orange curd, the gnawing inside her having little to do with hunger. "You and Philip will have to come down for the christening . . . act as godparents."

Cosima's brows slanted inquiringly as Lily Cate switched subjects. "Aunt Cosima says I must visit her in Philadelphia."

Nodding, Cosima brushed a crumb from her bodice. "I was asking about her former governess. If you cannot secure another, there's a fine day school in the city founded by Quakers."

Curious, Sophie looked again at Lily Cate. "Would you like to go away to school?"

Her head shook so vigorously her curls wobbled. "I would miss you and Papa—and Sassy."

Sophie rued the way her eyes darkened like Seamus's did when considering something dire. How would they break the news to her about the coming week in Williamsburg? "Perhaps when you're more grown up you can attend, like I did at Mrs. Hallam's."

"A lovely idea. As for me, I shall be leaving all too soon," Cosima said with a dramatic sigh. "Will you miss me—and Shrub?"

Lily Cate giggled again, eyes on the pet bird, her wary mood fading. "Yes, though Papa said he won't miss Shrub at all."

"Well!" Cosima said in mock offense. "I shall leave Shrub with your uncle Philip next time. Or talk your father into having better manners."

The parrot squawked, and the three of them dissolved in unladylike laughter.

※

The next evening ushered in the bittersweet. For the time being, Seamus felt at peace. Blessed. Able to keep the world out. Cosima had left for Philadelphia that morning, and the house was tranquil. Tomorrow seemed years away. Then the clock struck nine, reminding him that time could be a tyrant.

As if sensing the moment had come, Sophie gave him a pensive smile, and he reached for Lily Cate, taking her on his knee. Looking up at him, she smiled and touched his bristled cheek. His heart turned over. She'd made such strides in accepting him. Would he now see it all undone?

"Tomorrow we're going to Williamsburg to see your aunt and uncle." He spoke slowly, voice emptied of emotion, gauging her reaction. "They want you to stay with them for a few days."

There was a surprised pause. She sat looking up at him like he'd done her some injury. "Without you and Mama?"

"We'll be back to bring you home in a week."

She leaned into him, her fingers picking at his coat buttons. "Promise?"

His chest went cold. She felt so small, the separation so large. "Aye, I promise."

"Will you come in the night like last time?"

So she hadn't forgotten. "Not in the night." His fury with the Fitzhughs rose up and nearly choked out his reply. "Early in the day. Mayhap at first light."

Sophie spoke, a smile in her voice. "Jenny will be with you."

"Jenny?" She looked up, still bewildered. "How many days?"

Sophie held up seven fingers. "Once you return, we'll start school. Won't that be a delight? All those books you've been wanting to read . . ."

Seamus didn't miss the emotion in Sophie's words. He shouldn't have confessed his dread of Lily Cate leaving. In the hours since, his turmoil had quickened, overtaking him like an enemy he couldn't shake off. Could Sophie sense that?

Lily Cate yawned, and Sophie held out a hand. "For now 'tis time for a bedtime story."

Turning toward him again, she reached up, cradling his chin in her fingers. "Goodnight, Papa."

The brush of her lips was warm. Heartrending. He fought the urge to hold her too long, too possessively. He released her reluctantly, watching as Sophie led her away in what had become a touching nighttime ritual. He tried not to dwell on another separation, both tonight and in the days to come.

Sophie stood in the Fitzhughs' grand parlor, biting her lip lest she blurt out something she'd regret and add to the bitter feeling filling the room. Charlotte was making a scene about Jenny, demanding she return with them to Tall Acre. Standing behind the sofa on which Charlotte sat was Fitzhugh, looking bored and saying little, staying beyond the fray.

"I tell you, she is an unfit companion for Lily Cate." Charlotte addressed Sophie as if she were to blame. "Nor is she welcome in my home. I—"

"Then we'll take our leave, the four of us." Seamus's calm overrode her complaining. He took Sophie by the elbow and turned to go out when Charlotte erupted all over again.

"But the court order—"

"The girl—Jenny—will stay." Fitzhugh spoke at last, taking a snuffbox from his pocket. "Next time we shall insist on Lily Cate coming alone."

"There will be no next time if this visit is less than I hope." Seamus's grip on Sophie's arm never lessened, but he continued in his low, measured tone. "We'll return a week from today at first light."

"First light?" Charlotte brought a silver vinaigrette to her nose, rife with the heady scent of cloves. Her sulky frown left Sophie wondering if Anne had been half as petulant.

"First light," Seamus stated again.

They went out without another word, having already said their goodbyes to Lily Cate and Jenny, who were now playing in the garden under a servant's watchful eye.

Once in the coach they said little, the unwelcome separation heavy, the sour encounter uppermost. Sophie leaned back against the leather seat, shoulder to shoulder with Seamus.

The Fitzhughs wouldn't mistreat Jenny, surely. The thought turned her sick inside. Myrtilla had been good about her going. Did Charlotte somehow know about Myrtilla and Anne's bitter past? Could that account for her resistance about Jenny? Or was it simply because they still considered Jenny a slave?

Through the coach's open window, she lost sight of the Fitzhughs' townhouse when they turned onto Francis Street. Seamus was quiet. Too quiet. Knowing she could say little in the way of comfort, she leaned her head against the leather seat and shut her eyes, counting days instead of sheep. In only a week they'd be a family again.

Once they were home, the silence echoed. As the evening sunset flamed scarlet-pink, Seamus came in from a visit to a tenant, no more hungry than she. He soon excused himself again, going to the dovecote to oversee the renovations.

Alone in her room, Sophie contented herself with a bath instead of supper, sinking deep into the copper tub, her skin slick from fragrant French-milled soap. Florie helped wash her hair, pouring pitcher upon pitcher of fresh water till every strand came clean. A finely embroidered nightgown lay across the settee, a wedding gift from Cosima.

So clad, she sat by the fire and dried her hair, listening for Seamus's step, her heart in her throat. Once Florie left, she cracked open both doors, the one in back of the stairs and the one leading to the hall and small parlor. The subtle invitation—or was it brazen?—brought the blood rushing to her cheeks.

'Twas nine o'clock, the time she'd always thought of as hers and Lily Cate's. *Aesop's Fables* lay on a near table. She couldn't imagine Charlotte reading fairy tales. She didn't seem the type to pay children much attention. And Fitzhugh? She shivered. With his stiff pomp and polish, he reminded her of her father. Thoughts of Curtis crowded in, magnifying her angst. Still stung by his betrayal, she shoved down her longing to see him again.

An open door creaked, raising hope it was Seamus, but 'twas only a stray draft. If he was as unsettled as she, couldn't they draw comfort from each other? A snatch of Scripture sprang to mind but held no solace either.

By night on my bed I sought him whom my soul loveth; I sought him, but I found him not.

∞

His callused hand held fragile wildflowers. Field pansies and lilies of the valley. Standing outside the stillroom, Seamus took a breath, feeling the fool, wondering if anyone was watching. He might have gone into the formal garden and gathered far more showy ones than these, but he'd been drawn to the pasture where the wildflowers bloomed. They seemed more Sophie's style, like the pearls.

Behind him, two maids hurried past, giggling all the way down the colonnade connecting the summer kitchen to the main house. His skin prickled with warmth beneath the linen of his cravat.

The master of Tall Acre had far more pressing matters to tend to than gathering posies, no doubt. But still he stood there, convicted.

With his free hand he pushed open the stillroom door to . . . emptiness.

Disappointment knifed him. And then Mrs. Lamont's voice broke over him from the rear, abject apology in her tone. "Mistress Ogilvy has gone to Roan, sir. To see about something for Miss Lily Cate."

With that she swept away, her yellow skirts swirling as she walked. Flustered, he stepped into the stillroom's shadows, an avalanche of memories overtaking him. Then, as now, bunches of dried lavender and herbs perfumed the close space. His mother's housekeeping book lay open on a table. He could almost see her beloved head bent in concentration, hear the scratch of her pen against paper. In the margins, Sophie's own handwriting abounded. His new wife took her duties very seriously.

If he had quill and ink, he'd leave her a note. But what would he say? His mother's gentle whisper came.

Let your actions speak louder than your words.

The flowers already seemed to be fading, choked by his damp grip. Should he get a jar to put them in? Fetch water from the well? Leave them for her? Beset by second thoughts, he placed them atop the book. When he started back outside, he nearly bumped into Riggs, who was waiting impatiently.

"Sir, you're needed immediately at the mill. The new tumbling dam's given way in the recent rain and is jamming the watercourse."

Setting his jaw to curb his frustration, Seamus started for the stables, all thoughts of courting relegated to the far reaches.

At dusk, Sophie came into the stillroom. All was as she'd left it when she'd ridden to Roan with her groom. Or was it not? The door was slightly ajar. Her stool was out of place. A bouquet of wilted blooms lay on the wide trestle table.

Seamus?

Did he have a particular fondness for wildflowers? Even with acres of garden at his back door? Bending, she breathed in their fading fragrance, the sweetness rivaling his gallant gesture. Likely he had no knowledge of their meaning. Lilies signified a return of happiness; pansies bespoke loyalty.

Oh, that she had been here to take them from his willing hands. Give him a few words of thanks, a tiny piece of her heart, in return. The luxury of being alone with him seemed an extravagance she would never know. She'd missed his presence today by mere minutes, perhaps, all in a silly quest for underpinnings.

The next few days swept past with scarcely a glimpse of him, but she had little room to ponder it or show her thanks. Tall Acre seemed determined to wrest from them every waking moment and ounce of strength they possessed. And more.

27

O n the Sabbath, Sophie sat side by side with Seamus in the Ogilvy pew for the first time since they'd married. Her gaze drifted from the kirk's old English organ to a wide window framed in sunlight. A lamb looked down at her, its stained-glass shepherd leading. Again she was reminded of Lily Cate, who had a special fondness for lambs. She'd soon be home for all the fullness of spring.

The benediction was said, and before they'd turned out of their row, the questions flew. Church members who'd turned aside without a word now greeted her openly. Marrying Seamus had given her a measure of respectability, a new presence.

"General Ogilvy and Mistress Ogilvy, where is your little daughter?"

Sophie smiled at the once unfriendly seamstress as Seamus answered. "In Williamsburg visiting relatives. She returns home on the morrow."

"Such a charming child. You've been missing her, no doubt."

"Very much," Sophie said. "Counting the hours, even."

They moved outside into a misting rain where the coach awaited. A number of parishioners were missing, the churchyard oddly empty. A smallpox outbreak on a neighboring plantation had Seamus intent on inoculating them all. They returned home, and the house nearly yawned without Lily Cate, most of the staff absent on the Sabbath. They entered the small parlor where a quiet meal awaited, with hardly a word between them.

Suddenly tongue-tied at being alone with this husband of hers, so near she could almost hear him breathing, Sophie hardly recognized her answered prayers for what they were. She and Seamus were entirely alone. The day was theirs to do with as they wished. And she was naught but . . . numptie.

He'd removed his coat, for it was a warm day despite the damp. In turn she'd not worn a shawl. They sat in their respective chairs, so close his leg brushed the edge of her gown. Finished with his own simple meal, he reached for *The Gentleman Farmer*, and she remembered she hadn't thanked him for the lilies and pansies he'd left for her.

Her voice came soft in the stillness. "How did you know lilies of the valley are my favorite flower?"

He smiled, gaze never leaving the book in hand. "Would you neglect the poor pansy, Sophie? Admittedly, they are no match for your lilies. But they are the hue of your eyes."

Delight enveloped her from head to toe. Was he toying with her? She was cast back to warm, witty Williamsburg days shimmering with silk and candlelight, fluttering fans and secret flirtations.

She took a breath. "Both are exquisite." Did he know she'd kept them, even wilted? She couldn't bring herself to throw them away. "I'm sorry I wasn't here when you picked them. Sometimes I think we are too busy. Too busy for the finer things . . ." Dare she say it? "For each other."

He set the book aside, his low voice like a caress. "Would you have more of me, Sophie?"

She kept her eyes on her lap. "I would have as much of you as you are willing to give, Seamus."

The silence lengthened as if he was sifting through her words, every nuance, every syllable. Could he sense that she was holding out her heart to him, nearly spelling out what she could not say?

Seamus, there is no other man. Only you.

He took her hand. The strength of his fingers was surprisingly gentle. Slowly he pressed his lips to her palm and then her wrist, moving up her bare arm to the lacy waterfall of her sleeve. She shut her eyes, well beyond thought. Beyond words. His kisses lingered like a trail of fire on her skin.

Was this how love began? Softly? Unexpectedly? With pangs of aching sweetness? 'Twas nothing like his careful, self-conscious wedding kiss. This was . . . bliss.

From somewhere far off came the unwelcome intrusion of hoofbeats. The shutters were open to the front lawn, but the rain made the view a hazy gray. Sophie fastened on the frail, flowering dogwood trees Seamus had planted with his own hands nearest the road. A rider was coming hard and fast down the carriageway, oblivious to the mud.

An express on the Sabbath?

This usually meant dire news . . . death.

Seamus let go of her hand. She had no recollection of leaving the parlor and hurrying to the foyer. Seamus was ahead of her, pulling open the wide front door.

He turned round, wary. "Go into the study, Sophie."

He was the general again, stoic, giving orders. She stood rooted, defying them. Waiting to hear bad news secondhand was somehow worse. His words of days before flashed to mind and struck her like a fist.

Why do I feel such dread at her going?

She wanted to protect him, spare him whatever was coming. Mute, she looked on as he went out and down the steps into a pelting rain, the wind tugging at his coattails.

The express handed him a post before riding away. Slowly he opened the paper. For long moments she waited while he stood, oblivious to the rain beading his handsome features and turning his chestnut greatcoat black.

"Seamus . . . please." Her heart already felt fractured with the waiting, her mind bent out of shape with half-frantic assumptions.

When he looked up, she read the worst in his eyes. "'Tis Lily Cate. She's missing."

⁂

The coach lurched and heaved, the coachman driving the horses over mud-mired roads to Williamsburg on the heels of the express. The post was merciless in its brevity. Sophie was beginning to think Fitzhugh had a cruel streak.

Your daughter is missing. Sheriff is combing both country and town. Come at once.

Come at once? As though they wouldn't? Was it her imagination or a subtle taunt about the war years when Seamus hadn't come at all?

Beside her he sat like stone, saying nothing, eyes straight ahead, locked in a world where she wasn't welcome. What had just passed between them was swallowed up by the blackness of disbelief and loss.

Questions that had no answer circled without end. When did Lily Cate go missing? Were they not watching her? Perhaps she'd been found by now and this race to get to Williamsburg would end in thankful tears.

Their arrival at the Fitzhugh townhouse was far different from when they'd come the week before. Men combed the grounds and passed in and out of the house, glancing at Seamus, their expressions closed, even grim. Seamus left her in the foyer and closeted himself with Fitzhugh in the study while she was shown into an adjacent parlor, the door closed between them.

A tearful, terrified Jenny was brought to Sophie straightaway. Charlotte, a maid told her, was indisposed and abed.

For a few minutes Sophie just held Jenny close. Even comforting words seemed to stick in her throat. "Can you tell me what has happened with Lily Cate?"

Jenny's eyes welled. "Mistress Charlotte kept us apart, said we made too much noise, so I stayed out back with the servants. When I went to wake Lily Cate this morning, she was gone."

"Had her bed been slept in?"

A brief nod. "She left her doll behind."

Sophie said nothing, fears mounting.

Chin quivering, Jenny continued brokenly, "When we first came here, Lily Cate cried to go home and made Mistress Charlotte angry. She said Lily Cate likely run off, back to Tall Acre."

"Did Lily Cate mention anything to you about running away?"

A firm shake of Jenny's head removed all doubt. Sophie

took out a handkerchief and dried Jenny's tears as the men's voices escalated in the next room. Seamus was in a fury and she didn't blame him, but their high tempers lent to their loose ends. Could they not be reasonable?

Wanting to spare Jenny their heated talk, she sent her upstairs. "Can you bring Lily Cate's doll to me?"

With a nod she was off. She returned just as Seamus filled the doorway, the storm in his features never lessening. "The coach will take you and Jenny to Tall Acre. I'm staying on at the Raleigh Tavern till this is resolved."

She opened her mouth to protest, but the sheriff appeared, asking to speak with Seamus and making her reconsider. She'd received her marching orders. Tall Acre. With Jenny. Now. There was no arguing. But truly, she wanted to be home if somehow Lily Cate arrived there. Perhaps she was even there now and they'd just missed her . . .

"Pack your things, Jenny, and we shall go." Sophie mumbled the words, wanting a last minute alone with Seamus. But he was deep in conversation with the sheriff, as grieved as he was angry, his back turned.

She waited, glad when the sheriff left and he faced her. "Seamus, I—" She struggled to speak, her voice giving way.

He swallowed, his own eyes awash. "There's nothing you can say, Sophie. Just go home and wait and pray."

His gaze fell to the doll in her arms, and his face flashed such terrible pain it sent her heart to her throat.

She stood mute as he passed through the open back door to the garden, where two men were looking into the well, raising fresh fears.

Hugging the doll to her chest, she stayed stoic till she climbed into the coach. There, waiting for Jenny, she cried as she'd not done since her mother died and Curtis had written.

All the heartache that had gone before seemed a tiny drop of anguish compared to this.

Where could Lily Cate be?

⁂

Without Seamus and Lily Cate, the heartbeat of Tall Acre was missing. Two days passed, then four. Another express came, nearly choking Sophie with anxiety as she opened it, but it was only word from Seamus that nothing had turned up, even with a small army of men and dogs combing Williamsburg and beyond.

In the long silences Sophie prayed and fasted, but in truth she had no heart for eating. Only at Mrs. Lamont's insistence did she take broth and bread. Visitors started to arrive, expressing their sorrow, the reverend and his wife staying longest. It was like a death, only it wasn't. Few children went missing. 'Twas strange . . . unnatural.

Without warning, a portrait painter arrived from the east. In the confusion of events, either Seamus had forgotten to tell her he'd been commissioned or he'd wanted it to be a surprise.

Unaware of the turmoil he'd walked into, Mr. Peale bowed. "I've come to paint the new mistress of Tall Acre's portrait, a wedding gift from the groom."

How could she turn him away?

For hours on end Sophie sat in her wedding gown, serene without and at war within. When she wasn't posing for her portrait, she went up to Lily Cate's room, where the doll dresses Sophie had sewn for her lay across a little chair, the doll beside them. The beloved toys haunted.

If Lily Cate had run away, why hadn't she taken her doll? It went everywhere with her, even to the necessary. Sophie smoothed the silken dress worn soft by small hands, the dark hair a bit thin, the eyes lackluster.

Lord, bring Lily Cate home. I'll not even ask for Seamus's heart. Just return her. Restore our family. Please.

The irrational prayer made little sense, nor did the continuous fire she insisted be kept burning in the grate before her. The days were getting longer, warmer. But if she let it go out, lost hope, Lily Cate might not come back. Desperation twisted her mind and emotions. She could only imagine how Seamus must feel. He'd won a war yet lost his daughter. Could he live with the heartache if she never came home?

✧

The sweet song of a lark rent the April air. Sophie leaned against a column of the garden folly, the whimsical little clapboard building Seamus's father had built for his mother. Perched at the far end of the garden, it overlooked the river and courted a sultry breeze, its pagoda roof a shelter from the sun. Fragrant wisteria twined with climbing roses and decorated its exterior, smothering her in shade and scent.

She'd lost all track of time, almost forgotten the season. Though another week had passed and Seamus was still away, Sophie felt disoriented. Everything in her world revolved around Lily Cate and Seamus, and without them her world had shrunk to shadows.

Blind to the beauty, her gaze traveled across the water, past the long weathered dock and bobbing rowboat, to Early Hall. It sat silent and empty while Tall Acre was humming and thriving.

A litter of foxhound puppies had just been born, as well as the first crop of lambs. They dotted the pasture like dandelion down, scattered bits of white, their sweet bleating carrying on the wind as they followed their mothers. Watching them, Sophie felt her heart trip. This was the season she and Lily Cate had looked forward to most, making plans for picnics and rides and games out of doors. Seamus was even going to teach Lily Cate to swim.

"Mistress Ogilvy . . ."

She turned away from the river when Myrtilla's voice reached out to her, unmistakably kind. "We thought you might like these." Jenny stood behind her mother, her face marked with sadness, holding out some pussy willows.

Sophie took the offering, her cold fingers touching the velvety nubs that had burst into bloom. Numb as she was, the gesture was not lost on her. Whatever Myrtilla's feelings about Anne or even Sophie herself, there was no doubt she cared for Lily Cate.

Myrtilla came nearer. "Jenny has somethin' to tell you. Somethin' she remembers."

The folly came sharply into focus. Sophie looked at Jenny, hopeful yet afraid.

"I 'member Lily Cate saw that man again in Williamsburg." Jenny swiped the wetness from her eyes with a linsey sleeve. "The bearded man who used to come here."

Sophie's heart seemed to stop. "And you? Did you see him too?"

Jenny shook her head. "Just Lily Cate. She said he was watchin' us across the fence when we played in the garden, and then he was gone."

Sophie put her arms around Jenny's bent shoulders and hugged her, suddenly aware of how different she was than Lily Cate. Bony and tall and smelling of wood smoke. Not soft and lavender-scented and small. "Thank you for telling me. 'Tis important."

Jenny leaned against her, her words a whisper. "Granny Bea says God knows where Lily Cate is, even if we don't."

Sophie nodded, needing the reminder in light of their helplessness.

"Come along now," Myrtilla said in her no-nonsense way. "I need to return to my spinnin'." Her face was a dark mask again as they left the folly.

Sophie fetched a vase from the stillroom, went to the well, and drew water for the pussy willows. Tall Acre's back door was ajar, the maids busy beating rugs in the open air. She was used to seeing Seamus striding about. He needed to know what Jenny had told her, flimsy as it was. Though it might not help locate Lily Cate, Sophie felt sure this unknown man played a role in her disappearance. It couldn't be coincidence. Wishing for something more substantial, she went to Seamus's study to pen the news to Williamsburg.

28

Sophie stood with Mrs. Lamont in the Palladian room turned studio. The smell of oil paint was strong, the large canvas facing the riverfront windows for the best light. Brushes and jars abounded, but Mr. Peale was taking a walk in the garden. Sophie focused on the bare place above the mantel where the new portrait would hang when done. What had become of Anne's portrait, Sophie did not know. Not even Florie had told her.

"Well, I must say, Mr. Peale has remarkable talent." Beside her, Mrs. Lamont stared at the work in progress, her expression already pronouncing it a success. "Certainly a fine feat for a saddle maker turned artist."

Sophie stared absently at the canvas without comment. Would she always associate this portrait with heartache and loss?

"I forgot Peale was coming."

Seamus's low voice spun Sophie around. He studied the painting, his expression unreadable. He'd been gone a fortnight, the longest two weeks of her life. And now he'd returned but had no answers. She could tell just by looking at him. His unshaven jaw, the weary lines about his eyes, and his rumpled clothing and muddy boots bespoke sleepless nights and hours in the saddle.

Mrs. Lamont excused herself, leaving them alone.

Seamus looked at her, but his blue gaze seemed washed out, without focus. "We know little more than we did. She vanished sometime the night of the second. The servants deny any wrongdoing. Nothing was disturbed in the house. The Fitzhughs state the doors were locked and they don't know what happened, but since they're the prime suspects, they're still being questioned."

"And the man Jenny told us about, the one here and in Williamsburg?"

"We have little to go on, I'm afraid. Lily Cate is the only one who's seen him."

"And so we . . . wait?" For days, months, years. She saw the futility in his eyes, and it shook her to her soul.

"I've posted a substantial reward. The sheriff and constables are doing all they can. They even questioned me."

"You?"

He gave a weary nod. "Has anyone threatened me or my family? Just a trespasser. Is there anyone who bears me a grudge? Aye, the whole British army. Do I get along with Anne's relations? Nay. Did I harm my daughter?"

"Oh Seamus . . . they didn't."

"I keep thinking of her hungry. Cold. Bewildered." His voice wavered. "Wondering why I don't come."

She pressed trembling fingers to her lips. Such torment, all this wondering. Where was God amidst such anguish? Would it drive Seamus away from Him? Or bring him closer? His fierce reserve left her more undone. He seemed so strong.

Unbending. Or had war so hardened him that he was able to stay standing while inwardly he was coming apart?

His low voice was raked with exhaustion. "I have known pain. But I have never known pain like this."

"Mistress Ogilvy, there's a matter that needs discussing." Riggs stood before her, hat in hand, gaze on the stillroom floor.

Surprised, Sophie took him in, seeing echoes of Jenny in his pockmarked face though his daughter mostly resembled Myrtilla. Sophie's hands stilled on the mortar and pestle she was using to blend herbs for another needed tonic. "Of course, Riggs. Speak freely, please."

"It's the general, ma'am. Says he saw another light late last night at Early Hall." He looked up at her, stark worry in his eyes. "Trouble is, nobody else saw that light." He swallowed, clearly ill at ease. "I'm not nay-saying him. I just know the master's a mite touchy about his first wife. I thought maybe it would help to do away with the riding chair. He mentioned it once but never gave me the order to be rid of it himself."

She hadn't forgotten finding Seamus's note about it. Did he know the history behind that chair? She'd hoped to have it painted. Use it for outings with Lily Cate. But now in light of Riggs's words she saw how unwise a wish that was. "I've seen it in the coach house."

"Aye. With your permission I could have it moved to Three Chimneys."

Locked away, like Anne's diary? Riggs was clever and clearly wanted to help Seamus.

He continued. "The general is meeting with his tenants this morn. Now might be a good time."

"By all means, move it immediately. Three Chimneys' coach house is empty."

Thanking her, he left, leaving her to ponder his words.

The master's a mite touchy about his first wife.

Just how much did Seamus know about Tobias Early?

⁂

At sunrise, Sophie was awakened from a fitful sleep by the slamming of the riverfront door. Seamus? Rattled by the sound and what it meant, she flew to the window and caught his agitated stride before he disappeared behind the boxwood hedge.

When she lost sight of him, inexplicable panic set in. She tore off her nightgown and began dressing, her frantic fingers working the hooks of her gown. There was no time for stays or stockings or minding her hair. Stuffing her feet into the nearest pair of slippers, she left her bedchamber and went out into a day so soft and hushed it only magnified her turmoil.

Was he at the stables? One of the dependencies? He'd been home but two days. He was barely sleeping or eating. He was always armed—never a worry till now. Sometimes shock, grief, drove people to extremes. Something urged her to action, but she hardly knew where to begin.

Half sick with alarm, she finally found him at the river's edge, untethering a rowboat. "Where are you going?"

He turned, his bloodshot eyes like a blow. "Across the river."

To Early Hall? She looked toward the shuttered house. Had he seen another light? "I'll come with you."

"Nay, Sophie." His back to her, he shoved the boat into the current and jumped in with an ease that belied his exhaustion, leaving her little choice but to wade in after him.

Clutching her skirts, she held them high as the current

tugged at her and wet sand engulfed her slippers. Heedless of his disapproval, she climbed into the bow unaided, rocking the boat as he took up the oars.

Their glide across the river was silent save the splash of the water, a few dragonflies darting about, their incandescent wings the bright blue of the river. Seamus ignored her, his angry paddle strokes bringing them swiftly to the opposite shore. Gripping the sides of the boat, she steadied herself as he ran aground. In a gesture more angry than gallant, he picked her up and planted her on the grassy bank as if she were little more than a hogshead of tobacco.

Shaken, she smoothed her rumpled clothes as they started up the hill, her skirts dragging in the dew-damp grass. Seamus's face darkened the nearer they came. Together they took in the crumbling brick outbuildings before fastening on the abandoned house. Ivy wove a thick web across a multitude of doors and windows. Early Hall looked unwelcoming and forbidding even in broad daylight, making Sophie want to tug on his sleeve and retreat.

When they reached the edge of the garden, once carefully laid out in elegant parterres, she felt a sadness she couldn't explain. It was a ruin of weeds and vines, impassable. They skirted it, Seamus leading. Every door was locked save a side entrance with a broken latch.

His tone was terse. "Stay here while I go in."

Uneasiness rising, she waited a few seconds then followed. Inside, the house was still as a crypt. Pale with dust, the spacious, well-appointed rooms held once-treasured ceramics from Europe and the Orient and fine oil paintings on peeling walls. Dust covers draped a crush of furnishings. Mice and bats had had a heyday and were still. She walked about slowly, touching nothing but perusing everything.

Had Seamus gone upstairs?

The startling sound of breaking glass was her answer. Spinning round, she took the grand staircase by twos, slipping in her haste and skinning her knees on the landing. "Seamus!"

Her cry was smothered by more violence coming from a distant room. Chest heaving, she ran toward the sound till she found him, a sea of shattered glass between them. Every window in the once-lovely chamber had been destroyed. A humid wind buffeted moth-eaten drapes, brushing her flushed face.

Seamus stood looking at her, stance wide and hands fisted at his sides. Face ravaged with a consuming misery, he seemed one step away from madness.

Her voice broke. "Seamus . . . please."

She started forward across the wreckage, barely aware of the sharpness beneath her thin soles. In back of him was a marble hearth, an abundance of ashes within. A recent fire? Perhaps the explanation of the strange light? Some passing vagabond or gypsy, likely. Many were homeless and wandering with the war won. She tore her gaze away, searching for some tenderness, some familiarity, within the face she loved so well.

His eyes were on her, his own chest heaving, staring at her as if she were little more than the enemy, the wife no longer wanted, no longer needed. The truth of it didn't have to be spoken. It resounded in the glittering chasm between them as if he'd shouted it. Without Lily Cate, what purpose did she serve? She was naught but a burden, a reminder of his loss, his heartache.

With three quick steps, he closed the distance between them, glass crunching beneath the hard soles of his boots. Still taut with fury, he picked her up and carried her out of the battered room and down dirty stairs into a day so brilliant she squinted beneath its fierce glare.

300

Again he set her down roughly. "I told you not to come, Sophie."

He said nothing more as he rowed them across, the fine linen of his shirt torn and stained, knuckles bleeding. When they touched the southern shore, he sat listless at the oars, head bent, his unkempt hair a tangle of neglect. She shut her eyes, her heart empty of all but the simplest plea.

Lord . . . help us.

Once they started up the hill to Tall Acre, Seamus ahead of her, a servant met him about some matter needing immediate attention. Seamus walked away from her without looking back.

Benumbed, Sophie spent the rest of the morning in the stillroom, trying to plan the physic garden, a replica of Seamus's mother's in its heyday. Sitting on her worn stool, she tilled and planted the fertile acreage in her mind, counting seeds, all the while wondering where Seamus was.

High above, the roof was half shingled. The din of hammers stole her concentration and lent to her aching head. Setting aside her seeds, she opened the housekeeping book, gaze landing on a receipt that said *Mistress Ogilvy's Water.* In the margin, Seamus's mother had written, "John's favorite scent." Made up of thirty-three herbs and flowers, the concoction was distilled in white wine.

Never had she so needed the stout, soft-spoken Cornish woman who'd been Lilias Ogilvy. What would the former mistress of Tall Acre say or do about her granddaughter's disappearance? What would she concoct to soothe her son's bleeding hands and heart?

Early Hall raised a hundred questions she couldn't answer.

Why had Seamus gone there? Would she ever know? Was it simply to give vent to his blinding fury? Or did some secret knowledge of Anne and Tobias Early account for every shard of shattered glass?

As the needs of the day closed in, she met them as best she could. Two children in the quarters were down with croup and needed camphor and hartshorn. The child sickest with worms had recovered, thanks to prayer and constant nursing, but another child had fallen from the dovecote and broken his arm. The wants never seemed to end.

Basket on one arm, Sophie left the sanctuary of the still-room and headed down the shell path to the spinning house. She'd timed her visit carefully. 'Twas the noon hour and dinnertime. She didn't want to interrupt the workday. Riggs didn't like it, and what's more, Seamus didn't like it.

She entered the building, her practiced calm eroding at Myrtilla's frown. They were alone in the large room, the silence thick.

"I've come to see how things are faring here."

Myrtilla stood by her idle wheel. "The weaver's turnin' out a fair amount of woolen cloth and linsey. I'm trainin' a tenth woman to spin." Her chin tipped up, eyes dark with discontent. "Molly's been raisin' a ruckus again, just so you knows."

"Yes, I know. I've sent her to the laundry." Done with Molly's quarrelsomeness, Sophie moved on to other matters. "I'd like you to bring all the children to the small parlor to be measured for new clothes. This afternoon would work best, if you can manage it."

"To the house?" Myrtilla's dark hands caressed the distaff of the spinning wheel. "Mistress Anne never did abide any slave children near at hand."

"Well, I'm not Mistress Anne, nor are there any more slaves here at Tall Acre."

Myrtilla's gaze sharpened. "Word is the general freed us on account o' you. Makes me wonder why."

Sophie set her basket on a near table. "I simply mean for you to live as the general and the good Lord intend, as a free woman, with all the rights and privileges that brings."

"I may spin fine, but I can't read nor write. Riggs says a body ain't worth much without such."

"Would you care to learn? You and Jenny?" For the first time since they'd met, Sophie sensed some common ground. "As a free woman, you have that right."

Myrtilla's eyes narrowed to suspicious slits, snuffing Sophie's hopes. Had Myrtilla been so impudent with Anne? With Seamus she was docility itself.

Sophie tried again. "There was a woman in Williamsburg, a friend of my mother's, who founded the Bray School. She taught enslaved and free children before the war. We might do the same here."

Myrtilla started to speak, then clamped her mouth shut. The other spinners were coming in, ready to resume work, all giving Sophie a respectful greeting. Without waiting for Myrtilla's answer, Sophie left to finish her rounds, thoughts of Seamus as heavy as the iron keys in her pocket. Another hour inched past as she emptied her basket, dispensing tonics and advice, speaking with servants who bore none of Myrtilla's moodiness.

Bypassing the coach house, she paused briefly to look down the wide corridor that sheltered the Ogilvy conveyances. Anne's riding chair was now at Three Chimneys. Out of sight if not out of mind.

She flinched as pewter clouds released a cold, stinging

rain. The work on the roof had come to an abrupt halt as men scrambled down ladders and gathered up tools. Hugging her basket tighter, she hastened back to the house as a west wind began an uneasy rising.

Mrs. Lamont met her in the foyer. "The general has left for Williamsburg."

Williamsburg. Again.

29

The gentle knock on his study door could be none other than Sophie.

Seamus did not answer. He was in no mood for company or questions after another fruitless week in Williamsburg. Sophie's very presence drove home a great many things he wanted to forget. Lily Cate's absence. His destruction at Early Hall. His rude treatment of her. He owed her an apology, but he felt bankrupt, nearly soulless, consumed by stark, embittered fury and a deep, never-ending need for his daughter. He turned his back on the door and focused on the storm beyond the windows.

"Seamus?" Her soft call was nearly lost beneath the patter of rain. She came in unasked, further fraying his loose ends.

He faced her, noting the strain in her features, the sleepless nights and weeping he wasn't privy to. Her careful entreaty tore at his forced composure. "Is there any news?"

His own throat ached. "Nay." Tears glazed her eyes, turning him more on edge. With an effort, he took control. "What is it, Sophie?"

Her voice was nearly lost beneath the rumble of thunder. "I'd like to reopen Tall Acre's schoolhouse. Teach Jenny and whoever else wants to learn to read and write."

He listened grudgingly. She was trying to bury her hurt beneath a blur of work. He couldn't fault her. Was he not doing the same—losing himself, or trying to, shutting their circumstances out? "Don't you have enough to do?"

Was it his imagination, or did she almost wince at his harsh tone? "I—'tis important to keep busy, to not think . . ." She paused, hands coming together over her heart in a gesture that only wrenched him further. "The schoolhouse might give me some measure of peace."

He looked away, glad of her request if only because it made room for his own. "Now seems a good time to tell you I'm considering taking part in the Virginia Assembly."

"The Assembly?"

"Aye, there's much that needs to be done. I'll be away in the capital much of the time when I'm not in Williamsburg." He moved to the sideboard and poured himself a brandy. He rarely drank this early, but lately it seemed the only thing he could stomach. "The states are bickering for power, and Congress is considering a new constitution. Meanwhile Britain is laughing at us as we conquer ourselves with petty rivalries and jealousies." He took a fiery swallow. "All this leaves me wondering what we fought for in the first place."

"Do you have political ambitions then?" There was an odd edge to her voice he'd not heard before. He welcomed it. Anger was far preferable to tears. "Is your being general not enough, Seamus?"

He shrugged, a cold callousness taking over. "Away from Tall Acre, I might forget for a time, be of benefit elsewhere. You just said as much yourself."

"What will be next? Attorney general? Governor of Virginia?"

He lit a second taper as thunder rolled and the room grew darker. "Why are you so opposed?"

"My father's politics were our undoing. I hardly see you now. I would be a political widow then."

His hand shook as he moved the taper nearer. "So you want more of me, Sophie?" The once tender question, now phrased bitterly, brought a crimson stain to her cheeks.

He sensed she was thinking of the man she loved. He certainly was. He'd racked his brain for a name, a neighbor, someone who might be the one. Like a splinter, the wondering lodged inside him, painful and distracting, compounding the hurt of losing Lily Cate. Making him feel an unfit husband as well as father.

"You have free rein to hold your school if you want to," he said evenly. "I'll be in Richmond and Williamsburg for the most part. Riggs will oversee things in my absence just as he did during the war." He set the empty glass down. "I suppose the matter is settled."

Only it wasn't settled. He read the questions in her eyes, even though she'd retreated into a tear-stained silence. *Have you given up on Lily Cate? Is that why you're leaving, Seamus? Will you make a life without her? Without Tall Acre? Can you really outrun the pain?* In truth, Richmond and the Virginia Assembly were the farthest things from his mind.

She hugged her arms to her chest as if chilled. "When will you be leaving?"

"Tomorrow morn." He sat back down at his desk, bringing an end to the conversation. "I don't know when I'll be back."

The next morning Sophie kept to her bedchamber, determined to avoid Seamus's leaving lest she come apart completely. A quick look out the window told her what she had no wish to know. Through the shimmer of the rising sun, she saw his silhouette as he turned in the family graveyard beneath the oak grove. He went more often of late, though he never stayed long. There was simply too much to do at Tall Acre.

Her emotions were so worn, so sore, she simply sat amidst the pungent company of dried herbs and flowers, wishing for something to ease her heart. His heart. The distance between them had never been greater. Had she only dreamed those tender words and Sabbath kisses, half-stolen bits of heaven, before everything came crashing down?

His leaving, this sudden political bent, seemed an outright rejection of her. Yet despite the heartache of Lily Cate, he was still her husband. Her hero. The man she loved. How would she find her way back to him?

The following days loomed long and lonesome. In Seamus's absence, she began meeting with Riggs and Mrs. Lamont, but it was no substitute for the master of Tall Acre. Questions that only he could answer were put to her, and she found herself growing wearier. Not even prayer seemed to sustain her.

"You must eat, Mistress Ogilvy," Mrs. Lamont urged at nearly every meal.

But Sophie had no heart for anything with a husband and child both missing.

⁂

"We've searched for weeks, sir, and have exhausted all leads."

Seamus stared at the sheriff, thinking how no amount of

money or begging would sway him. The case was no longer paramount. Other, more pressing matters awaited. Seamus didn't blame him. But he couldn't rest.

"Then I'll hire another search party. Go over the ground we've covered once more. Take out further notices in the papers."

The sheriff nodded. "I understand, sir. 'Tis not easy to move on with a child missing. We've done all we can and questioned the Fitzhughs repeatedly. They maintain their innocence, and oddly enough, I believe them. Till something more is uncovered, there's little to be done."

Truly, there was little left to do but return home once he'd finished in Richmond. He rode south without any sense of direction or purpose, letting Vulcan take the lead. When Tall Acre came into view, he felt nothing, the pride and pleasure it had once wrought now a memory. Thirsty and winded, he took a side alley to the stables, glad the staff were at supper. The familiarity of hay-strewn stalls, the tack on the walls, and the nickering of his favorite horses were hollow, holding none of the welcome of before.

No sooner had he dismounted than his stable manager emerged from a back room. "Evenin', General."

"Evening, Abel." He forced the amiable words past the leadenness. "How goes it since I've been away?"

A slight pause. "I'm loath to be the bearer of bad tidings, sir. But the morning after you left, I found this here note tacked to the back of the new mare's stall. Mistress Ogilvy's mount, ye ken."

Seamus's hands stilled on the bridle. "A note?"

Abel passed him a battered paper, the ink heavy and nearly illegible. Bracing himself, Seamus read the words thrice, his stoicism slipping.

*The lady who rides this mare, take care. The mistress
of Tall Acre shall be no more.*

Seamus's gaze shot to the house, to the open river door.
His next words were choked as he folded the note and put it
in his waistcoat pocket. "How *is* Mistress Ogilvy?"

"None the worse for it. We didn't want to worry her so
said nothing. She's not been riding, busy as she is."

"Wise to keep the matter quiet. I don't want her alarmed.
Any idea who might have made the threat?"

"None, sir."

"I'll double the guard. Make sure you bring any more
mischief to me straightaway."

Removing his saddlebags from the lathered stallion, he released Vulcan to Abel's care and made for the house, the weight
of Williamsburg returning with a vengeance. By the time he
reached the river door, he'd broken into such a sweat he felt
light-headed, almost feverish. Dropping his load on the steps,
he hurried into the foyer, nearly colliding with Mrs. Lamont.

Startled, she looked up at him. "Welcome home, General.
Is something the matter?"

"Where is the mistress?"

"On a walk as of a quarter of an hour ago. I don't have
any idea where."

He went out again, eyes everywhere at once. Garden. Stillroom. Schoolhouse. River. He felt pulled in every direction.
His pulse thrashed in his ears as his worst fear stared him
in the face. Sophie hurt . . . Sophie dead.

*Lord, am I to lose everything? My hand . . . my daughter
. . . my wife?*

Anguish, ever near, became sheer physical pain.

God, please. Sophie.

Was time ever felt as keenly as in a graveyard? Sophie stopped just shy of the surrounding stone fence. Overhead a stand of oak trees convulsed in a sudden wind, making her miss her shawl. Slipping inside the enclosure, she rubbed the goose bumps from her bare arms and glanced back to make sure no one followed. She wanted to be alone when visiting Anne's resting place. She wasn't sure how Seamus would feel about her coming.

The two largest stones belonged to Seamus's parents, side by side in death as they'd been in life. Each marble slab bore a fuzz of pale green moss. As Sophie stood before Lilias Ogilvy's grave, a lump formed in her throat at the chiseled inscription.

Once she was all that cheers and sweetens life. The tender mother, daughter, friend, and wife. Once she was all that makes mankind adore, now view this marble and be vain no more.

The words blurred. Despite everything that had happened, was she not called to cheer and sweeten life, be a tender mother, a tender wife? Was she wrong in wanting to carve her name on Seamus Ogilvy's heart, not just on some cold slab of stone?

Two small markers rested behind his parents' imposing ones. Babies? Seamus and Cosima's siblings? Her gaze swung wide, searching, but all that met her eye was untrammeled grass and thick blackberry vine reaching a thorny arm through the crumbling fence.

Bewilderment pummeled her. Where was Anne?

"Sophie."

She spun round, eyes wide as Seamus came toward her.

Stripped of his coat, he wore shirtsleeves and breeches, his mud-spattered boots indicative of a long ride. He'd returned home without warning.

His voice was low. "What are you doing here?"

"I'm—" Why had she come? "I'm looking for Anne's grave."

"Anne's?" He looked startled. "Why?"

"Because you keep coming here, and I—" Her voice caught and nearly broke. "I thought if I came too, it might not haunt me so."

He looked to the ground, struggling visibly for a response. "I come here to think, Sophie. To remember what my parents had. Not try to hold on to something—or someone." His next words came low, nearly inaudible. "Anne died in Williamsburg and is buried at Bruton Parish Church. She had no wish to be here even in death. She hated Tall Acre."

She blinked, a tear falling free. He'd rarely acknowledged Anne's unhappiness. "Seamus, I'm . . . sorry." Sorry for a failed marriage. For the irreparable stain of war and torn loyalties and a too long separation. Catching up her apron, she dried her eyes.

"Come back to the house, Sophie." He grasped her fingers, surprising her. Turning her on end. "We have some things to discuss."

Hand in hand they left the graveyard. Her gaze roamed, taking in Tall Acre, the surrounding hills and fields. The chill racing over her had nothing to do with the wind's sudden stirring. Even with the tall, stalwart soldier beside her, she felt strangely vulnerable. On the verge of some further calamity. And very much afraid.

30

S ophie sought the haven of her bedchamber, thoughts crowded with Seamus's unexpected return and his per-plexing words. *We have some things to discuss.* Disquiet gained a stranglehold as the supper hour neared. Had he come to tell her he was going to Kentucky? Might he leave her as her father left her mother? Their marriage, distant and unconsummated, seemed flimsy at best. 'Twas Lily Cate who had brought them together. In her absence, little remained to keep them from coming apart.

She stared in dismay at the hat boxes and parcels littering the room. Her trousseau had arrived from Roan earlier that day, something she'd forgotten about completely. Though she'd once anticipated it with pleasure, the very thought of its expense now taunted her. Seamus had spent an untold sum on her new wardrobe and was no doubt regretting every shilling.

Mrs. Lamont sent Florie in to help unpack, but there was a great deal more examining and admiring than putting away. She realized anew she needed a lady's maid but wouldn't burden Seamus with that. As the supper hour neared, dresses and shoes and stays were strewn about the room like confetti.

Florie came to a complete stop as she held up a dress meant for Lily Cate. The rose lustring fabric was exquisite, the lace sleeves a work of art. A matching gown for Sophie was spread across the sofa. "Do you want me to hide this one away, mistress?"

Sophie paused from layering clocked stockings in a cupboard, the simple question thorn-sharp. "Take it to her bedchamber, if you would, please."

With a nod, Florie left up the back stair, the gown in her arms. For a moment Sophie stood amidst the disarray, spying yet another dress for Lily Cate beneath a stack of underpinnings. She held it close, burying her face in its linen folds, barely aware of Seamus in the hall. Lifting her head, she overheard his conversation with Mrs. Lamont in preparation for supper. Would they dine together again after so long?

Setting the wee dress aside, she faced the looking glass. 'Twas easy enough to pin a stray curl into place beneath her cambric cap, but there was no help for her lusterless eyes, the shadows beneath. Even though Florie had dressed her in a new gown, it did little good for her spirits—or Seamus's. With a last distressed look in a mirror, she went across the hall to the small parlor.

He was standing by the hearth where a fire burned, his expression unreadable. "'Tis good to be back, Sophie."

Unsure of him, she looked to the rug. So he was glad to be back? For a few hours? A few days?

"You should know straightaway that I've reconsidered my role in politics." His unexpected words nearly sent her back a step. "I've sent my regrets to Richmond."

Her head came up, a dozen questions clamoring. "You're staying home?"

"I'm most needed here at Tall Acre." He was looking at her in a way he hadn't in weeks. As if he sensed her turmoil. Her questions. Her deep need of him. "The new government will go on with or without me." He took something from his coat pocket, his expression so earnest, so contrite, it hurt her. "I found this for you in the capital. It comes with an apology. My behavior at Early Hall was unconscionable. I treated you rudely besides—"

"Please, Seamus, think no more on it." Shaken by his bewildering reversal, she took the package from him and slowly unwrapped it. She expected a fan or a thimble. Some other trinket. Not a . . . busk. Busks were intimate, worn next to the skin, usually given by sweethearts. She beheld its painted design, a bit awed. "Why, it looks like Tall Acre."

"Mayhap it is."

"I—I don't know what to say." She felt all thumbs, nearly dropping the gift on the rug at his feet. Once in the privacy of her bedchamber, she'd slip it in the front of her stays, tie it in place with a lace busk point. "Thank you. I'll treasure it."

He smiled and her eyes smarted. He'd not smiled at her since Lily Cate went missing. She'd feared he'd never smile again.

At the clamor of dishes in the hall, they took their usual seats. A maid served them, and Seamus said a halting grace. Would they never get used to being without Lily Cate's buffering presence? She longed to be easy with him, to regain even a shadow of what they'd had . . .

"You've been—" He swallowed and surveyed his plate, looking no hungrier than she. "You've been well while I was away?"

Saying she had been was more lie. Even now she was reeling from his sudden about-face and what it foretold. "I'm relieved you're back," she finally murmured. "When you leave, things seem to happen." Taking up a fork, she poked at her chicken and new potatoes and spring greens. "There's been a rash of thieving of late."

"So Riggs told me." He took a drink of cider. "Someone broke into the smokehouse again, and a few sheep are unaccounted for." He glanced at the open door leading to her chamber. "I need to change rooms with you, if you would. For a few days, mayhap, just till we catch the culprit." At her alarmed look, he shrugged. "I'd simply feel better if you were on the second floor."

"'Tis no trouble." But even as she said it, she remembered her normally tidy chamber was a shambles. If there was one thing she'd learned about Seamus, it was that he liked order.

"You've noticed nothing amiss?"

She hesitated. "Nothing near at hand." Dare she share her fears? "I've not quite gotten over the war years. Sometimes I still feel a bit . . . haunted. Mostly after dark."

He looked at her, his expression grieved. "If you need me in the night, Sophie, don't hesitate to come to me."

His earnest words broke over her, stirring and sweet. She steeled herself against the rush of emotion sliding through her. "I'm not frightened, Seamus. Not with you here."

He set down his fork. "I promise you this trouble will have an end."

She looked to her mostly untouched plate, the knot in her throat expanding. Would it ever end? Would Lily Cate find her way back to them? Would they somehow find a way back to each other?

He said nothing more, just took a few more halfhearted

bites of supper before setting both their trays aside. She watched as he opened his father's Bible. Before Lily Cate had left, they'd made an attempt at family devotions, reading a Psalm aloud each evening, a blessed end to their busy days. But she was unprepared for his resuming the readings tonight.

"Except the LORD build the house; they labour in vain that build it . . . Children are an heritage of the LORD; and the fruit of the womb is his reward. As arrows are in the hand of a mighty man; so are children of the youth. Happy is the man that hath his quiver full of them."

His voice cracked. And then he stopped reading without explanation.

Heartsore, she waited. That terrible sadness had descended, driving out all peace, however fleeting. She got up and lay a hand on his shoulder as she passed behind. Not trusting herself to say goodnight, she left the small parlor, the dilemma of separate quarters tugging at her again.

Upstairs, she passed down the hall to his room, struck by its starkness. She'd had no cause to come here before. 'Twas completely masculine, a shock to her feminine senses. No doubt he'd find her chamber just as strange with its frills and flourishes. She shut the door and allowed herself a few luxurious liberties. A linen shirt hung from a near peg. She reached for it as hungrily as if it had been Seamus himself, burying her face in its soft, scented folds. Her fingers grazed the razor and leather case on his shaving stand, the soap and toiletries scented with lime and sandalwood. A linen stock lay beside a clothes brush and a nest of queue ribbons. Across the room a cupboard door stood ajar, revealing fine broadcloth suits. She wondered where he kept his uniform. His cocked hat with its finely worked cockade rested in a window ledge.

The bed . . . it was so big. Did a man need so much room?

Once Florie brought her a nightgown, she used the bed steps to climb atop the high tester, the lush feather mattress sinking beneath her weight.

She'd rather have Seamus than his room, the comfort of his arms rather than the warmest coverlet. But even this was far more than she'd ever dreamed of.

⁂

After working at his desk till midnight, Seamus checked all the doors in the house. Once in Sophie's bedchamber, he nearly forgot the threatening note. Evidence of her trousseau—a hat and gloves and stockings—lay about in provocative disarray. Two dresses he'd never seen were draped across a love seat. He studied them, tongue in cheek. Was she trying to tempt him? Or had Florie just left things untended?

He was more undone when he lay down. The bed linens held her subtle scent, the pillow a slight indentation. A lone candle threw light around the room, calling out all the ways she'd made it hers. He rolled over, facing the wall where the shadows were the thickest.

She was overhead, sleeping in his very bed. Did she ever think of him in a more than practical way? Need him . . . desire him? Did she ever long to embrace the life God meant for them as husband and wife? That holy, mysterious intertwining marriage wrought? Not just in body but in soul?

Despite his ongoing anguish, his visceral need of her was unrelenting, but it strayed well beyond that. 'Twas more the depth of his desire, his wanting more of her. Her friendship, first and foremost. Her companionship. Her devotion. The thought of it being ripped away, the loss of her, had flipped his world on end again.

Prayers for her protection crowded in, desperate and beseeching. He finally slept, and then, like getting a face full of icy water, he jerked awake. Lily Cate? Cold reality rushed in as he recalled the loss. The rousing cry held a woman's strength, sharp and strangled, before snapping short. He was on his feet, grabbing his pistol before taking the back stairs to his room. Its familiarity was his advantage. Even in pitch blackness he quickly determined there was no danger.

A single taper burned on a low table. Sophie sat in the center of his bed, knees drawn up to her chin. With a little moan of dismay, she seemed embarrassed at his appearing. Her hands went to her unbound hair in a show of modesty before circling her knees again. She looked touchingly girl-ish. He found himself wishing she'd open her arms to him like she often had Lily Cate.

"Sophie?" The tenderness of his voice seemed to ease her. What had she said?

I'm not frightened, Seamus. Not with you here.

He sat on the edge of the bed, determined to still her shaking. When he leaned nearer she almost seemed to startle, making him second-guess what he was about to do. He ached to hold her. To make amends with more than words, gifts. The busk he'd given her seemed a paltry thing.

Go slowly. Don't scare her.

The reminder was at odds with his need. The glint of her wedding ring caught the candlelight as he took her hand. She lowered her eyes, thick-lashed and black, and the last of his reserve cracked. How could he have ever thought her undesirable or plain?

The feel of her was so unfamiliar it shook him. He rested his chin on the crown of her bent head, aware of a great many things at once. Her wildly erratic heartbeat. Her shallow breathing. Her skittishness.

His pulse began a slow climb. Their unexpected closeness begged him to do something.

If she wasn't so uneasy, he would tip her chin up and kiss her . . . Aye, he wanted to kiss her. He wanted her to kiss him back. Fully. Feverishly. He wanted his everlasting misery over Lily Cate to abate if only momentarily in the sanctuary of her arms.

He went still, wrenched back to reality as she slipped free of him. "Just a bad dream, Seamus. No more."

Though her words were reassuring, he sensed something else at play. He sat silent for several moments, listening. Gauging the darkness.

"You're all right . . . alone?" At her nod, he made a reluctant exit, casting a last, uneasy look at her from the doorway.

🐚

When Seamus left, Sophie started toward Anne's former bedchamber. Taking up the candle, she shouldered aside her dread. The adjoining door opened soundlessly with the turn of the knob. Her hand shaking, the light wavered and threatened to go out.

There on the floor was the vase she'd heard fall from its perch on the nightstand, jarring her awake. She held the candle higher. In the deepest shadows, the chair to Anne's desk was pushed back. Fumbling, afraid, she felt beneath the familiar panel and released the secret latch. The drawer was empty.

Anne's diary was gone.

🐚

Returning to bed, Sophie lay awake till dawn. Seamus reappeared, surprising her yet again, trying his best to be quiet.

320

Broad back to her, he was fumbling in a cupboard, clad only in breeches, feet bare. Clearly they'd thought too much about Tall Acre's thief and not enough about the practicalities of switching rooms.

She lay quietly. This was how it would be . . . should be. Not separate rooms or separate lives. Not wondering when he'd gotten up or where he was.

He turned round and she shut her eyes. Soon he came to stand by the bed. She felt him there—his presence, his warmth, the wholeness of him. The heat of the blankets reached her face. Did he find her lacking, all mussed by sleep? Was he remembering last night?

Her breathing thinned when she felt his touch. Gently, almost imperceptibly, his fingers stroked a strand of her hair. The gesture, simple though it was, brought healing. Rekindled something lost.

Oh, Seamus.

She wanted to open her eyes. Her arms. But he stepped back and left as quietly as he'd come.

31

Sophie recited the alphabet, thinking *The New England Primer* too melancholy. "A, in Adam's fall we sinned all . . . G, as runs the glass our life doth pass . . . Y, while youth do cheer death may be near . . ." But Myrtilla and Jenny seemed not to mind, dutifully repeating each verse after her and scratching out letters on their slates.

She'd begun teaching in Seamus's absence. Now that he was home again, the lessons continued. With its fresh paint and repaired chimney, a crate of new slates and books, the schoolroom had a bright, expectant feel. Above the mantel were colorful prints of animals. On the walls were maps. A window was open wide to the garden, ushering in a welcome breeze. Word was spreading in the quarters that lessons were not only pleasant but a blessed reprieve from work.

Sophie looked up as a stable hand darkened the doorway. "Come in, Jim." Pleased, she gestured to an empty desk, retrieving a slate and stylus for him to use.

Mumbling his thanks, he sat as Jenny murmured a greeting and returned to her work. For the next half hour, Sophie taught the lanky boy to spell his name, introducing him to a picture book that had been Lily Cate's.

If Lily Cate returned, what a help she would be. *If.* Biting her lip, Sophie prayed for a miracle. *When* Lily Cate came home, the joy of the schoolhouse would be complete.

As she thought it, a slightly sheepish Granny Bea entered, a baby on her hip. "I suppose I ain't too old to learn my letters . . . read a book."

Taking the baby from her, Sophie assured her that age had nothing to do with it. Busy minutes passed, the warmth of the day calling for Sophie to open the door. When the bell sounded from the blacksmith's announcing the noon hour over, all returned to their work reluctantly.

The sudden emptiness seemed lonesome, the mosquito whining about her head assailing her as doggedly as the events of the last hours. Seamus's unexpected return. The change in their rooms. Anne's missing diary. What would happen next?

She straightened slates and books, craving order, wishing she could do the same with their unsettled circumstances. A bit woozy, she remembered she hadn't eaten breakfast. Days and nights of neglect were taking a toll. She felt wrung out, benumbed, but for those fierce bursts of grief that ambushed her at every turn. She knew it went harder on Seamus. To lose a child, not to the grim, irreversible grip of death, but to be forever undone wondering . . .

Bear up, lass.

Her mother's voice came clear as daylight. But this time it brought little calm.

Closing the schoolhouse door, Sophie paused on the sunlit stoop, bone weary. Before her, Tall Acre was spread like a lush landscape in oils. She stood unmoved by its beauty. She'd lost sight of the wonder of being its mistress, married to the man who was just now coming through the river doorway, sunlight framing every hard-muscled line of him. Unaware of her, Seamus took the shell path to the stables.

Her gaze trailed after him as he called to a groom before entering a far paddock where a new horse had recently been broken. The high-spirited bay shied at his approach, but he spoke a few words and began checking the horse's girth with a sure hand. She nearly held her breath as he, in that effortless way he had, took the reins and swung himself into the saddle. Immediately the proud horse reared and danced, stirring up a whirlwind of dust.

Riveted, she watched from her porch perch, sensing Seamus warmed to the challenge, was adept at courting danger.

Or had ceased to care what happened to himself.

He held fast for a few breathtaking seconds, and then he fell, one booted foot caught in the stirrup. With a shrill whinny, the bay bolted round the paddock, dragging him through a storm of dirt and rock.

Her life—their life—flashed before her eyes. Every misspent second, every withheld word.

With a little cry, she jumped from the porch and ran toward the paddock.

⁂

A nimble groom gave chase and grabbed for the reins, finally bringing the agitated horse to an uneasy stop. Another groom disentangled Seamus's boot from the stirrup, but for a few moments he simply lay on the ground, chest heaving and head spinning. Slowly he pulled himself to his feet, more mindful of his pride than any injury. He spied a flash of blue and saw Sophie—calm, competent Sophie—running toward the paddock, a look of terror on her face.

"You all right, sir?" The nearest groom was regarding him as if he doubted it, apprehension foremost.

"I wouldn't be if you hadn't gone for the bridle," Seamus said with a small smile of thanks as he bent and retrieved his hat. "Turn Prince loose in the far pasture, aye? I'll not do any more riding today."

The stallion was led away, still shying and snorting, as Sophie entered the dusty paddock, looking even more frightened than when he'd come to her in the night. "Seamus, you're hurt."

He touched his temple, his fingers warm with blood. "A scratch."

"Come, let me look at you." Taking his arm, she was intent on the stillroom, reminding him of the flowers he'd left for her that long ago, half-forgotten afternoon.

For a moment he stayed dizzy, and then the sharp tang of herbs cleared his head as she led him to a chair. Unused to being on the receiving end of her care, he stayed silent while she took out rags and salve and, with the finesse of a physician, set about cleaning him up.

Her touch was light and capable. She stood so enticingly close he had to clench his hands lest he reach for her as he had last night.

"Seamus, you might have been killed." Emotion flooded her eyes, turning them a darker blue. "I saw you fall—"

"I'm fine, Sophie."

"Well, I'm not." The words came in a rush as if she'd been holding her breath since she'd seen him tumble. "I-I was thinking how life is passing us by, how sometimes there are no second chances." She choked and stumbled over the words, though her ministrations never ceased. "All is well one minute, and then everything is turned on its head the next." He smelled something strong but not unpleasant as she uncorked a bottle. "I could be here with you now, only you might be laid out on this table instead, broken and lifeless and—"

"Sophie, what exactly are you saying?"

"'Tis not what I'm saying, Seamus. 'Tis what I'm feeling." She set aside the rags, nearly spilling the tonic. "I . . . I . . ."

He felt a jolt of alarm at how pale she was, all the blood drained from her face. Unthinking, he caught her wrists and pulled her toward him. There was no other chair in the room but his lap.

She sat down without a protest, with a willingness that had been missing last night. This close, he marveled how he could no longer chase her from his thoughts. Her wealth of dark hair, the memory of her bell-like laugh, her ongoing eagerness to please him combined with her befuddling distance, had worked a spell on his hardened heart. Despite everything that had happened to them and between them, he longed to touch her, to know her inside out. He wanted her and her alone. He wanted her intimately and lastingly and forever. Could she not sense that?

Mayhap she did.

Her gaze held his, open and honest, conveying things too deep for words. Leaning ever nearer, she took hold of his shoulders and pressed her mouth to his. His heart seemed to stop. She tasted sweet. Pure. True.

"Seamus"—the words came on a rush of air—"I love you."

He fought for a response. For clarity. A question rose inside him, but his throat closed, denying him. Dazed, he tucked a strand of loosened hair behind her ear, his fingers grazing her pale cheek.

"There's no one else. There never was. I told Captain McClintock what I did because of my feelings for you. At the time I knew you didn't love me—might never love me. I could not tell you then, but I tell you now because sometimes there are no second chances . . ."

He took the confession in, every stunning syllable. His thoughts cut to Lily Cate. It seemed almost a betrayal to feel even painfully happy without her. The hole she'd left never lessened. But joy was here, in this very room, calling out for him to claim it.

"Sophie, I believe I loved you long before this. Till now I don't think I even knew what love was—"

"Hush, Seamus." She put gentle fingers to his lips. "We shan't waste another second."

He kissed her hungrily, even fiercely, afraid he might startle her. But her response held a willingness he'd not anticipated. For long minutes they lost themselves in each other, passionately and unashamedly, till their breath was spent. He'd forgotten the wonder of this kind of closeness. He'd been without it so long he was stunned by the power of it, the way his blood raced, the way it left him shaken.

Someone was coming. Yet another interruption. He could hear a footfall on the walk. They drew apart, flushed and breathless, and he felt the distance between them like never before. His thoughts raced full tilt to the sweetness of tonight. Being alone with her again couldn't come soon enough.

✦

His wedding night had come.

He took a breath, the razor in his maimed hand less steady than usual. He was a bridegroom . . . again. Though the war had ground sentimentality out of him or at least forced it into retreat, he found himself wanting to stop time, hover on the edge of this hallowed moment. Come morning his world—and hers—would have shifted. They'd be one in the truest, most biblical sense, never to be undone.

At not yet ten o'clock, the house was locked, the servants settled. Finished with shaving, he ran a hand through freshly washed hair, feeling a bit self-conscious in bare chest and breeches. The floor was cold against his naked feet. He felt young and in love and uncertain again, not an experienced widower and soldier.

His mind kept traveling downstairs. From this night forward they'd share his parents' bedchamber. Was Sophie readying for him, wondering if he'd come? At supper she'd said little. A silent current had pulsed between them, as felt as lightning, making words unnecessary. Ever since she'd first kissed him in the pungent shadows of the stillroom, he'd thought of little else.

He left his bedchamber, passing by Lily Cate's and feeling the familiar ache. But for the moment Sophie was waiting. He took the back stairs to her bedchamber slowly, a sconce on the landing lighting his way. Thankfulness warmed him, pooling in his chest till his eyes smarted. Sophie was God's gift to him. For years of war. Griefs unspoken. Heartaches on the field and at home. He paused at her door, head bent. Humbled.

His heart had never beat like this for Anne.

⚘

Sophie could barely breathe. As she shook the pins from her hair, the candlelight called out her expectant, pensive expression in the looking glass. She wasn't sure of Seamus till she heard his footfall on the stair. She'd forgotten to leave the door ajar. Would he think she meant to turn him away?

Self-consciousness flooded her. She was unsure of what was to come. The intimacies of marriage were unknown to her, but this melting ache inside her was becoming all too familiar. Did Seamus feel the same?

As her hair tumbled past her hips, she reached for her nightgown, little more than a skim of lace, the fabric was so sheer. It fell into place as his light tap on the door turned her round. She called to him and he pushed the door open, standing on the threshold, a final question in his eyes. With a shy but joyous smile she doused the candle flame and opened her arms to him.

By morning it seemed they had always been this way, she curled against him, her head on his hard shoulder, he on his back, his relaxed features barely visible in dawn's feeble light. Nothing in the big house stirred. A rooster crowed beyond the shuttered windows, but it barely intruded on her happiness.

In the drowsy haze of half sleep, she remembered it was the Sabbath. Lily Cate was not with them. They would go to church without her. And then all the wonders of the night rushed in, making her rue the morning.

Seamus's sleepy voice roused her completely. He turned on his side and looked down at her with a new tenderness that was her own special possession. "I must be dreaming . . . you . . . this."

"If this is a dream, I never want to come awake," she whispered.

The intoxication of their closeness lingered, making her wish it was nighttime again. As she thought it, he took her in his arms, showing her she needn't wish for anything at all.

32

A tumultuous month passed, half of it spent in Williamsburg. This time Sophie went with him. Seamus hadn't told her about the note found in the stables. He'd simply given it to the sheriff, who now knew that the threat extended beyond Lily Cate. The strain of her disappearance never lessened, but life went on its relentless, consuming way, tarnishing his beloved memories of her.

Sophie filled the emptiness, a tonic for his fury and loss. They returned home to Tall Acre, determined to start anew. Once again he was pitched headlong into the needs of the estate from dawn till dusk. But his priorities had altered. His evenings, his every waking thought, were hers.

He left his study their first eve home, the strike of the clock and his own rumbling stomach announcing supper.

Mrs. Lamont met him in the foyer, a worried pinch to her brow. "We're ready to serve, General, but Mistress Ogilvy is sleeping."

Sleeping? At this hour? He said nothing, and she continued on genially. "I'll delay the meal till you're ready."

The aroma wafting from the summer kitchen convinced him Cook had prepared a feast. He thanked her and moved to the private hall of their bedchamber, the door ajar.

Sophie lay atop the counterpane, a letter from Cosima near at hand. His heart clenched as he took in her abandoned slippers on the rug, so small compared to his own brawny boots. She was on her side, one arm curved beneath her head, her lovely features at rest.

He knew every inch of her yet couldn't look enough at her. Couldn't touch her enough. Her skin was soft as lamb's wool beneath his ravaged hand. Even now he wanted to take the pins from her hair. They winked at him in the light, tiny pearls amidst piercing blackness like stars in a night sky.

He'd grown so used to men. Soldiers. Their vile habits and weaknesses. Their wild snoring and smells. Living with Sophie was bliss. Even in sleep she was ladylike. Delicate. He forgot all about supper.

He sat down carefully on the edge of the bed, a new worry scratching at the surface of his conscience. Was she ill? Fever, an ever-present malady, was spreading in the quarters, though they'd quarantined those most sick. In truth, she'd never looked healthier. She seemed to give out light like a candle.

Flushed from sleep, she turned on her back. "Seamus?" She raised up, and he realized he was blocking her view of the clock. "What time is it?"

"The supper hour."

Her face dimmed as awareness rushed in. He knew she was thinking of Lily Cate, reliving the heartache all over again. Every morning upon awakening he did the same, spirits sinking as he faced another day without her, the ache never lessening, only lengthening.

"'Twill be our last meal together for a time. I leave for Williamsburg again in the morning. The sheriff wants to see me."

Her sleepiness fell away. "Oh Seamus, do you think . . ."

Touching her cheek, he reined in his own disappointment. "He said it's not urgent, to come when I could."

"I'll go with you."

"No need. I'll be away a day or so at the most." He weighed the implications of telling her about the threat and decided against it. All seemed to know but Sophie and were on alert. "You're most needed here."

"Then I shall count the hours till you come back."

Bending near, he kissed her. "I'll do the same, aye."

⁂

Smothering a yawn, Sophie rummaged through glass bottles in the stillroom, some highly decorative and some plain. Essential Salt of Lemons. Hill's Balsam of Honey. James's Fever Powders. Daffey's Elixir. Though she was intent on some help for the fever toppling the staff, nothing she'd found or concocted had curbed it yet.

Seamus had left that morning, but she'd hardly had time to ponder it, not with so many servants ill. So far Jenny had been spared, though a baby had died, adding to Tall Acre's melancholy. Myrtilla was a tireless nurse, working close as Sophie's shadow. They trod back and forth to the icehouse, applying cold cloths and changing bed linens and dispensing medicine, trying to make the sick more comfortable. Dr. Craik had been summoned but was slow in coming, busy with a smallpox outbreak elsewhere.

Sophie's bleary gaze fastened on a bottle of absinthe. Anne's diary had been riddled with its mention, and she shrank from the sight. She shut the cupboard quickly, her

332

breakfast of toast and tea rising to the back of her throat. Swallowing hard, she left the stillroom but made it no farther than an iron bench against an ivy-clad wall. If she was perfectly still, the wooziness might pass. She couldn't fall sick herself, not at a time like this. She'd rest for just a moment, not long enough to be missed.

The gentle drone of June's bees and the heady scent of honeysuckle lulled her, and she dozed, unmindful of her missing hat or the way her complexion freckled in the sun. Sleep was a refuge, a world beyond the worries of the present.

"Mistress Ogilvy."

Sophie stirred on the bench. How long had she napped? Too long, her overwarm skin told her.

Mrs. Lamont hovered nearer, still a bit wan from falling ill herself. "I'm sorry to disturb you, but you have a visitor. She's in the Palladian room as the large parlor is being painted."

Sophie nodded and thanked her. Probably a neighbor expressing concern and asking about Lily Cate. Standing, she smoothed her skirts and started up the shell walkway to the house.

The shadowed foyer was cool, the door to the Palladian room open. Sophie's eye was drawn to Peale's finished portrait above the mantel. She always felt a little start when she saw it, as if staring into a mirror. She, Tall Acre's unlikely mistress.

The visitor's back was to her, and she was looking up at the portrait too. Her polonaise skirts were drawn up over lush petticoats trimmed with fine ecru lace, her matching hat trailing periwinkle ribbons.

Sophie's greeting carried across the elegant room. "Welcome to Tall Acre."

Slowly, the woman turned, a lace veil obscuring her features. "The general isn't in, the housekeeper said."

"He's away, yes."

"How unfortunate." She looked about as if getting her bearings, gaze returning briefly to the portrait.

Sophie gestured toward a settee. "Would you care to sit down?"

"Perhaps . . . I suppose we should make introductions."

Raising gloved hands, the visitor pulled loose a pin and removed her elaborate hat and veil. Sophie fought to place her, shaken by a strange familiarity she couldn't quite grasp hold of. Her eyes—were they brown? The woman wasn't smiling. Her pale, blue-veined features seemed more ice, but even their coldness couldn't blunt her beauty. She was the most dazzling woman Sophie had ever seen.

"I well remember you." The words were clipped. Precise. Thoroughly British and unmistakably condescending. "You're the daughter of Midwife Menzies from Three Chimneys."

Sophie opened her mouth to reply, but her throat felt like dust. Again, that odd sense of familiarity settled over her then spun away.

"'Tis clear you do not remember me . . . or do not want to." With a graceful gesture, the visitor settled her hat upon the settee and sank down beside it, chin tipped up proudly. "I am Anne Howard Ogilvy. The mistress of Tall Acre."

⁂

Urging Vulcan on, Seamus fixed his gaze on the road to Williamsburg and ignored the quiet tug that told him to turn back. Lately his battle sense seemed to sharpen, his every instinct on alert. It had served him well on the field but was hardly needed at home, yet here it was again, following on his heels like some faithful, misguided dog.

His thoughts veered to Sophie. She'd been restless in the

night, murmuring in her sleep. She seemed preoccupied of late. More emotional. He feared she was taking the fever. He'd had a brief bout of it himself but had worked his way through it despite her protests to stay abed.

Squinting into bright sunlight, he scanned the lay of the land as he rode. Blooming magnolia and catalpa spread across the valley on both sides of him, commanding his attention and making light of his fears. All the extravagance of early summer held sway, a warm wind drying out the muddy ruts in the road.

Another tug to his conscience. *Sophie.* Having become one with her in the truest sense, was he now able, even away from her, to sense her need of him?

Heeding it, he reined his stallion sharply round in a turn reminiscent of battlefield retreats. In less than an hour of hard riding he'd reached the borders of Tall Acre, his practiced eye moving past beloved fences and fields to the long alley where an unfamiliar coach waited near the front steps.

Cutting across the sheep pasture, he cleared a sunken ditch and came to the stables, a noisy rooster crowing his arrival. He stopped long enough to wash up in the laundry where the new bath was nearly in place, then started for the house, casting a last look at the strange coach as he did so.

I am Anne Howard Ogilvy. The mistress of Tall Acre.

Sophie heard the words but couldn't take them in. They made no sense. Nothing in her mind and heart had prepared her for this moment. Her hands clutched the back of the chair she stood behind, her nails digging into the lush blue brocade.

Anne was dead of a fever, buried in Williamsburg during the war. Seamus had told her so himself.

"I'm obviously the last person you expected. You're looking at me as if I'm a ghost." Anne's cold half smile was locked in place, her composure seamless, as if she'd rehearsed their meeting. "To reassure you that I am indeed Seamus's wife, I shall provide you with a few details. My husband bears a scar on his jaw given him by his sister during childhood. More intimately, he has a saber wound on his left thigh from early in the war. He also—"

"*Don't.*" It was the only word Sophie could muster. The wooziness she'd fought for days was winning, tiny flecks of black staining her vision as the blood left her head.

Anne stood and began a slow walk around the room, fingering objects on tables as if reacquainting herself with them. "I don't know what Seamus has told you. While he was away fighting, threats were made against me. He had so many enemies during the war that I became a target. Fearing for my life and that of my child, I left Tall Acre and fled to Williamsburg. Unfortunately, the danger followed me there, so I sailed for England."

"You left Lily Cate behind." In the shock and confusion of the moment, Lily Cate stayed foremost. Was Anne behind her disappearance?

Anne lifted slender shoulders in a shrug. "There was simply no other choice. Crossing the ocean with so small a child . . ." She gave a shake of her head. "My sister and her husband took Lily Cate to raise as their own. They erected a gravestone to quell questions. Once in England I went to Bath, where I have relatives, to gain some safety. Peace."

Peace? Sophie stared at her. Had she left Seamus peace? Or Lily Cate?

"Now that the war's been won, I've come back to reclaim my rightful place."

Her rightful place? After leaving a wide swath of lies and brokenness in her wake? Was she . . . mad? Anne paused to look up at the portrait again, clearly vexed. Her thoughts were plain. Sophie was the imposter, the pretender. The real mistress of Tall Acre had returned.

"You must understand I was one of many who fled in the wake of war. But now, peace has come . . ." Anne's voice trailed away. She was looking past Sophie to the open doorway, expectancy in her expression.

Seamus.

Sickened, Sophie shut her eyes, unwilling to turn around and witness his reaction. The prolonged, stunned silence told her enough.

Seamus entered Tall Acre's foyer, gaze on the open Palladian room door. He heard Sophie's voice, clear and lilting yet strained. She was speaking with someone whose tone and inflections stirred some vague, uncomfortable recollection. Not bothering to change his boots or greatcoat, he walked their way.

In seconds he stood on the threshold. Overcome. Ambushed. Recognition rushed in like smoke clearing. His eyes made the connection, but his reason . . . nay. Like a barrage of musket fire, Anne's appearance sent him reeling.

His gaze swung to Sophie, who'd begun a slow retreat. She looked dazed, like she might faint. His chest was so tight he couldn't breathe. The room lost its focus, spun wildly, and resettled, but his heart stayed at a gallop. "Sophie, wait."

Her hand grasped the doorknob of his adjoining study door. There was a plea in her eyes—a hundred questions— begging him to make things right.

He returned his attention to Anne. His voice was so choked he nearly couldn't speak. "What have you done with my daughter?"

The flash of fury in Anne's face told him he'd get no easy answers. He looked again at Sophie. She'd pressed her back against the door to his study as if it was the only thing holding her up.

Anne waved a hand, her cloying cologne sparking tattered memories. "I was explaining to Miss Menzies—"

"*Miss?*" He spat out the word, stepping into the room. "'Tis Mistress Ogilvy, my wife."

"Your wife?" Her voice hardened. "More your mistress, Seamus. I am your wife—"

"Nay." His voice came grieved and broken. "You are nothing more to me than a ghost of the past, and I've a gravestone to prove it."

A crimson stain spread over Anne's finely wrought features. "Be that as it may, I was explaining how I fled for my life—"

"Then you've been spouting a good many lies and excuses."

"Those threats were real, every one of them. Ask any of the plantations surrounding us or Tall Acre's slaves—"

"You were the only one who ran while they remained." His curt indictment only fueled her ire. "Nothing you say can explain your absence—or your reappearance."

"How dare you!" Taking a step closer, she raised a gloved fist, returning the memory of all her fits and whims he'd buried at the back of his conscience. "'Twas you—"

He clasped her wrist, imprisoning it. "Where is my daughter?"

"Safe and sound where she rightfully belongs." She wrenched away from him with renewed rage. "I am her mother—"

"You, who abandoned her to begin with."

"Who abandoned whom, Seamus? 'Twas *you* who left me with a baby and a miserable plantation to fight a war!"

"You knew my politics when you wed me."

"That's past." Like quicksilver, Anne softened her stance and placed a hand on Seamus's chest, dismissing his words with a turn of her head. "We can look to the future now—"

"Where is she?" he repeated.

"I'm not here about Lily Cate." Her breath released in a pent-up rush. "I've come about us."

"Us . . . *nay*." The word held an unwarranted intimacy. He looked toward Sophie, but she turned away, going into his study and shutting the door. Their hard-won happiness was beginning to fail like a faulty redoubt along enemy lines. He turned toward Anne unwillingly. "Why in heaven's name did you come back? If you went to England and had a life there, why?"

"Because I came to my senses in Bath, Seamus." She blinked, eyes wet. From regret? Or the injury she felt he'd done her? "Surely you can forgive me that."

Seamus focused on Sophie's portrait and set his jaw, the pressure so taut it ached. He'd do well to remember what he'd often told his men.

Never let your emotions overrule your reason.

He spoke slowly. "I may forgive you, but I'll not stand by and let you destroy the life I've built here and now."

"Then I'll go to the courts."

"On what grounds?"

"On the grounds that I want my husband and daughter back—"

"You've already thrown that away, declaring yourself dead and fleeing to England."

"So what will you do, Seamus? Divorce me? Our union is still legal as I'm very much alive." She moved away, backtracking to retrieve her hat and making a wide circle around him. "I'm staying with old friends, the Alexanders, a few miles from here."

He yanked his gaze back to her. "The Alexanders who are now accomplices in your kidnapping scheme."

"Be that as it may, our daughter is well but is proving rather inconsolable as she is so attached to your mistress."

He left the barb unchallenged, wanting to be free of her. Only he wasn't free. And he might never be.

33

He expected an ugly confrontation. More fight. Anne was a formidable opponent, after all. But he saw no sign of her carriage or her manservant as he rode up the drive to the Alexander estate soon after she fled Tall Acre. British to the bone, Artemus Alexander and family only paid lip service to the American cause. His ivy-coated home was the perfect refuge for Anne. Artemus was, he remembered dully, a cousin of Fitzhugh.

Dismounting, he fixed his eyes on the carved pineapple finial adorning the mansard roof, an ironically hospitable symbol. Before he'd set one foot in its direction, the front door swung open and Lily Cate ran out as if her heels were on fire.

"Papa!"

Never was a word more sweetly spoken. He caught her up, choked and overcome at the sight and feel of her. He'd thought she was lost to him. Gone forever. But here she was, as warm and wiggly as a puppy, burrowing deeper into his arms before covering his bristled jaw with a flurry of kisses.

"Papa, I knew you would come. They told me you wouldn't but I knew better."

He wondered at the *they* she spoke of. The Alexanders . . . Anne. For a long moment he didn't speak, so torn with emotion his eyes smarted and he couldn't focus. "I've come to take you home. Soph—your mother—is wanting to see you straightaway." He pulled back from her, eyeing her disheveled dress and lank hair. "They didn't mistreat you?"

She laid her head on his shoulder. "They fed me a little—and locked me in a room."

Behind him, two of his grooms waited silently on their mounts, pistols drawn, their attention riveted to the house as if expecting a fresh outburst of opposition. But all was quiet. Eerily quiet. Seamus had the distinct impression they were being watched from myriad windows, but the Alexanders didn't dare intervene.

"To Tall Acre," he told the grooms, setting Lily Cate atop his own saddle before swinging up behind her. "I'll deal with the Alexanders in time."

'Twas candlelight. The supper smells were thickening, the clatter of cutlery and dishes oddly comforting, penetrating Sophie's pain. Her mind felt broken, replaying the afternoon's events endlessly. Despite everything, Lily Cate slept in her arms, having grown noticeably taller in the weeks she'd been gone.

The hours following Anne's leaving were a frantic blur. All Sophie knew was that Seamus had gone to an estate a few miles east, where close friends of Anne had been sheltering her and Lily Cate. Seamus spared Sophie the details of just what had occurred when he'd arrived there, leaving her to sort through her scattered thoughts and emotions while he sent word to Williamsburg to call off the search.

Now, every few minutes Sophie pressed a kiss to Lily Cate's brow as if to convince herself she'd truly come home. As the night's shadows lengthened, Lily Cate stirred and yawned, looking about as if unsure just where she was. Then, finally, "Mama, who was that strange lady who kept me? She looks like Aunt Charlotte."

Sophie was at a loss for words. Should she say it was her mother, the woman Lily Cate had no memory of? Had Anne not identified herself as such?

Lily Cate filled the uneasy silence. "She is very unhappy with Papa."

"Yes, sometimes grown-ups quarrel. Your father is upset that she took you away from us."

"The bearded man took me away, the one who used to come here and watch me." She sat up and hugged her doll closer. "But I'm home now. I'm ready to start school and play with Jenny and ride my pony."

"Oh aye," Sophie replied absently. She rested her cheek against Lily Cate's hair, wishing matters would end so happily for herself and Seamus.

With supper over, Sophie tucked Lily Cate in once prayers were said. After a joyful reunion, Lily Cate begged Jenny to stay close and sleep in the trundle bed. Myrtilla, ever devoted, had positioned herself outside Lily Cate's bedchamber to stand watch all night. At Seamus's bidding? In the light of a single candle she knitted, her ebony face unusually serene.

Sophie went below, going through the motions of undressing without Florie. She couldn't risk the maid's questioning.

She had no answers and felt so at odds—elated that Lily Cate was finally home, anguished over Anne. Tugging at her front-lacing stays, she pulled them free, standing in her shift before the candlelit mirror. That old, insidious dissatisfaction swept in with the evening shadows. In light of Anne's sheer physical beauty, she felt lacking. Second best.

Listening to the old house settle, she wondered if Seamus would come. What he might say. Panicked prayers, a cup of chamomile tea, did nothing to ease her. All normalcy had fled. Benumbed, she could only climb into bed alone, a new awkwardness overtaking her.

At midnight the door opened. She stayed quiet as Seamus's tall shadow moved in the moonlight shining through shutters she'd forgotten to close. The feather mattress sagged beneath his bulk when he finally undressed and came to bed. The silence was rife with tension.

"Sophie."

Tears close, she couldn't answer. He had become so gentle with her. So tender. Would that end? Was it wrong to be here, in this intimate moment, wanting what only a husband could give?

He lay down beside her, the quaver in his voice matching the one in her spirit. "I want you to know I didn't suspect any of this with Anne. I never once doubted she was dead. I would not have wed you had I any inkling—"

"I believe you." She turned away from him, the wall a poor refuge when all she wanted was his arms. "But what are we to do?"

"We will hope. Pray. There shall be no barriers between us." The strength in his voice, honed from years on the battlefield, brought little comfort. He placed a careful hand on her bare arm. His reassuring touch was like fire, like salt to

344

her rawness. "You are my wife, Sophie, heart and soul and body. There is no one else."

He lay back, releasing her. But his words went deep, echoing into the sleepless night. Enduring, heartfelt words she'd long dreamed of, but ones that held no promises nonetheless.

※

The next morning Seamus went away without warning. When he returned the day after, he faced her across the expanse of his desk, its bulk symbolic of the deep chasm between them.

"We need to talk this out, Sophie." He went and closed the door. "Away from Lily Cate."

She sat down on the edge of a Windsor chair, her poise deserting her. "She's—" Unshed tears made a hot knot in her throat. "She's not yet awake. After breakfast she'll be in the schoolhouse with Jenny and the others. 'Tis important to keep to a schedule, I ken."

He nodded absently, sitting back in his chair. His cravat hung loose and he was in his shirtsleeves. Black fringed his angular jaw, giving him the look of a rogue. She could trace in his face a sleepless night and more. The old Seamus was missing, lost in the depths of some fierce, internal struggle he might not win.

"I met with both an attorney and a judge yesterday in Richmond. They advise filing a petition with the Virginia court."

She took the words in, sensing a long, complicated fight looming. She knew little about Virginia law in light of the Revolution. 'Twas Seamus's own words that kept coming to mind in regards to Curtis. *He's family. The war is won. We should be glad he's alive, all loyalties aside. One day it won't matter.* Rational. Humble. Wise.

Shouldn't the same be said of Anne?

Although she stayed silent, he was regarding her in that uncanny way he had, gained from years on the field when he'd read men like maps. "Anne has deserted. Falsified her death. Grounds enough to keep my marriage to you intact."

She pushed back a strand of hair she hadn't bothered brushing, praying for calm. "Answer me this, Seamus. If not for me, would you take her back?"

"Take her back?" He leaned forward and his eyes held hers, stunned. "Why would you even ask such a question?"

Nearly flinching, she bit her tongue. He was too angry, too sore, her careful question like flint against steel, igniting his temper.

"Anne and I—" He broke off, fighting for words. "'Twas a marriage gone wrong from the start. Suffice it to say there is far more at play than first appears."

"I sense that . . ." Nay, she *knew*. Anne's diary was proof. But it was also missing, unable to prove Anne's misdeeds. She wouldn't mention it. He'd been hurt enough. "But I—I cannot remain here at Tall Acre. Not when I'm little more than—"

"*Nay.*" His gaze held hers, daring her to defy him.

Defy him she did. She who had been reared a Menzies and finished with Mrs. Hallam's airs and graces was little more than his mistress. "I *am* your—"

"You are my wife. I wed you and made you mine in good faith before God and all of Virginia."

She shook her head. "Your first wife is alive, making a second marriage invalid. I am not your wife no matter how much you or I wish it to be." Her voice frayed, but she clung to reason. "Nor am I Lily Cate's mother."

"You are both a mother and a wife in all the ways that matter."

"That changes nothing." She stood, too worn to argue. "Anne is back and I—I must go."

"Where?"

"To Three Chimneys."

"You realize your absence lends credence to Anne's claim. That you are not the rightful mistress of Tall Acre."

In the anguish of the last few hours, she'd not thought that far. She looked to a shuttered window as all the repercussions came crashing down.

"Sophie, look at me." He'd left his chair and now stood too close. "This is not about Lily Cate any longer."

"Seamus, please . . ."

The feel of his hands on her shoulders sent a shiver of longing through her. "Whatever our beginnings, Sophie, I love you. I have never loved a woman the way I love you. Nothing can change that."

She gave another shake of her head, trying to build a wall his tender words kept tearing down. Now that she had his love, what did it matter? She took a step back. "Seamus, feelings aside, I cannot stay, no matter the reasons."

"Then you should know about the note that was found in the stables when I was away in Richmond last. Someone left a threat concerning you. I've since given it to the sheriff, who feels it is a part of this business with Anne."

"You didn't tell me . . ."

"I didn't want to frighten you. I only tell you now because if you leave, I cannot guarantee your safety even with a guard posted."

"Then I'll take extra care myself and rely on the Lord." She turned away and thought he might reach for her—stop her leaving—but he was a man of honor and would let her go.

Even as she walked the hall to their bedchamber, she felt

the ache to be close to him. Would she never know him as her husband again? The threatening note bothered her but little. How to sever two fiercely woven hearts, two bodies made one in the truest biblical sense?

She shut the door to their room, overwhelmed with where to start. Her personal belongings, all she'd brought from Three Chimneys, were scattered about, mingled with that of Seamus's own.

She pulled a worn trunk from beneath the bed and began packing essentials. Smallclothes and underpinnings and a few simple dresses. The lovely busk he'd given her. Her comb and hand mirror. She clutched the pearls that were his mother's then put them back. Her movements were slow, unwilling. She didn't stop till a beloved voice sounded in the doorway, turning her cold.

"Mama, where are you going?" Lily Cate stood in her nightgown, clutching her doll.

The plaintive question, couched in alarm, hurt more than anything that had gone before. Dropping down on a loveseat, Sophie took Lily Cate in her arms. She'd make this no harder than she had to. "Remember when I lived at Three Chimneys and you used to come visit me?" At her thoughtful nod, Sophie continued quietly, "I need to return and take care of matters there."

Sorrow engulfed the girl's small face. "May I go with you?"

"I wish you could, but your papa needs you here." The words rang hollow. How could she explain such a tangled web? Forcing a half smile, she gestured to her trunk as if she were going on little more than an outing. "Can you help me pack? Fetch my clean linens from Florie?"

With a nod Lily Cate was off, leaving Sophie to look about the room for anything she might have missed. Seamus would have to explain her leaving to the staff. She had no heart for it and couldn't answer the awkward queries sure to follow.

She moved to her desk and took Curtis's letter out of a drawer, the money neatly folded. More money than she'd had need of till now. Was this what was meant by the Almighty bringing good out of all things? Somehow the Lord had provided for her through her brother's and father's desertion when she thought nothing good could ever come of such twisted circumstances.

She bent her head in silent thanks, unwilling to think beyond this painful moment.

Lord, I am Yours. Yours alone. Not Seamus's. Not Lily Cate's. None but Yours.

᷒

Three Chimneys was no longer home. Home was Tall Acre. But at least Mistress Murdo and Henry were waiting. Since wedding Seamus, Sophie had only returned to visit a few times. But this . . . this was different. Shameful. Humiliating. She walked up the front steps, the groom carrying her trunk on one broad shoulder, her conundrum written on his solemn face as they entered the empty foyer.

Sophie straightened her shoulders and weighed what she would say, only to have it unravel in seconds. The moment Mistress Murdo spied her, the housekeeper burst into a torrent of tears. Thankfully, word traveled fast among the staff, sparing Sophie an explanation.

"I've heard the news but can scarce believe it." Mistress Murdo dabbed at her eyes with her apron hem. "I knew 'twas something shifty behind Lily Cate's disappearance. Mistress Anne and her manservant are to blame." At Sophie's silence she rushed on. "His name's Blackaby. 'Twas him who snatched Lily Cate in Williamsburg and him who was trespassing and scaring folks here. I've no doubt he's behind the light shining at Early Hall. When the sheriff nabbed him, he confessed in hopes to gain some sort of pardon." She sniffed. "Shows how little allegiance he had to Mistress Anne."

Seamus hadn't told her this. What had he said?

Suffice it to say there is far more at play than first appears.

"Yer in need of refreshment, looks like." Taking Sophie's hand as if she were no older than Lily Cate, Mistress Murdo led her out the back door toward shade and fresh air. A bench was situated beneath a sprawling magnolia tree nearly as old as Three Chimneys.

Sophie surveyed the kitchen garden, the tidy rows a patchwork of green. "Have you any ginger tea?" Her request seemed more a weary guest's. "I recall some in the larder."

"Ginger, is it?" With a nod Mistress Murdo hastened back inside, then returned shortly with a tray bearing a buttered scone and porcelain pot.

Sophie sipped the tea cautiously, not trusting the scone.

"Ye've nae turned down a sweet yet." Mistress Murdo's eyes were penetrating as an owl's. "But under the circumstances . . ."

"There's a fever going round Tall Acre. I'm feeling a wee bit . . ." She left off. If her innards were chancy as a butter churn, it was because of Anne, nothing else.

Mistress Murdo released a mournful breath. "Well, peelywally or no, you look right bonny. I'll go back into the kitchen and see about supper."

When she'd returned to her tasks, Sophie braved another sip of tea, the gold glint of her hand nearly making her sputter. She set her cup down and twisted her wedding ring off, sorrow overriding the nausea as it came free. She pocketed the ring, torn between keeping it and returning it, glad there was only one wedding band and Seamus was spared doing the same.

If the Almighty could bring good from this predicament, then He was Almighty indeed.

∞

Her presence had filled Tall Acre and now her absence emptied it. Though she'd taken only a few of her belongings, he'd rather she have taken them all. After two days of legal counsel, Seamus returned from Richmond to find Sophie gone. Despite her warning that she would be at Three Chimneys, he felt foolish in his grief. Standing before a corner cupboard, he'd taken her wedding dress in his hands and buried his face in its silken folds and wept.

Later, lying on his back in bed, an arm thrown over his eyes to block the sight of her remaining things, he heard the door open with a telling creak. Lily Cate's small form was a flash of white as she rushed toward him in her nightgown. *Papa, where is Mama?* he expected her to say. But she climbed the bed steps and burrowed into his arms without a word as if sensing he had no answers.

She'd asked him about Anne but once. "Who was that strange lady who took me away?"

He'd replied, "Her name is Anne Howard, sister to your aunt Charlotte." He would not call Anne *mother*. Or *wife*. Lily Cate had merely nodded at his choked answer, the confusion in her face finally giving way.

Now he held her close, her warm breath tickling his cheek as she lapsed into sleep. In Sophie's absence, Myrtilla mothered her as much as she did Jenny. He need not worry about

Anne or her manservant causing more mischief, not with Blackaby sitting in the Richmond jail on kidnapping charges.

In the hours ahead, he suspected Anne would come to Tall Acre just as she had before he'd left for Richmond, uninvited and without warning, wanting to wear him down amidst the scandal to ensue. No longer blindsided by her beauty, he'd faced her, immune to her threats and cajoling and tears. Years of war and ongoing reports from Riggs of her absinthe-induced rages had stripped him of all gullibility and sharpened his vision. He'd turned her out before she'd uttered a single sentence.

Furious, she'd flown to Richmond and charged him with bigamy. He almost smiled at the bitter irony. If he did have two wives, she was to blame, resurrecting herself from the dead.

꙳

In the waning afternoon light, Seamus's legal counsel wore a look of resignation and regret. "You understand that your case could take longer than expected, General Ogilvy."

Seamus's gaze roamed the rich mahogany walls of Henley and Stokes' paneled study on this, his third trip to Richmond. He feared over time the chamber would become as familiar as his own. "How long in your estimation?"

"A year, perhaps . . . years." Stokes rubbed his chin, his red-rimmed eyes indicating a lack of sleep. "The defendant, Anne Howard, has made it clear she is determined to turn this into an extended battle if you don't give in to her demands from the outset."

Seamus set his jaw. "I will not relent."

"I'm afraid there is more than Mistress Howard at play." Henley, the elder of the two attorneys, paused to take a pinch of snuff. "States such as ours are scrambling to establish new laws, making marital matters civil court proceedings rather than state proceedings, requiring action by the legislature. All of this takes time. Despite the war being won, many are staying true to English law and advocating no union can be dissolved, none more so than Virginia." He met Seamus's eyes. "Yours is a complicated case, General, and you may well be caught in the crossfire."

"What more can be done?" Seamus's tone knotted with impatience. After his years of being in command of a situation, the maze of legalities baffled and frustrated him.

Henley put on his spectacles and removed a paper from atop his desk. "You're aware your first wife has filed her own petition, charging you with neglect and abandonment—"

"Because I was serving my country, a charge that will not hold up in court."

"True enough, but one that must be dealt with nevertheless, including the more recent charge of bigamy." Henley's thin mouth twisted. "Take heart, General. You're not the only man involved in a bigamy scandal. Others have done the same during the war, quitting their first families and starting second ones, though none are quite as well placed as you."

Seamus failed to find even grim humor in it. "I did not quit my first family, mind you. Nor did I falsify my death, abandon my daughter, and flee to England." Despite his best efforts, he spoke with a rancor that soured his stomach. "I am simply asking for a full dissolution with the right of remarriage."

Henley pulled another paper from a hefty stack. "As matters stand, the innocent party will be set free from the bonds of marriage while the guilty party will be unable to remarry during the lifetime of the innocent spouse."

"And my daughter? There is no question about custody?"

Henley met his gaze full-on. "Absolutely none. Virginia law is clear about paternal rights. Even Fitzhugh, all bully and bluff, hasn't a leg to stand on."

The reassurance rang hollow. "I want all that can be done to move this forward as if there were no expected delays, no impediments."

Stokes rose from the desk to open a window as the sticky, early summer heat blanketed them. "Depositions from friends and relatives are needed, of course. Both Henley and I will be coming to Tall Acre to collect those with your consent."

"What sort of depositions?"

"Statements from friends and relatives, even trusted servants, that may help in the case regarding your first wife's conduct, among other matters."

He felt a qualm. The newspapers would waste no ink printing every sordid detail. "There's no avoiding dredging all this up for public consumption?"

"I'm afraid not," Stokes said.

Seamus looked down, the ensuing silence rife with questions. Where had it all gone wrong? He was far from blameless, but he had tried to be a worthy husband. Faithful. Honorable. He'd put Anne's needs above his own in the matter of a second child. He'd been a good provider while he was away fighting. But somehow it wasn't enough. Now, as then, he was back in the thick of battle, sweating and harried, uncertain of the outcome.

Henley wiped his brow with a handkerchief. "You understand that the court might not consider any of the above things I've mentioned sufficient grounds for dissolution. Under colonial law, marriages are seldom dissolved unless there is evidence of cruelty or infidelity, though prior cases do exist in New England where abandonment for three years or longer is justification enough."

Seamus stood, returning his cocked hat to his head. "You simply need to determine the truth."

Henley and Stokes looked at him. "The truth?" they said in unison.

"Aye, the truth behind Anne's leaving Virginia. The truth behind her years in England. The truth behind her return. I don't know what that entails, but given time the facts will stand."

He looked at them, a strange peace flooding his soul, so at odds with the anguish twisting inside him. Only that morning he had read a verse that seemed an anchor for his shifting circumstances.

And ye shall know the truth, and the truth shall make you free.

34

Sophie stood in the mulberry grove after a week at Three Chimneys, no longer spinning dreams of silk production. Would the estate revert to Clementine Randolph's kin once again? If so, she'd be without a home, in the same predicament she'd been in at first. Nay, 'twas far more tangled now. She'd simply been a spinster then. Now she was a wife set aside. And a guarded one, at that. Her protector lurked nearby, back turned as if to give her some privacy, at least.

She pressed her palms to her bodice, so snug she'd soon have to set it aside. All her dresses seemed smaller, her bosom fuller. Despite her unsettled stomach and circumstances, she was blooming right before the eyes of anyone who cared to take a second look.

Leaning against a mulberry's rough trunk, she shut her eyes. When she opened them, the guard was gone and Seamus stood before her. Sunlight skimmed his handsome features, warming his gaze and shimmering off his dark hair. He always carried himself like a soldier, tall and stalwart no matter their situation. Her heart gave a little leap. Might he bring . . . good news?

"I've been in Richmond. Matters are moving slowly." He swallowed, the cords in his neck taut. "I'll spare you the details."

Her disappointment went bone deep. "How is Lily Cate?"

"Missing you, but busy in the schoolhouse with the new Scots tutor. I expect she'll speak with a Scots brogue ere long."

"So he's come." She smiled past the irritation of feeling excluded, unnecessary. "And Jenny, everyone else?"

"The fever is finally subsiding." He tucked his hat under one arm. "Myrtilla is back in the spinning house again. The planting, all the seining for shad and herring, is done, but my correspondence is getting out of hand."

"You need a personal secretary."

"That would be you, Sophie."

"Send over your papers and I'll see to them gladly."

His gaze sharpened, and he brushed her cheek with the back of his fingers. He was looking at her as if they'd been apart weeks, not days. His touch told her the same. "Mistress Murdo said you've been ill."

Self-consciously her arms went round her waist. "Nothing for you to worry about. Just missing you and Lily Cate."

"She's missing you." His eyes darkened to a deeper blue. "She needs you in a hundred ways I cannot answer."

"She's welcome to walk across the meadow now that it's spring." Saying it brought back the sweetness of that first time, when they'd met gathering chestnuts. She kept her voice light. "I'm always right here."

He tipped her chin up with his hand. "Do you have need of anything?"

"What could I possibly need? You've stuffed Three Chimneys' larder with more goods than Tall Acre since my arrival. At least bring me your papers so I can earn my keep."

"You'll have them by tonight."

"Tonight? Send them by way of the staff, then." The surprise in his face begged explanation. "Because if you bring them yourself, you might be tempted to stay, and I—we—cannot."

"By the staff, then." He took a careful step back as if ready to leave, then tossed aside his tricorn and gathered her in his arms.

"Seamus, I—" Words of caution died in her throat at the beloved scent and feel of him. He was naught but fresh linen and fine soap, muscle and sinew. Her refuge.

He kissed her like a man who couldn't remember what she felt or tasted like, with an urgency, a sweet fierceness, that had been missing before. "Sophie, love, this is nearly beyond enduring. I walk into the house and it feels empty. I feel empty. I reach for you in the night and you're not there." His tone was oddly tender and brusque. "By heaven, if I'd known you before the war, I would have been a failure on the field. You take up my every thought."

"There was a time when I wondered if you'd ever love me."

"Then wonder no longer." For long moments he held her, saying nothing, and then his gaze fell to her hands resting against his chest. "Where is your ring?"

In answer, she fingered the fine chain about her throat, pulling it free of her bodice. "Near my heart if not my hand."

His features tightened and he turned away, walking through the haze of sunlight to his waiting horse. When he rode off, it seemed he rode right out of her heart. Wooziness, once held at bay, now overcame her, and she barely made it to the bushes in time to empty her roiling stomach.

Sophie took out her sewing, the needle and thimble glinting in the firelight. The flannel fabric in her lap had been gotten in Roan by Mistress Murdo, who said not a word but seemed to know it was needed. Sophie rubbed it against her cheek. Soft as a rose petal and the blue of Seamus's uniform coat, it seemed reassurance of a boy. Carefully she cut an infant's gown from an old pattern kept by her mother with newly sharpened scissors.

Her thoughts drifted and refused to settle. Just yesterday, the day after Seamus had surprised her in the mulberry grove, Lily Cate had come. They'd spent an afternoon sewing together in the garden, Sophie full of praise for the little sampler Lily Cate was working. The alphabet was interwoven in a simple floral pattern, Lily Cate's initials at the center.

"When I grow up, I want to sew as well as you, Mama."

Sophie leaned nearer and kissed the sun-warmed crown of her head. She'd forgotten her hat, but Sophie didn't want to scold her. Their time together was too precious to squander on foolish reproofs.

"I asked Papa if I could stay here with you till you come back." She was chattering now, swinging her legs beneath her skirts, her sewing forsaken. "But he said you'll be home soon."

Oh Seamus . . .

"He's teaching me to play chess. He says he misses you, that you are very good company. He even moved the painting of you."

Sophie stopped her stitching. "Out of the Palladian room?"

Lily Cate nodded. "He put it over the mantel in the small parlor. 'Tis almost like you're there with us."

The guileless words left a mark. *Lord, I cannot do this any longer.*

"Florie says I might have another mama. But I don't want another mama. You're my mama."

Florie, nay. She'd often spoken to Florie about being discreet. To no avail.

Setting aside her sewing, Sophie gathered Lily Cate in her arms, biting her tongue to keep from mouthing flimsy reassurances. *I'll be home soon. We'll have a tea party in the garden and read fairy tales and say bedtime prayers . . .*

Her stomach was churning again along with her emotions. She looked to the bushes. She would *not* be sick in front of Lily Cate. She would stay strong. She would remember the promises in Scripture. She would hope and pray and not give way.

⁂

The depositions had begun. One by one the servants who had been at Tall Acre during Anne's brief tenure as its mistress were called to make a statement, Henley and Stokes presiding. Seamus kept to his study, hearing only a low murmur of voices through the closed door as he tried to work on ledgers and tally accounts.

He'd awakened at dawn, surprised he'd slept. Without Sophie, his humid nights were a tempestuous stretch of wartorn dreams and pulse-pounding regrets, leaving him half sick, unfit for work. Without her, even the staff seemed on edge.

At day's end an abrupt knock pulled him to the present. The attorneys came in, hands full of papers, expressions grave as they took seats opposite him.

"We've finished the depositions under oath," Stokes told

him, his youthful zeal in sharp contrast to Henley's mature caution. "Your overseer, Riggs, provided the most comprehensive testimony, but 'tis your spinner Myrtilla's that is most advantageous."

Seamus gave a nod. "I'm glad to see it done but don't care to hear the details." 'Twas punishment enough that his people, his staff, were subjected to this. A humiliation for everyone involved.

Henley fixed solemn eyes on him. "Though the spinner's testimony is certainly the most damning, I doubt it will be admissible in court given she is an enslaved woman—"

"Myrtilla is enslaved no longer. She was manumitted prior to my marriage to Sophie Menzies." His tone was saber sharp, regrettably so, but his legal counsel's continual presence put him on the defensive even if he had retained them. Henley had even had the nerve to remind him on more than one occasion that he'd not wed Sophie, at least legally.

Stokes gave a wan smile. "Her manumission may prove helpful. I intend to push for consideration of her entire testimony, even if it means calling her as a witness."

Henley grunted his doubt. "That is highly improbable. We need more than a statement. We need something tangible. A letter, perhaps, or something written that supports the spinner's words. You have no such evidence, I suppose."

Seamus shook his head. "The Fitzhughs moved Anne to Williamsburg when she fell ill and took all her personal effects. There's nothing remaining." Though glad of it at the time, he now saw just how damaging the lack was.

"We'll go to Williamsburg, then, in hopes of recovering something." Henley removed his spectacles and returned them to a leather case. "The Fitzhughs are more cooperative than we'd hoped given the pending charge of falsifying a death and erecting a gravestone before them. We've also threatened to have the judge removed from the bench."

Seamus drew in a breath. He could only guess how the haughty Fitzhugh reacted to that. All these accusations and bad feelings were stacked like ammunition between them, between him and Anne. But not between him and Sophie. He had to keep reminding himself that he'd done nothing wrong. She'd done nothing wrong.

"No one is forgetting your reputation as a decorated war hero. That alone should carry weight." For once Henley looked almost smug. "The ensuing press, all the papers, might work in our favor. You helped win a war that seemed to have no end. That's fresh in American minds at present, including the Virginia courts."

Seamus listened, steeling himself against false hope. What if Anne won? What if the testimony of Tall Acre's staff and Anne's misdeeds weren't enough to dissolve their tenuous tie? What if everything was excused because their lives had been torn apart by war and the court was willing to let it go at that?

"We have your first wife's statement, of course." Henley reached into a satchel and removed another document. "Therein she claims your Patriot sentiments conflicted with her British sympathies, and she fled to England after threats were made on her life, leaving your daughter in the care of Williamsburg relatives."

Sane words. Sensible words. All believable, even understandable. But what about desertion? Betrayal? Cleaving together for better or worse? Seamus looked to the mantel where his guns and saber rested, the wounds inside him festering again. Only the years on the field under impossible conditions kept him from tearing the papers from Henley's hand and feeding them to the fire.

Be not hasty in thy spirit to be angry: for anger resteth in the bosom of fools.

Henley tugged at his stock. "She also cites your neglect during that time—"

"Which has been explained sufficiently, I should think," Seamus interjected. Would Anne have everything dragged into the public arena? Every intimate detail better left behind closed doors?

Another hour ticked by, crowded with legal terms and speculations that left his head pounding.

"General?"

In the aftermath of Stokes's and Henley's exit, Myrtilla stood before him. She raised dark, liquid eyes to his. "Sir, is a freedwoman's word no better than that of a slave's?"

He swallowed, feeling the injustice like a burr. "'Tis more your word against that of a white woman's." Another inequality he could not remedy. "Virginia law is slow to change. One day, mayhap, matters will be different."

She nodded, lips pursed in contemplation. Curiously, a glint of satisfaction shone in her dark eyes, so at odds with what he had just told her.

35

Sophie came awake, snatched from sleep by Mistress Murdo's frantic words. "'Tis Lily Cate—the general has sent for you. She's worsened."

Worsened? She'd had but a summer's cold, someone said. By now Lily Cate should be better. Guilt and anger rushed in as Sophie's head came clear. Guilt she'd not been there from the first. Anger that matters with Anne had kept her away. She'd seen neither Seamus nor Lily Cate for nigh on a week. The lapse loomed large in her already troubled mind.

Her fingers shook and fumbled as she dressed with Mistress Murdo's help. The Ogilvy coach was waiting out front beneath a gibbous moon, the horses restless. A young groom jumped down to open the door for her as light cracked open dawn's dark horizon.

Mrs. Lamont met her in Tall Acre's foyer, her usual calm decidedly stirred. "Dr. Craik's above with the general. I'll be here below should you need me."

Sophie's spirits tumbled. Calling in Dr. Craik meant that every other means had been exhausted.

The sturdy Scotsman stood at the bedside, obscuring Sophie's view. 'Twas Seamus who turned her way, expression inscrutable, their emotional parting of days before hanging between them. One glance at Lily Cate and Sophie was ready to fall to pieces, but Seamus was looking at her, expecting more than panic. He was never more the general than in a crisis, but she sensed his silent anguish was as great as her own.

Half a dozen candles flickered around the room, illuminating bloodletting equipment and vials of medicine. The reek of onions boiled in molasses and a steaming kettle of vinegar and water told of hours spent to no avail. Myrtilla had been here. These were her remedies.

Craik moved aside as Sophie leaned over Lily Cate, his voice ragged with fatigue. "I could bleed her again."

"Nay, please. Let us try something else." Neither she nor her mother had ever believed in bleeding the life from a person struggling to live. Instead she felt the need to move Lily Cate, hold her, despite her frightening pallor and rattle of breath. When she suggested it, Craik frowned.

Undaunted, she eased onto the feather mattress. Lily Cate stirred, her eyes coming open then fluttering shut as if the simple effort stole all her strength. Sophie kissed her forehead, finding it cool, her lips a queer bluish-gray. Pneumonia . . . or quinsy?

Panic rising, she racked her memory for some remedy. Perhaps if Lily Cate sat up, head on Sophie's shoulder, she wouldn't struggle so to breathe. The nightgown she wore was stained with medicine and more. Was she coughing up blood? "Help me undress her. There's a clean shift in the cupboard."

She reached deep into her pocket and brought out a tin

of salve, her mother's mainstay, as Craik went below and Seamus rummaged for a shift. Together they undressed her, smearing the salve thick on her throat and chest before easing the clean shift in place, the herbal scent driving back the smell of sickness.

Sophie eyed the rocking chair, the place of many a heartfelt evening. "I want to rock her."

Gently Seamus picked Lily Cate up and resettled her on Sophie's lap, then pulled a blanket from the bed and tucked it around them both. Sophie settled in while he went below, the creak of the chair masking Lily Cate's labored breathing.

Tears swelled Sophie's throat, nearly stealing the hymn she sang over the girl. Lily Cate grew more lax, her breathing shallower. "You must get well, lamb. I cannot manage without you." She whispered the words that till now had only warmed her heart. "There's a new baby coming. Your very own brother or sister. I'll need your help. We must choose a name and sew clothes and prepare the nursery. There'll be a christening with cake and punch . . ."

A footfall on the stair hushed her. Seamus returned and took a wing chair across from them, his profile in sharp relief in the candlelight. She'd never seen him so undone. All the signs pointed to Lily Cate leaving them, yet Sophie kept rocking as if the steady motion kept death at bay.

She wouldn't let Lily Cate go. She had no say over Anne or the court or much else, but she loved Lily Cate like her own, and for this night, this moment, she would be her mother, even though there was no guarantee of tomorrow.

She looked to the shuttered window. If this was as dire as her spirit told her, Anne needed to be informed. "Seamus, though it hurts me to say it—"

"Anne has been sent for. She has not come."

366

Sophie began another hymn as if he'd never spoken, her foot pushing against the floor to keep the gentle rhythm of the rocker steady. And if Anne came? How strange it would be, the three of them in this room, in this marriage.

Lily Cate began to cough, a great racking cough that seemed a storm let loose inside her. Tensing, Sophie held her as Seamus brought a basin. Her frantic struggle brought Sophie's own stomach racing to her throat.

Spent, Lily Cate slumped against her, and Seamus set aside the basin to lay hands on his daughter. Was he praying? Or simply touching her before the last of life flowed out of her? The helplessness she felt, the hopelessness, was strangling. She couldn't help Lily Cate. She couldn't help Seamus. She had no power to undo this complicated knot with Anne. But God had promised to bring good out of all of it, even if it broke her heart and sent her to Edinburgh. Even if Lily Cate died. Even if Anne became mistress of Tall Acre.

All she had left was faith. Belief. God Himself.

⁂

Seamus splashed water into a basin as dawn lit the windows outside his and Sophie's bedchamber. He felt battle-weary, so torn in spirit he couldn't speak. Dr. Craik had left on another urgent call, declaring with his Scots candor that there was nothing more to be done. Sophie remained upstairs with Lily Cate, but he fully expected to see her at his door telling him it was all over.

Only it wasn't.

He'd bury his child and quietly prepare to face a court that seemed set against him. Virginia law, as it stood, would not allow a former slave's oral testimony against that of her former mistress. His legal counsel's attempts to wrest the truth from their British contacts regarding Anne's where-abouts and circumstances there were slow in coming, having to cross an ocean and back before bearing fruit. He'd forgiven Anne for whatever it was she'd done, but he could not resume a life with her.

"You could, General, bring the second Mrs. Ogilvy into the courtroom, to gain sympathy with the judges, even if she, being a lady, is unwilling," Stokes had urged in the hushed confines of his Richmond office. "Though the marriage rite is in question, she did promise to obey and serve you as your wife."

"And I vowed to love her, comfort her, and honor her," he replied. "Not force her to appear in a demeaning scandal that would make her public fodder and besmirch her own reputation."

That had shut Stokes up, but it hadn't helped the situation. With Virginia law being more firmly English and Anglican than any of the other new states, the case was hindered from the start. Not even citing more liberal laws in New England would likely sway these tradition-bound judges. Nor could a word from General Washington aid him. He was at the mercy of the court and Almighty God.

Bending over, he splashed water onto his unshaven face, then dried it with a linen towel embroidered with his and Sophie's initials. The reminder of how intimately they were tied sent him outside.

He passed through the west door into a morning so beautiful it seemed to magnify his grief. A whip-poor-will sang out overhead as he walked uphill to the cemetery. He sent his gaze into the overhanging oaks' deep shadows, finally fastening on his parents' gravestones.

Aye, there was room enough to bury a child. Room enough

to lie down himself. Years of trying to stay alive in combat seemed to mock him. What he'd give to rest beside his father and mother and end the pain and darkness of the present, the prospect of a life without his daughter.

The prospect of a life without Sophie, his wife.

⁂

Stiff from sitting, Sophie kept watch over Lily Cate as one day bled into the next. When she could stay awake no longer she dozed, unaware of whether Seamus was in the room or out, ever terrified of waking to Lily Cate's limp, lifeless body in her arms. And then . . .

"Mama, I'm thirsty."

Raspy and weak though they were, the stunning words were the sweetest Sophie had ever heard. Joy dawned as she looked into Lily Cate's lucid face. With trembling hands, Sophie fumbled with cup and pitcher on a near table, hardly believing it as Lily Cate downed the water and asked for more. When she began to cough, Sophie tensed, but it no longer held the threat of before.

Holding her close, careful not to upset the cup, Sophie kissed her hair and cheeks and chin till Lily Cate's giggle erupted into another spate of coughing. When she finally quieted she whispered, "When is our baby coming?"

So she'd heard the hushed secret, after all. A tear fell. For a moment Sophie couldn't speak.

Lily Cate touched her damp cheek. "You told me last night when I was sick. I saved it in my heart till I could ask you this morning."

"'Tis our secret. I haven't told your papa . . . not yet." Telling him too soon would only add to his burden. Saving the news till the proper time would be best, if . . .

Pressing a finger to her lips, Lily Cate looked to the door where Mrs. Lamont stood in joyous disbelief. "Well, praise be! Our little miss is up and talking!"

"Indeed!" Sophie eased, releasing the worry that Lily Cate might somehow worsen. "Please ask Cook for some broth and bread. Tea."

"Straightaway," she answered, disappearing.

Seamus filled the doorway next, hair lank and bloodshot eyes wary. Sophie's heart swelled when Lily Cate held out her arms to him with a husky, "Papa!"

Looking amazed, he reached for her, tickling her and nuzzling her neck despite another wrenching round of coughing. In his arms she looked content, happier than Sophie had ever seen her.

Thank You, Lord. Your mercies are new every morn.

36

Y ou've a visitor."
A visitor?

Mistress Murdo's wary expression told Sophie everything as she met her in Three Chimneys' foyer. After two nights and days at Tall Acre, Sophie had just returned through the back door, disheveled and worn but thankful beyond belief. All that mattered was that Lily Cate was well. Even Anne's unexpected arrival couldn't diminish that.

"She's waiting in the front parlor."

Sophie looked toward the open parlor door, forgoing changing her rumpled clothing. Seeing Anne so composed and queen-like, just as she'd been that first unforgettable day she'd returned to Tall Acre, sent Sophie reeling all over again.

"So how is my daughter?"

Shutting the door, Sophie faced her, fury and fatigue nearly making her lash out. Not once had she heard Anne say Lily Cate's name. She only spoke of her in possessive terms, as if to remind Sophie that Lily Cate was not hers and never would be. "Far better than when I arrived, though her cough needs to mend."

Anne nodded and smoothed a lace sleeve. "I suppose Myrtilla is dancing attendance on her in your absence." Bitterness laced the words—and blatant dislike. "At least she's of some use, ill-natured as she is."

Sophie measured her response, too weary to prolong the visit with an argument. "Why are you here?"

"Why?" Anne arched a pale brow, reminding Sophie of Charlotte. "The court proceedings begin tomorrow. Or didn't Seamus tell you?"

He hadn't. Sophie felt a qualm. "I didn't know. My presence isn't required."

"*Your* presence is the very reason this matter is so tangled."

Stubbornness squared Sophie's shoulders. "My presence—or your absence?"

Anne waved a dismissive hand. "Such a tiresome matter. I don't care to discuss it. Besides, that's not why I've come." Sitting down on a fraying sofa without invitation, she settled her reticule in her lap. "I feel it only fair to tell you that I spoke with your father before I left Bath. He was there taking the waters, and we had an unexpected meeting. I fear he is . . . unwell. He and your brother are anxious for you to join them in Edinburgh."

Sophie listened without comment. Bath had long been a favorite retreat of her father's, but it held no temptation for her save seeing Curtis again. She longed to tell him about her marriage to his commanding officer and onetime friend, but given their separate loyalties . . .

"Even though we are at cross purposes, Miss Menzies, I want to be of help." Anne studied her as if she were an annoyance to be dealt with, little more than a pesky fly. "There

372

is a ship sailing for England in two days' time, the same one that returned me here. The *Umbria* has better accommodations than most, and the captain is an experienced seaman."

Sophie moved a hand to her bodice, to the life already beginning to swell her middle. "You expect me to flee at the first sign of trouble?"

"Ah, Miss Menzies, how foolish you are." Anne's smugness was laced with pity. "My legal counsel assures me that you have little hope of returning to Tall Acre. My case is nearly foolproof. You know nothing about what I've been through—"

"What *you* have been through? What of Seamus? Lily Cate?" Exasperation gave Sophie the fire she'd lacked upon entering the room. "I know more than I care to. I know you left Tall Acre when you were needed and should have been of benefit. I know about—" The hated diary came to bear. "Tobias Early."

The name was no more than a whisper, but Anne was looking at her as if she'd shouted it.

Sophie plunged ahead, heedless. "I know why you left Tall Acre."

Pulling her gaze from Sophie's, chin still high, Anne seemed unconcerned. "Myrtilla told you, I suppose."

"Myrtilla, nay. She said nothing to me, nor have any of the servants. 'Twas your own words that exposed you. You left Tall Acre because you were expecting Tobias Early's child, a child I believe you must have lost because you cannot carry another babe to term—"

"Your mother broke confidence about that, I'd wager." Anne's eyes were ice, the anger that always seemed to lurk beneath her flawless facade threatening. "As for all the rest, my relationship with Tobias Early, you have no proof."

How right she was. The diary had never resurfaced, despite Sophie making careful inquiries among the staff. Misery twisted inside her. "Nay, I have no proof, but I have wondered . . ." How often she'd been preoccupied by what had happened to Anne, trying to stitch the missing pieces together like a garment that begged mending. "I believe you sailed to England with Tobias and took up life with him there. The Earlys are a prosperous, titled family. Bath would be one of their haunts. I'm guessing that somewhere along the way you and Tobias had a falling out, some sort of separation, leaving you destitute. You had little choice but to return here, though I'd dared to think it was a hope for reconciliation, a true heart's change that brought you back—"

"A true heart's change? What nonsense! 'Tis I who have been wronged most of all!" Anne stood, bringing a close to the conversation. "You have little to recommend you, Miss Menzies. In light of that, I advise you to return to Scotland and honor your father's wishes."

Sophie spoke to Anne's rigid back as she made for the door. "I am, in heaven's eyes if not the law's, Seamus Ogilvy's wife. Nothing can change that. Not even you, Anne."

With a last, contemptuous look, Anne went out.

❧

The chill in the courtroom matched the chill in Seamus's soul. Hours of testimony and legal posturing had played out before him as he marked time by a wall clock. His every breath was a prayer. For peace. Protection. Truth.

Thy will be done.

But it was his will, his need for Sophie, that consumed him. He pictured leaving the courthouse, the dust of Richmond on his heels, and riding straight to Three Chimneys be it daylight or dark. Sophie would be waiting, the wounds of the past no longer between them. There he'd hold her as he'd not done for weeks, triumphing over circumstances that had pushed them apart, then return her home to Tall Acre, where they would live out their days in uncontested privacy.

For now the judges sat before him in their robes and powdered wigs like relics from another century. One, Eustace Adams, had been a close friend of Sophie's father. Seamus's hackles rose as soon as he saw him. Years before, Adams and Lord Menzies had been involved in dishonest political dealings. Seamus doubted the war had cured him of that any more than it had whitewashed his tarnished reputation.

Anne was sitting across the room, facing forward. He'd brushed by her in the hall outside and noted the dilated pupils, the faint anise smell. She was too calm, too confident. What else but absinthe could still her shaking hands and high-strung nerves? Did she honestly believe he'd welcome her back in his home, in his bed? The attraction he'd once felt for her had withered to pity and outright revulsion. God knew he could not make a life with her. Could not trust her with their daughter. Could have no more children by her.

"I would like to cite the state of New Jersey, in which abandonment by one spouse for three years is sufficient justification for dissolving the union . . ." Stokes's voice filled the courtroom, raising Seamus's hopes.

Anne had been gone for more than four years. Stokes was presenting the most incriminating evidence so far, that she'd declared herself dead and Bruton Parish Church had a gravestone to prove it. His threat to haul the marker from Williamsburg to Richmond as evidence was met with grim laughter. Seamus didn't crack a smile. In his world, where fidelity and honor were the code, desertion was an offense punishable by death.

Back and forth the voices droned. One volley for Anne. Another for himself. His gaze sharpened as Reverend Hopkins was called and sworn in, driving home his and Sophie's wedding day. An objection was made that no banns had been read prior to the ceremony. Stokes countered that this was allowable now by special license. Anne's counsel intervened, stating the certificate Seamus and Sophie had signed and filed with the county clerk was now missing. Reverend Hopkins raised upturned hands to signify he did not know what had happened to the document, though he had delivered the certificate to the county clerk himself following the wedding.

A murmur rippled through the room. Anne turned her head and cast a slight smile Seamus's way. Behind him were many of his officers, some who had traveled great distances on his behalf in a show of support. He himself was in uniform. Though missing his usual accoutrements, he had dressed for battle, the wool nearly suffocating in close quarters.

But being a general, even a hero, no longer mattered. The judges were looking at him, weighing him, as Anne's counsel charged him with neglect, even cruelty, for his lengthy absences. Each charge was dismissed by Stokes immediately, who cited the war and Anne's medical condition after childbirth. Yet the damage was done. He had been cast in the role of a negligent husband, no matter the Revolution or Anne's precarious health.

He sat still, stoic, as Anne's failings were brought to light. The humiliation of it made him want to sink beneath the bench he sat upon. Cutting across his conscience was the problem with the missing marriage certificate. Missing . . . or mishandled? Mayhap maliciously?

The drone of voices stopped. Three days of testimony

and deliberation were at an end. The judges convened in a small chamber as tense minutes ticked by. On their return, the lead judge stood. Seamus heard the verdict as through a fog.

"By the power invested by the state of Virginia, we the council hereby declare the marriage between Seamus Michael Ogilvy and Anne Howard Ogilvy to be upheld according to colonial law—"

Seamus shot to his feet, slamming his maimed hand on the table in front of him. "Do you think I will not fight? Appeal? Do you think your ruling can undo years of absence and betrayal and unfaithfulness?" Every eye was on him, every face taut. "Am I to be bound by archaic colonial law—*English law*—that I gave eight years of my life to upend? Nay!"

There was a stunned silence as he spun on his heel and left the courtroom.

⁂

"She's gone, sir." Mistress Murdo stood before Seamus in the glare of a summer's afternoon. "I came home from market late yesterday to find this note waiting. I would have gotten it to you sooner, but you were in Richmond."

At that, she left him alone in Three Chimneys' foyer to read the note privately. Apprehension, thick and potent, overtook him at the first line.

Dear Seamus,

I must go. By the time you return from Richmond and read this, I will have sailed to Scotland. Please forgive me. You must remember, no matter where I am, my heart will always belong to you and Lily Cate.

Sophie

Shaking, he turned the paper over, wanting more. More words. More time. More chances. A soaring ache, unlike any he'd ever known, took hold of him. He'd been betrayed. Twice. Only he'd never believed Sophie capable of such. She had gone behind his back. She had given up. She had . . . left.

The vacant foyer, the unceasing ticking of the longcase clock, echoed the emptiness inside him. He crumpled the paper, his gaze fixed on the elegant clock's maker. *John Scott, Edinburgh*.

Sophie, what have you done to me?

She'd put an ocean between them. He could not get to her. He did not know exactly where she'd gone. How would he find words enough to tell Lily Cate?

In one severe thrust, the clock's sparkling front gave way beneath his fisted hand. So anguished within, he barely felt the cutting and bleeding without. The jarring shatter of glass brought Mistress Murdo running.

Rage vented, but no easier of mind, he turned and left Three Chimneys without apology, the words sticking in his throat . . .

Seamus awoke, drenched with sweat, the bedsheet in a fierce tangle. The nightmare fled. For a few disorienting seconds he couldn't grab hold of where he was. And then the stench of burnt meat and stale spirits from the taproom below stormed his senses. 'Twas an overwarm summer's morn in a comfortless Alexandria tavern. On the day of his appeal.

The dream faded but the panic remained.

37

Sunlight drenched Sophie's shoulders as she sat by the open parlor window. Silver thimble on one finger, she planted tiny stitches in the blue flannel with her best needle. Every so often she would pause, turn toward the glass, and search for some sign of Seamus in the green landscape. Four days it had been since he'd left for Richmond. Four days with no word.

Did the delay spell a denial? An end to their life together? Her every nerve stood on end, her hopes nearly spent. She almost wished theirs had stayed a marriage of convenience. There'd be no severing of hearts and souls and bodies. No baby.

Dropping needle and cloth to her lap, she pressed her hands to her middle. This was her one comfort, her sole joy. God had given her a child even if she had no home and no husband. No secure future.

Yet how was she to raise this child? On what funds? If the courts ruled against them, she could still sail for Scotland and plead her father's mercy. There she'd raise their baby, holding on to a part of Seamus if she could not have all of him. But by law the child was his, not hers. If they had a son, he would be heir to Tall Acre, perhaps taken away from her and raised by . . .

Nay. She lowered her head as if to deflect the piercing thought. Better to flee to Scotland and face her father's wrath. The truth was she bore Anne no ill will. She'd even begun to pray for her. Yet they were not prayers for reconciliation but repentance and restoration. God could bring blessing out of anything, but He would not rewrite the past. Betrayal and absence exacted a high price. Anne's actions had cast a long shadow and carried lasting consequences.

Swallowing down a bout of nausea, she uttered another silent prayer. For Seamus. For the court's wisdom. For truth. But in fact she was already moving away from him. Forced to think of a life without him. Without Lily Cate.

What choice did she have?

※

He had appealed. And now he returned home to Tall Acre to wait. No sooner had he come in than a dozen matters needed settling. Riggs was waiting, as was Mrs. Lamont. But he put all else aside till he could see his little daughter.

Lily Cate was awake despite the late hour, driving every pressing need from his head.

"Papa, have you been to Three Chimneys to see Mama?" Her face held joy and wonder as she sat on his lap and fingered his bewhiskered jaw. "Did she tell you our secret?"

"Secret?"

"Our baby is coming. She told me so when I was sick. She said I must get well to help her . . ."

She rambled on while his breathing slowed and his mouth

went dry. Sophie. Expecting. She'd been ill while he'd been . . . preoccupied . . . blind. Or was it just the hope of a sister or brother?

"Are you sure?"

She nodded so hard her curls bounced. "'Tis time for Mama to come home." She nestled into him again with a little sigh, sounding more grown-up than her years. "Our baby should be born here at Tall Acre."

⁂

"She's out walking, sir," Mistress Murdo told him in Three Chimneys' foyer, her ready smile banishing his previous bad dream. "I'm not sure which direction she went today."

Thanking her, he went out into brilliant July sunlight. As he walked toward the river, he thought of all he had to tell her, all she'd missed—all he'd missed—being away. The threshing floor of the new barn was newly laid. A second litter of hound pups had been born. The folly had been damaged by lightning, and rain had flooded the lucerne field. Schoolmaster McCann was making strides in the schoolhouse despite falling prey to ague, a common malady of newly arrived immigrants. He was even following Sophie's lead and continuing to teach Jenny and Myrtilla and others.

Tall Acre's demands never lessened. Sometimes he felt pressed against a millstone, ground and crushed by responsibilities. Never had he missed Sophie more than now. In the brief time they'd been married, she'd stood beside him, sharing the burden, lightening it in myriad ways. He craved her steady, sunny spirit. Her honesty and industry. Her gentleness.

A virtuous woman is a crown to her husband: but she that maketh ashamed is as rottenness in his bones.

Squinting in the glare, he cleared a copse of trees and saw her at the river's edge, sitting in the grass. Head bent, she was unaware of him, making a daisy chain from those tiny yellow flowers he'd always considered more weed. Other than acting as his secretary, she was forced to be idle when a world of need awaited at Tall Acre.

A fragrant wind tousled her upswept hair and carried her voice to him. She was humming a lullaby, low and sweet. He allowed himself the tender moment, taking her in unawares, and then all sentiment fled. She was no longer his. Might never be again. She was the woman he wanted to spend the rest of his life with, yet he might have to spend the rest of his life without her.

If he were a lesser man, a rebellious believer, he'd take Sophie and Lily Cate and go west. Flee to the Kentucky territory and the lawless frontier where men made their own rules and courts held no sway. But he was a redeemed man and seasoned soldier and would stay.

Come what may.

⁂

Sophie sensed him before she saw him. She looked up from her lap, aware the guard was missing, and saw Seamus instead. Flowers forgotten, she stood and began a slow walk toward him. The sudden wooziness inside her had nothing to do with the baby. The slanting sunlight seemed a barrier between them. She couldn't get a fix on his features to gauge whether he brought good news or ill. And then she knew. A closer look told her everything. Richmond had gone hard on him.

He took her in his arms and held her. "I've appealed. To the legislature."

For a moment the weight of it overwhelmed her. Weeks,

months, loomed before her, each a mountain she had no strength to cross. "How long then?"

His hand dropped to the lace of her bodice and traveled to her waist. "You answer me, Sophie. How long?"

She placed her hand over his, the miracle of new life upending her all over again. "Late winter by my reckoning."

The tension left his face and tenderness took its place. "That's why you've been ill."

She gave him a small, sad half smile. "'Tis worth every trip to the chamber pot or bushes."

"The thought of you here, away from me at such a time . . ." He left off, the sheen in his eyes saying more than words ever could.

Her good humor returned. "You've little to worry about with Mistress Murdo clucking over me and the men standing guard."

"Does anyone know?"

"Mistress Murdo likely suspects, though I've told no one but Lily Cate."

"You're a far better tonic than Dr. Craik. No doubt that piece of news pulled her through."

"That and prayer."

"Aye, prayer."

She linked arms with him, walking along the gravelly riverbank, its soothing rush like music. "You should know that Anne came here with word of my father."

He went still.

"She saw him in Bath. He and Curtis want me to join them in Scotland. I only mention it in case Anne speaks of such."

"I'll keep it in mind. If this isn't resolved in the legislature, I will appeal to a higher court. I want you home at Tall Acre, and I won't rest till that's done."

She listened, uncertainty sweeping over her. His was the conviction that had won a war, but she'd begun to doubt this would become a personal victory.

"I don't want you burdened by any of this." Misery framed his face. "If anything happens to you, our baby . . ."

"No matter what has happened or will happen, I will never begrudge knowing you, loving you—and Lily Cate."

"You deserve far better. Far more." The regret in his words turned her inside out. "I'll always begrudge our beginnings, Sophie."

"I shan't, ever. 'They lived happily ever after' is the stuff of fairy tales, Seamus. At least in this life."

He raised a hand, tracing the flushed curve of her cheek. "Keep praying. Hoping. Truth will prevail."

38

Seamus was in court again. A month from the day he had appealed. The event had been well publicized, stealing every headline in Virginia, and now the courtroom was once again crammed and breathless in July. Anne sat in her usual place, color high and brandishing a fan, a maid beside her. Throughout the proceedings, the Fitzhughs had been conspicuously absent. Seamus thought it as a door opened at the back of the room and they made an unexpected entrance.

The judge took up his gavel and brought the room to silence with one decisive pound to the podium. "The Virginia court is hereby in session to resolve the case of General Seamus Ogilvy of Tall Acre and Anne Howard Ogilvy lately of England."

Perspiring beneath his wool uniform, Seamus forced calm. His fellow soldiers sat behind him, so many it seemed his whole regiment was assembled. He could feel their tension much as he had on the field, in the hours and minutes before a decisive conflict was at hand. Now his own dread went as deep as it had then, when he'd wondered which of his men he would lose and which would stay standing after the storm of battle. If he too would survive.

His attorneys, especially dour this morning, were prepared to cite Sophie's pregnancy if their appeal was denied. Seamus balked against making such a personal matter public, but there was little to be done about it. He already felt exposed to the utmost, though Anne seemed not to care. She fluttered her fan and chatted with the woman beside her as if this were of no more consequence than a horse auction.

Seamus fixed his eyes on the judge, whose attention was pinned on the doorway at the rear of the room. Turning his head, Seamus saw a slave woman enter the courtroom, her head bound with a bright kerchief, her homespun dress neat if plain. A slow awareness dawned.

Myrtilla? All the way from Tall Acre?

She looked neither to the right nor the left as she walked the narrow aisle to the front of the courtroom. A hum of murmuring began. She clutched a book to her chest so tightly it seemed no one could pry it loose from her bony, work-worn fingers.

A bailiff intervened, trying to deter her, but she continued unswervingly toward the judge's bench, her bearing confident yet respectful. The presiding judge leaned forward to hear something she said, and then he gestured toward Seamus's and Anne's legal counsel.

"The proceedings are momentarily adjourned."

With that, the judge led the counsel and Myrtilla out of the courtroom as the hum of the crowd grew louder.

◈

A quarter of an hour passed, and Seamus felt he would melt from the heat. Giving a tug to his stock in a bid for air, he watched the door that Myrtilla, the judge, and the counsel had retreated behind. Beside him, Cosima whispered something, but he barely heard her.

God, help us. The truth, please.

Try as he might, he couldn't fathom what had brought Myrtilla to Richmond when she'd never been more than five miles from Tall Acre her entire life. But as a freedwoman, she now had liberties she hadn't before and no longer needed a signed pass from him.

He squared his shoulders as a bailiff called his name and then Anne's. A private meeting? Anne cast him a pensive look and moved into the antechamber ahead of him. He followed, curiosity overriding dread. A near-smothering longing for Sophie settled over him, though he was glad she was far removed from the courtroom drama. Lily Cate intruded next, her parting words to him haunting.

Papa, won't you bring Mama and the baby home soon?

As the door closed behind him, he found himself facing Myrtilla across a battered table. Stark white light from a window illuminated a leather-bound book at the table's center. The book she'd clutched to her chest?

With their legal counsel looking on and the judge still presiding from a corner chair, Seamus and Anne took their seats, though Myrtilla remained standing. Anne was regarding her former servant with a telling wariness, defiance in the jut of her chin.

"General Ogilvy, is this woman known to you?" The judge gestured to Myrtilla in an unnecessary formality.

Though Seamus wanted to cut to the chase and reach for the mysterious book, he steeled himself and answered, "She is a freedwoman, once a slave at Tall Acre and now in my employ as a spinner."

The judge nodded. "Since she is at liberty, she can speak for herself in the presence of these witnesses."

Myrtilla swallowed and met Seamus's eyes. "If my word as a black woman ain't good enough, General, I thought maybe I could help you some other way." She reached for the book and held it out to him. "This was in Mistress Ogil—" Her eyes flared at the slip. "This was in Mistress Anne's desk, in her old room at Tall Acre, on the second floor."

Seamus took the book and opened it. Recognition stirred. His own heavy, sprawling hand was on the flyleaf. *To my beloved, Anne, wife of my heart*. "I gave her this on our wedding day but have since forgotten. 'Tis a diary, a journal."

Nodding, Myrtilla continued at the judge's prompting, voice steady if low. "I used to watch Mistress Anne write in this book while you was away fightin' in the war. I wanted to know what it said, but I couldn't figure out the words till now. I always believed it might help you if I could."

Seamus waited, on edge.

"Now that I can read—"

"How dare you!" Anne lunged for the little book.

She had but touched it when a bailiff intervened and the judge barked a sharp rebuke.

"You shall be seated, Mistress Howard, and refrain from speaking until I deem otherwise." The judge turned back to Seamus. "Is the writing in this book that of your first wife, General Ogilvy?"

Seamus paged through the contents, noting entries and dates in Anne's unmistakable hand. Details that left him feeling winded and half sick, secrets long suspected but better left unspoken, unwritten. Buried. "Aye."

He shut the book. His legal counsel was studying him, pensive and stone still, as he returned the book to the table.

"I do not expect you to read it. I would advise otherwise," the judge said. "But it contains evidence that is the deciding factor in this case."

He stood, and Seamus's legal counsel stood with him. To their left, Anne's attorneys were strangely silent. Anne herself had turned ashen.

Seamus felt wonder take hold. Could it finally be over? Swept behind them for good? If so, he owed the freedwoman before him an immense debt of gratitude. But the shine in Myrtilla's eyes told him that turning the case in his favor was payment aplenty.

"This entire matter has dragged on long enough. I, for one, am glad to see it end." The judge held open the door to resume the proceedings. "Shall we, General?"

Overcome, unable to murmur even an aye, Seamus followed him into the stifling courtroom. He looked up, eye drawn to the back where a lone figure stood against one paneled wall. Riggs? He had obviously brought Myrtilla here. And Myrtilla, ever faithful, had saved the day.

The true mistress of Tall Acre could come home.

❧

Was she imagining it or did the day feel different? Walking down Three Chimneys' long drive without reason or explanation, when the slant of the sun made her feel she was melting from the heat and should be indoors, Sophie took in Tall Acre. She longed to see signs of Seamus back from Richmond. Longed to see Lily Cate at play like it was an ordinary summer's day and their whole world didn't hinge on a Richmond courtroom.

She caught her breath as the baby moved beneath her airy muslin shortgown. She was growing used to that flutter, more a tickle, soon to be an outright kick. The delight never dimmed. She ached to decorate Tall Acre's nursery right down to the pincushion Glynnis had just sent her, charmingly embroidered with "Welcome Little Stranger."

But much had to be settled. And there was no promise she would ever set foot in Tall Acre again. Fear welled within her, but she kept it at bay by remembering the words she'd awakened to at dawn.

Joy cometh in the morning.

It was that hope, that belief, that propelled her now. She walked on, intent on a dusty cloud in the distance.

Seamus had said he would send word of the outcome. But this rider, going at full gallop, *was* Seamus, not some post rider.

Glad she wasn't heavy with child, she began to run toward him, unmindful of the dust she herself was kicking up or the trickle of sweat beneath her loosened stays.

The distance denied her any hint of his expression. But his speed suggested pleasure. Hope. Glad news.

He dismounted by Tall Acre's gate. She was nearly there, out of breath, but so full of expectation at his return she never slowed. When he started toward her, he was . . . smiling. She'd not seen him merry in so long she had begun to think he never would be again.

They collided, nothing gentle about it, but there was a deep tenderness in his embrace. "Come home, Sophie."

Questions gathered into a knot in her throat. She touched his cheek, noting the shadows beneath eyes that were now a shining, triumphant blue.

"The judge put Anne on the first ship back to England. The court order forbids her return to American soil." He took a breath, a great lungful of air, before continuing in staccato beats. "The Fitzhughs have sailed with her. I stayed myself to see it done."

Done. The word brought release. Disbelief. Joy.

"Nothing stands in the way of your being my wife. Lily Cate's mother. The trouble is over, never to be resurrected again."

She began to laugh but she wanted to dance. Turning toward Three Chimneys, she bid it goodbye in her heart and head. Clasping her hand, Seamus began tugging her gently toward his waiting mount. Toward Tall Acre.

Home. At long last.

Epilogue

Nearly March, a skiff of snow was melting, proclaiming winter's end. Sophie looked toward the bedchamber windows, unshuttered now that her travail was over. During the long, pain-ridden night, she'd all but forgotten what season it was. She was finishing her first winter as Tall Acre's mistress, and in such fine company too. She looked down at the infant in her arms, swaddled in new linen, only minutes old.

Seamus had just gone to get Lily Cate, who was at breakfast. The whole house seemed to be holding its breath, waiting for a baby's triumphant cry. Only this baby hadn't cried but had emerged plump and pink and politely, turning them anxious till he'd opened eyes the shade of Seamus's Continental coat.

Elation crowded out exhaustion as Sophie counted ten flawless fingers and toes, breathing in the babe's intoxicating newborn scent like some sort of heaven-sent cologne.

"I'll step out and enjoy a cup of punch," Dr. Craik was saying, "while you and the baby greet Miss Lily Cate."

He left the door open as Myrtilla wiped her brow and Florie took pains with her hair, rebraiding the lengthy plait that had frayed in the night. Their own pleasure was apparent—they could hardly look away from the heir of Tall Acre.

Mere seconds later, Sophie thrilled to the sound of rushing feet. Lily Cate soon hovered in the doorway, gaze riveted to the bundle in Sophie's arms. She approached the bed with near reverence, Seamus just behind, as the women left the room.

Still clad in her nightgown, Lily Cate climbed the bed steps and settled on the feather mattress with care.

Sophie placed the bundle in her arms, delighting in Lily Cate's rapt expression. "Our baby is in need of a name."

Lily Cate looked up at Seamus. "Papa, is he truly a boy? How can you be sure?"

"Trust me," he said with a wink.

"He is so small!" Leaning closer, Lily Cate kissed his reddened nose. "Brothers should be big, but he is more like a puppy."

"He'll grow in time," Seamus said, bending to kiss Sophie full on the mouth.

She touched her dry lips as he pulled away, mindful of the anxiety in his eyes. The night had been long and he'd been pacing, coming in once when she'd cried out despite Craik and the women having all in hand.

"Why not call him Seamus?" Sophie offered.

He quirked a brow. "One of us isn't enough?" When she shook her head, he relented. "Seamus, then. But the lad still lacks a middle name."

"Let's call him Adam." Lily Cate cradled the baby closer. "After the first man God made."

"Seamus Adam Ogilvy," Sophie echoed, gauging Seamus's reaction. At his delighted smile, joy sang through her. "A bonny family we make—Seamus, Sophie, Lily Cate—"

"And baby Adam!" finished their wee daughter.

AUTHOR'S NOTE

The Mistress of Tall Acre was a joy to write because of my own family heritage in Virginia, but mostly because of my continued awe and appreciation of those first American Patriots. From the comforts of our twenty-first-century homes and a world of instant everything, we often forget how long the Revolutionary War was and how very turbulent and passionate that time period. In the span of a novel I've attempted to portray a tiny slice of that era through the tenants at Tall Acre. Their stories are mere echoes of the flesh and blood lives of real colonials who often did not share the Ogilvys' happy ending. However, through their sacrifices, courage, and vision they leave us an enduring, historically rich legacy.

It was a joy, too, to spend time researching and reading George Washington's journals and letters as well as the diaries and correspondence of fellow planters and Virginians, including the Jeffersons, Byrds, and Carters. I also became fascinated with George Mason, an often overlooked founding father, and his elegant estate, Gunston Hall. The story of his life and his loving tribute to his wife, Anne Eilbeck, on her gravestone are also a part of this novel.

When writing a book I usually have character names picked out long before the story begins, but this time I asked savvy readers for help. I was delighted when Emma in Michigan chose Miss Menzies as a heroine's name, and in a heartbeat Jennifer in New Brunswick came up with Seamus Michael Ogilvy. I was left to dream up my littlest heroine, Lily Cate, but oh what fun that was! Heartfelt thanks also to Whitney in Ohio for befriending me and telling me about Elswyth Thane's works. One of my favorite sources was a vintage copy of Thane's *Potomac Squire*, a truly praiseworthy book. For other primary sources and visuals used in the writing of this novel, please visit https://www.pinterest.com/laura frantz/.

Many thanks to all the other hearts and hands who were a part of this work—you know who you are!

> Now therefore, our God, we thank thee, and praise thy glorious name.
>
> 1 Chronicles 29:13

Laura Frantz is the author of *The Frontiersman's Daughter*, *Courting Morrow Little*, *The Colonel's Lady*, and the Ballantyne Legacy series. She lives and writes in a log cabin in the heart of the Kentucky woods. Please visit her at www.Laura Frantz.net.

MEET

Laura Frantz

Visit LauraFrantz.net to read
Laura's blog and learn about her books!

 see what inspired the characters and stories

 enter to win contests and learn about what
Laura is working on now

tweet with Laura

"Laura Frantz surely dances when she writes: the words sweep across the page with a gentle rhythm and a sure step."

—LIZ CURTIS HIGGS,
New York Times bestselling author of *Mine Is the Night*

"Riveting plotline, dynamic characters, and flawless historical accuracy will vividly transport the reader to another time and place."
—*Library Alive*